# THE OTHER SHOES OF

# LARRY MARTIN

## BOOK ONE:
## REVELATION OF LIES

## Pavane Ravel

COMING SOON *in the series of …*
**THE OTHER SHOES OF LARRY MARTIN**

Book Two – *On Becoming Laurie Roberts*

Book Three – *The Board Extraction*

Book Four – *Decisions and Diversions*

Book Five – *Revenge Served Cold*

# FORWARD

To my good friend and editor, John E. Wildermuth, thank you for all your patience, help and guidance. I couldn't have written my books without you. That is a fact.

To my family, thank you for all of your support. I know I've ruined a couple of vacations, but please take me on vacation again. I don't promise not to work, but I will try to be more fun. And thank you for all your professional roles in helping to get this book published.

While I have tried to keep the politics of this book accurate from a progressive stance, it is a work of fiction.

In building the contemporary creation of Larry Martin—something I enjoyed—I have used 'literary license' to build his world according to my imagination. This includes any media, newspaper, pundits, medicine, architecture and accounting in this series. It needs to be said that all mistakes are mine. And I am sure there are many. My apologies.

# CHAPTER ONE

**Atlanta, Georgia**
**April, 2017**

Larry Martin sat up in bed, his mood dark. He could barely open his eyes after a bad night's sleep. He glanced at the morning sun streaming through the blinds and flinched. He had slept badly because he was worried. Because he was worried, he wasn't feeling well and didn't want to get out of bed. Not yet. He let his head hang low as he procrastinated and reflected. He was twenty-three years old, living in a crappy duplex on the southside of Atlanta. His rent was due. Yesterday, both the check engine light and the oil light had come on in his old 1992 Toyota. He would have to get them looked at. Even as the thought formed, he knew he wouldn't do anything. He never did.

Larry massaged the temples of his pounding head. He forced his eyes open and gazed at the wreckage of his home. Dirty clothes were strewn over furniture and across the floor. The coffee table and kitchen counters were hidden under moldering stacks of takeout containers and pizza boxes. The garbage can in his kitchen was overflowing and smelled foul. The sink was piled high with unwashed pots, mugs, plates and silverware. He hadn't been able to use his faucet for some time now. The sour stench of unwashed clothing and decaying garbage wafted to his nostrils.

Larry sighed. None of this concerned him. Sometimes the mess even comforted him, like he was a just a real guy roughing it. Real men lived rough. He thought of his father's home growing up. It was worse than his apartment.

On the rare occasion he'd brought a woman home, one or two had tried to help straighten the place. But no relationship had lasted. He knew only rejection. He had learned while women loved that he was a reporter for a high-profile political site, they also expected him to pay for their dates. He loathed this. He could barely afford his own rent, much less pay for a girlfriend. He viewed women as money-grubbing whores. He hated them and his hatred festered deeply and bitterly. Women didn't understand that they owed him. They didn't get the only reason for their existence was to give him sex when he wanted. To be subservient to his every wish. To take care of him, clean for him, make him food and just shut up about their own wants and needs. He was active on a lot of online message and chat boards telling him this was the way it should be. Men were owed their rightful place in the world. Women shouldn't be allowed to work. They sucked jobs away from men. Nor should they be allowed to vote. As for rights, they should get none, especially any reproductive choices. Hell, he knew that some guys even debated whether women were human. In his opinion, they were — but less than a man.

Larry believed that women had only two functions: to have babies and to take care of men. That was it. He knew a lot of other guys who felt exactly the same way. He often wrote comments on various men's rights websites. Other guys loved his vicious words. These men were men's rights activists, incels, and white supremacists. They all agreed feminism was fucking things up and making men feel emasculated. He knew it was true. His father had pounded all this into him as a boy. Especially after his mother had abandoned him as a baby, barely over a year old.

Every fucking time he told any girl about her role in his home, the bitch had walked out on him. One had even slapped him. Another had nearly broken his nose. That had been Marney. While she hadn't exactly been his girlfriend, they had gone out a half-dozen times. He wasn't sure about her; she was no beauty, with her chubby body and dark, curly hair.

Worse, she'd even had the nerve to complain about his place when she picked him up for their dates. The fucking bitch wouldn't even ride in his car because she said it was too filthy. Larry knew he'd eventually have to slap some sense into her. He only had to bide his time, reel her in real solid before he did. He had to make her respect his rightful dominance. It was just a matter of training her properly.

Inviting Marney back to his duplex the night of their sixth date had been a mistake. But damn, Larry thought, she'd been to his place and knew what it looked like. He remembered how she had stepped inside, glanced around, and made instant sound of revulsion.

"Jesus, Larry, you're disgusting."

"Aw, come on," he cajoled. "Didn't we just have a nice dinner —"

"Which I paid for because you never pay," she returned bluntly. "It's always some lame excuse, like, you've forgotten your wallet or lost your credit card. Besides being filthy, Larry, you're cheap. And, oh wow, I can't believe I caught you stealing the waiter's tip tonight! That was way low, just unbelievable!"

"Yeah well, people like that don't know how to handle money anyway."

*"People like that?"* Marney countered, her voice rising. "You stupid son of a bitch, I am 'people like that'! Where do you think I get the money to pay for the dates you never pay for?"

Larry became angry. Stepping closer, he gripped her arm tightly. "A woman's place is to take care of her man, Marney! Just like the reason this place is such a mess is because you didn't clean it!" His voice grew harder, his free hand starting to rise. "You should be buying groceries and cooking for me! But do you? No! This place should be clean, but is it? No! And that's your fault!" He slapped her. Not hard enough to hurt her, but hard enough to get her attention.

Marney's mouth opened in fury, but Larry wasn't done. "You finally get a man and what do you do? You whine about having to pay for a few dinners instead of being grateful as hell that I'm with you! And in spite of my being so good to you, you haven't even screwed me yet." He tightened his grasp on her arm, wanting to hurt her. Roughly, he jerked her to him, enjoying her gasp. In command now, he backed his voice down. "Well, that's about to change. Tonight. Now. And after we have sex, I want you to scrub this place from top to bottom so we'll both be happy. When you're done, you can come back to bed and we'll take it from there."

Marney dropped her eyes away from Larry's intense gaze. Larry looked and sounded absurd to her. He was crazy. She pretended to shrug. "You can let go of my arm now, Larry," she murmured, slipping her hand into her shoulder bag.

Larry let his hand drop, his anger receding. He was feeling masterful. Watching her, he assumed she was going for lipstick or something to please him. Instead, her fingers were seeking out a smooth, inch-thick metal bar. Gripping the metal so Larry couldn't see, she withdrew her hand from her bag. Lowering it to her side, she stood silently.

As she stared at the floor, Larry nearly smiled at her apparent acquiescence. This is gonna be easy, he thought. He lifted her chin to look at him. "Listen Marney, you have to learn that men control the world — you know, dominate it — and it's a woman's duty to submit to that. It's the natural order of things. You might say that women owe men anything they need or want. *Anything*. And that's how it's going to be between you and me, all right? You do as I say and we're going to be happy." Larry searched her eyes. "Let me hear you say okay. That you understand. That you agree."

Taking a smooth step back from Larry, Marney arched abruptly and furiously connected her fist to Larry's nose. The contact came with such force, Larry keeled backwards to the floor. Taken by surprise, he immediately started backing up crab-like, staring at her in shock. Blood poured through his fingers as he held his nose. Yanking the door open, Marney snarled, "Get the fuck away from me, and don't ever call me again, you asshole! I hope you bleed to death!" She slammed the door.

Cradling his nose in pain, Larry considered calling the cops to report the assault. It would be humiliating to explain how a girl had punched him and he quickly decided against it. Fuck her. Staggering to his feet, Larry stumbled to the bathroom to look at his nose. It was swelling rapidly but the bleeding wasn't so bad now. He wasn't sure if it was broken, but it didn't matter. He had no money to see some expensive goddamn doctor anyway. All he'd done that night was pack his nose with toilet paper and ice. He had stumbled to his freezer, rolled some cubes into a paper towel and molded the ice to his nose until it felt frozen. The ice had brought some relief, even as he was hot with resentment and anger.

The next morning at work, he lied about being jumped by thugs for his wallet and fearlessly fighting off the thieves. His nose had been a sickly blue for three days before finally turning yellow and easing back to normal. In spite of Marney hurting him, he still missed her. But he was also afraid of her. She wouldn't give into him, and she had become violent. He was lucky she hadn't broken his nose.

He wanted a woman. Sex was on his mind twenty-four seven. He was feeling the ache of it even now. But that's not my main concern this morning, he thought. He glanced again at the sun pouring through his blinds and groaned. This morning was going to be rough.

He'd have to confess to his asshole of a boss that his story on Atlanta's homeless wasn't written. He couldn't meet Ellison's deadline. The problem couldn't have happened on a worse day either, he thought. Today was also his review and he desperately needed the raise.

The trouble was, Ellison had an unbearable ego. He saw himself as some important media god. His father had loaned him the money to start his business. Ellison hadn't graduated from Georgia State University, where he had met Larry, although they had taken a few journalism classes together. Ellison had offered Larry a job as a journalist while he was building his new website. Larry had taken Ellison up on his offer. He'd begun to work for Ellison immediately, even before graduating. That was two years ago. Ellison Bart ran an extreme alt-right news blog called The Bart Data Report out of a brightly-lit office off Jimmy Carter Boulevard. It took Larry a traffic crazed hour — and often much longer — just to get to the office. The cost of gas was killing him.

While Larry generally agreed with everything Ellison's site published, he also knew Ellison had no interest in factual reporting. Ellison lied as easily as he breathed. Everything he promoted was based on his loathing of minorities, the government, women, the poor and especially the homeless. But Ellison's website had a good following and was growing. At twenty-two years old, Ellison was a white nationalist who felt strongly that all liberals should die, and he did everything he could to pound them hard on the Internet. So hard, The Bart Data Report was making a name for itself. This made Ellison intolerable. Larry had come to despise the man's pinched face, skinny frame, and snap-finger attitude.

Last Wednesday, Ellison had ordered Larry to go downtown and interview homeless people for a strict Monday deadline. He had demanded photos this time, and that's where things had gotten sticky. If it had just been an article, he could have fudged the kind of story Ellison wanted by trashing the homeless as evil, lazy, drug-addicted losers who deliberately infested the streets to hunt for victims and handouts. But the photos had made this assignment impossible.

Larry knew the kind of photos Ellison was after. The kind that portrayed the homeless as worthless and ugly. The kind that illustrated them as shiftless panhandlers with their palms out, or passed out on a city sidewalk. The kind that showed a butt in the air while dumpster diving. Or a close up of a black dude's scary face. Or a cart-pushing, old woman that Ellison could tag with the headline "Hag on the Street!"

Ellison had a real cruel streak. He wanted his readers to loathe street people. He wanted to whip up their animosity, get lots of site traffic and thousands of derisive comments. But Larry had no such photos and so, he'd written no story.

Ellison paid Larry two thousand lousy bucks a month, less taxes. Between Larry's rent of nine hundred a month and his utilities, internet, phone, food and car insurance consuming the rest, he didn't have the gas money to drive downtown, much less fork over an absurd parking fee to get those photos. He just didn't have it. He was fucking starving. Now he was going to have to maneuver not getting fired along with getting a desperately needed raise.

He hated Ellison Bart. He hated him with a passion. He hated his superior attitude. He hated that Ellison was a year younger than him and doing so well. He hated that he was going to have to brown nose the supercilious sucker just to keep his job, never mind get more money. He wasn't up to it. He needed a drink.

Climbing out of bed, Larry headed to the fridge for a beer. There was one Yuengling left. He anxiously twisted off the top and chugged it down quickly. Then, hunting for a t-shirt that stank the least, he pulled it on along with grimy jeans. He flipped on the light in the bathroom and glanced at himself in the mirror. At five foot eleven, he wished he were taller. He hated the way Ellison's skinny frame loomed over him, especially when Ellison was yelling at him.

Larry didn't have to worry about his hair. It was buzzed so short, he could hardly tell it was brown. His brown eyes looked bloodshot and dull. His stubble of a beard was three days old. He debated whether to shave and even picked up the razor, but his hand was shaking so hard, he quickly abandoned the idea. It was then he realized that he was scared. Truly scared. He had to make Ellison see things his way. He just had to.

Under the dim light of his bathroom, Larry blankly stared at his reflection for a few seconds longer. He pinched some fat at his waist. He never exercised. He had no muscle tone.

I look like shit, he thought. Sighing, he bent over the cruddy sink and splashed his face in cold water, drying it with the sour-smelling towel hanging by the mirror. He brushed his teeth, grabbed his keys, and headed for the car. He let his ancient Toyota run for a minute to warm up. Finally, he knew he had procrastinated enough. Shifting his transmission into reverse to back out of his parking spot, he got on the road.

He was already late.

# CHAPTER TWO

The drive to the office was awful. Traffic on the highway was crazy. The late April morning was heating up fast. Ignoring the red warning lights on his dash, Larry drove like a man possessed to get to the office on time. He knew it was hopeless. He would be late.

As traffic bottlenecked to a halt, Larry swore loudly. He wondered if an accident was the cause. People always gotta look, he thought bitterly. As he waited, he began to envision the scene in the office he was about to enter. Various so-called 'journalists' would be coming and going, so smug and self-important, it made him want to vomit. He despised their back-stabbing ways, fake smiles, and phony self-confidence. The girls in the office would be clacking away on their computers and answering the phones with the same air of arrogant impatience. In some ways, they were worse than the men. When he tried to talk with them, they often wouldn't answer. They would roll their eyes and turn away. This stung, leaving him humiliated, his hostility towards women intact. Ellison would be in his office with his door shut, daring anyone to bother him. Ellison kept the office freezing cold and the lights so bright it hurt his eyes. The office was well furnished and professional, and did its job of being intimidating. Larry found it to be a miserable place. He was also intimidated. He just couldn't let anyone know it.

Traffic started moving again. Picking up speed, Larry maneuvered his way through the sea of semis and other vehicles as fast as he dared push his decrepit car. Fifty-nine minutes later, sweating from anxiety and a lack of air conditioning, he arrived at the brick buildings of his office complex. He parked, took some deep breaths and arranged his game face.

Sauntering through the front door as though he hadn't a care in the world, Larry bid the girls standing around reception a loud good morning. No one responded. He clenched his teeth in insecurity. It was all part of that intimidation thing. Like they were too good for him. Sliding into the chair of his cubicle, he turned on his computer. While it was starting up, the phone buzzed on his desk. Pretending to be annoyed because he was a busy man, he snatched it up and gruffly barked, "What!"

"Get in here," Ellison Bart snarled. He slammed down the phone.

Rising, Larry glanced at the receptionist. He knew her name was Lucy. He tried to smile at her, but she quickly looked away. Striving for his best casual walk, he opened Ellison's office door and stepped inside. Making for the hard metal chair in front of Ellison's desk, he sank into it, his mouth dry.

"Where's the story?" Ellison demanded, pushing his laptop aside.

"I'm working on it. I had problems with my phone, you know, the camera —"

"Phone camera? What the hell, Larry. I told you to use a real camera. To check it out of production. What the fuck are you talking about?"

"Okay, okay. I'll check it out today. You'll get your story tomorrow. Relax, man. It'll be good. Listen, Ellison, downtown parking is too expensive. I can't afford it. You know I can't. I can barely survive on my salary. I gotta have more money if I'm going to take trips downtown — "

"You live on the south side, you moron. You can drive through downtown on your way home."

"Look, Ellison, there are parking fees, gas and other expenses too. These are your business expenses; you can deduct them. I can't. And since you charge to check equipment out of production, I can't afford that either."

Ellison stood then, his jaw working in agitation. "Tough shit, Larry. You guys break equipment, you pay for it."

"If I don't break my camera, I shouldn't have to pay for someone who does."

"I don't care. My company. My policy. Anyway, you don't meet deadlines. I'm fucking tired of it. The thing is, Larry, you're a good writer, but I've had enough of your whining. You hear me? I'm fucking done. You're fired."

Larry scrambled to his feet, hands spread wide. "Aw, come on, Ellison! Fuck man, I can't make it on two thousand a month! All this shit adds up. Sometimes it's over a couple hundred a month. It's too much, man. Help pay for the parking, or, help me out with a raise here and you'll get your story. It'll be fucking great too. I won't be late again."

"Get out of my office," Ellison said harshly, sitting down. He pulled his laptop close and started to work again.

"Ellison! Don't fire me. I'm one of the best journalists you have." Larry stared at his boss, panic stricken, his brown eyes filled with fear. "I won't let you down again. Come on, man! Please!"

Ellison was pointedly scrolling his inbox. "You disgust me with your begging, Larry. I'm busy. Get out!"

"Please, Ellison —"

"NOW!" Ellison screamed heatedly, pointing at the door.

Larry stumbled towards the door, trying not to sob. Opening it, he went to his desk to clear out his things. No one looked at him. Not one friendly or sympathetic face was there. Averting his eyes in humiliation, he grabbed an empty box by the printer, dumped his few belongings into it, and left the building.

Driving home was nearly impossible. He could hardly see through the tears in his eyes. The fear in the pit of his stomach was also dangerously distracting. Once he got to the south side of town, he pulled into a liquor store and bought a cheap bottle of rye whisky.

Pulling into his duplex, he parked, as usual, on the concrete pad right outside his front door. Leaving the office box in his car, Larry clutched the bottle to his chest. With a trembling hand, he let himself into his apartment. The sight of it, to him, was suddenly depressing in its discord and filth. Irate at Ellison, his apartment, and his life, Larry swept the pile of crap covering his armchair onto the floor. Sinking into the grubby, green upholstery, he twisted the top off the bottle and took a long, burning gulp. Eyes watering, he remained there for hours, dazed, drinking, and thinking about what to do.

About eleven that night, Larry stood, surprisingly sober, and took a shower. Then he began the process of washing dishes and picking up his clothes. Those that weren't wearable went into the dirty clothes bin. Those that passed the smell test got hung in his closet. He worked until four in the morning scrubbing his apartment knowing he wouldn't be able to sleep. Finally, crawling into his freshly made bed, Larry found that he was feeling some better. Setting his alarm for 8:00 in the morning, he fell back on his pillow. Sleep took him quickly.

Lying on his side, Larry opened his eyes to the clock. It read 11:00 a.m. He sat up, feeling disoriented. He must have turned off the alarm somehow. He didn't remember doing it. He remembered that he had lost his job and needed to find another fast. Waking to a clean apartment, at least, was mildly uplifting. He walked to the kitchen, made himself an instant coffee, and ate the last pieces of a stale loaf of bread topped by the last scrapings of jam.

Sitting down at his freshly clean desk, he scrolled through the contacts in his cell phone. He called everyone he knew asking if they knew of any work and to keep him in mind if they did. No one knew of anything. Some had even hung up on him. He got the impression that no one cared and he wasn't well liked. There was one more call to make.

Larry stared at Peter Bennett's number for a while.

Peter was a straight up kind of guy, all honesty and integrity, as if that mattered. Peter was also some kind of contributing editor at a wide-ly-read progressive news site. Larry didn't know his exact title, but he could research it. Years ago, they had gone to high school together, although Peter had been two years ahead. They had even shared some journalism classes at Georgia State. So, he and Peter had some history, but they had never been friends.

Larry had never associated with Peter in high school. All he knew of Peter was that he was the guy who always won the academic awards. Peter was the kind of guy who always showed up to class, assignments completed, while he'd been the complete opposite. He was the guy who skipped out of class whenever possible and did the least amount of work he could get away with. He wasn't proud of it, but since he could do the work with very little effort, it was all he did. If his father had guided him or pressured him to do better, he would have. But his father was too busy watching television to ever help him.

In sophomore year, Larry heard that Peter was leading his class in an environmental team effort to clean up a section of the Chattahoochee River. Peter was also helping to build houses for Habitat for Humanity. He had sneered at this. Poor people were always mooching off other people's efforts, and according to Fox News and the right-wing radio his father listened to, these kinds of handouts just kept them poor. He heard it continually. His father loved conservative news and always had the TV or radio blaring in the house.

Larry knew Peter's high school history. Everyone loved the guy, so they talked about him. He knew that Peter had been the captain of the debate team in his junior year. And in addition to all of Peter's activities, he'd also become the editor of the yearbook in his senior year. He remembered this very well because he'd been deeply envious. At the time, he'd still been writing stories in his bedroom in the middle of the night with the door locked against his father and the relentless barrage of his talking-head programs. He remembered being heartily sick of the frothing rants that invariably followed. His father hated everyone: Blacks, Latino's, gays, Jews, Asians, Native Americans, feminists and Socialist-liberal pigs and he never stopped yelling about it.

During the years Larry had loosely followed Peter's rise, Peter had no idea of Larry's interest. Since Peter was everything Larry was not, they had never socialized or even talked. But college was different.

In college, Larry hated seeing all the girls who hung on Peter's arm. It had twisted him with bitterness. He remembered that Peter was tall and fit. He remembered that Peter had chestnut colored hair, dark brows and light blue eyes. Women loved him. His envy had run so deep that, one evening, he had even dared to follow Peter and his latest date as they had left campus to stroll down an Atlanta city street to a bar called McMullan's. Standing at the bar, he had watched Peter take a table and seat his date before sitting himself. He remembered how he had rolled his eyes in disgust. That kind of treatment only spoiled a girl. You had to tell them what was what.

Spying on Peter over his beer, Larry noticed all the people who stopped by the table, talking and laughing with the couple. Peter had a hearty laugh that showed straight white teeth. So fashionable was Peter, he had even worn a sharp black blazer over a crisp black t-shirt. The look was so cool, so right, he'd felt his insides churn with envy.

After a few more sips, Larry finally summoned the guts to stroll over to Peter's table. With a smile on his face, he leaned towards Peter, hand out, saying, "Hey. Do you remember me? We went to high school together. And now, we share some journalism classes at the university. I'm Larry Martin."

Rising slightly, Peter had shaken Larry's hand, confusion on his face. High school? Larry Martin? His mind drew a blank. There was nothing. No memory at all. "I'm sorry, Larry — I don't remember. My fault. But I'm Peter Bennett and this is my friend, Shelby."

"No problem. We're in Professor Boynton's class?" Larry replied smoothly, his eyes on Peter, ignoring Shelby.

"Sure, okay," Peter said, trying to remember. "Come to think of it, yes, I have seen you in class. Nice to see you again."

"Say, I'm alone. Do you mind if I join you?" Larry asked hopefully.

Peter glanced at Shelby, then back to Larry. "Well, truth is, we're about to go to dinner. So, maybe some other time, okay?"

"Hey, no problem, man. See you around."

Although Larry started going to McMullan's regularly, Peter never did sit with him. But they had talked on several occasions while standing at the bar, the first of which Larry had immediately gotten Peter's phone number. But beyond those few conversations, Peter had taken to avoiding him.

Maybe, Larry reflected, he didn't like my crude gay jokes. Maybe he didn't like my talk of how to train a woman properly. Maybe he didn't like my position of burning down the government and ripping the safety net out from under all those fucking welfare queens. Then Larry recalled that while Peter had listened to his rants — which he suddenly realized were just like his father's — Peter had never laughed with him like he had with other people. He knew that Peter was quick to laugh. He'd seen it. As for the girls that had surrounded Peter, none of them had ever spilled over to him. His effort from that angle had been a total bust. But, for some reason, he had liked Peter Bennett. He still did.

Looking at Peter Bennett's number now, Larry wondered if Peter would remember him. Worse, what would he remember? He felt his jaw constrict at the thought.

He wished he hadn't run his mouth about his political beliefs. Politics was a funny thing, a touchy thing. A great divider. A destroyer of relationships.

Then, he remembered all that he had said to Peter about women knowing their place and the necessity of training them to be subservient to men. Closing his eyes, he vividly recalled Peter's narrow-eyed look of tight amusement. What had Peter said? Something like, "Yeah, good luck with that. The women I know would serve you your heart on a platter for such antiquated thinking."

Peter had never spoken to him again after that night.

Larry dropped his face into his hands.

# CHAPTER THREE

Larry leaned his elbows on his desk, covering his eyes in self-loathing and reflection.

Antiquated thinking? Was he so wrong? He sighed hard, lowering his hands. He needed a drink to screw up the courage to call Peter. It wasn't that he was afraid of Peter. Well, he was. But it was more that the other phone calls hadn't gone well. Not one. None of his conservative friends had any interest in his problems or in talking with him. Peter was the absolute last contact he had. More importantly, if Peter allowed him to write for The Political Standard, he'd be back in business. He'd have to write remotely, but that would be fine. Perhaps they would be interested in some right-wing balancing to their liberal shit? Maybe he could sell himself that way?

Standing, Larry grabbed the whisky bottle off the end table. He was pleasantly surprised to find it half full. Taking a long swig, he went online to read The Political Standard. As he scanned through a range of articles, he shook his head in contempt. Christ, they were for easier voting and against the Republican gerrymandering of districts. They were for reproductive rights of women and against the privatization of jails, education and national lands. He sat back, thinking. From a young age he'd been taught that the government doesn't work. What was wrong with privatizing jails and education? Why wouldn't Republicans gerrymander districts if it helped them win elections? Now, he was trying to understand a different perspective. Privatized prisons had contracts to keep them full?

Some prisons were serving just two meals a day — sometimes with rotten food —cruelly keeping inmates hungry? Charter schools also had issues; some schools were scamming the government in various ways? He read that redrawing districts was a Republican method for obliterating minority voting. All this was the opposite of what he thought he knew. Sighing, he continued to research on his computer.

Larry kept reading. He saw there were all manner of articles covering the supposed corruption of the Trump presidency. They ranged from the potential investigation of Trump's obstruction of justice to the potential of Russian mob ties and money laundering. There were also many articles devoted to the question of Russia hacking the 2016 presidential election. There were interviews with senators. There were other members of Congress stating their opinions on various issues, including the raging debate over healthcare. The Political Standard was a serious news-site, publishing many in-depth articles based on "aggressive investigative reporting." These people apparently had real D.C. contacts. They closely followed lobbyists and legislation. They interviewed scientists and economists. They followed global affairs and climate change.

All this scared him.

Fuck, Larry thought, all I do is write hit pieces on helpless homeless people who never hit back. He had never written anything close to the level of reporting in The Political Standard and maybe . . . well, shit, maybe he wasn't qualified. All he knew of writing was within the narrow, mean-spirited confines of The Bart Data Report. Suddenly, Larry realized that Ellison's site seriously sucked, with its lies, innuendo, and conjured up crap. It dawned on him that it was a lot easier to sell hate, chaos, and destruction than it was to actually try to solve the world's problems. Bart's site wasn't about solving problems. It was about agitating people, whipping up conspiracies, and being provocative. People ate it up. Ellison was making a fortune because they did. He had real power because of it.

Larry's head sank to his desk. He felt his eyes burning from frustration and fear. The enormity of his situation was setting in. He was in terrible trouble, serious trouble. He needed to call Peter. He needed to wash his face and summon some courage. Heading to the bathroom, he turned on the faucet and let the water run until it finally got warm. After brushing his teeth, Larry grabbed a washcloth and soaked it with hot water. He spread the steaming cloth over his face. He did this a few times. The heat felt good on his swollen eyes. With his stubble softened, he decided to shave. When his face was smooth, he put on a touch of aftershave. Peter was the most neatly groomed man he knew. He couldn't talk to the man feeling filthy, even on the phone. It was bad enough that he was feeling weak and desperate.

After one more deep breath, he went back to his desk and lifted his cell phone. He was afraid and ashamed, his finger shaking as he touched his finger on Peter's number.

Peter answered promptly, "Peter Bennett."

Larry was so astonished that Peter had answered, he couldn't find his voice. Since Peter had not asked for his number, the man was actually taking an unknown call. He, personally, would never have answered, but was grateful Peter didn't feel the same way.

"Hello?"

"Peter?" Larry asked, his voice catching.

"Yes? Who's this?" Bennett's voice was low and crisp.

"It's Larry Martin. You probably won't—do you remember me?"

"Sure, Larry. What can I do for you?"

At least Peter had not hung up on him. Unsure of how to start, Larry asked, "Do you have a minute?"

"A minute, Larry. What's going on?"

In that instant, Larry decided to be straight up and not bullshit Peter. It wouldn't work anyway. "I need a job, Peter. Writing. Do you have any-thing open?"

Silence. "Don't you write for Bart? I've seen some of your . . . words."

Larry winced. Words. Peter had seen words, not pieces or articles. Just words. "No. No. Not anymore. Let's just say, I've seen the error of my ways. I don't like Bart's approach to issues, so I've left him," he lied.

Peter was silent on the line. The long silence was too much for Larry. He began to babble, "Peter, I'm a good writer. Honestly. I can write anything you want. I can do research and I've been reading The Political Standard and I promise you . . ."

"Listen, Larry," Peter cut in quietly, "I'm not sure you have the skill set to write for TPS. But if you want to send me a fresh perspective on two important political issues, I'll read them. Fair enough?"

Larry swallowed hard. He wanted to ask about money, but now wasn't the time. Instead, he said, "Yeah. Certainly. Very fair. Any suggestions?"

"I'll leave that to you."

"Does it have to be a political issue or can I do a human-interest story?"

"I've made my suggestion, Larry. If you get something together, just upload it as a PDF to the Tips and Information tab at the bottom of the site. It's secure. Put a cover letter on it to my attention."

"Okay, Peter . . . thanks."

"No problem, Larry. Good luck." Peter ended the call.

Larry lowered the phone to his desk. Peter had been generous. And kind. He didn't know any decent human beings, but Peter had just showed him that he was one. He also knew that if it were reversed, he wouldn't have given Peter the time of day. He would have acted like he was too busy and too important to give a guy asking for a job a break. He would have been a real asshole because . . . that's what he was.

With Peter's suggestion, Larry also realized that he was out of his league. Fear gripped his throat. He was woefully behind on major issues of the day, preferring to spend his spare time commenting on men's rights activist message-boards that reinforced his low opinion of women. He had never read progressive blogs. He started reading through TPS, discovering what he didn't know. He had no idea of the Left's vehement resistance to

Trump. He had no idea that Trump had pulled out of the Paris Climate Accord. Or, that Congress was doing its best to destroy Obamacare. He didn't know about Republicans slashing Medicaid or their defunding of Meals on Wheels for seniors. Larry had no idea that the Trump administration was intent on destroying National Public Radio and The National Endowment of the Arts. He had no idea that the Republican Congress was working to eradicate environmental and consumer protections and kill net neutrality. He was clueless that Trump's EPA was working to allow increased industrial pollution and eliminate the regulations that kept drinking water pure for all Americans. This actually shocked him. Who doesn't want good drinking water?

As he skimmed through several progressive sites, Larry discovered there were a lot of issues that he was clueless about. He had much research to accomplish and much to learn. He was overwhelmed. He also had some professional writing to do. He didn't know how he could do it. It could take a while, days, weeks . . . he didn't know. Even more pressing was the need to find paying work immediately. He would wash dishes if he had to, or maybe he could get a job at Walmart.

For the sake of his sanity—if not desperation—he drew up a simple schedule to live by. On a piece of notebook paper, he carefully wrote:

| | |
|---|---|
| 8:00- 11:30 a.m | Read progressive news and pick subjects to research/develop to send to Peter. |
| 11:30 - 12:30 | Shower, shave and lunch |
| 12:30 on | Look for a job. |
| 7:00 - 11:00pm | Formulate facts/organize/outline topics. Write. |

The short list activated more depression. But he couldn't afford to stay depressed, so he dug in deeper, determined to live by his list.

Rising from his chair, Larry glanced at the list one last time, grabbed his jeans jacket, and went to his car. First, he applied to Walmart on their computer kiosk. Then, he drove around to a number of restaurants hoping to bus tables or help in the kitchen. The chain restaurants told him to apply online. The smaller restaurants were willing to talk to him for a minute, but had nothing for him. Discouraged and hungry, Larry returned home. It was nearly 7:00 p.m. and starting to get dark.

Walking into the kitchen, Larry opened his refrigerator. He sighed in frustration. There was a box of his latest leftover pizza, but not much else besides a nearly empty carton of orange juice, a bag of rice, and a half-eaten bowl of macaroni and cheese. Lifting the bowl, he sniffed the rubbery orange glob. He was afraid to eat it. It was so old, he didn't even remember making it. Food poisoning was the last thing he needed right now. After scraping the bowl into the garbage, Larry returned to the fridge and withdrew the pizza box. Lifting the lid, he stared at the remaining two pieces of deflated pepperoni pizza. Except for the slight curling of the edges, they might still be edible if he warmed them in the oven. Turning on the oven, he placed them on the rack and set the timer for ten minutes. As the pizza was heating, he returned to his desk and began the process of filling out online applications for the chain restaurants he had visited earlier in the afternoon. He was surprised by their complexity. They wanted to know his personality, people skills, capacity to memorize and background. Worse, under the experience category, he had nothing to say. He had never worked in a restaurant. He'd never had any job but The Bart Data Report and he didn't want to even mention it. His father was right. He was stupid, just damn stupid. How could he be twenty-three years old and have done nothing in his life — no school awards, no hobbies, no volunteering, no work history and zero accomplishments? But, Larry thought, there it is. That's me, a zero.

Eating old pizza between typing, Larry tried to find something positive to say. He was a writer after all, wasn't he? Certainly he could find clever words to make himself shine. Words like: "I have a great desire to break into a new industry. I'm a team player." Words like how he looked forward to learning something new and growing. Or that he liked people, had a great personality, a dedication to work, was reliable and could be counted on to do a great job. *Blah, blah, blah.* His neck ached. He was suddenly weary, suddenly out of words. Staring at this laptop, he saw that it was nearly 1:00 a.m. Standing, Larry stretched, brushed his teeth, and fell into bed. With his head on the pillow and covers pulled to his chin, he gazed at the heavy moon shining outside his window. I'll begin again tomorrow, he thought.

Rising early, Larry poured himself a glass of orange juice. He went to his computer to read the news and search for a compelling article topic for Peter. That afternoon, he went out job hunting again. He hit retail stores, fast food restaurants, and even two pet stores. All had required online applications. Diligently, Larry applied until he was exhausted. Why was it so damn hard to find a simple job?

For the next few weeks, Larry stuck tightly to his schedule. For all his applications, he had yet to find a position, much less get hired or frankly, even interviewed. He lost count of the days as they ticked by. He had tried Monster.com, Zip Recruiter, and Craigslist for every entry level position he thought he was qualified for, but no one ever responded. No one ever thanked him for applying. There was nothing but frustrating internet silence. With no background in anything but writing, no practical experience of any sort, that's what he got — nothing. No replies.

One thing was changing for Larry though. He was starting to get the hang of the progressive sites, their thinking, concepts, and positions on issues. For Larry, it was like experiencing an alternate universe. The research for his articles had been mind-expanding. He had lived so long in the narrow, rigid viewpoint of The Bart Data Report's hatred of everything progressive, he'd never once thought beyond it. Now he was less intimidated by new insights and education. Learning isn't easy, he thought, but then, mind-bending never is.

Finally, Larry settled on the subject of traditional public education versus charter schools. After reading extensively on the issue from different perspectives, both conservative and progressive, Larry actually grew afraid of for-profit charter schools. He titled his first article:

## *The Ultimate Peril of Ending Public Education for All Americans.*

He began to type, opening with a personal viewpoint:

> *While my own public high school experience was not great, much of that was my fault. I was far too often lazy or uninvolved. Looking back now, I can't imagine where I would be without that education or access to it.*

Leaning back in his seat, Larry considered his father, Ray, an ignorant fuck of a man. Yes, they had been poor but, in his case, there was more to it than that. Ray hadn't just been stingy, he was also a sick, evil bastard. His father would never have paid a penny for him to be educated. Larry could see how millions of kids could be in the same situation, even if their parents were good people, but too poor to afford the costs of for-profit schooling. Lifting his fingers to the keyboard, he continued to type:

> *Access is the key word here.*
>
> *I mean this in terms of a fundamental right. Right now, it is still possible for any child in this country to receive an affordable, quality education no matter who they are or how much their families earn. This is what public education delivers — or what it once did. But no institution can be financially starved and remain healthy, viable, and accessible for everyone. What we are seeing now is a willful attack on that fundamental right.*
>
> *Today, charter schools — often private and religious — are siphoning off critical tax dollars from public schools. As federal funding is intentionally slashed, public schools are closing at an alarming rate. The obvious intent is to end the time-honored tradition of free education for all American children.*
>
> *There is every possibility of this continuing to happen.*
>
> *Prior to 2008, public schools were doing fairly well. After the recession, funding for public education did not recover. At*

*least twenty-nine states were providing less funding overall to their educational systems, and local funding was not making up the difference. It is apparent the federal government does not care. Federal funding for almost all forms of state and local aid has continued to fall, especially under Trump's administration.*

*The problem isn't just charter schools themselves. The problem is that Republicans are seeking to kill public education.*

He took a sip of water and continued:

## PUBLIC EDUCATION AFFECTS OUR COUNTRY

*What will happen to the quality of public education in grades K-12, should they continue to decline from deepening funding cuts? What will happen in the long run if public schools continue to close?*

*If this continues — and Betsy DeVos is doing her best to ensure that it does — it will affect the future economic growth of our country. We know business must have a well-educated workforce in order to function, much less prosper. How can anyone support weakening our future workforce by intentionally cutting funds to education? Now, more than ever, we must ensure Americans have the skills to master new technologies and acclimate to the increasing pressure and complexities of a global economy. We have to grow and adapt. Or we fall behind.*

## CHARTER SCHOOLS ARE NOT DELIVERING

*For-profit schools do not serve the public. They serve only their own bottom line. They have to. They are, after all, for-profit. For-profit schools can also select and choose which students to admit. This means that millions of marginalized students will never get past those hallowed doors. Maybe they are black. Maybe they are fat. Maybe the interviewing administrator just doesn't like them. Discrimination can run rampant without governance. If we have a thriving public school system to fall back on, this isn't a problem. If we don't, then it certainly is.*

## PUBLIC SCHOOLS ARE ESSENTIAL

*Public schools will take any child regardless of race, creed, disabilities, gender or grades into their school, as long as that child lives within their district. Any parent can afford free. Any parent can know their child will get an education because their child **will** be admitted. Their child **will** have a school.*

*However, as public education is slowly being decimated in favor of charter and private schools — although tuition may be partially subsidized — the poor still won't be able to afford the expenses beyond this subsidy. I can apply this to my own situation. Growing up, my father was a poor man. If he had to pay precious dollars to educate me, I would not have received an education. The money was just not there.*

Larry stopped typing. He needed some water. Sliding his chair back, he went into the kitchen. He found a large plastic cup and filled it from the faucet. He stood there, gulping and analyzing. He returned to his chair and set the water on his desk. Then he continued to type:

## CHARTER SCHOOLS ARE GROWING AND OFTEN SCAMS

*Aside from the problem of affording education, let's look at the rapid growth of charter schools. Today, there are approximately 7,000 charter schools with a combined attendance of more than 3.1 million students.*

*These schools tout themselves as private schools, but when they accept federal dollars — our tax money — they are no longer truly private. And look at what has happened. These schools have virtually no government oversight of either curriculum or finances. These schools have already wasted over a billion dollars in government funds. They are often complete scams, set up to accept federal money, without ever opening! They are supposed to be nonprofit organizations, but they enter into contracts with other for-profit companies —companies they happen to own. These companies profit tremendously off of students supported by our tax dollars. These companies overcharge for leases, facilities, and school supplies. Charter schools sometimes pay these "contracted" companies twice the market rate for rent, bilking billions of dollars from this system. When it comes to their teachers, they are underpaid. Many are uncertified. The same goes for the lack of support services to students. Worse, there is no evidence that students perform better at charter schools.*

*It is troublesome that, at the alarming rate of diminishing free education, these schools may end up being our only form of schooling unless they are stopped. If they are not, the result will be, rather than lifting all boats for the necessary and critical intellectual growth of America, there will simply be no boats unless a child can not only get admitted but can afford the costs beyond what is being subsidized.*

*But there is a reality and it's this:*

## THE REALITY OF AMERICAN SAVINGS

*According to a 2017 government survey, more than half of Americans (57 percent) have less than $1,000 in their savings accounts.*

*Think about that. It means that the majority of Americans — nearly 60 percent — are close to being broke, with little to no savings. So how do they afford expensive private school tuition?*

*They don't.*

*When and if private schools ever become all that remain of our educational system — where we seem to be currently headed — there will be a terrible consequence.*

Larry rolled his neck, feeling weary. Leaning forward, he began to type again.

*It will lead to the literal death of our once fully educated nation. This isn't conjecture. To test the truth of this assertion, all one must do is compare the number of people living in relative poverty to the number of those who don't.*

*Extrapolating the trend of diminishing public schools, eventually, free education will be over. Admittance for all will be over. Education will be accessible to only those who can afford it. This will only widen the gulf between rich and poor. It will amplify inequality. It will produce avoidable mass poverty. It will produce increased crime. It will produce the jailing of those of whom, had they not been left behind, would have avoided being sucked into drugs or crime or worse.*

*The fact is, hopelessness kills.*

*We all know this.*

*If poverty leads to despair — and it does — what kind of thinking leads this Administration and Congress to purposefully inflict such misery and mayhem when it doesn't have to? Why is the funding of unnecessary wars and giving tax cuts to the wealthy a priority over the educational health and intellectual growth of our country? When leaders refuse to invest in the citizens of their country, just what are they investing in? War? Debt? The rich? Prisons?'*

He took a sip of water and continued:

*The loss of education for young American minds is also a loss for the innovation, diversity and the future of America. Condemning a massive segment of America's youth to hopelessness is beyond folly.*

*It is dangerous. It is destructive. It is ruinous.*

Larry paused, thinking. So, what is the solution to all this, he asked himself. Fingers moving, he continued:

*The only solution, the only antidote to poverty and sustained economic growth, is a greater investment in public education. Failure to do this is to fail our children. And, should this happen, we will ultimately fail ourselves.*

After writing three pages, Larry leaned on his desk, staring at his article. Hitting the spacebar a few times, he typed a note to Peter:

Peter, I feel I should leave it there. But, if not, here is further ending . . .

*Knowing all this, what kind of leadership does such gross harm to its country? I'll tell you. It's a Republican administration that, according to Trump, loves the poor and uneducated. After all, poverty has no voice to the powerful and the ignorant will fall for anything. It's the perfect plan for the few to reap it all, leaving the rest of America to fight over the scraps.*

Standing abruptly, Larry snatched a book off his desk and threw it angrily across the room. *God!* He didn't know himself anymore. What the hell was he writing? He felt like his brain was distorting, causing his head to hammer. He was acutely aware he'd been forced to learn quickly. He knew his articles had to succeed. If they didn't, he would lose the only hope he had for now of writing for a living. If they failed, he would lose his connection with Peter. He didn't want that. But he was personally troubled. Half of him had believed what he was writing. No. More than half. He had been angry over the charter school issue. He had tried to write with passion. Sighing, he picked up the book and set it back on his desk. Shaking his head, he no longer knew what he believed. He was a mess. His life was a mess. *That* was all he knew.

Striding away from his laptop, Larry grappled with his foul mood. Snapping off the lights, he fell into bed, worried and stressed over his own predicament of poverty. He was still hungry. His rent was long past due. He hardly slept that night.

The following evening, Larry sat at this desk to write his next article. As his thoughts formed, he found himself holding his head. The topic and his approach were once again going to be excruciatingly difficult for him. The reverse of everything he had believed —especially about women. Hadn't he always hated women and wanted nothing more than to beat them into submission? Well, it had never worked for him. He thought of how Peter loved women. And, they loved him back. From what he had seen, Peter's method of treating them well had worked out real good for the guy. But the notion of men loving women was a tough one for him. He realized then that much of his hatred of women stemmed from the one woman who was supposed to love and protect him. His mother. She had abandoned him, leaving him at the mercy of his abusive father. No wonder I am so messed up, he thought unhappily. Leaning forward, he slowly began to type the title of his theme:

### *"Destroy Reproductive Rights of Women? Reap The Consequences."*

Staring at his title, Larry dove into its implications. Aside from the arcane notion of forcing a woman to birth a child she didn't want or shouldn't have, there was a significant possibility of her dying as a result. That's just cruel and absurd, Larry thought with new insight. Anyway, forced pregnancy wasn't just a female problem either. There were plenty of men who would be furious over a compulsory child they objected to or couldn't afford. Larry now knew that red states like Texas were relentless in their attacks on women, abortion clinics and especially Planned Parenthood. The result was obvious. Women were no longer receiving enough care and as a consequence, maternal mortality rates had doubled. Doubled! Larry shook his head. How do you see a hundred percent increase in women dying and do nothing about it, he wondered. It all goes back to men's attitudes toward women, he reflected. Like the discussion on the men's sites about whether women were human. Man, he thought, if I were a woman, I'd be seriously pissed.

But the issue was only growing worse and more hostile.

Women were being attacked all over the country by hundreds of conservative anti-women bills passed under the guise of 'pro-life.' But, from all that he had read, it appeared to him that Republicans didn't give a rat's ass about what happened to a child once it was born. They were eviscerating Medicaid, children's healthcare, food stamps, school lunches and public education — anything that would help a child grow up healthy and happy.

Still, this wasn't the focus of Larry's article. Rather, he intended to angle his article to the dangers of what would happen to the United States if, annually, approximately 80 million child-bearing age women were forced to give birth. The numbers would be staggering and it wouldn't take too many years for these numbers to pile up. Who would care for these millions upon millions of unwanted babies? The strain on states coping with cast-off children would be monumental.

The financial strain on hospitals would cause many to close, especially in rural and high poverty areas. Poor people wouldn't have insurance and they sure as hell wouldn't be able to afford fifteen to thirty thousand dollars for a normal hospital birth. What if the child wasn't normal at birth? The costs could run into the hundreds of thousands per fetal anomaly. Children born with heart conditions or other serious problems would drain the system drastically and rapidly. What choice would a poor family have but to abandon such a child to the state? Especially when the alternative might mean being jailed for child abuse when they couldn't provide proper care for a situation into which, by law, they had been forced.

At what point would the state decide these children were not worth saving? And, at what point would states start to notice children piling up on the streets and turning to crime to feed themselves?

The result of all this was obvious. Forcing women to reproduce at an unmitigated rate would cause the dangerous destabilization of society. It would plunge Americans into massive, inexorable poverty. It would shred families, feed the prison complex and create millions upon millions of uneducated, hopeless, jobless people with virtually no chance of success. Outsourcing and robots were already claiming many jobs. With the rise of artificial intelligence, entire industries were going to be wiped out in the near future. With no answers to this, no solutions being created, laws which would force millions of more people into the world were unthinkable. Larry's conclusion was that forced reproduction was a recipe for a painful, dystopian human disaster. And, America would buckle under the weight of the misery and its costs.

After reading and editing his article for the twentieth time, Larry finally sent it to Peter.

He fell asleep hungry and drained. He had nightmares of starving children clawing at his face as they tried to climb over him. He woke up fuming and fearful of the future. With no money to buy groceries, Larry was, himself, close to starving. He needed coffee but had none. Instead, he mixed up the last of his oatmeal and then, went to check the mail he'd neglected for days. Throwing away all the coupons and circulars, he landed upon an official looking letter from the management company for his duplex. Opening the envelope, his hands began to shake. His heart began to race as he read the eviction process had begun against him. Sinking into his desk chair, he lowered his head to his crossed arms.

Larry wanted someone to save him. He wanted someone to commiserate with him. He wanted friends like those of Peter Bennett's to walk through the front door this instant, saying that they'd heard the news of his being fired and it really sucked.

Larry wanted them to be loaded down with fast food and coffee and pat him on the back saying everything would be okay. That he could even stay with any of them if he needed to for a while. You know, until he got on his feet. They would eat and laugh and he would feel immensely better. Safer. More secure. Loved.

Immersed in his fantasy, Larry began to smile. Raising his head and through bleary eyes, he gazed at the front door expecting them to walk in at any moment now. Yes, the door would open any second now.

It never did.

# CHAPTER FOUR

Larry closed his eyes. No friends were coming. He had no friends. No one was going to save him. Numbly, he glanced down at the letter on his desk which defined him as a loser. He had hunted down every job and stayed neat, clean and sober. But it was not enough. He was going to lose his apartment in a handful of days. If something didn't change soon, he *was* going to be homeless. His empty stomach growled in pain.

For lunch, he heated up his last can of stewed tomatoes and poured it on the last of his boiled pasta. After wolfing it down, he felt a bit better. Contemplating his circumstances, he decided to stay in his apartment until the final hour when there was nothing more to do, nothing left to fight. At least, until then, even if hungry, he would be sleeping in a secure bed. Try as he might, he could not see himself sleeping in his car or worse, under some bush out in the open air. And somehow, still surviving.

The thought was too much for him and he walked to his bathroom.

Staring at himself in the mirror, he was dimly aware that his buzzed hair had morphed into a weirdly flat mess hanging nearly an inch long from his scalp. Larry staggered out of the room and back to bed, clutching a soft blanket to his cheek and chewing on his lips. He slept the afternoon away, and finally woke up around 5:00 p.m. He was hungry again but too disoriented and upset to dwell on it. Pacing around the room, he came to his front door. Swinging it open, he stared at his car parked in front of his duplex. A few weeks ago, he had found a container of oil in his trunk and added it to his engine. It had been enough to turn off the oil light but his check engine light was still on. He knew his car was developing a serious oil leak and he was worried about it.

A nervous energy began to bubble inside of him. He felt as though he needed to do something like run around the block. Instead, he decided to clean his car. His decrepit Toyota looked much like his apartment had: filthy and filled with fast food containers and other trash. Grabbing a bucket from under his sink, he filled it with water and carried it out by his car. Returning to his kitchen, he gathered dish soap, a sponge, a trash bag, glass cleaner and a roll of paper towels. He piled them in a large metal bowl. With his arm around the bowl, Larry turned on his stereo. Leaving the front door open so he could hear the music, he set about scrubbing his car.

When he was finished, the Toyota looked much better. With the sun now setting in the distance, there was nothing to do but pack up his cleaning supplies and drop the bag of car trash into a nearby dumpster. Standing by the dumpster made him ill. Would he soon be dumpster diving too?

Dinner was a small bowl of dry Cheerios he took to his computer. He spent the rest of the night searching online for any new job postings. He didn't see any. The pain of anxiety caused him to sweat. It caused him to feel ill. It caused him to despair.

In the morning, he drove around to various businesses, a car wash, a mechanics shop and others, asking if they needed help. He stopped at a mom and pop burger joint asking for work. The owner had nothing for him. The delicious aroma of cooking meat tore at his gut. He was so hungry, he was lightheaded.

Stepping through the doors to return to his car, Larry noticed a couple rising to leave their table in the outdoor seating area. The girl had barely eaten her burger and fries. The second they were gone, Larry jumped to the table and lifted her plate. Clutching the dish to his chest, he walked briskly away. He fully expected someone to stop him. No one did. He kept up his hurried pace, passing other stores of the strip center, until he came to a grassy area with a large tree at the end of the sidewalk. Circling the tree, he sat with his back against the trunk so that he faced a lightly forested area. Feeling mostly hidden, Larry ravaged the food on the plate. Part of him couldn't believe that he had just eaten a stranger's food. The other part of him was too grateful for a real meal to analyze what he had just done. Leaving the plate by the tree, Larry stumbled back to his car. The mid-June heat was unbearable; his car was an oven. Turning the ignition, the old Toyota sputtered to life. Laying his hand on the burning steering wheel, he noticed his gas tank was perilously low on gas. He needed money fast. But how?

An idea formed in his mind. It was awful, but he had seen other people do it. He could do it too. Desperate times call for desperate measures. Driving home, he swung by a liquor store to get some cardboard boxes. Once at his apartment, he cut the boxes into flat cardboard for signs. He made four. They read:

*Homeless - Anything helps. Please.*

His plan was to go begging on Ridge Avenue near South Atlanta Park. Placing the signs on the backseat of his car, Larry drove to Ridge Avenue and Center Street. He parked his car at an apartment complex not far from the corner where he intended to stand. There was a traffic light at the corner so people would see his sign as they stopped for a red light. They would have time to give him money. He wanted the money, but he hated what he was going to do and was profoundly embarrassed.

Dressed in a plain white t-shirt, jeans and scuffed sneakers, he looked the part of a homeless person. Since he had not shaved since yesterday, the stubble added to his look. He tried to think of this as a job. He tried to not be so depressing in his manner that people avoided him. He discovered that a small questioning smile helped. Being stone-faced didn't work and too broad of a smile made people think he was too happy. He made $14.80 that afternoon. It took him three hours.

Driving to the gas station, he put ten dollars into his tank. He moved on to the grocery store. Kroger always had a bin or cart with aging fruit or vegetables. Bless Kroger, Larry thought, and headed there first.

These fruits or vegetables were covered by a red net bag containing three to six pieces per bag. Maybe more. Each bag sold for .99 cents. This time they had summer squash and apples. He placed two bags, one of each, into his cart. Hunger on his mind, he moved to the deli and dropped a pre-made turkey sandwich into his cart. After grabbing a single bottle of orange juice, he made for the men's room. There, he ate the sandwich on the toilet, gulping it down with the juice. Stuffing the sandwich packing into some paper towel by the sink, he left the men's room and sticking his hand into the women's room, dropped the paper lump into the trash can by the door. He had to eat, even as his heart was racing with guilt. But they would find no evidence on him. Next, he went to the bakery section. He got a loaf of Italian bread on sale for .99 cents. Last, he went to the milk section and got a small bottle of whole milk for .99 cents. He had four dollars and eighty cents in his pocket, just enough to cover his bill with pennies to spare.

As he checked out, he waited for someone to stop him. It was possible a security video would show him taking the sandwich. When no one did, he drove home in relief with his bread, milk, squash and apples. The milk would give him some wet cereal again. The bread and squash would make a good dinner as he still had some butter. Apples for dessert would be good too.

Larry was drained from his day. He was already sick of the fear.

Entering his apartment, he set the groceries on the kitchen counter and rinsed his face and hands in the kitchen sink. Standing over the sink, hands braced on the edge, he allowed the water to drip off his face. He decided then and there that he would go begging again tomorrow. It had been utterly humiliating but it had worked. At least he was doing something. Glancing at the groceries, his resolve solidified. He had something real to show for his mortification.

Suddenly, he thought of Peter Bennett. The Political Standard was based in New York and that's where Peter was. What must his life be like there?

Had he read his articles yet? Larry wondered. What did he think? Was Peter out on the town tonight with a beautiful woman? Did she look like a model with shoulder length blonde hair, dressed in a classy black cocktail dress? Was Peter stylishly dressed in designer pullover and pressed slacks? Was he ordering an expensive bottle of wine over a carefree candle-light dinner? Did he pay a tab of several hundred dollars without thinking about it? Did he make love to her on scented sheets? Did he live in a hand-some, masculine apartment of glass, rich woods, and plush leather sofas overlooking the city?

Larry had no idea how Peter lived. But, knowing Peter, it would be like that. Without envy, Larry hoped so. He could envision Peter's life so clearly and wished these good things for his only friend. A friend with whom he had a one-sided relationship. Peter would not be thinking of him, he was sure. The contrast of their lives was also sadly jarring to him. He was a loser. Peter was not. If Peter saw him now, he could only feel contempt.

Drying his face with the kitchen towel, Larry realized that he was already beginning to feel homeless. Not just thinking about it. Not just being frightened of it but actually feel it. The intensity of it sucked the life out of him.

Without warning, he suddenly felt very, very old.

# CHAPTER FIVE

Waking the next morning, Larry decided his new schedule would be to continue his job search in the morning and spend his afternoons begging. Over the next two weeks, he found other corners to stand on. He was determined to never be on the same corner more than two days in a row. Moving around was best. He wanted no trouble from the cops. Being predictable was the fastest way to gain unwanted attention. Even seeing a cop car sent his heart racing. He could so easily be arrested. He did not want that.

Larry had learned to bring his old denim jacket when he was panhandling cars. He used it to cover his sign whenever he saw a cop. Then, he would quickly move on and disappear somewhere behind a tree or building. He prayed that he would always be fast enough. The threat was always there. He lived in terror. My begging is worthwhile though, he reflected. It yielded him sometimes as much as thirty dollars in an afternoon. He was no longer hungry and now, he could also afford to keep his car filled with gas.

One evening in late June, weary and sweating from the sun pounding him as he worked to collect money from cars, Larry drove home to his duplex. During the drive, he imagined the fresh roasted chicken and corn on the cob he would have for dinner. As he pulled in, he was horrified to see that his front door was wide open. Two large men were dumping his belongings onto his parking pad. Screeching into his neighbor's space as his own was being rapidly filled with a mounting pile of his junk, Larry jumped out of the car, waving his arms, screaming at the men, "No! No! Stop! Please, no! Please stop!"

The man carrying Larry's green armchair dropped it roughly on the asphalt parking pad. "Don't come any closer," he warned Larry, his tone ominous. "We're just doing our job. Now, stand back and let us finish. Or, better yet, help us."

"Is this legal?" Larry cried out, his heart shattering. "This can't be legal!"

"All I know is we have our orders. I don't know anything about your legal situation. Sorry. Now, get out of our way."

Larry ran into his apartment to collect his personal papers and laptop. Loading them on the passenger side of his car, he hurried back in, glancing wildly around, trying to think what he could save and what he would need for his first night on the street. He grabbed his pillow, a few blankets and towels. He loaded up one of the men's cardboard boxes with groceries and condiments. He grabbed some of his favorite books. He filled his backpack and another box with clothes. He also went for his toothbrush, toothpaste, razor and comb. It was all happening so fast. Too fast. The chaos around him was mind-numbing. Degrading. Soul-crushing. The men knew their business and were dismantling his place at an alarming rate.

An hour later, it was over. The contents of his apartment were now heaped on the parking pad. The men were just finishing up, bagging the last of the trash in his apartment.

As the men drove away, Larry stood gazing at the miserable mountain of his pathetic belongings.

He was convinced the management company had dumped him illegally. He hadn't even gone to court. He figured being muscled out as he had just been was probably commonplace. He couldn't know. But he did know that he had neither the energy nor the means to fight his shockingly rapid displacement. Picking up a broken plate, Larry stared at it, his hands shaking, holding the two pieces. This represents my life, he thought in anguish. Broken . . . totally broken. A sob escaped his lips.

Through his haze of misery, it occurred to him that he might need a plate or two, a mug, a pot, a can opener and maybe some silverware. He began to sift through the pile to look for these items. He was numb; in a daze. Finding them in the rubble, he emptied a small box of now useless books and placed the more necessary items gently inside. He also spied a roll of toilet paper. Adding it to the box, he set the box in the trunk of his car. Tears were streaming down his face, his breath reduced to harsh jags.

He was now everything he had despised and mocked and hated. Standing there, he rolled his head back and with his right fist striking his chest, let out a primal scream of frustration, anger and disbelief. He had no friends. He had nowhere to go. He was truly homeless. He was a loser. In agony, he dropped to his knees, his sobs shaking him, his tears pelting the ground.

Larry didn't know how long he stayed there. But slowly, his vision began to clear. Slowly, he began to regain control of himself. Slowly, his thoughts began to churn. What was he going to do? What was his plan? What did he have to work with?

Wiping his eyes on his sleeve, Larry considered the hundred and three dollars in his pocket. He also had his car. That made him not entirely destitute. For now. Stumbling to his feet, he moved to his car and climbed into the seat.

His neighbor pulled up then, grimacing at the sight of the disreputable mound of Larry's belongings.

Larry backed out sluggishly to allow the man into his space. His neighbor parked and turned off his car. Opening the door, the man stepped out and walked over to Larry's car window. "I'm sorry for you," he said kindly, leaning down to talk with Larry better. "This is really tough, man."

Larry nodded mutely, not trusting his voice.

"Listen," the man said, "we've never really spoken. My name is Nick. I hate to see this happen to anyone. Do you have anywhere to go?"

Larry shook his head, ashamed. A tear leaked down his cheek.

Nick sighed, pulling out his wallet from the back pocket of his slacks. "Okay. Let me at least buy you a motel room for the night." Opening his billfold, Nick pulled out a hundred-dollar bill and handed it to Larry.

"Thanks, man," Larry mumbled thickly, taking the money. "I very much appreciate your kindness."

"Sure." Nick glanced over at the pile of Larry's stuff. "What will happen to your things?"

"I don't know. They're lost to me now. Help yourself to anything you want. I imagine our landlord will come and cart it all away soon. Sorry for the mess."

"Yeah. Yeah, it must be hard," Nick said softly. "Okay, then . . . best of luck to you, my friend."

"I'm Larry. Larry Martin."

"Larry," Nick repeated. "Yeah. Well, take care." He patted Larry's shoulder lightly and turning, went into his apartment.

The sun was nearly gone and twilight was setting in. Traumatized, Larry started his engine and drove to the nearest strip mall. Sitting in the parking lot, he felt weak with hunger but at the same time, he wasn't sure that he could eat anything. He focused dully on the Mexican restaurant in front of him. Thinking of food, he settled on getting a couple of beef tacos and a beer. Maybe then, he would have the strength to make future plans.

He lowered his head and cut his engine. He sat for a while, breathing out of his mouth, trying to regain himself. His nose was still stuffy from crying. He didn't want to go into the restaurant looking upset. He sat quietly for over half an hour. Finally, he went inside, his eyes still swollen and his spirit still utterly shattered.

# CHAPTER SIX

Entering the restaurant, Larry nodded to the hostess who told him to sit anywhere. The place wasn't busy. He chose a booth in the back corner where he could be relatively private. Sliding into the booth, he was relieved the eatery was cool and dim and soothing. He needed cool, dim and soothing. His head hurt so badly.

The waiter placed a basket of warm tortilla chips and a bowl of freshly made salsa on his table. Larry told the man he was just getting a snack and just wanted a beer and two beef tacos. The waiter left. Larry dug into the crisp chips and spicy salsa like a deranged person. Minutes later, when the waiter returned with Larry's beer, the basket was empty. So was the salsa. The waiter, sure he'd make no money on this table, silently cleared away the bowl and basket without offering more. Shortly later, a table runner set a plate of steaming tacos in front of Larry. He ate them slowly remembering that once he left the restaurant, he had nowhere to go.

As he sipped his beer, Larry decided he would drive up the street to the Kroger parking lot and spend the night there. He was pretty sure no one would bother him. Cars were always in the parking lot at all hours. First, he would go into the store and buy a small flashlight so he could read in his car. Then, deeper into the night when traffic at the store was quiet, he would reorganize the contents of his car. He would find his toothbrush, comb and maybe his razor. He would find his pillow and blankets and sleep if he could. Come morning, he would wash up in the bathroom and buy some coffee from the Starbucks inside. After that, he would consider what to do next. Baby steps.

It wasn't much of a plan, but it calmed him. Long after Larry had finished his tacos, he remained in the booth, nursing his beer. Eventually, the waiter returned to ask if Larry wanted anything else. When Larry said no, the waiter gave Larry his bill; $5.00 for the tacos and $2.50 for the beer plus tax. All things considered, Larry knew the bill was reasonable, but he loathed parting with the money. However, he also knew he could get more money from his begging. He still had his four signs.

Something shifted in Larry's attitude. It was an insightful shift for him. While he ate, he kept coming back to the all-important question of why he was completely without friends. He could lie to himself or be honest. Lying would get him nowhere. Frowning, he considered his personality and general nature. Somewhere in the middle of the second taco, he hit upon the answer. It was simple, really. He did not treat people right. He had never treated them well. He had never been a good person. He was a racist, misogynist, and a stingy, mean-spirited man. These self-realized truths were enough of a clue to his friendless state to make him cringe inwardly. He thought of Peter. Peter was a better person. Somehow, he had to change to become more like Peter. But how could he do that? How did he become a better person?

Suddenly, Larry was determined not to stiff the waiter. Reaching into his wallet, he handed the Mexican man a ten-dollar bill saying, "Keep the change."

"Gracias," the waiter replied, leaving Larry to finish his beer.

Giving the waiter a full twenty percent tip was a small but significant milestone in Larry's life. He had always stiffed his waiters figuring in his arrogance that if being a waiter was all a person aspired to, they deserved to be poor. It had never occurred to Larry that they were working to earn a living. To pay their bills. To support themselves and their families. The old, self-important Larry would never have understood this. But, the new Larry did. Oh god, I am about to start a new phase in my life, Larry thought. The old saying about walking a mile in another man's shoes took hold in his mind. He wished it hadn't. But that was exactly what was going to happen and what he would do. Wear the shoes of a homeless man.

Draining the last of his beer, Larry left the restaurant.

A few minutes later, he was circling the Kroger parking lot in search of the right place to spend the night. He chose a spot under a tree at the edge of the lot. Tucked into the space, he left his car. Passing other parked cars, he traversed the length of asphalt into the brightly lit store. It didn't take him long to locate a small flashlight pack that came with two batteries. He also bought a gallon of drinking water, a cheap roll of paper towels and a box of doughnuts on sale for a buck. Returning to his car, he found a book to read for a couple of hours while eating stale donuts washed down with water.

Around midnight, when the parking lot was quiet, Larry quickly pissed under the tree. Pouring water from his gallon onto his doughnut sticky hands, he dried his hands with a paper towel. Then, unloading the contents of his car onto the asphalt, he found the personal grooming items he was looking for. Grabbing his backpack, Larry removed the clothes he put in earlier and folded them neatly on top of his other box of clothes. He would go through them later. He packed his comb, toothbrush, toothpaste, razor, deodorant and a fresh pair of underwear into his backpack. He set the backpack on the passenger seat for the morning. Repacking his car and trunk, Larry arranged his belongings in such a way that he could lower his driver's seat to an almost horizontal position. Then, he layered the driver's seat with three blankets and his pillow. The last thing he did was cover his windshield with a black towel to prevent the sun from blasting him at first light.

Climbing into the bed he'd made on his seat, Larry lowered the window halfway for circulation before laying down his head. Exhausted and numb, he settled back on one soft thick blanket folded under him and two others covering him. Though comfortable enough now, he burned with the feeling that this was the worst night of his life. He rocked in shame and pain until he finally stopped moving.

Morning came gently. The blackout towel on Larry's windshield had been genius. As the sun began its eastern rise, it was sixty-eight degrees, clear and sunny. But the car remained dark and Larry slept through the glory of early morning under the snugness of his blankets. He woke up several hours later on his left side, his nose tucked deep into his pillow. He opened his eyes slowly in awe. He was feeling so peaceful, he didn't want to move. A quick check of his cell phone showed it was 10:00 a.m. He might have drifted off to sleep again except for a new urgency to pee. Shaking off his blankets, he pulled the towel off the windshield. He grabbed his backpack and headed for the store. The parking lot was already busy with customers.

In the bathroom, Larry pulled a few paper towels from the dispenser and soaked them in the sink. Then, he pulled a few more which he kept dry. Stepping into a stall, he set the backpack on the ground and placed the wet and dry towels on it. After using the toilet, he opened the backpack and pulled out his fresh underwear. Laying the plaid boxers over his shoulder, he stripped off his jeans and old underwear. He rinsed and dried his groin and pulled on his fresh underwear. When his jeans were back on, he lifted his t-shirt and rinsed his armpits. Next, he rolled on some deodorant, liking the spicy masculine scent.

Leaving the stall, Larry went to the sink and turned on the hot water. Splashing his face several times, he lathered his stubble with the foamy soap from the sink dispenser. Shaving quickly with a nervous eye on the door, he followed the shave with brushing his teeth. Lowering his head into the sink, he wet his hair and then stuck his head under the hand-dryer for a while. Returning to the mirror above the sink, Larry combed his damp, growing hair away from his face. He was done. He could breathe again. He was thankful no one had disturbed him. A quick glance in the mirror told him he didn't look too bad. At least he felt cleaner. Sliding his arms into the straps of the backpack, he left the bathroom.

As Larry was heading to the coffee counter to buy a cup, he realized his face was beginning to itch. This rerouted him to the personal products aisle where he found a simple bottle of skin lotion with a pop-up top. He took the bottle from the shelf and walked away with it. As he headed down another aisle, he squirted some lotion into one hand. Turning back to the personal products area, he put the bottle back in the same spot from where he had gotten it and kept going. Intent on getting coffee, he spread the lotion over his hands and face as he walked. The lotion did the trick and stopped the itch.

At the Starbucks counter, Larry bought a large black coffee to go and left the store. Returning to his car, he placed his coffee on the roof of his car. He folded up the blankets of his bed. Opening the back door, he set the pillow, blankets and towel in a neat pile on the empty seat. Retrieving his coffee, Larry settled in behind the wheel. Sipping his coffee, he stared, unseeing, at the parking lot in front of him, contemplating his next move.

If he was going to be homeless, it would be better and safer to be homeless in a richer area where there weren't many homeless. Too many homeless in any area set people on edge, got their guard up. He wanted to go generally unnoticed. A wealthier, more relaxed area might allow him to move around more freely with no one eyeing him suspiciously. It might offer better opportunities too.

He had once been to Balfour on the northwest side of Atlanta with a coworker. He had liked it. It was clean and neat with a small town feel. In reality though, it had numerous grocery stores, gas stations, restaurants and a Walmart all in close proximity. Larry figured the city of Balfour was at least sixty miles away. To get there, he would have to negotiate several major highways. He wondered if his old car would make it. What if it died on the highway? He would lose everything, the last of what he had. And, as bad as last night had been, he had slept both relatively secure and comfortably enough. He would lose that too.

The perilous thoughts attacked Larry's nervous system. He began to tremble. Fear ate at him again, sucking the life from him, making him tired. My situation is so damn scary, he thought. He knew he was still cold from trauma. He shook his head. He felt so out of control.

Gulping the last of his coffee, Larry made a valiant effort to breathe deeply and summon some courage. Starting his engine, he sat for a minute, his eyes closed, trying to imagine his route. He didn't want to use his cell phone GPS. The battery was already getting too low.

Slowly, he steered himself out of the parking lot and turning towards Balfour, he began his journey.

# CHAPTER SEVEN

By the time Larry reached I-285, he was a nervous wreck. Traffic was fast and dangerous. His old car was shaking at seventy miles per hour. He didn't know this route or this highway. Cars and tractor trailers were whizzing by him. They bounced his creaky little vehicle around in their back draft. His oil light suddenly flashed on. To Larry, it resembled a red-eyed demon. He was instantly terrorized. Eyes wide with stress, he tried to get off the highway. An exit was coming up fast, but he missed it. A monster eighteen-wheeler was blocking his path. Screaming profanities, he turned on his blinker. He tried to maneuver into the right lane. He could not miss the next exit. He had to get oil. His life depended on it. His car was all he had now. Seeing a small opening in traffic, he aggressively jumped lanes. The car behind him laid on the horn long and hard. Keeping an eye on the road signs, he saw the next exit was in one mile.

Exiting off the highway, Larry careened into a large, busy gas station and cut his engine at a pump. He sat for a minute, wrestling down his blood pressure. His heart was still pounding in his head. Finally, he entered the store. The intoxicating odor of oven-roasted hotdogs, burritos, and rolled chicken tacos made his stomach leap in response. He'd eaten nothing yet this morning and his gut was rumbling. Turning abruptly, he headed for the men's room, palming a packaged sandwich on the way. Entering the stall, he sat on the toilet and devoured the egg salad sandwich in four bites. Larry wanted more food — he didn't care what — but he didn't dare steal anything more from this store. As busy as it was, it was also small and probably had cameras in every corner. He might be new to stealing, but he knew better than to get greedy. Rolling the skimpy sandwich cellophane in toilet paper, he flushed it down the toilet. On his way out, he bought ten dollars of gas for his tank and a bottle of motor oil.

Larry was terribly nervous as he pumped his gas. He prayed that no one was calling the cops on him this very minute. While the gas flowed, he popped his hood and poured the oil into his thirsty engine. As he slammed the hood shut, the gas meter clicked to a stop. Shoving the gas nozzle back into the pump, he jumped into his car and raced away.

Driving up the street, Larry searched for a restaurant with outdoor seating and soon, he noticed a Mexican place that fit his bill. Parking away from the entrance, he reached for a black hand towel in his backseat and tucked the edge into the front waistband of his pants. Between his white t-shirt and black towel as an apron, he hoped he looked like a busboy. Studying the various tables, Larry's eyes landed on two girls talking. One of them had almost a full plate of refried beans and maybe enchiladas? It didn't matter. Stepping closer to the table while keeping an eye out for real waiters, Larry asked softly, "May I take your plate?" One girl shook her head. The other, still talking, handed Larry her plate without looking up.

Leaving the eating area, Larry glanced over his shoulder. No one was paying attention to him. Covering the plate with his towel, he made for his car. Starting it, he drove a little further down the road to a strip center where he could eat in peace. The food was cold but good. The only problem was, he had no water to wash it down. He had drunk the last of his gallon on the highway, fighting off his freaked-out, dry-mouth. Then and there, he decided to never run out of water again, that to be without it was both stupid and dangerous. He also decided to keep the plate and set it on top of his stuff on the passenger seat. His hunger satisfied; Larry left the parking lot. Since he wasn't anxious to get back on the highway, he became intent on looking for a store to buy a cheap gallon of water.

A few blocks up the street, Larry pulled into the parking lot of a small food market. Entering, he saw there was just one cashier busy with a line of six people. As he searched for water, he slipped a candy bar into his pants pocket. An apple went into the pocket of his jacket. Pulling a gallon of water off the shelf, he found himself wanting to steal more. The thing was, he had to stop spending. Out of his two hundred and three dollars, he was already down thirty dollars from yesterday. He had to start conserving for emergencies. He wasn't sure what that meant. Only that the possibility existed. The candy, apple and water would hold him for the next thirty miles or so until he reached Balfour, but not much after that. He knew he would steal again. And, realizing this truth with certainty, his shaky pact with peace unraveled.

Standing in line, his thoughts began to needle him. What will happen once I reached Balfour? Where will I spend the night? In what lonely parking lot will I park my car? Will there be light or will it be dark? Which is safer? His apprehensions felt so surreal, Larry began to tremor again. His hand shook, paying for the water. Leaving the store, he climbed into his car, sick at heart, afraid of taking on the highway again.

Getting back on the highway turned out to be blessedly easy. Larry urged his car up to speed and rattled along at sixty miles per hour. Settling in for the last half of his journey, he saw a police car slide in behind his Toyota. He wasn't doing anything wrong, but the cop's presence worked his nerves, causing him to sweat. He tried to relax but his knuckles were white around the steering wheel. Driving as steadily as possible, Larry exhaled in relief when the cop, after a few miles, moved on. The rest of the ride was uneventful. He consumed his apple followed by the candy bar. Trying to hum to a rock song on the radio, eventually, he saw the signs for Balfour and exited towards the town.

The main drag of Balfour, Larry soon discovered, was set up like a 'T'. The stem of the T was a handsome four lane street called Town View Parkway. The road was about eight miles long. The median was nicely land-scaped with grass, brick landings and flowering trees. The sides of the road were loaded with banks, gas stations, grocery stores, various retail shops and restaurants. A Walmart was located at the bottom of the stem. The top of the T was downtown Main Street.

Main Street was mostly two lanes bordered by wide sidewalks meant for strolling. The sidewalks were lined with antique and gift shops, boutiques and restaurants, many of which had outdoor seating. Main Street was clean and charming. Beyond Main Street, the area turned fairly rural.

Turning his car around, Larry left Main Street and headed back to Town View Parkway, fairly confident that he had passed a coffee house there. Driving slowly, he noticed numerous streets leading off the Parkway and imagined they led to residential areas. He would check out those areas later. Right now, he wanted a cup of coffee and even more, an electrical outlet so he could charge his laptop and phone. Both were nearly dead.

Pulling into the parking lot of The Coffee Connection Cafe, Larry saw the restaurant was packed. People were even mingling outside. Scoping out the small parking lot, he saw no available spaces until he suddenly spied a car backing out just a few spots down. He was there in a flash. Turning off his car, Larry grabbed his equipment and walked inside. The freshly baked pastries and exotic ground coffees made the cafe smell delicious. Sofas and easy chairs were artfully arranged. Sets of small tables and chairs lined the walls. People were milling around talking, some sitting in groups and others quietly working. The music was light jazz but it was barely audible as the place was alive with laughter and chatter.

Larry got in line to place his order. Eyeing the glass case of pastries, his mouth watered over the scent of hot cinnamon buns. He wanted one badly. But not bad enough to shell out five bucks for only one bun. He would just get a small black coffee. At four dollars, it was already robbery. Once he paid for his coffee, Larry turned and scanned the place. He saw a girl stand and start to gather her things off the table. Moving quickly, he asked if she was leaving. She was. Before she had even finished packing, Larry sank into the chair clutching his laptop and phone. He looked under the table at the wall. As he suspected, there was an outlet. As the girl moved away from him, he opened his case, pulled out his cords and plugged in his equipment. It was a small moment of triumph. For a few brief seconds, he felt normal. He had a car, he had a laptop, he had a phone and he had coffee. He belonged. He looked the same as everyone there.

Sipping his brew, Larry powered up his laptop. By the third sip, he was feeling an urgent need to use the men's room. It's all the water I drank on the highway, he thought. Glancing around, he wondered if it was safe to leave his laptop and phone on the table. If he took them, he would lose his table and outlet. If he left them, the coffee and electronics would mark the table as occupied and remain his. Staring at his equipment, he was filled with indecision. He decided to leave them. He would be gone for seconds, no more. Then, he could settle in for as long as he needed to get his equipment fully charged. Rising, Larry quickly pushed through the crowd to the bathroom. Relieving himself hurriedly, he exited and pushed his way back through the crowd again.

He came to his table.

Larry stared in disbelief. At his table, an older man sat, dressed in a white polo shirt. The man was typing on a new HP laptop he knew wasn't his. He saw no trace of his own equipment. Panic clutched his throat. His heartbeat roared in his ears. "Where is my laptop and phone?" he demanded angrily.

The man looked up, startled. "What? Excuse me?"

"I left them on this table while I used the men's room. I was only gone for thirty seconds!"

The man shrugged sympathetically. "I don't know what to tell you. Really, I don't. After I got my coffee, I saw this table empty and quickly sat. It's hard to get a table here, you know."

Larry went pale. Turning from the man, he yelled, "Please, everybody . . . did any of you see what happened to the laptop on this table?" Pointing at the table, he raised his voice, upset, "I went to the bathroom and left my phone and computer on this table. I was gone for just seconds! Anybody? Please, please help me!"

For a moment, the chatter and laughter died down. The people closest to Larry shook their heads. "Oh my God," Larry shouted, "my laptop and phone have been stolen! Anyone see who took them? Anyone?"

People backed away from Larry. No one wanted to get near his growing rage. Swinging around the room, he furiously surveyed their faces.

"You fucking latte drinking pigs! Not one of you saw something? Not one?" Larry screamed heatedly.

Leaping around the crowd, Larry began to shove people, searching their hands for his technology. Backing away from Larry even more, no one spoke. The innocent had nothing to contribute. The guilty would remain silent anyway. Some people though, looked understanding, even sympathetic. Dashing out of the cafe, Larry elbowed the customers blocking the door. From the sidewalk, Larry looked sharply to the left and then to the right, hoping to glimpse someone sneaking away with his stuff. He saw no one. He didn't want to talk to the police. They would do nothing anyway.

Head low, and so distressed that he almost couldn't breathe, Larry stumbled back to his car. Climbing in, he slammed the door and stared out the windshield. Hot tears spiked down his cheeks. He had always been an easy crier. As a little boy, he had often cried himself to sleep after his father had hurt him. Ultimately, he had learned to cry in front of no one. But no one was watching now. He leaned over his steering wheel and sobbed openly.

In the midst of his tears, he bitterly thought, *Welcome to Balfour*.

# CHAPTER EIGHT

Larry sat in his car, crying off and on for more than an hour. He had nowhere to go anyway. The theft had been so swift, he wasn't able to wrap his mind around it. He felt mowed down, completely flattened. His two most vital assets were gone; the ones that would have kept him connected to the world. He hadn't even made it through his first day of being home-less without getting destroyed. He had stupidly thought things were going to be okay. Sure, he had eaten a stranger's food again and stolen a few small items, but he had made it to Balfour without his car blowing up. That had made it all bearable, until this . . . this, disaster. Using his busboy towel to blow his nose, he wiped his eyes with a dry corner. But he couldn't stop crying and he resented even considering whether his tears were manly. He didn't give a damn. He'd like to see anybody else in his shoes not cry.

He knew his tears weren't just over his laptop and phone. They were over everything . . . the loss of his job and his self-worth. The loss of his apartment and all his possessions. The loss of his comfort and security. The loss of his footing in the world. It was all of it combined. And it was all too much for him. He felt like a low-life. He felt like trash. And, he cried until he was empty of tears.

He needed a drink.

Leaving The Coffee Connection parking lot, Larry drove down the street to a liquor store where he bought a cheap bottle of whiskey. Driving on, he steered his Toyota down Town View Parkway and made a right into the Walmart parking lot. The day was hot and his dried tears made the skin on his face feel hard. I have to get myself together, he thought, feeling miserable. It's my first night in Balfour and I better damn well get ready for it. He laid his forehead on the steering wheel to rest for a moment.

Sighing, he climbed out of his car.

Entering the store, he glanced around, trying to concentrate on what he needed to get through the night. He knew he wanted a candle. He didn't want to drink in the dark. He figured putting a candle on his dash would give him a comforting glow of light that his flashlight could not. Locating the candle display, Larry examined the various kinds on the shelf. He didn't know anything about candles. Finally, he selected a small round candle encased in glass. He slipped it into the pocket of his jacket. A little later, a lighter went into his back pocket.

Moving to the grocery section, Larry artfully opened a box of plastic sandwich bags and pilfered a few. Grabbing an empty cart sitting in the aisle, he moved to the deli and put an eight-piece box of fried chicken into his cart. As he walked to the men's room, he shed his jacket and dropped it over the container of chicken. Entering the men's room with the box under his jacket, Larry took the opportunity to relieve himself. In the stall, he transferred a crispy breast from the box into the sandwich baggie and shoved it in the other pocket of his jacket.

Approaching the sink, Larry set the container covered by his jacket on the counter. Gazing at himself in the mirror under the harsh fluorescent light, he thought he looked terrible. His eyes were red and swollen and his hair was greasy from running his fingers through it all day. Turning on the cold water faucet, he rinsed his sour mouth, face and hands. Then, he turned the hot water handle to see if the water was actually hot. It was. With a small bit of hand soap, Larry soaped the crown area above his forehead and rinsed it with the wonderful warm water. It felt so good. He would have loved to get his whole head wet, but there was no way to really do it. This had to be good enough. Grabbing paper towels from the dispenser, Larry squatted beneath the hand blower and rubbed the front portion of his hair nearly dry. Then, he went back to the sink and with cupped palms, soaked his face and eyes with more cold water. He began to feel a little better.

Returning to the deli, Larry set the box of chicken in the same spot from where he had taken it. After placing a box of marked down doughnuts and a gallon of water in his cart, he checked out and went to his car.

Leaving Walmart, Larry turned right and followed the little winding road with no destination in mind. He came upon a few new subdivisions and driving further down the road, he saw an older neighborhood. Passing it, he continued down the road for a few minutes. Then, he came upon a large forested area on the right side of the road. Pulling off the road, he let his engine idle on the wide, flat shoulder. He studied the tree filled thicket. The trees were tall and huge and far apart. He wondered if he could drive his car into it. He decided he would try.

Moving forward slowly, Larry entered the forest, bumping along cautiously, listening to the sounds of branches and underbrush crunching beneath his tires. He prayed he wouldn't blow a tire. Negotiating the tall old trees, he kept going, his car jostling about as he went. Finally, he stopped. Stepping out of his old Toyota, Larry looked back towards the road. He could no longer see it. Standing there, he felt a chill breeze sweep around him. He heard the twitter of birds above him. He figured it was about four in the afternoon but the trees made it seem darker. He would have to make camp fast.

Searching for some heavy rocks — of which there were plenty — he worked to form a fire pit. The effort made him sweat. He was getting cold, mostly from his own moisture and the eerie strangeness of the woods. When the small boulders were in place, he set about gathering firewood. He broke the pieces as evenly as possible to create a neat stack about two feet high by two feet wide near the pit. He had no idea what this meant in terms of burning. Would it last one hour or five? How could he know? He had never done anything like this in his entire life. Staring at the empty pit, he decided to set an initial fire within the stones. Loading the pit with twigs and larger wood droppings, he wished for the thousandth time that he knew what he was doing. But he had done the best he could. Now, the fire was set to be lit when he was ready.

Opening his trunk, Larry rooted through his box of groceries. He located a can of baked beans, a spoon, a can opener and a pan. Setting these things by the fire pit, Larry also laid a towel on the ground. He didn't want to sit on the bare earth while he heated the beans and sat next to the fire for warmth. The idea of spiders and insects freaked him out. Next, he moved to make his bed on his driver's seat like he had the night before. Feeling chilled, he returned to his trunk and located a navy hoodie in his box of clothes. Slipping it on, he tried to ignore the sour stench of the garment. It smelled like his old apartment before he had cleaned it.

Shaking and weary from his exertions and the whole rotten day, he badly needed to rest.

Slipping under the blankets, Larry set the glass candle on his dash, ready to be lit when he wanted. Curling into a fetal position, he pulled the blankets over his head. Between the shock of the theft, his lousy situation and the falling temperature, he couldn't stop shaking. His intention was to sleep just a short while. Then, he would get up, light the fire and eat a dinner of cold fried chicken and hot beans with doughnuts for dessert. He tried to think of the good things. He had a bed, a dinner and a fire. It was more than some people had. Latching onto these thoughts, he fell into a dreamless sleep.

Several hours later, Larry opened his eyes. Darkness surrounded him. He felt uncomfortable and disoriented. His knees were cramping from being pulled up to his stomach and his ankles were aching from hanging off the seat. The air was stale in the car from no circulation. He had no idea of the time. He lay there shivering from the numb disbelief that this was happening to him. As his teeth clacked, his gut rumbled with hunger. He began to consider hot beans and the warmth of a fire. All he had to do was get up and light the thing. The fire pit was ready to go. But it meant leaving the small warmth of his blankets. It meant negotiating the night, trying to see and not trip. And, what if he burned down the forest?

He knew nothing of managing a campfire. He was frozen with indecision and dread. But it boiled down to getting up and doing something or doing nothing and staying cold and hungry. Finally, the notion of hot beans and hot flames won out.

Sitting up, Larry drew the lighter from his back pocket and lit the candle on the dash. Holding the candle tightly in the palm of his hand, he pushed his blankets aside and stepped out of the car. He limped from the pins and needles of his deadened feet to the fire pit. Setting the candle down on the towel, he lit the dry leaves and twigs in several places. The fire took hold and started to whistle and burn. Within minutes, the blaze became wild and high. At first, Larry was frightened by the ferocity of the leaping flames. But, as he watched, fascinated, he realized the fire was settling down into a steady source of heat. Satisfied with the light from the fire, he blew out the candle. Keeling on his towel and holding out his hands to the blaze, he sighed in pleasure. As the crackling heat warmed him, he fed the fire a few more pieces of wood.

Opening the can of beans, Larry placed the pan at the edge of the flames. While the beans were heating, he pulled the piece of fried chicken from his pocket. Opening the baggie, he touched the meat to his dry lips. The fried coating was soggy but the taste was there. Tearing into the breast with hunger, Larry stirred the beans, tasting them intermittently. The fire was too hot and the beans rapidly became a gooey muck. Eating the mess straight from the pan, Larry devoured both the breast and beans too quickly. He was surprised when there was suddenly nothing left but a blackened pan and some well sucked bones in his hand. He wished he had more. Aside from the food he had stolen in the morning, he'd eaten nothing all day. Downing a couple of doughnuts, he rinsed his mouth and hands with his gallon of water. Then, pouring water into the pan, he rinsed it and set it by the dwindling fire to dry.

Lighting the candle again, Larry staggered to the trunk of his car intent on finding something to place under the steering wheel to support his ankles while he slept. His ankles were still killing him.

The chilly, moist air of the forest made his breath come out in labored huffs. Rolling a bunch of clothes inside a shirt, he tied them into a bundle and shoved the pillowed lump onto the floor of the driver's seat. While his hunger was eased, Larry was still shaking as he climbed back under his blankets. He lowered the window a half inch for air. His chill was bad enough to make him turn on the car and run the heat for a short time. Any small loss of gas was worth it. As the fire went out near his car, Larry pulled the covers over his head, still traumatized over the loss of his laptop and phone. Their absence from his pathetic life loomed so large and depressing, his eyes leaked again onto his pillow. It's only my second night of being homeless, he thought morosely, and I don't know how I am going to make it. I can't stand this. I can't stand it!

Overcome and undone, Larry began to sob in earnest in the privacy of his car, his solitude and the shadows surrounding him. He was vaguely aware of feeling embarrassed. Men weren't supposed to cry. How many times had his father slapped it into him? How many times had his father burned him with cigarettes? How many times had his father withheld food in punishment? But his father wasn't here now and he was too upset to control himself. His tears flowed and his sour hoodie sleeve became gummy from his running nose. He didn't hold back, didn't even try. He wept until he was worn out.

Eventually, he grew quiet. He became aware of the mechanized sound of blowing heat. Leaning up, he turned off the ignition. His car was warm enough now anyway. Settling back, he lay listening, eyes open, to the black of night around him and all the odd noises of the woods. He felt so strange to be in this strange place. He lay silently until he heard nothing more than his own heartbeat.

His eyes slowly closed in the hollow night.

An abyss of darkness overtook him.

For the next few hours, he found some peace.

# CHAPTER NINE

Larry's eyes opened to sun dappled trees and the twittering of forest birds.
Lying on his side, he gazed up at high oaks through the window. The tall
trees were beautiful with their long branches lightly swaying. The morning
was gentle and golden leaves were listing downward here and there, the
result of late summer morphing into early fall. He was suddenly too warm
under his blankets. Pushing them aside, he stepped out of his car. Yawning
loudly, he raised his arms and arched back to relieve the pain in his low
back. Looking around, he was thrilled the day was much warmer than yesterday. Stripping off his sour smelling hoodie, he tossed it onto the backseat
of his car and replaced it with his thinner jeans jacket.

Larry walked to his ash filled fire pit and noted that his wood stack
was low. He realized he had to gather more wood. From last night's fire,
he had learned that while thin sticks burned well, they didn't last long. He
would have to find bigger pieces if he wanted a fire that would burn without constant feeding. But first, he needed some coffee and supplies.

Larry got into his car, started the engine, and let it warm. Putting his
car in drive, he moved slowly forward, crushing more bramble and branches
under his tires. His car rocked and bucked as he cautiously circled a few
trees intent on joining the newly broken path he'd already made entering
the forest. Back on the path, he slowly came out of the forest. Stopping, he
wondered if he could find the opening again. Sliding his transmission into
park, he climbed out and surveyed the landscape for anything that could

mark the entrance. He spied a rock about the size of a flattened basketball. Grunting from the weight, he carried the large, heavy rock closer to his entrance. Then, he laid a large branch on it so that it was raised slightly, pointing toward the street. Satisfied that his path was sufficiently marked, he drove onward, unsure of where to go.

Larry mentally reviewed his needs. First, he needed more pans and soap. He needed a way to heat water to wash and clean his pans. He didn't want to live on just cold food. He also wanted to be able to heat a few things at the same time like pasta in one pan and sauce in another. So, he needed pasta, sauce and more water. Lots more water . . . and a sponge. And a strainer. He frowned as the list grew longer.

Second, he had to find a way to wash his clothes. He could smell himself and found it unpleasant. The sour odor of his hoodie still clung to him. Cleaning his clothes presented a problem and made him feel more homeless than ever. Without his computer or phone, he could not look up a local laundry. He felt the tears well again over the loss. But he was sick of crying and forced his eyes dry. He needed to focus on his immediate needs to survive and find some level of comfort.

Third, he needed to start begging again. He still had money but he was aware that it was slowly dwindling. Glancing at his dash, he noted his half tank of gas. He would get gas tomorrow. The check engine light was still on but at least his oil light wasn't. He also needed more blankets. What he had wasn't keeping him warm enough, especially with the window cracked for ventilation.

While he was thinking, Larry found himself cruising the residential area he had passed to get to the forest. Unlike the newer subdivisions of the area, the homes he was seeing were mostly older brick ranches spaced far apart. Turning down a narrow street lined with towering oaks and pine trees and wide yards —some more scruffy than others—he slowed, idling, as he spied an old man in a faded flannel shirt and jeans shuffle to his car. Larry's interest peaked when the old guy backed out of his driveway, leaving the garage door open. As the old man's car barreled down the road,

Larry made a split-second decision to pull into the drive. Climbing out, he quickly entered the garage and tried the doorknob. It was unlocked. He had heard of people who didn't lock their homes, but he had never encountered one before. Turning the knob, he stuck his head into the house.

"Hello, anyone home? Bill? You here?" Larry called loudly. There was no Bill. He had a story he'd instantly conjured . . . that his friend Bill had asked him to pick him up and to just come in if he didn't answer. But he needed no story; the house was empty.

Stepping in, Larry hurriedly entered the old-fashioned kitchen, his heart hammering. Opening the cabinets at break-neck speed, he rounded up a large metal bowl, a strainer and a few pans, including a very large one, and ran them out to his car. Moving fast, Larry burst through the kitchen door again, straight to the living room, where he grabbed a few blankets off the living room sofa and made for his car again. His last trip led him to the pantry. Finding grocery bags under the sink, he bagged a loaf of bread, strawberry jam, a box of pasta and a jar of spaghetti sauce. Into more bags, he loaded a sharp knife, some stirring spoons, a bottle opener, a couple of ceramic bowls, a head of iceberg lettuce from the refrigerator, a bottle of ranch dressing and a few beers. Lastly, he stole the mesh basket from the coffee maker and nearly a full pound of coffee.

Clutching the bags tightly, Larry tore out of the house and jumping into his car, he sped down the road. He was breathing hard, warring with emotions of shock over what he had just done and his elation over gaining a large haul of necessities. He was especially excited over the wide metal bowl and the large, deep pan he had just stolen. These meant he could boil enough water for bathing, making coffee and cooking his pasta, all at the same time. The pasta was important to Larry. It was filling and he very much wanted to be filled. And now, he could not only boil water in preparation, he also had the pasta and sauce too. Tonight, he would have a real and fine dinner.

Traveling up Towne View Parkway, Larry pulled into the far edge of the Kroger parking lot to reorganize his car. Shifting the contents of his trunk, he was now able to fit his new pans loaded with his new utensils. Condensing his groceries into two bags, he set them on the floor behind the passenger seat. He worked to straighten his backseat by folding his bedding tightly, including his new blankets. He had a vision of going to a liquor store and getting boxes for storing his food and one to serve as a table. Now, he could do so. He had room for them.

But first, he wanted to get water. Parking near Kroger's entrance, Larry entered the store and bought four gallons which he placed on the floor behind his seat. Then, he drove to the local liquor store. From a pile of discarded boxes in the service alley, he easily loaded his car with five of the sturdiest.

His adrenaline was plummeting. Larry badly wanted a cup of coffee. At a donut shop up the street, he bought a cup. With coffee in hand, he guided his car next door to a little strip mall featuring a nail salon, an ice cream shop, a pottery place, a pizza parlor and a gift store. Sipping his coffee, Larry gazed at the line of stores through his windshield, wondering if it would be safe to leave his stuff at the campsite. It would be liberating to be free from carrying his pots and pans and groceries around in his car. He fantasized about building himself a small shelter with a table and chair underneath. He knew which table and chair too . . . because he was looking at them. The ice cream shop directly in front of him had several small sets of tables and chairs on the sidewalk just outside its doors. The little furniture was the type that folded, made of lightweight metal and thin wooden slats. He could envision himself pulling to the curb, quickly snatching a table and chair and tossing them into his soon to be empty trunk. The thought excited him. He would have furniture. But, not now. Not yet.

First, he had some other things to get before he could return to camp and get organized. Camp. He liked the sound of that. It held the promise of somewhere to go, kind of like a home. Now, he really was a guy just roughing it. For the first time in days, he smiled.

Getting back on Towne View Parkway, Larry made for the dollar store located across the street from Walmart. Entering the store, he glanced around, checking out the number of cashiers and stockers who might be there. He could see only one frowning female cashier busy with a long line of impatient customers. A quick scan of the store revealed no other employees. Grabbing a basket, Larry strolled the aisles. He tossed into his basket four packages of white plastic table cloths, a ball of kite string, a bottle of dish soap, a package of cheap washcloths and a crime novel. Into his pockets went a thin, red plastic box cutter, a pen and a small pad of paper, a bar of soap and a couple of small packages of chocolate and nuts. Pockets bulging, Larry checked out and moved on to Walmart.

At Walmart, Larry grabbed a cart and set his backpack carefully into it, standing the canvas bag up, zipper open. Heading to the grocery section, he used his new box cutter to pilfer a few more sandwich baggies and brown paper lunch bags from their packages. Shoving them into his backpack, Larry spied a six pack of diced peaches in syrup. He loved peaches. Slicing open the bottom of the package, he slipped two of the small plastic cups into his backpack and returned the package to the shelf, tucking it deep to the back.

From the deli, Larry placed into his cart a plastic wrapped plate of four freshly made turkey roll-ups with lettuce and tomato rolled in soft flour tortillas. Heading to the men's room, he hid the turkey rolls behind his backpack and opened the door. A man was at the urinal but Larry ignored him and slipped into a stall. Sitting on the toilet, he split the four turkey rolls into two baggies. Getting out two brown paper lunch bags, he wrote on the first, 'Your Lunch, Love Mom.' On the second, he wrote, 'Same snack for later. Love Mom.' Putting a peach cup and a baggie of turkey rolls into each bag, Larry folded the tops neatly and placed them into his backpack. Breaking the styrofoam tray into small pieces, he wrapped the broken bits compactly in toilet paper and flushed the balls of tissue.

Leaving the men's room, Larry strolled to the office supply aisle where a roll of tape ended up in his pocket. Pushing on to the men's section, he dropped three packages of underwear, white t-shirts and socks into his cart. A collection of cotton turtlenecks and plaid shirts were followed by several dark, fleece hoodies. His cart was piling up just as he intended. Moving on to the dressing room, Larry appeared to be fumbling with all the stuff as he surreptitiously filled his backpack with the packages of underwear and a hoodie.

"How many can I bring in?" Larry asked the dressing room attendant.

"Six," she replied, looking away, disinterested. Her boyfriend had just broken up with her. She couldn't support her son on what she was earning. Her problems were huge, her bitterness even larger. She hated her job.

Larry turned from her. His cart was filled to overflowing. He chose from the selection two black cotton turtlenecks and four plaid button-ups. Leaving his cart filled with clothes, Larry stepped inside the dressing room. Swiftly, he withdrew the packages of underwear, t-shirts and socks and the hoodie from his backpack. Silently, using his box cutter, he sliced into the three packages and withdrew two garments from each. He neatly taped the bottoms of the packages.

Stripping quickly, he relegated his dirty underwear to the bottom of his backpack and pulled on the new undergarments. Their freshness caused him to immediately feel better. Stepping back into his jeans, he sliced off the tags of a new black cotton turtleneck and yanked it on over his new undershirt. Dressed again, Larry laced up his grungy sneakers and then pulled out another brown lunch bag from his backpack. On it he wrote: 'Stay clean. For later, Love Mom.' Into this paper bag, he stuffed the other t-shirt, socks and underwear he had stolen from the packages. Finally, he turned his attention to the hoodie. Cutting off all the tags — even the one in the collar showing the brand — he picked at the floor of the dressing room for pieces of lint and threads and rubbed them into the chest of the hoodie. For an added measure of ownership, he rolled his spicy scented deodorant over the garment. Now, it looked and smelled like his . . . and, no longer new.

On the empty hanger from the turtleneck he was now wearing, Larry carefully hung his ratty old shirt and concealed it in the middle of the new shirts. Wrapping the clothes around the underwear packages, he clutched the bundle to his chest and left the dressing room. He glanced at the dressing room attendant and saw she was still on the phone. Grabbing his cart, he casually dropped the bundle on top of the other garments and kept going.

Returning to the underwear aisle, Larry filled his cart with even more packages of underwear, tees, and socks. For the sake of the security cameras, he went back to the men's department and put the shirts and hoodies back on their respective displays. His old shirt, he crammed into a messy clearance circular where it would likely go unnoticed for a long time. From there, he went to the grocery section and put a gallon of fruit punch, two gallons of water, and a cherry pie into his cart. Pretending that he was about to check out, Larry pulled up to the end of a cashier line six people deep. Rifling through his cart as he waited, he suddenly shook his head as though he had changed his mind. Turning his cart away from the line, Larry ambled back to the underwear aisle. Taking care to put the taped packages on the hooks first so they would be farthest back, he re-hung all the packages.

He had done all he wanted to do.

Using the self-check out for his pie and bottled liquids, he nervously rang them up as cheap produce by scanning an abandoned head of leaf lettuce sitting by the register. Holding his breath, he pushed his cart through the doors to leave the store. Being arrested for shoplifting was his worst nightmare. He had tried to be diligent in covering his tracks. Maybe it was overkill, he thought. But if he was stopped and searched, he was fairly confident that all his 'Love, Mom' bags would work. He couldn't know. It didn't matter now, he thought, the warm morning air rushing through his nostrils. His theft was successful. No one had stopped him. Loading his car quickly, he pushed the cart aside and drove away.

He had survived a morning of intense petty thievery.

Now, all he wanted was to get back to camp, sort out his supplies and get set up. With his turkey rolls, peaches, pie, nuts, and juice, he had plenty to eat without having to light his fire pit. He could work without being hungry.

He wished he had stolen a battery-operated radio for some music. But then, he would have to steal batteries too. He rolled his eyes at the thought. Christ, he was getting brazen. It scared him how little time it had taken.

Driving back to camp, Larry began to feel a glimmer of excitement.

It was still early in the day. Once he got to his camp, he could tuck in and spend the rest of the day there working happily, safe and secure, without having to leave. The forest was private . . . and his. There, he could cry all he wanted. Or, not. The best thing was, no one was there to pass judgment on him. Nor, did he have to feel guilty about not having done enough today. Instead, he would work to make the camp his own. He would enjoy setting it all up. He would make the place home. The thought brought a sense of contentment. Yes, it was all about having somewhere to go.

# CHAPTER TEN

Finding the entrance to the forest was not as easy as Larry had thought it would be. The line of cars behind him kept pushing him faster than he wanted to go.

Head bobbing, Larry's eyes roved for his landmark while trying to keep his car straight on the curvy two-lane road. Finally, sure that he had gone too far, he turned his old Toyota around and tried again. He couldn't find the entrance from the other side of the road either. Too many cars were whizzing by for him to get a clean look at the forest's edge. Driving cautiously, he kept searching. As Walmart became visible, Larry knew he had overshot his mark once more.

Cursing, Larry pulled into the parking lot, pounding his fist angrily and petulantly on the steering wheel, frustrated and breathing hard. He sat for a while, rubbing his eyes. He had to stop this. He needed to get some self-control. And, he needed to do it now. His upset was doing him no good. He took another breath, laying his forehead on the steering wheel, waiting for the heat of his tantrum to pass. He would not let it happen again. It clouded his mind, making him unable to think. He didn't want that. He had to do better.

Wheeling his car around, he got back on the road again, determined to go more slowly and even pull off the street if necessary, to let any faster cars go by.

Passing two new subdivisions, Larry came upon the older residential area where he had committed his earlier burglary. Suddenly, he recognized the low brick ranch on the corner. Pulling off onto the shoulder of the road, Larry crept forward slowly, seeking his elusive marker of branch and stone.

A few hundred yards ahead, he found it. Elated and triumphant, he waited patiently for traffic to die down. He scanned the area around him to learn landmarks. He would not miss his marker again. When the road was clear and no one would see him, he entered the forest.

Driving forward slowly, Larry gripped the steering wheel tightly. His car rocked as it had before over the coarse, uneven floor of the forest. Finally, he spied the ringed stones of the fire pit and stopped. Climbing out of his car, he stared at the blackened hole. Maybe he had built it up in his mind, but the reality of his 'camp' in the harsh light of day was underwhelming. There was nothing here but an insignificant ring of stones. Overhead, the birds were raucous in their song. The hollow breeze ruffled his hair. What had he been thinking? Camp? There was no camp. Abruptly, he felt shaken and disheartened. He was deluding himself that he could stay here. Freezing weather was only months away. Still, the other harsh truth was, he had nowhere else to go. Nowhere.

This is all I have, he thought. I must get this camp together. There is nothing more. Setting his jaw, he lowered his head, huffing deeply in despair. Staring at the stones, he felt his eyes glaze over. Sinking to his knees, he knelt by his fire pit. It smelled of fire and ash. The scent sparked in him some primordial memory and slowly, little by little, he felt a peace settle within him. People had existed by a pit of fire for millennia. He could do this. He had to stop being so negative and weak. He had to stop whining and take action.

Whimpering involuntarily, Larry stripped off his new clothes and replaced them with the dirty ones from his trunk. Folding his new underwear, socks, t-shirt, and turtleneck, he set them on his seat for later. Standing by his car, he surveyed the land and decided his first priority was to replenish his firewood. As he gathered kindling and thicker wood to restock the firewood pile, Larry also pulled to the fire pit area any branch he found measuring seven to eight feet in length to use later for a lean-to. When his firewood pile reached three feet wide by three feet high, he figured he had enough to last two nights, burning for four hours per night. Staring at the stack, he wondered how accurate his assessment was. He would find out.

Turning, he moved to find more fuel for the pit itself. Once the pit was set to be lit, Larry sank cross-legged on the ground next to the stones, his head hanging down. His hands hurt. He was tired and hungry. Staggering to his feet, he returned to his car for his backpack. Opening the canvas bag, he pulled out one of the brown lunch bags containing a baggie of turkey roll-ups and cup of diced peaches. Grabbing the gallon of fruit punch, he returned to sit by the stones to eat. He was too hungry to bother rinsing his hands. He devoured the two rolls and peaches almost without tasting them. Lifting the gallon of fruit punch to his lips, he took several deep gulps before wiping his mouth with the back of his hand.

Sitting quietly, his hunger sated, he listened to the calling birds. As the breeze teased the boughs of the trees, Larry's eyelids began to droop. He wanted nothing more than to spread a blanket by the stones and nap for a while. But with no way to control how long he might sleep, he knew he couldn't risk it. He still had a lot of work to do.

Reluctantly, Larry climbed to his feet. He examined the longer branches he had collected. There were eight of them, some longer than others. Selecting the four tallest, he worked to strip them of extraneous branches until they became somewhat matching poles. He repeated the process with the remaining four shorter branches and set them aside.

Next, he unloaded his car, placing his supplies in a neat row on the forest floor. Now, he could see everything he had without having to dig for what he needed. With this done, he scanned over the liquor boxes, food, metal pans, utensils and other things he had stolen. Finding his ball of string, he set it aside. He would need it for his plan.

Then, picking up a plastic white table cloth from his stack of four from the dollar store, Larry opened the bag and removed the cloth. Unfolding the thing, he was disappointed by how thin and flimsy it was. Whatever. It was all he had to work with. Scanning the area, he contemplated where to build his lean-to. He decided to build it on the roadside of his fire. It would help block the flames of his fire from being seen at night. He grabbed a heavy stirring spoon and tucked it in his waistband. He walked to his chosen area and spread the white plastic cloth on the forest floor. With the cloth spread, he could see where he needed to sink the four corners of his poles. The cloth measured four feet by six feet, so he would dig a little further out, about five feet by seven feet. He didn't need the plastic sheet, which he would use as a ceiling, to fit tightly. He just wanted to feel something above his head.

It took Larry over an hour to dig the four holes with his spoon, grunting as he dug. He wanted to sink his poles at least ten inches deep. This would leave six feet or so above ground, just enough for him to stand up in the structure. Any rocks and stones he pulled from the holes, he set aside. As soon as he planted his first pole, he knew he would have to load heavier rocks around the base to keep it upright. He needed more rocks. Picking up his big metal pan, Larry set off to fill it with the best rocks he could find. Carrying the full, heavy pot back to his construction site, he worked from it to ring all four holes with layers of rocks.

Once he had sunk all four posts, Larry used his string to tie the tops of the four poles together to prevent their rectangle shape from listing. Then, to further steady the poles, he tied the sides and the back around the center, leaving the front open so he could walk in and out. The front would also face the fire and he wanted his view unobstructed. The last pole he tied lengthwise across the top to give the overhead plastic cloth some height and prevent it from dipping in the middle. With his lightweight ceiling beam tied securely in place, Larry laid the cloth over the wooden beam. He moved quickly. The breeze kept blowing the lightweight plastic out of place. He quickly looped the four ends of the plastic cloth to the four standing poles and pulling them tight, created his ceiling.

Standing back, Larry admired his work. It didn't look half bad and it definitely gave the illusion of a small room. Still, he could imagine that the first windy rain would likely destroy his structure. He wanted to shake a pole to see how secure they felt, but he didn't dare. Not now anyway. The earth was too freshly dug and needed time to harden. He was exhausted and dirty. He felt his hands burning. He wondered briefly what the hour was. From the sun, he figured mid-afternoon, 3:00 p.m.? It was time to light his fire and boil some water. He needed to bathe while it was still warm enough to do so. Drawing the lighter from his pocket, he went to the pit and set the wood aflame. Pouring a little water into his large metal pan, he rinsed out the stone dust. Then, he filled the pan and set it at the edge of the beginning blaze to heat.

While the water was warming, Larry continued to work. First, he searched for four larger rocks. Finding them, he laid the stones in a row on the left side on his future dwelling about five feet away. With his ball of string, he looped the top of the back-left pole and ran the string six feet in length to tie it to the small boulder at the other end. He did the same with the front left pole and rock. The two middle rocks, Larry tied to the initial rectangle string of his new construction. Then he cut ten lengths of string a little over five feet each. With this string, he tied the four long strings together every six inches until he had created what looked like a net. Over this net, he tied on another white table cloth as a roof. Under this slanting structure, Larry lined the floor with another table cloth. Next, he carried over four cardboard liquor boxes and after removing the inserts, pushed their flaps inward. Stacking the boxes faced open, big ones on the bottom, smaller on top, he now had shelves to store his food. Hopefully, the plastic lining on the floor would keep the cardboard fairly dry when it rained.

Stepping by the fire, now crackling cheerfully, he stuck his fingertip into the water. It was warm but not yet hot enough for a bath. He decided to stack his food on his new shelves. He had a lot of food now.

With satisfaction, he loaded into the top boxes his dish soap, coffee, beer, lettuce, ranch dressing, bread, strawberry jam, box of pasta and a jar of sauce. He added the few other cans, salt and pepper and condiments from his car as well. In the bottom left box, he placed his plates, mug, metal and ceramic bowls, mesh coffee basket, silverware, openers and other utensils. In the final box, Larry placed his pots and pans. Standing back to look at his work, he smiled contentedly. With his last tablecloth, he lined the floor of his home and placed the last box upside down in the middle for a table.

Turning, he added more wood to the fire and tested the water again. It was hot enough now. Returning to the shelves, he got his dish soap, metal bowl and another pan. It's a beautiful thing, Larry thought, knowing where my supplies are and not having to struggle to get at them. Setting the pans and dish soap by the fire, he returned to his car for a wash cloth, towel and a bar of soap. Carrying them to the fire, he removed his clothes and tossed them a few feet away. Standing naked in the forest felt a little weird to him, but it was also exhilarating. For a moment, he felt oddly free.

Using the smaller pan as a ladle, Larry filled the deep metal bowl with hot water from the large pot by the fire. From this metal bowl, he bathed. He soaked his hair and lathered it with a small amount of dish soap. With the small pan, he dipped into the metal bowl, then back to his head, rinsing out the soap. His hair now clean, he dropped the washcloth into the remaining water in the metal bowl. Pulling out the sopping cloth, he wet himself down. Shivering slightly, Larry picked up the sweet-smelling bar and soaped his entire body. Setting the washcloth and soap on a stone, he used the small pan to ladle water over him like a shower. He felt clean now. His bath finished, Larry dried up quickly with his towel. He was starting to get cold, but, oh man, did he feel better!

Running to his car with the towel around him, Larry hurriedly dressed in his new underwear, turtleneck and hoodie. Picking up his old jeans, he sniffed them. God, they're rank, he thought. The dirty clothes cluttering his old apartment rose in his mind. He had rarely done laundry. Some of them hadn't been washed in years, including the jeans he was holding. Sighing, he shoved his clean legs into his dirty jeans, followed by encasing his fresh socks in dirty sneakers.

Warm again, Larry nuzzled the soft fresh fabric of the hoodie against his cheek. For one moment, he marveled at the pleasure of such a simple thing. As his stomach rumbled, his focus changed.

He went to his shelves to get another pan along with his stirring spoon, pasta and sauce. Back at the fire, which he fed more wood, he ladled some hot water from the big pot into the midsized pan he was now carrying. He set it into the fire to boil. Then he poured some sauce into the small pan he had used as a ladle. Gently placing the sauce pan into the water of the midsize pot, Larry decided to heat his sauce with this improvised double boiler. He knew the hot water would heat the sauce rather than the fire. He figured this method would prevent his sauce from turning into scorched muck like his beans had last night. What a rotten night last night had been, Larry thought, but today is better. He had built something. Turning from the fire, he contemplated the final securing of his structure.

Larry knew the wind could easily flap — and break — the thin table cloths, so he busied himself with tying down both plastic sheets on the outside in a crisscross fashion so they couldn't flap. Lastly, he tied the string to the top of the back pole on the right. Letting out the string as he circled a tree, he pulled the string tight as he walked. He ended up at the front right pole where he cut the string and tied it tightly to its top. Since he had no stakes, this would have to do to further stabilize and secure his new room. Although the kite string was thin, it was surprisingly strong. If he stayed, perhaps he would build something more permanent in the future. But for now, his efforts brought him a desperately needed sense of comfort. A sense of belonging. A sense of having some type of home.

His water was boiling. His sauce was gently bubbling. Setting the sauce pan aside near the fire, Larry opened the box of spaghetti and dropped a hefty handful into the boiling water of his midsize pan. As they softened, he gently stirred the noodles. Without a timer, he decided to stay close. Sitting on his towel, he watched the long strands of pasta boil. Stirring them now and then, his mouth began to water as he waited for them to be done. He was hungry again. But now, he thought, I am always hungry.

He thought of his old apartment pantry filled with boxes of macaroni & cheese, cereal, peanut butter and canned goods and his refrigerator filled with eggs, bacon, bread, jam, orange juice and milk. He had never thought about food then . . . because he had food. But now, it was different. Now, it was harder, whether paid for or stolen, he could see how getting food could become a struggle. He stared into the boiling pot, trying not to think too much or be impatient. Self-control. He had to find it. He had to learn it.

When he thought the spaghetti was close to being done, Larry rose to get the strainer and a ceramic bowl. He had already set his box table with a fork, a beer and a washcloth for a napkin. Straining his noodles, he slid them into the bowl and poured on the sauce. Taking the bowl back to his newly built room, he sat cross-legged at his cardboard table and ate. The beer was warm but good. The pasta was hot and fresh and tasty enough. He devoured it more quickly than he intended. Licking the bowl clean, he sighed in disappointment that his anticipated meal had ended so quickly. He wanted more, but his bowl had already been generous. He wasn't going to have more because he had to conserve. Conservation was his life now. Swallowing, he thought: *I have to think this way now. From now on, this is how I have to live until something changes.*

After dinner, Larry washed his plate and pans and returned them to the cardboard shelves. The big pot, though, he decided would live by the fire pit. He wanted his camp to be neat. Neatness was close to decency. To be decent was getting close to being normal. It was the most he could strive for. After adding wood to the fire, he added more water to the big pot to boil again.

Moving to his car, Larry opened the trunk. Gathering all his clothes, he sorted through them and folded them neatly. His dirty underwear, he set aside. They would go into the pot now heating to be boiled clean. Finished with organizing his clothes, Larry dropped his dirty underwear into the pot. Watching them sink into the water, it occurred to him that he needed a place to hang his laundry to dry. Looking around, he saw the place, ten feet or so to the right of his structure. Using the last of his string, he made a clothesline between two trees that stood about eight feet apart. As he passed the fire walking to his Toyota, he nudged the large pot a little deeper into the flames to boil faster. The late day temperature was starting to fall and he wanted to get his underwear boiled and hung to dry overnight.

Opening all the car doors, Larry found his bottle of whisky and put it on the front passenger seat. He cleaned out any trash and shook out all the blankets. After setting his candle and book on the dash, Larry made his bed in the usual way but added the two stolen blankets. The third blanket was actually a thick quilt. He folded it tightly and made it level with his seat to provide badly needed support for his ankles.

Taking three washcloths from the cheap pack of ten, Larry arranged them in a row on the edge of the driver's side roof, holding the trio in place with six small rocks. He hoped that the cloths covering the window crack at night would let in the air but keep out some of the cold. Later, he would find a better cover but right now, he only had what he had.

The water was boiling. He went to get his large metal spoon and strainer. Stirring the pot, Larry let his underwear boil for a couple minutes. Then, he carefully dumped the pot into the strainer and using the spoon, pressed down on the steaming underwear to squeeze out more water. Allowing his briefs to cool, Larry sat by the fire, looking at his construction. He had discovered that sitting on its floor hadn't been remotely comfortable. The ground was rough and bumpy from layers of stones, sticks and leaves. The plastic tablecloth wouldn't stay put either. Larry decided that the room had to be raked out before he could put a table and chair in there. He also needed better tarps before the thin tablecloth ceilings fell apart. It would also make the fire less visible from the road. He wondered if anyone had noticed his fires. He hoped not and he frowned at the danger it would bring. He touched his underwear. They were cool enough to handle now.

Rising, Larry stepped over to his new clothesline to hang his under-wear. After draping the nine pairs on the string, he returned the strainer and spoon to his shelves. Going to his car, he grabbed his whisky bottle off the front seat and returned to the fire.

Seated on the towel again, he fed the voracious pit more wood. Twilight was upon him. The air was cool and the crickets were humming. Sitting cross legged, Larry took a sip of whisky as he watched the flames grow higher again. He went back to his mental list. He needed more food and water. He needed plastic shelves instead of cardboard. He needed a real coat, a warm winter coat. He needed more towels and tissues and toilet paper. He needed a sturdy bucket and trash liners so he could take a proper shit and dispose of it the next day. Larry sighed. He needed so much. Tomorrow, he would also boil some socks and a few t-shirts. He would have more clean clothes. That would be good.

Staring into the fire as darkness seeped in around him, Larry began to fantasize about building a real home in the forest. It would have a front porch, with a wooden rocker. Inside, he would have a fireplace and a bathroom. It wouldn't be a real bathroom, but it could have a tidy makeshift toilet and a handsome stand that held a water pitcher and basin. There could also be a metal tub big enough to sit in and next to it, a shelf of thick towels and masculine soaps for bathing and shaving. Maybe it would have a window. He would like a window. Outside, there would be a rain barrel for collecting water and a neat stack of firewood.

The cabin itself, would be essentially one large room with his bed near the fireplace for warmth. The bed would be large and comfortable with several pillows and soft blankets. The kitchen area, tucked in another corner of the cabin, would be filled with warm bread and butter, hot coffee, and spices. It would have a wood burning stove perfect for roasting corn and a fat, whole chicken. In the mornings, there would be the smell of bacon frying as the sun rose. In front of the stove, he'd have a sturdy wooden table with four chairs. Centered on the table would be a bowl of fresh fruit.

He'd have colorful rugs on a smooth wooden floor. On the far wall, there would be shelves of clean, warm clothes. And, by the fireplace, there would be a wooden rocking chair. Rocking and reading by the fire on a cold winter evening . . . he would like that. And maybe at Christmas, he would line his mantle in evergreen and on the stove, steam mulberries and cinnamon to scent his cabin. It was all so wonderful, he could see it clearly. His home in the forest was perfect; all his own, hidden from the judgements and pressures of the outside world.

"Yes, yes, I would like that," Larry mumbled. He slowly opened his eyes as his fingers reached out to the fire, the scent of cinnamon lingering in his dreams. The last of the glowing orange embers were a blur to his eyes. His vision cleared and he became aware of the hollow night air around him, the vague buzz of crickets and the distant hooting of an owl. He had fallen asleep. He wasn't in the cabin of which he had dreamed. As real as it had seemed, it did not exist. Instead, he was somehow curled on his towel on the chilly forest floor. The fire was nearly out. Shivering and dizzy, Larry tripped to his feet under the early September moon, hanging large above the trees. The air was still and silent. The car, my bed, he thought groggily, gotta get to my car. He was not completely awake. He felt disoriented and light-headed.

Stumbling along, Larry covered the short distance to his Toyota. Opening the door, he tossed his whisky bottle onto the passenger seat and climbed gratefully into bed. The interior of the Toyota was chilly. Starting his car, Larry intended to let the heat run for a few minutes before cracking the window. To pass the time, he flipped on the radio, thinking he would let the car warm to a few songs. Leaning back, he listened to the music. He couldn't name the song but it was slow and soothing and it calmed him.

Finally, when he did lower his window an inch, the washcloths hung over the crack like a short drape. Turning off the ignition, Larry shifted and lay his left side, staring out into the darkness. He pulled the covers high over his head except for his face. His list of needs began banging around in his brain again. He needed money. He couldn't do all he wanted and needed to do without more. Murmuring to himself, he said, "Tomorrow, I must start begging again. I just have to." He moaned slightly at the thought, hating that he had to, hating that he had sunk so low.

Clutching the blanket to his cheek, he closed his eyes. It had been a day and he was completely drained. He knew nothing more until morning.

# CHAPTER ELEVEN

With the dawn, Larry woke feeling content and amazed at how well he had slept. Apparently, he had not moved all night. Still lying on his side, he gazed out the window. Enjoying his comfort, he was content to linger in bed a few minutes longer. The morning was crisp, clear and bright. Eventually though, the thought of hot coffee stirred him.

Lifting his blankets, he opened the door and swung out his legs. Standing, he looked down, surprised to find himself still in his shoes. Well, he thought in good humor, that's one step saved.

Looking around, Larry slowly smiled. The structure didn't look as ridiculous as he had feared. The room was standing straight and emanating an impression of permanence, something he knew wasn't true. But this morning, he was more than pleased to embrace the illusion. The attached sloping section covering his cardboard shelves made the overall configuration appear even larger than it actually was. He enjoyed seeing his wealth of food and pots displayed so neatly. It made his camp feel cozy and organized and real. His eyes moved beyond the dwelling to the clothesline draped with his underwear. It was such a homey touch, it almost seemed like a prop to complete the authentic feel of the camp. It telegraphed that, yes, someone lived here. Joyfully, Larry did a happy dance around the camp. He was surprised by his easy movements. He didn't know he had it in him.

Coffee. He needed coffee. At the fire pit, Larry quickly laid in dry leaves, twigs and wood. He lit the bundle. As it smoked and started burning, he went to his shelves and filled the mesh coffee basket half full with coffee grounds. Placing the basket in the small pan, he grabbed his mug and returned to the fire. Pouring two cups of water into his pan, he set it at the edge of the flames. While the water was heating, Larry opened his backpack and pulled out the other 'Love, Mom' brown bag containing the last of his turkey rolls and peaches. Sitting on the towel by the fire, he ate his breakfast and swigged from his gallon of fruit punch to wash it down.

Enjoying the warmth of the fire, he touched the water with the tip of his finger. With so little in the pan, it was getting hot quickly. When it boiled, he poured the water slowly over the grounds in the basket. As the water seeped out of the basket into the small pan, the water turned a dark brown. Larry let the grounds steep for a minute before lifting out the basket and setting it aside. Then he poured the coffee from the small pan into his mug.

Sipping the strong brew, Larry considered his morning. As much as he hated the idea of begging again, he knew he had to get himself to a corner and get started. *Self-control*, he thought. *I've got to do this.* The money would keep him in food and water and other necessities. Maybe he could get himself together enough to eventually look for a job. He touched the stubble on his face. He shouldn't shave if he was going begging. His begging signs were still on the backseat of his car. He poured himself the last of his coffee. His small fire was dying down and he decided to let it go out. Gulping down the last of his cup, he stood to collect his boiled underwear off the line. They were dry and stiff, but clean. That was all he cared about. Folding them neatly, he added them to the rest of his clothes in the trunk. After folding his bed and moving it to the backseat, he pulled the washcloths and stones off his roof and changed into his dirty clothes. He despised the feel of them.

Sliding behind the wheel, Larry stared out the windshield, thinking about where to go. Maybe he could ease into things by standing on a lesser corner. He would make less money but at least he'd get that 'old begging feeling' back again. Right now, he couldn't summon it. Starting his car, he left camp.

For the next three weeks, Larry begged in the mornings. The month had rolled into the beginning of October. His early afternoons were spent shopping and finding other necessities. He bought numerous gallons of water and kept his food supply steady. He bought a ten-dollar rake from Walmart, figuring it was too hard for him to steal. From the dollar store, he got a box of tall kitchen trash liners and more candles; some paid for, some stolen. From a local hardware store, he bought a bucket to shit in and two sturdy tarps, one ten feet by twenty feet and the other six feet by eight feet along with a hundred feet of synthetic clothesline rope.

After his daily supply shopping, Larry spent the rest of his afternoons working on his camp. He gathered wood. He raked out the ancient floor of the room, no easy task. Over the thin plastic ceilings, he tied down the larger of his tarps. The twenty-foot tarp was long enough to cover both the rectangular room and the attached sloping section. It was also wide enough to create a back and side wall to the room, giving Larry a new sense of privacy. While the outside of the enclosures were now brown, their ceilings remained white. The white was nicely visible at night, making the room and the sloping section feel larger and brighter.

With the floor of his dwelling now clean and level, Larry laid down the smaller tarp, silver side up, to cover the bare earth. Since his room was only seven feet long by five feet deep, he folded under the edges of the eight-foot tarp to fit the area. Finished, Larry walked on the tarp to try it out. It worked, neither buckling nor moving around. Satisfied, he installed the table and chair he had stolen from the ice cream store several nights earlier. In the middle of the table, Larry placed his candles. In the back left corner, he'd set his shit bucket and box of liners on the floor so he could go to the bathroom even if it was raining.

He had redone the clothes line with the thicker rope. And, using forest stone, he had formed a relatively level pad, a foot square, at the edge of the fire on which to heat his pots. It worked. The stones absorbed the fire's heat, causing the water to boil faster, not only from one side but underneath the pot as well.

Early evenings were spent washing his clothes and hanging them to dry. Aside from his underwear, he could only wash a couple of shirts and towels at a time, but he had found a method. Now, he was clean and keeping up.

He roasted hot dogs and chicken on a stick over the open fire. He heated soup and made sandwiches. While he bathed every other night to conserve water, he brushed his teeth and washed his face and hands daily.

The last number of evenings, he'd sat in the chair at the table to read his book by candlelight while sipping whiskey and watching the fire, waiting for the laundry water to boil. Nights were chilly, but he was coping by wearing extra layers of clothing. The fall leaves had become a steady struggle though. They never stopped falling and they covered everything. It was an unrelenting battle to keep his tarps and car clean. But overall, Larry was content. He felt as though he had a home, rough as it was. He had plenty of food and a hundred and fifty-seven dollars in his wallet. He had gas in his car and he had just added more oil. So far, the check-engine light hadn't caused him any problems.

After hanging his laundry that evening, Larry fed the fire more wood and returned to his table and chair to read. As the dark of night and its noises set in, he lit a few extra candles for more reading light and warmth. His bed was already made, his dishes were washed and the camp was as neat and secure as it could be. With his chores done, Larry just wanted to relax. It had been a busy, good week. He wasn't ready for bed yet and he simply wanted to enjoy the evening and his general sense of wellbeing. He poured a touch more whisky into his mug. The bottle on the table glimmered in the candle light. A blanket on his lap kept him cozy against the cool breeze from the night air. The fire and the candles were mesmerizing. He was at ease. After a half hour, Larry couldn't stop his eyelids from drooping. That's it, he thought, time to close up shop.

Glancing at the freshly poured whisky in his mug, Larry decided he wouldn't drink it. It would be a waste just to gulp it down. He poured the liquid carefully back into the bottle and screwed the cap closed tightly. Gathering his book and blanket under his arm, Larry blew out the candles except for the one to light his way to the car.

Stepping out of the room, a raindrop hit his forehead. Moving quickly to the Toyota, Larry set the candle and book on the dash and spread the blanket over his bed. Sliding under the cold blankets, he shivered. The car was chilly. Turning on the ignition, he let the heat run for a few minutes. When he turned it off, he cracked the window. The little washcloths were in place covering the crack. Laying back, Larry pulled the covers to his chin. He was okay now, warm enough. He fell asleep quickly.

Morning brought the rain. Dark, heavy, merciless rain.

Larry woke to thunder and spears of water attacking the roof of his car. Watching the grim, gray downpour through the windshield, he wondered how long it would last. There would be no fire for a while. His wood would be too wet. He prayed the structure would hold. He wondered if his cardboard shelves would hold too. Well, there's nothing I can do about it, he thought. He drifted back to sleep for another hour. When his eyes opened again, nothing had changed. It was then Larry realized that he had a problem. He couldn't leave the forest. He couldn't have his car getting stuck in the deepening mud. He didn't dare leave camp just to get stuck elsewhere. If he did manage to leave, with visibility so impaired by the intensity of the rain, he wasn't at all sure that he could find the opening again. Even if he did, how could he drive through the forest if he couldn't see the trees or his path through the rain? He didn't want to spend the night away from camp, especially if the rain didn't let up for several days. At this time of year, that could happen. Hell, it was likely to happen. Sighing, Larry raised the back of his seat to upright and lit the candle on his dash for cheer against the storm. Taking his book, he opened it and read for a while. But he was getting hungry. He needed to pee too. Ignoring his needs, he read for another hour hoping there would be a break in the rain. There wasn't.

Unable to wait any longer, Larry blew out the candle and returned his book to the dash. He folded his blankets, including the one underneath him and set them on the passenger seat. Slowly and unhappily, he stripped off his clothes. Leaving his shoes on the floor, he placed his clothes on top of his blankets. Sitting naked on the driver's seat, he hugged himself and stared at the bitter, relentless downpour. He really didn't want to do this. Slapping his chest to raise his blood and courage, he reached for the handle. Cracking the door partially open to keep the wet washcloths in place, he slid through the tight space. The wintry water spiked him instantly. Closing the door, he sprinted to his room. At least he had been smart enough to make sure the front was a little taller than the back so rain would run off, and so far, it was working. Cold and wet, he made it to his freshly lined bucket. Relieving himself felt so good. He hadn't wanted to pee in the freezing rain. When he was done, Larry tied the bag and laid it on the floor. Into the clean bucket went the nearby box of liners. Quickly, he grabbed two shopping bags and loaded them with toilet paper and paper towels. Setting the bucket on the chair, he packed it with his four candles, mug and whiskey bottle from the table. Grabbing the washcloth on the table as well, he pushed it between some of the glass.

Leaving the room, Larry moved left to his cardboard shelves. They were wet and starting to buckle. Into his bucket went bread, jam, peanut butter, crackers, a knife and a few other small snacks. Racing back to the car, he shoved the bucket and shopping bags behind his seat and slammed the door. Cold and shaking badly, he dashed to the fire pit and grabbed a gallon jug of water from his stash near the big pot. Dropping it on the back seat, he kicked the door shut. Jumping to the trunk, he grabbed a couple of towels and washcloths. Slamming the trunk, Larry moved to squeeze through the driver's door. Closing it firmly behind him, he sighed in relief, his heart hammering with exertion.

His window washcloths were miraculously still intact.

He was dripping rain water. Larry knelt on the driver's seat and quickly spread a towel and sat on it. Hugging himself, he cranked on the ignition, cursing his own lack of foresight. If he had left the heat running, he'd be warmer now. Lesson learned. Shaking out another towel, he briskly dried his body and hair. Grabbing his clothes, he slid into his socks, underwear, tee-shirt, jeans, turtleneck and finally, his hoodie. The air coming out of the vents was warmer now but his teeth were still slamming together. He noted with relief that the rain was not getting past the window washcloths. His body and breathing were starting to calm. Sliding the towel out from under him, he tossed it onto the back seat. It was moist but not soaked. He draped his drying towel over the back of the passenger seat. Breathing in the warm air, his body finally stabilized. Watching the rain pour down the windshield, Larry prayed he wouldn't have to go out into the storm again.

But now that he had, he was ready to get comfortable.

Maneuvering in his cramped car, Larry worked to make up his bed again. Getting it done, he knelt on top of his covers. He brought the bucket from the back to the front and onto his lap. On the passenger seat, he placed his groceries and whisky. The candles went on the dash as did his mug. Relining the bucket, Larry twisted to let it drop behind his seat. It was ready to use now, if he had to.

Sliding under his blankets, Larry extended his arm to grab the towel off the back seat. Sitting up, he covered his lap. He wanted no jelly or peanut butter or crumbs to soil his precious blankets. If they spilled on the towel, no problem. He could wash the towel, but not the blankets.

Settled now, Larry turned on the radio. He listened to chatter and music while he made himself a peanut butter sandwich. He realized that his birthday was somewhere around this time of year. He was turning twenty-four but he didn't even know the current date. He sighed. It didn't matter. He had never had a birthday celebration anyway. Growing up, his father had never acknowledged his birthday of October 20. It had been just another day. He had never had a birthday party. He had never had a birthday present. Not even a cake. So, he wasn't missing anything now. It was so ingrained into him that his birthday meant nothing, that even as he had gotten older, he had never mentioned his birthday to anyone. Thinking of his birthday now, Larry realized that it was just one more sad thing in his life. He watched the rain come down.

For a while, he enjoyed the music but hated the commercials. After a half hour, he turned off his ignition and read for another hour. Then he slept. When he woke, his windshield was dark with leaves. Late October rains did that. They brought down the leaves. Millions upon millions of them. As the leaves coated his car, he had a strong sense of being buried alive. He shoved the thought away. It was too dark, too painful. He could still see out of his side windows. As long as he could do so, he was okay.

Night was approaching. The last of the dim afternoon light was quickly fading. Lighting a candle against the gloom, Larry poured a small amount of whisky into his mug. Rolling the first sip around his mouth, he listened to the rain pound his car. It was mesmerizing. Ancient. Primordial.

He conjured his old apartment, clean and comfortable, the way it had been during the last few weeks of his time there. When he had had a roof over his head, he had never given any thought to when it rained. Or how hard it came down. Why would he? He could walk around, use his laptop, go to the bathroom, watch TV or cook whenever he wanted . . . and do it all while being dry, secure, and safe. If I had to go out, he thought, I could also easily get dry. These are all the things I can't do now.

In his little car, Larry was feeling the heightened impact of the deluge. He found it frightening. But at least he had his car. Cramped as he was, he had this small shelter. What did people do in bad weather with no shelter? He didn't know.

Sipping his whisky, Larry cringed at the terrifying electrical lashings of lightning in the sky. He listened to the powerful, rolling rumbles of thunder that followed. He was afraid of the eerie crackling of wind-whipped branches surrounding him. The resonance of water pounding his roof overhead was, to him, indescribable.

Blowing out his candles, he lowered his seat, and drawing up his covers, he listened until he could no longer keep his eyes open. Falling asleep, he dreamed that he was in a little boat adrift on a black, roiling sea.

His brain roiled. His stomach roiled. His shelter was so small and the storm was powerful, wicked and titanic. The whipping wind brought wave after wave of water.

He stayed in his Toyota for three days.

# CHAPTER TWELVE

On the morning of the fourth day, Larry opened his eyes. He was in pain. His back hurt. His legs hurt. His whole body was cramping.

The rain had stopped. Listening to the silence, Larry was grateful the deluge was over. He was feeling delirious and dehydrated and very, very hungry. He had allowed himself one peanut butter and jelly sandwich a day, along with a few nuts, a few chocolates, and a few sips of water and whisky. Since he had no idea how long the storm would last, he had conserved.

Moving slightly, he groaned again. God, he was stiff.

Raising his seat up, Larry pushed off his blankets. He painfully laced on his sneakers. No longer caring if the window washcloths came off, he opened the car door wide. Heavy with water, the washcloths slipped to the ground along with their anchoring stones. Stepping out into the morning air, he was glad it wasn't cold. The sun was shining cheerfully through the spires of the newly stripped trees. It occurred to Larry that the weather was like a manic person . . . all depressive and stormy one minute and all sunny and bright the next. He'd been aware of it before, but to experience it so up close and personal was: educational? Fascinating? Terrifying? He didn't know the word. Maybe all three.

Leaning weakly against the car, Larry surveyed the damage of his camp. His construction was still standing but the cardboard boxes hadn't made it. They were waterlogged and unraveling in layers. His food stuffs were on the ground and the bottom of the boxes were caved in. He could replace the boxes. The laundry hanging on his clothesline was also on the ground, smeared with mud and leaves. The fire pit was buried in leaves, the ring of stones now invisible. Larry could only find it because of the nearby stack of wood. He now knew that he had to wrap his wood to keep it dry. Had he done so, he could have had a fire once he cleared the pit of leaves. Lesson learned. I need to start thinking in advance, he thought desolately.

Feeling sour and clammy, Larry urgently wanted a warm bath but with the wood wet, it wasn't going to happen. What he had to do was leave the forest. He had to get to a restaurant where he could get something hearty and hot to eat. Then he could get more boxes from the liquor store, steal some wood bundles from a service station and pick up more groceries. After burning his candles for three long nights in the car, he needed more of those too.

Staggering around the Toyota with aching hips, Larry opened all the doors to air out the car. With his arm, he swept as many leaves as he could off his windshield. His car was completely covered in soggy forest droppings. He couldn't bother with that now. Shaking his arm free of water and brushing off his hoodie, he moved to the structure to retrieve his tied liner. The table and chair were okay, but the tarp floor was buried in forest debris. He'd have to rake it out. What he really needed was a broom. Walking back to the car, he dropped the shit bag in the bucket with the others. He would dispose of them in a dumpster somewhere later this morning.

Opening a new gallon of water, Larry rinsed his face and hands. He changed his underwear, brushed his teeth and combed his hair. Stepping around his car, he cleaned out the trash and moved his bed to the back seat. He set the whisky bottle on the table in his enclosure. He didn't need to be driving around with an open bottle even if it was nearly empty. Closing the doors, he slid behind the steering wheel and started his engine. Damn, he needed gas too. Suddenly, it all seemed too much. It's only because I'm feeling weak and hungry, he thought. After I eat, I'll feel better.

Moving the car slowly forward, he found the forest floor soft and unreliable, with mud pockets hidden under leaves that could sink his tires.

Worse, the leaves had covered his established path. The most important thing was to keep his speed slow but steady. Finally, Larry made it out of the woods with no mishaps. Coming to the road, he turned left, wondering where to go. He decided that Waffle House was his best bet. He wouldn't be noticed there and he could get a hot, inexpensive breakfast with unlimited coffee. The thought nearly made him smile, but he was feeling too unwell, dizzy, and disoriented. It's kind of like coming alive again after being dead, he thought.

Turning onto Town View Parkway, cars whizzed by him. The area was active with people coming in and out of stores, jogging along the parkway, and sitting in outdoor cafes. The vivid sun shone brightly in Larry's eyes. As he dipped his head to avoid the blinding light, he was engulfed by another wave of dizziness. Straightening up, he worked to get his focus back on the road. He had to get to the Waffle House soon or he would faint. He summoned some self-control and adjusted his focus back to the road.

Ten minutes later, Larry pulled into the parking lot. Turning off his car, he hurried in and slid into a hard booth. The restaurant wasn't busy and the waitress was immediately at his side.

"You want coffee?" she asked.

"Yes. Lots of it, please. And orange juice. I've been camping and I'm famished."

She started to turn to get the drinks, but Larry stopped her. "Can I just order now too?" he asked, trying to smile.

"Sure. What'll you have?"

"Three eggs over easy, hash browns well done, grits, bacon, and raisin toast with apple butter."

"Got it," she said. The pitch of her voice was so chipper it hurt his ears. She turned and left his table. She was back in two minutes with Larry's drinks. As she set the juice and coffee on the table, Larry grabbed the juice and nearly drained the glass in one long gulp.

"Wow, " the waitress exclaimed, "you are hungry! Where did you go camping?"

"The river," Larry replied gruffly. He didn't want small talk but he also didn't want any questions, so he added more gently, "I got rained out. The last three days were a real bad time. Do you think the food is ready?"

"It will be soon. I'll go check on it."

"Thanks," Larry murmured, looking away. He didn't want to talk to her.

When the waitress returned, her arms were loaded with food. Setting the plates on the table, she lingered, wanting to chat. She didn't know why she was drawn to the man, except for his rough handsomeness. But cleaned up . . . well, she could see it. She also liked his voice. But as Larry dug into his meal and paid her no attention, she left to let him to eat in peace. Larry tried to pace himself, but it was hard. He couldn't remember ever being so hungry. Eating steadily, it took him no time to consume everything in front of him. Finishing the last of his fourth cup of coffee, he rose to pay the check and left the restaurant. Time to drive to Walmart.

At Walmart, Larry left the store with an eight-dollar broom, which he paid for, and a bundle of wood from the pile outside the entrance, which he stole. Walking quickly, he got into his car and sped away. Next, he went to the dollar store. Tucking a pack of glass-encased candles into his waistband, Larry covered the theft with his hoodie. He grabbed two larger candles, a plastic white table cloth, and a box of trash liners and checked out at the register. Then he went to Kroger for water and other supplies. As he left the grocery store, he pilfered another bag of wood from the outside pile. Walking swiftly to his car, he got in and drove to the gas station. He pumped fifteen dollars' worth of gas into his tank and then steered his car to the side of the station, where he pinched another bag of wood from a pile on the far edge of the sidewalk. His last stop was the liquor store.

Entering the store, he saw the cashier at the register and asked, "Clearance?" She pointed to two shopping carts full of sale bottles a few feet away. There, Larry found a small bottle of bourbon for $9.99. Checking out, he drove around the back of the store, threw his shit bags into the dumpster and carefully selected his new boxes.

He could return to his camp now. He had a lot of work to do to restore his home before nightfall.

Finding the entrance easily, Larry maneuvered his car back to his camp. The sun and his hours away had dried the land enough so that the ground was a little firmer. He kept going until he could see the leafless rectangle where his car had been parked. Getting out of the car, he shed his new clothes for his old. At least they were clean. He grabbed his broom and rake and set about straightening his fire pit. He swept the leaves off his existing wood pile. With his rake, he cleared the area around the pit and a larger area around the wood stack. It was rough going because the leaves were still wet and heavy. Laying the new tablecloth on the ground next to his wet wood, Larry loaded the three bundles of wood he'd just stolen onto the end. Before he lay the plastic over the entire pile, new and old, he selected some sticks and the driest kindling he could find to ready his pit for later. Then, covering the stack, he set a few branches on top of the white plastic tablecloth to keep it from blowing away.

Walking to his room, Larry tightened the rope around the tree to make it stand a little straighter. Then he pushed on the ceiling with his broom to run off any pooled water. Moving the table and chair out of the way, he raked the floor clear of leaves and swept the remaining water and debris off the tarp. When the table was back in place, he put four candles from the stolen pack and one larger one on it. The other large candle he would place on the dash of his car. Next, he raked a wide path to his fire pit and did the same in front of the shelf area. This done, Larry broke down his old boxes and shoved the remains into two of his tall kitchen liners. He placed the bags in his trunk to dispose of later. Setting up the new boxes, he stacked them like before. After loading them with his groceries and pans, the cardboard shelves looked the same as they had prior to the rain.

Lighting the fire with the new wood, Larry poured bath water into the large pot. He was glad to see his stone pad by the fire again. While the water was heating, he raked a wide path to his car. A clear path would be easier to walk in the dark. Grabbing the bucket from his car, he returned it to the left corner of the structure. He stood his broom and rake in the right corner. Then he got his bath supplies together along with a fresh t-shirt, underwear, and socks to wear when he was done bathing. Setting them by the fire, he shook out his fireside towel and wrung it out as best he could. He would stand on it to bathe this time as it was already wet. Checking on his water, Larry found it getting warm. He had time to eat. Getting the beer and deli sandwich he'd bought for lunch, Larry sat at the table.

Glancing at the sun, he figured it was about 2:00 p.m. and the temperature in the mid-sixties. Biting into his sandwich, he contemplated the weather. The days are only going to get colder now, he thought. What am I going to do? Whatever he did, things were going to get difficult. The rain had showed him that. Eating silently, he looked around his camp. It was better now. He still had to clean off his car, rake a path to the clothesline and do a bunch of laundry, but that was okay. He'd get there. For now, he was just glad to be back to normal. Finishing his sandwich and beer, he threw the bottle and cellophane into the bucket. Walking to his car, he opened the door and turned on the radio. As the music played, he went to bathe. He was used to being naked in the forest now. He began to sing along as he washed his hair. He had the makings of a real beard now and he decided to let it grow. It might help keep his face warmer in the winter.

For the next three weeks, Larry settled into a routine. He would beg in the morning, get any supplies he needed in the early afternoon and work on the camp for the rest of the day. From this plan, he now had the entire campsite clear of leaves. His laundry was done and his car was clean. His boxes were now plastic instead of cardboard. He even had a new mat to stand on when he bathed and a fold out wooden bench by the fire. Somewhere along the way, he'd bought some real shampoo and a few solar lights which he had placed around the camp. Although it had rained now and then, the drops had remained light and not strong enough to disturb anything. Most days were sunny and clear and the early November temperature, still bearable. But it was time to get a winter coat. He had a hundred and sixty dollars in his wallet. He hoped Goodwill would have one cheap but if they didn't, he would spend up to fifty dollars at Walmart for a new one. I'll get a coat tomorrow one way or another, he thought, sitting at the table sipping his late evening bourbon.

From under his structure, Larry admired his camp. He was proud of the way it looked. He had put tremendous effort into it. He was worried about the freezing cold that was to come. He hadn't yet figured out a plan to deal with it. The coat was a start. But the days were slipping by. He had lost count of them again. Living in the forest, time didn't seem to matter.

An hour later, Larry saw that his fire had died. Setting his new mystery book on the table, he blew out the candles. Walking to his car with the solar lights showing his path, he suddenly became cold. Shivering, he climbed into bed and turned on the heat in the Toyota. Tucked in comfortably, he let the heat run while he listened to his two song limit on the radio before turning it off. The little washcloths that had covered the ventilation crack of the window were now replaced by one longer, heavier dishcloth to keep out the cold. Outside, the solar lights made the forest seem less formidable. Even his pillow case smelled sweet from being washed in shampoo yesterday. As he drifted off, Larry delighted in his small comforts. He fell asleep fantasizing about his imaginary cozy cabin in the woods, a recurring comfort for him.

Morning came clear and blue, and Larry's eyes opened early. He got out of his car feeling well-rested, and turned on the radio while making his fire to boil water for coffee. He heard the announcer say that it was November 19th and have you gotten your turkey yet? Turkey? Larry suddenly realized that it was getting close to Thanksgiving. In the past, he had gone to a coworker's house for the meal. He'd enjoyed the spread Chris's girlfriend had put out. She had been a fine cook. He wondered if he ever thanked her. Knowing himself, he wouldn't be surprised if he had not. Last year, when Chris had left Bart's for another job, no other invitation had been offered to him. He'd been left to find a turkey dinner by himself. He'd eaten his Thanksgiving dinner at the Cracker Barrel restaurant. The meal had been so delicious, Larry recalled that he hadn't cared about eating alone. He liked the nostalgic feel of the place and the cheerful fire burning on the restaurant's huge stone hearth. All in all, last Thanksgiving's dinner was a good memory.

Now he would have no turkey, just as he would have no Thanksgiving. He was a loser with no friends and nowhere to go. His mood turned sour as he ate a breakfast of two doughnuts and an orange. When his coffee was finally ready, it tasted bitter and he threw it out.

Leaving the woods a few minutes later, Larry stuck to his morning routine of begging. Maybe it was due to his dark mood, but he made less than usual. This further blackened his outlook. While the thought of buying a winter coat had once excited him, now it just felt like another expense. He suddenly felt bitter about the spending. He wasn't any closer to finding a job or getting an apartment. He was getting nowhere. He was just a stupid-ass, pathetic beggar.

Larry sank onto the grass on the corner of the intersection and sat cross-legged, his head low. He propped the sign against his knees so that people driving by could read it. He was vaguely aware that sitting like this would cause people to think he was a drunk, but he was just too sad to stand. Too disheartened. He had lost his energy. Staring at the stubby brown blades of dormant grass, Larry was aware that his depression was starting to dig in, its razor-sharp talons shredding his contentment. He had to stop it. He had to turn it around. He couldn't afford it. He had too many things to concentrate on . . . like survival. Still, he felt like crying. It was already raining inside him.

Suddenly, a twenty-dollar bill wrapped around a cheap ballpoint pen secured by a small rubber band landed at his feet. Jerking his head up, he saw the driver waving at him. Larry waved back, his arm in the air, moving wildly from side to side. "Thank you! Thank you!" Larry yelled. The man waved again and drove on.

Larry picked up the pen and looked at it. How is it, he wondered, that some people are so charitable while others are so stingy? I would have never thought of doing something like this. Never. What is wrong with me?

How did I get to be the way I am? God, I'm such an awful person. No, he corrected himself... that's the way I used to be. I am learning. I am changing. I am not that person anymore.

A car honked lightly. A woman was holding a bill out the window. Larry scrambled to his feet and ran to her car. Taking the bill, he thanked her profusely. She smiled at him and said, "Good luck!" Glancing at the bill as she drove off, Larry saw it was only a dollar. Still, it was given with genuine kindness.

He reflected on that deeply. Kindness changes everything, he thought.

He returned to his seat on the grass. Turning the bill over in his hand, it struck him that kindness was a towering essence of power. That even one small act of charity had a ripple effect on the economy. And that ripple would move to the world. I understand now, he thought, his eyes opening wide. People helping people is a good thing, even if I was taught that helping the poor only hurts them. But, it's not true. It's a lie. It is a lie. IT. IS. A. LIE. The generosity of others has helped me survive and stay fed. To make it through another day. And now, because of them, I'll get a warm coat so I can get through the winter without freezing to death.

His lips tightened in insightful revelation. I have been wrong, he thought. Every fucking thing I have been taught is wrong. He felt anger well within him. He thought of his father and his cruelty, malice, and his hatred. He thought of Bart and his wicked and gleeful promotion of chaos and loathing.

All the hatred has ruined me.

He felt like screaming. The urge was nearly beyond his control. He raised his eyes to the sky in pain. More money landed at his feet. The power of the sky hurt him. It was too big and bright. His eyes welled with tears. I must change, he thought desperately, watching the enormous clouds move across the vast horizon. I must change rapidly. And powerfully. It must be now. He lowered his eyes to the money at his feet. He closed his eyes. The pain of his life spread through him like rolling metal crushing him internally.

*I know how to do it. I know how to change.*

He knew what he was going to do. He was going to become a different person. Deliberately and attentively. Unconditionally and willfully. He was going to change until he no longer knew who he was. It would be hard, but somehow, he would come out on the other side. Then he would find himself. Maybe. He couldn't know.

I talk without thinking, he thought bitterly. I will change that too. I will learn a new way to communicate with others. I will slow my words down and give myself time to think between those words. I will talk slowly and I will talk thoughtfully. I will talk only when I need to and not otherwise. I don't do that now. I don't hear what others are saying. I'm too busy raising a defense before they even speak. *I've lost everything because of my close-minded ignorance.*

He heard his father's words: "You're just stupid, Larry. Just damn stupid." He *was* stupid. He acted without thinking. He was always reacting. He had no control. No discipline. No force of will.

Lifting his head, he watched the clouds as they floated and changed. He was sick of himself. He was lazy and weak. He was mean and rigid in his thinking. He was ill-informed and had no understanding. He was insecure and filled with hate. He had no self-control. He was ugly. *I will no longer lie to myself.* A tear slid down his cheek. He watched the clouds as they continued to shift; a massive supremacy that was way beyond him. He opened his eyes to it. The blueness of the morning sky nearly blinded him.

I am going to shed all of it. My anxiety, anger, fear, frustration, hatred and defensiveness. My meanness, ignorance, insecurity and laziness. They are like ancient scale armor dragging me down. I will let them all go. All I have to do is lower my shoulders from my ears and let them all fall off me. And then I will summon a calm. And, a *self-control.* And I will keep it to me.

Only then would he be able to see in front of him. Be open to hearing, thinking, analyzing, and seeing. All the things that he wasn't doing now. I have been wrong, he thought. Everything I have been doing is wrong. And it has brought me here. To nowhere.

He lowered his head from the blinding light. I am going to change. Now. This very minute. I will never be the same again.

He felt the dollar in his hand given in kindness. And I will become like this. I will become kind. I will move forward in kindness. I will bring that power to me. I will use it. I will become gentle and find a strength of character in it. I will become a part of the world in this way. It is all I can do, he thought with clarity. It is all I can do. *It is all I can do.*

He felt the breeze on him. He lowered his shoulders and shuddered. He knowingly shed his weighty scales of ignorance, laziness and hatred— all of it—then and there. It was his resolve to make. And he had made it. He slowly summoned within himself a force of self-control and a steady calm. He felt it when it filled him. It brought him a strong sense of peace. He felt his face begin to relax and his body become fluid. He could feel his fingers open. He breathed. He began to feel a determined strength. He inhaled even more deeply. He felt the morning air around him. He would have to continue to learn how to do this and do it until he understood it.

He was done here. He had to get a coat. Winter was coming. And it would hurt him.

He straightened the money at his feet and put it into his wallet.

Picking up his sign, Larry walked down the side of the street until he reached the donut shop where his Toyota was parked. He was still feeling faint. The walk had not cleared his mind. He waited for his light-headedness to clear. He leaned against his car. He blinked against the air and morning light and felt his lips part to take in more breath. He realized he was feeling emotionally broken. Torn. Spread out. His revelations were already impacting him. Knocking him off his feet. He realized then that no one could have a life-changing experience and just walk away. If it was real, it would cling and take hold. It was real. And it was taking hold.

He laid his hand on his chest. He felt the world dip as the newness of his self spread within his body. He was starting to feel fractured. His mind was opening. It didn't hurt. It was just disorienting. He stood there, gasping for breath. He bent, bracing his hands on his knees, waiting to regain his balance and breath. Everything about him was a lie. He was letting it all go. He was shedding more scales. He could see them falling on the ground, splintering in the sunlight as they fell. He could do this. He could learn. He could be open to understanding. He shook his head, trying to get his mind lucid. He knew he was experiencing a kind of delirium.

"Help me," he whispered to no one. "Oh God, help me." He didn't want to fall in the parking lot. He was close to falling. He felt tears in his eyes again. He felt the world shift as he sank against his car to the asphalt. He lowered his head trying to breathe. He would wait for this to pass. He would be okay. He just had to find his feet.

He felt a shadow over him. He heard the words: "I saw you looking ill and thought I would ask if you're okay. Do you need a hand to get up?"

Larry looked up. He saw an older man holding a donut box and a coffee. His face held an expression of concern. Larry saw that his hair was gray and his face was kind. He had on a navy t-shirt tucked into a neat pair of jeans. Larry had to say something. He couldn't find his voice. He was still too dizzy. Slowly, he shook his head. He began to rise to his feet. Standing, he straightened his shoulders. He blinked against the light. His voice returned. He remembered to speak slowly. He remembered to separate his contractions and to think between his words. It would be a new way for him to speak. But it would also force himself to slow down in his talking. It would feel odd until it became natural. It would take discipline. He remembered to be grateful for this man's kindness. He would speak and have the man move on. He really was okay. He would speak the truth this time.

"No. Thank you," he said softly. "I am okay. I was just thinking of my life. And for a moment, I was completely overwhelmed."

The older man nodded. "Yes. Life can be overwhelming. Well, I am glad that you are okay. If you're sure . . . "

"Yes. I am sure. You are very kind to check on me. I am grateful. But yes, I am sure."

"Okay. I'll leave you then. Have a good day."

"You too."

He watched the man leave. Opening his car door, he slid into his seat and pulled the door closed. He sat there quietly trying to regain himself. His balance. His vision. He could not drive until he did. He closed his eyes, letting himself doze. He had to rest. He did not kid himself that he would always know how to manage himself. He was acutely aware that it would be a process. That it would take time. He would still feel remnants of his old self until his new self took control and became his natural way of feeling. He would keep working on it until it did, even if it meant losing himself in the progression. A few minutes later, he opened his eyes. He took another deep breath and slowly let it out.

He was ready now.

He drove to the Goodwill located in a nearby shopping center. Looking through the racks, he found nothing that suited him. He was hoping for a thick coat, either dark blue or black, long enough to cover his shins. Most of the coats were blazers and bomber-style jackets that ended at the waist.

Leaving Goodwill, he got on the road again. Soon he passed a thrift store he thought looked okay. Making a U-turn, he drove into the parking lot and parked. Entering the store, Larry found the showroom brightly lit with a large selection of used furniture, framed pictures, lamps, and knick-knacks. He spied the clothing racks further back in the store and felt his hope rise as he headed to the area. He found the coat almost immediately: a single-breasted, dark blue, shin-length wool coat. The garment had some gently worn spots and was missing a button, but overall, it looked good enough. Larry tried it on and found it to be a decent fit. It was marked $20.00. Pleased, he paid for the coat and left the store.

Stopping by Kroger, Larry shopped for the dinner he would eat later in the evening. He selected a roast chicken, a few ears of corn for boiling, butter and to celebrate his new coat, a can of Thanksgiving-style cranberries. He left the store, stealing nothing on his way out. He had asked the cashier what time it was and she had told him it was 1:00 p.m.

He wanted to get back to camp to make some coffee and do some laundry. It was warm enough to take a bath too. The days were getting dark sooner now, so he'd better get to it.

Driving to camp, Larry heard a Christmas carol on the radio and started to sing along. As he passed Walmart, he continued down the winding two-lane road past the old residential area toward the entrance of his camp. He unloaded his supplies and spent the rest of the afternoon and evening content and happy. His dinner was good. He enjoyed reading and sipping his bourbon by the firelight. He learned that he loved cranberries. He knew he would buy them often during the upcoming holiday season.

For the next two weeks, Larry's routine stayed the same. He begged in the morning and worked on his camp in the afternoon. After eight weeks in the forest, he found himself generally happy. He loved the woods. He patted the trees. He knew every one of them. The wind in their boughs seemed to sing to him. His sense of well-being continued to grow. He was lulled into a sense of security. Larry didn't know it, as he lost track of time out here, but the days had rolled into December.

On December 5th, Larry drove home with a couple of new candles, another roast chicken, and a can of cranberries. He had everything else that he needed at the moment. His car had gas, he had plenty of food and water. His camp was neat and his woodpile was stacked high. Returning home, he felt secure and looking forward once more to his favorite meal.

As his turn-off came into sight, his mouth fell open in shock and his heart skidded to a stop. Fear rose within him like a tidal wave. He felt like he was having a heart attack.

The entrance to his camp was blocked by police cars, their blue lights pulsing and blinding. Five or six cars were there. Several men were walking around. As he drove by slowly, staring in disbelief, he saw that one police car was on the entry path, its headlights facing the road. That meant they had been to his camp. That meant they would destroy his camp. That meant they were on to him. Driving on, he dared not stop. His camp was over.

He was going to lose everything: his food and pans and supplies. His fire and shelter. He was going to lose his ability to bathe, do laundry and cook. He was also going to lose his forest, which he had grown to love. He was going to lose his home.

Gripping the wheel and trying to stay on the road, Larry began to scream. He couldn't stop screaming. "Oh God, please, no, no, no!" His own cries sounded agonizingly hollow in his ears. He couldn't stop his tears from flowing down his cheeks. He couldn't control his heaving sobs. He blindly tried to find a safe place to pull over. He ended up in the empty parking lot of a small Baptist church.

He spent the night there, without lighting his candles, in the dark. His heart was completely broken.

He cried all night.

# CHAPTER THIRTEEN

The morning light was dim when Larry opened his eyes. It had been an awful night of suffering.

His neck and hips hurt from sitting too long. He had fallen asleep without making his bed. His face felt crusty and his mouth sour. He had no water because he hadn't bought any yesterday. He hadn't needed to, as his camp already had a good supply. He ran the tip of his tongue over his dry lips and thought of his camp. He was afraid to go there and see what the police had done to it. Maybe they were still waiting for him to return. If they saw him, he had no doubt they would arrest him. On what charge, he didn't know. Vagrancy? Theft? Burning a fire in a forest? It does not matter, he thought dully. All that matters is that I don't go to jail. The thought, to him, was wrenching and terrifying. It could have easily happened. Had he been at the camp when the police arrived, he would be in jail this very moment, fingerprinted and locked behind bars. Larry closed his eyes, feeling sick. It had been a really close call.

Staring out his windshield, his stomach still twisting, Larry decided he would wait a day before seeing what had happened to his home. If his home hadn't been dismantled, maybe he could still retrieve some supplies. But now that the police were aware of his place, he knew he could never live there again.

Larry rested his forehead on the steering wheel. He tried to consider what to do next. He felt the pained rumble of his stomach. He had to come up with a plan. Slowly, his hand came up and turned on the ignition. Letting his engine warm, he decided that he would go back to the Waffle House, wash up and eat. Then he would be able to think more clearly.

Numbly, Larry made his way to the restaurant. Parking, he entered and went to the bathroom to wash. Turning on the hot water, he rinsed his face, mouth, and the front of his hair. Drying off with paper towel, he used his fingers to rake back his moist dark mane. It was longer now. Turning on the cold water, he wet two paper towels and folded them into pads. He applied them like cold packs to his stinging, bloodshot eyes. He repeated the process until some of the burning eased. Then he went to find a booth.

Larry was grateful that he was eating breakfast as a free man. He was acutely aware that it had been his developing kindness that had saved him. If he hadn't stopped to listen to the woes of an older man outside of the grocery store, he would have gone straight home from the store. But he had stopped. He had listened. The man had walked up to him, asking for food. The man had looked sad and lost. He had wanted someone to hear him. His eyes had held that dazed glaze of trauma. Larry knew the look well. The man had explained that both his wife and teenage daughter had been killed in a car crash some months back. He hadn't been able to pull himself together from his grief. He had lost his job and then his home. And now, he didn't know what to do with himself or how to live. And he was hungry.

Larry had given the man time to talk. He remembered that he had stayed mostly silent, just listening. He had given the man his grocery bag of crackers and cheese and orange juice. He knew it would help. He still had his chicken and cranberries. He still had his camp. He had more than that man had. He could share. He was learning to do that. He stayed with the man a good while. They had sat on the wooden rockers for sale outside of the Kroger entry. During this time the police had come to his camp. He hadn't been there because he had been absorbing the pain of another.

He had watched the man eat his food. He had seen the gratitude in the man's eyes. The relief of eating. The relief of someone being with him and treating him as a feeling human being. He had left the man with twenty dollars from his wallet so he could buy more food. He had left the man with no assurances that life would get better. He had done for him all he could. He couldn't adopt him. Couldn't take him home. He had met too many others along the way with their own sadness's. If he had taken them all home, he would have had a small community at his camp. All he could do was listen and give to them what he could. Since his revelation of kindness, his life had changed dramatically. He found that he rarely had to talk. He only had to listen. People were gravitating to him. He didn't necessarily want that, but neither did he push them away. He had already learned so much. They all had their own stories.

Now it was himself that was wounded. He was feeling vacant, fragile and distressed. He could not talk to anyone; it was out of the question. He was glad that his waitress was an older woman with a sour expression. Beyond getting his order of coffee, eggs, and toast, she had no interest in him. He needed to be left alone to think and recover. How, how, how did he recover?

Eating very slowly to make his time there last, Larry reviewed what he did have. He still had his bed and most of his clothes. What had been hanging on the clothesline was most likely lost to him. He had some towels, washcloths, and his coat. Two candles. Along with his chicken and cranberries, that was pretty much it. What did he need right now, immediately? Water. A can opener and some paper towels. He needed a plate, some silverware, and a mug. He would ask for a coffee to go at no extra charge when he left the restaurant. The styrofoam cup could hold anything, hot or cold. He could get everything else at the dollar store. Larry knew he should go begging this morning, but he wasn't up to it. He was wiped out. He needed to sleep. He would get his list and then find somewhere to tuck in, make his bed, and rest.

When Larry opened his eyes for the second time that day, the warm afternoon sun was bright. He felt sweaty and hot under the blankets. The air in the car was stifling. He hadn't cracked the window. Raising the seat, he pushed the blankets aside. A new gallon of water was on his passenger seat.

He pulled it to his lips and took a long drink. Looking out the passenger window, he could see in the near distance some boys trying to skateboard and a few adults walking about in their jogging suits. The boys were taunting each other and laughing loudly. The harsh clack of their skateboards against the concrete sidewalk felt sharp to his ears. The noise was probably what had awakened him. Watching the boys, Larry recalled that he was at some kind of city park, his car parked on the far edge of the lot, next to a shady tree. After his Waffle House breakfast this morning, he had driven to the dollar store and then past the entrance of his camp. The police cars weren't there. The entrance beckoned him, but he hadn't stopped. He had driven on, past the little Baptist church and finally into this park. Sitting there, he felt irritable and lethargic as he stared through the windshield at the small rising knoll of dormant grass in front of his car. His stomach growled. The light breakfast of the morning was no longer holding him. He remembered the roast chicken on his back seat.

Opening the car door, Larry stepped out and folded his top blanket into a square. Laying it on the grass under the tree next to the Toyota, he collected his water, paper towels, and the chicken. Sitting cross-legged on the blanket, he felt a bit better in the fresh air. Larry rinsed his hands with a small amount of water and dried them with a paper towel. Opening the plastic container of chicken, he tore off a leg. The scent of the roasted bird made his mouth water. He suddenly realized just how ravenous he was. He wanted the can of cranberries too. He had bought a can opener at the dollar store earlier, but had forgotten that to buy silverware. He had still been too dazed to think clearly. He cursed softly. He would have to use his fingers to dig into the can. Okay. He would deal with it.

Setting the chicken leg on a paper towel, he rose to get the cranberries. Returning to his blanket, he opened the can. With his car hiding him, Larry consumed his picnic in peace. As he ate, he realized that he was feeling something else. Anger. Anger at the cops. Why were so many cars there, he wondered bitterly. How many cops did it take to check out a guy living in the woods? Christ, it was like they were hunting some criminal.

Larry knew that he had been stealing, but it was small stuff. Not enough to send an army of cops to find him. Maybe it was the old man whose house he had robbed? Maybe he had made a police report. Or maybe it was just someone who had smelled his fires and was worried about it? He figured he would never know how the police had come to find his camp. Whatever the reason, their numbers had been ridiculous. Why couldn't he just have been left alone? Someone had reported him. Someone had known he was there. Why was it so hard to let a homeless person make a home where he could?

Lifting two fingers of cranberries to his mouth, Larry paused, sighing. He knew why. Because of him. Because of people like him. How many articles had he written mocking and demonizing the poor and homeless? He didn't know. Countless. Hadn't he spread the idea that they were bad people? Yes, he thought, but I'm not the only one to do it, nor the first. Hatred and loathing of the poor and homeless had been going on for decades in this country, and long before that. But that was then and now was now. He had been a horrible provocateur in provoking more disdain, disgust, and distrust against the truly vulnerable. The internet was a powerful thing. Who knew how many people had read his derisive words and used them as a bludgeon, a justification to reinforce their already low opinion of those who couldn't afford more than to live on the streets? He had once read that if something is repeated often enough, the lie will become the truth and people will believe it as fact. Hell, he had even believed the crap he was writing. Lowlifes. Beggars. Drunkards. Druggies. Thieves and frauds. And now it was probable that someone had turned his own opinions on him. Maybe, he thought, someone in the area had been watching him come and go from the forest. He had tried to be careful, but maybe he hadn't been careful enough. Maybe they didn't want his kind in their area, so they had called the cops to clear him out. And the cops, not knowing what to expect, had descended like a SWAT team. Yes, he thought, that made sense.

Larry shoved the cranberries into his mouth, appreciating the tartness and the way they tasted with the chicken. He was nearly done with the first leg. He reached down to the open container before him and tore off the other. Biting deeply into the meat, Larry became more convinced that his theory was very likely what had happened. Life's little ironies, he thought. Or was it Karma? Probably both . . . but now, he had to figure out what to do. Considering his limited options, he decided that he would spend the night right where he was. He could pee under the tree and his bed was already made. He was still feeling at a loss and terribly weak, so he would just sleep. In the morning he would start begging again. Perhaps something more would occur to him tomorrow. It wasn't happening at the moment.

Finished with lunch, Larry picked up the empty can of cranberries and half-eaten container of chicken and put them on the backseat floor. He rinsed his sticky face, mouth, and hands with his water. Standing, he shook out his blanket and carefully remade his bed. Locking his car, Larry brushed off his hoodie, combed his hair and took a long walk around the park, the same as any person would. He watched people jog and others talk and laugh in pairs or groups. He watched kids take to the air on the swings and play with their toys in the sandy area of the playground, immersed in their own childish fantasies. The adults in the area seemed so happy, so normal. Watching them, Larry felt like an awkward shadow. Invisible. These people were everything he was not. They all had nice homes to go to. Homes with tables and chairs and soft beds with thick comforters. Kitchens stocked with food and the latest appliances. Walls covered in tasteful art, the rooms all decorated. Rooms with electric light. Maybe some of them would have a fireplace burning with a warm fire. And a nice sofa or easy chair where they could watch a ballgame on a big screen TV. All these people were warm and fed and entertained.

A tear trickled down Larry's cheek. He seemed to be always crying. He had nothing. That set him worlds apart from the families here. They were worthwhile, while he, without a home, was not. He was just someone to be chased off. I have no one, Larry thought, while these people have friends and families. I am so sad, he despaired, I feel so low. I don't even have the words to describe just how low or how alone I feel. Oh God, I really am worthless. He closed his eyes in misery.

A sob escaped him. Drawing his knees to his chest on the park bench, Larry pressed a knuckle to his lips to try and stem the flow. He began to rock gently against his pain.

"You okay, buddy?"

Slowly, Larry raised his head. He stared at the stranger through his watery eyes. The man's voice had been kind. Larry tried to bring his face into focus. He saw that the stranger was about thirty, dressed in a sharp navy running suit. Larry opened his mouth to answer but nothing came out. How could he answer this?

"I mean," the man said, "you look kinda lost. Are you lost? You okay?"

Larry cleared his throat and found his voice. "I am not lost . . . just really sad." Thinking quickly, he connected his pain to his voice, "My girl-friend has just broken up with me and I did not see it coming. I am . . . not doing so well. Actually, I do not know what to do with myself. I just don't. I am a wreck."

The stranger's view of the man shifted. He had felt a little suspicious of the guy. But now he nodded in sympathy. "That's a tough one all right. I'm sorry for you. I hope it gets better for you." He turned to leave, then added, "Good luck."

Watching the man drift away, Larry closed his eyes. He had nearly blurted out that he was homeless and had nowhere to go. The urge to say so had been nearly uncontrollable. But why would he have said it? So the man might have pitied him and taken him home? Maybe have fed him and let him sleep in a real bed? How stupid, stupid, stupid, he thought. He had done the right thing. If he had spoken the truth, he might have opened a real can of worms. Maybe the man would have been repulsed and called the police. With all these kids around, Larry thought, people here would probably resent a homeless man watching them or being close to them, as if being homeless were the same as being a pervert. Thankfully his brain had engaged with a credible response. Getting to his feet, Larry decided to walk a bit to get his blood going. Being depressed was just soul-sucking.

As the sun began to set, the park quickly emptied out. The evening breeze was turning chilly. Larry returned to his car and climbed under his blankets. He wished he had something warm to drink. He lay there feeling vacant, his eyes staring until it was dark. After that, they didn't open again until morning.

At sunrise, Larry rose immediately, folded his bed, and laid the blankets neatly on the backseat. He was feeling stronger, more recovered, and sick of feeling sick. Leaving the park, he drove to the donut shop and bought a coffee. With cup in hand and his sign under his arm, he left his car behind and walked up the road to the grassy corner of the intersection. He planned to beg all morning, but first he wanted to drink his coffee. Sitting on the grass, he sipped his hot brew, feeling in need of a real bath. He felt oily, dirty, and ripe. He could smell himself; his sleep, his sweat, and his anxiety.

Racking his brain, he tried to think of where he could go to get clean. Suddenly, he remembered a hotel where his co-worker, Jeff, had taken him on his first visit to Balfour. Jeff had planned to meet a friend for lunch and since he didn't want to leave Larry with his folks, he had invited Larry along. The hotel had an indoor swimming pool. That pool was exactly what he needed now. He was pretty sure they had traveled up Main Street, maybe a mile or two to get there. He prayed it was true. After begging, he would go to the dollar store and get some silverware and scissors. He recalled that the pool area had a locker room shower area stocked with fresh white towels. He would bathe and trim his hair and beard there. He would also have to go to Walmart to buy a cheap pair of shorts for swimming. As the blue pool rose in his imagination, he could hardly wait to slide into the water.

Impatient now, and pumped with his plan, Larry set his coffee cup in the grass and began to hustle cars. His morning netted him $41.50. It was more than usual. People must be feeling generous because of the upcoming holidays, he thought. Squinting at the sun shining brightly overhead, he figured it was about noon. Tucking his sign under his arm, he retrieved his coffee cup and made his way back to his car. Starting his engine, Larry headed back down Town View Parkway towards the dollar store where he was in and out in just minutes. Crossing the street to Walmart, he quickly went to the men's department and located a pair of Hawaiian print swim trunks on a clearance rack for three bucks. He also splurged on a long sleeve black cotton pullover to match the black outline of flowers on his swimming trunks. Larry knew he had to look as decent as possible pool-side so he wouldn't be asked to leave. Paying for his clothes, he moved quickly to his car. Now, was the hard part . . . finding the hotel.

Traveling up Town View Parkway, Larry finally reached Main Street. Turning right on that road, he continued on, leaving the quaint shops and restaurants of the downtown area behind him. He couldn't recall the name of the hotel, but he was pretty sure that he remembered what it looked like. It had been a tall, square building, beige in color, nicely landscaped and surrounded by a wide parking lot. The enclosed pool was located in the back of the hotel. Larry knew this because after he and Jeff had finished lunch in the dining room, they had strolled through the lobby to the pool area and through the back doors to the lot where they had parked. He had stopped them before they had gone to the car because he needed to use the bathroom. The hotel had been crowded that day, so they had parked where they could. Interesting how small things can affect your life, Larry reflected. Had they parked in the front of the hotel, he wouldn't have known the pool existed. The minutes ticked by, and he felt unsure of where the hotel was, but he tried to remain calm. Suddenly, he spied The Balfour Inn just a little further up, on the right side of the road. Expelling a breath of relief, he thought, now, I just have to make it into the pool area.

Steering his Toyota to the parking lot in the back of the hotel, Larry saw there were plenty of available parking spaces as he parked. Moving to his trunk, he shoved his scissors and keys into his pocket and draped his new clothes over his arm. He selected an extra pair of underwear to wear once he was done swimming. Closing the trunk lid, he tucked the briefs between the clothes on his arm and proceeded to the gate surrounding the outside deck area. It was locked. He thought about climbing over the white metal fence. He could do it; it wasn't that high—but then he heard voices talking behind him. Stepping aside to let the group of four enter with their key, he moved quickly with them before the gate closed. Sticking with the group, Larry followed them through the keyed door that opened to the indoor pool area. Splitting from them, he made for the locker room. He was thrilled that he had gained entry so smoothly. Scanning the empty room, he noted a basket of black plastic combs sitting on the mirrored counter next to another basket filled with hotel soaps, lotions, and shampoos. A wicker shelving unit was against the back wall stacked with perfectly folded fresh white towels. It was just as he had remembered.

Slipping into a toilet stall, Larry stripped off his clothes and pulled on his new swimsuit. Leaving the stall, he stepped up to the counter and folded his clothes neatly. He hid them on the top edge of a row of lockers where they might not be noticed. Grabbing a small bar of soap and a couple bottles of shampoo, he moved to the shower and with hot water streaming down on him, he slipped out of his swim shorts and underwear and hung them on a shower hook. Pouring shampoo into his hand, he washed his greasy hair twice before lathering his body with the bar of Spring Bouquet soap. Larry used the remainder of his shampoo to wash his dirty underwear thoroughly. After a careful rinsing, he wrung out the water and pulled them back on, followed by his new swimwear.

Larry went to the mirrored counter and combed his wet hair down over his forehead and ears. With his scissors, he cut off a hank of two inches just above his eyebrows and angling down, cut the sides just below his ear lobes, leaving the back a little longer. Using a tissue, he swept the floor clean of his cuttings and dropped the clump into the trash can. Combing his hair back away from his face, he was relieved to see his cut didn't look half bad. His hair looked full and thick and very dark brown, like the color of burnished mahogany. That it appeared so dark surprised and pleased him. Bringing the scissors to his beard, he took his time trimming it close and neat. Satisfied that he no longer looked like a mountain man, he once again picked up and disposed of the hair. Staring at himself in the mirror, he felt renewed. He did not recognize himself. He was looking at a stranger. He looked suave, muscular, lean, and handsome. It truly surprised him. He didn't know how it was possible.

Moving to the lockers, Larry slid the scissors on top of his folded clothes. With a towel around his neck, he left the bathroom with three more towels draped over his arm along with his new black shirt. Confident that he looked okay, he scanned the pool area. A few younger kids were in the water and two single adults were on chaise lounges. The woman was reading a book, the man staring at his phone. He also spied a table with dirty dishes and a bill. Walking to the table of four chairs, Larry calmly studied the bottom of the check without touching it. It was signed M. Hansen, Room 215. The check listed three hamburgers, two baskets of fries, one order of chicken fingers, and four sodas. His mouth watered. After only coffee for breakfast, he was very hungry. Turning, he strode back to the locker room to get his wallet from the pocket of his jeans. Moving quickly, he returned to the chaise lounge next to the table so he could see the server when he or she came to clear the table. Casually spreading a towel over the lounge, his heart beat uneasily as he waited. He would eat well today. He hoped there would be no drama. He would get a hamburger, fries, and a cold beer. His stomach growled in anticipation. Fifteen long minutes later, the waiter—a young man—showed up to clear the table.

Immediately, Larry rose off his lounge to stand beside the waiter. "Hello," he said pleasantly, greeting the young man. "Before you go, will you bring me one more burger with fries and a cold Bud?"

The server glanced at Larry. "Okay. Do you have a room number?"

Larry spoke very slowly. "Yes. Hansen, 215. But I will be paying in cash. I do not want any more put on my room. If it is okay with you, I have been in meetings all morning and missed the meal with my family. I have not eaten today and am seriously starving. Could you do your best to hurry it along? Just bring it to this same table. I would really appreciate it."

"Alright. I'll get it out to you as soon as possible," the waiter replied, gathering the dishes and check onto his tray.

As the man walked away, Larry swept his towels and shirt from the lounge and placed them on the table to show ownership. He hid his wallet between the towels. Turning, he entered the pool with a smile of relief. The water felt as he knew it would, warm and spirit-soothing. The kids ignored him as he ignored them. Swimming to the deep end, Larry let himself sink into the caressing cool blueness. Only coming up for air, he sank again and again. It felt so good, the water was heaven. Eventually, he swam to the shallow end and lolled on the concrete stairs to wait for his food.

Keeping an eye on the glass door to the lobby, Larry stayed where he was, although he was ready to get out and towel off. Without a book or phone to look at while sitting at the table, he anxiously considered that he might look a little weird, a little off. Everyone had a phone. They would carry it with them even to the pool. After another few minutes, the wait became agonizing. He was getting chilled. A sharp pain was developing in his stomach. He waited for ten minutes longer before deciding that he could lie on the lounge by the table and pretend to snooze. Rising, he stepped out of the water. He moved to the table, where he dried off and pulled on his shirt, grateful for the warmth of the long sleeves. Less chilled now, he draped his wet towel on the back of a chair. Leaving a towel on the table, he believed the table still looked occupied. Taking the remaining two dry towels, Larry spread one over the lounge and used the other to cover his legs. Lying down, he got comfortable. He closed his eyes. Better now.

A short time later, the waiter came with a tray and set it on the table. Rising off the lounge, Larry held his wallet in his hand. The waiter handed him the bill. Taking the check, Larry glanced at the charges: $12.00 for the hamburger and fries and $5.00 for the beer. With a tip of a little more than twenty percent, the bill came to $21.00. He tried not to wince. Between his new clothes and lunch, he had spent almost his entire earnings from the morning. But I really need this, he thought. I must recover. He was clean, freshly groomed, and now about to be well fed.

"Thank you," he said gently as he paid the waiter.

"You're welcome. I'll be back to check on you. Let me know if you need anything more."

"Yes. I will," Larry replied, sure there would be nothing more.

As the waiter left, Larry sat and lifted the silver cover off his plate. The hamburger was large and had lettuce, tomatoes, onions, and pickles. His basket of fries was sizzling hot. On the tray sat small bottles of ketchup, mustard, and a few packets of mayonnaise. He eyed them, knowing he would keep what he didn't use. After dressing his burger with the vegetables and all three condiments, Larry took his first bite. He rolled his eyes in ecstasy. He was positive he had never tasted anything so damn good in his entire life. The trick now was not to gobble it down like a pig. *Self-control.* He commanded himself to eat slowly and savor every bite. For the next fifteen minutes, Larry gradually consumed every last thing on his plate. Using his finger, he licked up every remaining drop of ketchup and mustard. When he was finally finished, he dug into his pocket for his wallet and counted the money in his billfold . . . $138.00. He wanted dessert and coffee. He wanted the afternoon to last. He did not want to think about his homelessness or where to spend the night. He was feeling nearly normal, and reveling in the feeling. The waiter came back, asking, "Anything else, Mr. Hansen?"

"Yes. Please. What desserts do you have?"

"Apple pie, chocolate drizzle brownie with vanilla ice cream, carrot cake, and hot peach cobbler."

"I will have the brownie and ice cream . . . with coffee."

"Okay, but it might take a while. The dining room is getting busy."

"No problem. I am full anyway, so please, take your time. I am just going to snooze here by the pool. I need to relax. Would you be so kind as to wake me if I am not up when you get back?"

"You got it. My name is Seth. I apologize for not saying so earlier."

"No worries. By the way, do you have the time? I left my cell phone in the room."

Seth dug into his pocket for his phone, "One forty-five."

"Okay," Larry said gently. He looked at Seth. "Seth, I must close my eyes now. I have a meeting tonight. Please, wake me if you must when you return. Do you understand?"

"Yes, sir. I will," Seth promised.

With a nod, Larry watched Seth walk away again. Settling on the lounge with a towel for a blanket, Larry fell asleep lightly but comfortably. Twenty minutes later, Seth arrived with a tray containing a pot of coffee, a silver set of cream and sugar, and a hot brownie topped by vanilla ice cream and drizzled in chocolate sauce. Larry heard him and came awake. Setting the tray on the table, Seth handed the bill to Larry. The bill listed $8.00 for the dessert, $5.00 for the pot of coffee and calculating a generous tip of $3.00, Larry was looking at a total of $16.00, which he promptly paid to Seth. As much as it galled him to pay so much, he promised himself that he would make it up in the morning. It was more critical that he recharge himself now. The afternoon of swimming and good food felt like a vacation from the hard work of being homeless. It wasn't like he did this every day. Digging into the chocolate brownie, Larry tried to think of nothing more than the rich dessert he was enjoying at the moment. He would contemplate where he would spend the night only when he was through.

Ten minutes later, Larry noted that the pool area was empty. Without hesitation, he licked the last of the chocolate sauce off his plate. Setting the plate down, he stood and lifted the burgundy cloth napkin, mug, and coffee pot off the tray. Walking them over to the small end table, he arranged them neatly and settled back on the lounge. Lying there, he dozed a bit, but his thoughts kept returning to his plan for the night. He envisioned his camp and wished he could go home to it. It would have been the perfect ending to a good day. I can't go home to it, Larry thought, but I can swing by and see what's happened to it. It has been long enough. The cops should no longer be there. Why would they be? After that, I can return to the park and spend the night in the same spot by the tree again. He found some comfort in the small familiarity.

Larry considered the time. It got dark early these days. If he wanted to see his camp he would have to leave soon. He also needed to stop by Kroger to pick up water and a few other items. For the next fifteen minutes, he drank his coffee, draining the pot. Finally, knowing he couldn't dally any longer, he went to the locker room, dressed, and left the pool area to go to his car. He took with him a comb, some bottles of shampoo, lotion, and a couple bars of soap. He also took the burgundy cloth napkin and the small bottles of mustard, ketchup, and the packets of mayonnaise from his lunch tray.

Larry went straight to the grocery store and entered with his backpack. He quickly stole a premade deli sandwich and a bag of thinly sliced ham. In the men's room, he discarded their packaging and wrapped them together in his burgundy napkin. The bundle went into the side pocket of his backpack. He bought two $1.00 beers, sliced deli Swiss cheese, a can of peaches, a loaf of bread on sale and a gallon of water.

Driving towards his camp, he felt his heart pounding with anxiety. Passing Walmart, Larry continued down the two-lane road past the new subdivisions until he reached the old rural area with the low brick house on the corner. The entrance to the forest was just a few hundred feet ahead on the right. After a hundred feet or so, Larry steered his car off the road onto the shoulder. Moving forward slowly, he searched for his marker and found it. While the large branch had been thrown aside, the stone was still there.

Turning into the forest, he gripped the steering wheel tightly, expecting his car to start jostling about. When it didn't, he suddenly stopped and stared out the windshield. He could see a clear tire worn path . . . which meant that many cars had come and gone from here and the thickly layered floor of stones and branches had been crushed by vehicles far heavier than his old lightweight Toyota. Sadness squeezed his heart for both himself and the proud old forest. His forest. Larry pulled up to where he knew his camp had once been. He recognized the various trees that had surrounded his living space. He had often patted their trunks and talked to them. They had spoken to him too. He respected them and their towering strength. It was more than that, Larry thought. I love them.

Standing there in the early twilight, Larry felt faint. It was like he was looking at another time, only it wasn't another time—the loss of his forest had just happened. The birds were chattering as usual and the forest seemed to welcome him. There was nothing left of his camp. No tarps or structure. No fire pit or clothesline. No solar lights or clothes or boxes of food. No table or chair. No pots or pans or rake or broom.

Everything was gone, wiped away as though they had never been there. He had expected the killing of his camp, but to see it left him feeling bereft, deprived, and robbed.

Half of him wanted to immediately gather new stones and wood to quickly build another fire pit and spend the night under the trees by the heat of a crackling fire. He could still smell the homey scent of smoke. But he knew that he couldn't risk it. It was just too dangerous.

He had to leave the forest now. It could be that someone had already seen him entering the woods and was at this very moment calling the cops.

Yes, he had to leave. "Goodbye, my friends," he murmured sadly. He took one last sweeping glance of the leaf-covered land and tall, barren oaks. He bowed his head to them and sighed in pain.

Turning reluctantly, he got into his car and circling the trees, he left the forest.

# CHAPTER FOURTEEN

Coming out of the trees, Larry felt like he was suffocating. He had nowhere to go. He didn't know what to do. His chest was tight and he couldn't catch his breath. Huffing for oxygen, he was overcome by fear, despair, and anger all at once. He couldn't sort them out. Slammed by his emotions, he recognized that he was having a full-blown panic attack. It was killing him. This was how a person died little by little.

He didn't know how long he sat there, knuckles white on the steering wheel, facing the road, wrestling himself under control. When he could finally breathe again, he made a right turn onto the street with a focus on getting back to the park. Once there, he could cry his eyes out all night if he had to, but first he had to get there.

The gathering gloom of the early winter evening was setting in. It wasn't dark yet, but the temperature seemed to be in a free fall. The ribbon of dark asphalt loomed ahead of him, empty for as far as he could see. Why not, he thought dully. If I had a warm, brightly lit house to be in, I wouldn't be here either. He began to shiver. Damn, it was cold. Cranking up the heat, he thought of his coat, glad that he had it. He was going to need it. Driving slowly for a few minutes, Larry began to look for the left turn to the park.

A snowflake hit his windshield. Squinting at the tiny speck of ice, Larry's mouth opened in disbelief. While he didn't know the exact date, he did know it was around the first week of December. Snow just didn't happen in December in Atlanta. Another dozen snowflakes hit his window.

"No. I don't believe this . . ." he murmured softly to himself. This was bad. Very bad.

Suddenly his engine bucked. Smokey silver vapor began pouring in through the vents. An acrid smell hit his nostrils. "Oh my god," Larry screamed, "Fuck! Oh god, no!" Fearful and distracted, he continued onward down the winding two-lane road, missing his turn. His car was dying and he needed to pull over, preferably into some spot where it could be hidden.

Coming around a long bend, he spied an abandoned shack made of rough, decaying plank wood just up ahead. Turning right up the scruffy dirt drive, Larry saw a forgotten place riddled with poverty, small and square, with an attached open-faced shed. Steering his smoking car towards the sagging garage, he could see the house had been deserted for a long time. Nature was in the process of cruelly consuming what was left. He parked and swiftly killed his engine. A roaring silence filled his ears as he peered at the vile, decrepit place around him. He imagined the rotten room was infested with spiders, most likely black widows. But it was winter. They should be gone, asleep, or dead. Still, it had been warm enough these past months. Some could be alive.

Scared and trembling, Larry realized he was now in mortal danger. Behind him, the snow was starting to drift downward more heavily, frozen and white. It would have been beautiful in other circumstances, he thought, watching the glimmering veil of flakes through his rearview mirror. But now he was trapped. With his car blown, he was truly broken. And there probably were spiders. He hated spiders almost more than anything. He was going to spend the night in this godforsaken place. He had no way to escape except on foot. He couldn't do it in the snow. Life's about to get a lot harder, he thought grimly, that is, if I don't freeze to death tonight. Night was encroaching with a bluish tinge from the snow. In minutes, it would be completely dark. Sitting there, Larry felt paralyzed and utterly undone. He couldn't believe this was happening to him.

Larry thought he might truly go insane. He felt the hot sour juices of his stomach surge to his throat. His panic attack had already twisted his gut to the breaking point. With his car killed, his potential death in this snowstorm and his being trapped in this perilous place, he felt pushed to the brink of madness. He *couldn't* bear his hopelessness and pain. It was all too much. He felt his mind starting to break. He sat there, blinking, unable to think.

His inner strength stepped up and commanded without pity: "Get a grip. You're so used to being cold, you have a higher tolerance now. Get up and get busy. Take stock of what you do have and use it." Larry found himself nodding mutely in agreement. Yes. Yes. He had to get up. He had to get busy. There were things he could do.

Turning his ignition slightly to engage his battery, Larry clicked on his headlights and the radio. He wanted light and human voices so he didn't feel so alone. Finding a soft rock station, he set the volume on low. He wanted to hear the music but he didn't want it to distract him as he tried to recover his wits and concentrate on the small things he had to accomplish. With the headlights on, he was able to see more of his surroundings. He noted the massive messy webs in the upper front corners of the shed. Black widows had no style when it came to their webs. That no spiders were on the sticky threads meant nothing to him. He had no doubt they were tucked in somewhere trying to keep warm. The webs were proof that they were here. His stomach lurched violently.

Opening his car door slowly, Larry cautiously stuck one leg out. The bile in his throat rose thick and burning. Heaving hard, he vomited, gagging and retching, onto the dirt floor. The freezing wind tore at him in gusts, causing him to glance out of the open end of the dilapidated structure. The snow was coming down solidly and starting to accumulate at the lip of the shed near his tail lights. Sliding back into his seat, Larry pulled the door closed, feeling ill and feverish. This is no light snow, he thought. It's a dumping. Turning the dial on his radio, he searched for a local weather station. He learned that it was December 8th and Atlanta was expecting nearly a foot of snow tonight. Schools were closed tomorrow and the governor was warning everyone to stay home if possible.

Balfour is an hour and a half northwest of Atlanta, Larry mused grimly. Which means it will be colder here and the snow even heavier. It's going to be a very cold and very long night. Shuddering in fear, he could see his icy breath filling the interior of his car. Reaching forward with a shaking hand, Larry turned on the heat. He needed to get warm. He needed to regain some strength. He decided that he would chance closing his eyes while listening to a limit of two songs. Just two songs and he would get moving again.

He was true to his own promise. At the end of two songs, rather than feeling better, he was actually feeling worse. He was still cold and wanting very badly to sleep. Forcing himself into gear, he tumbled out of his car. He opened the back door and swiftly slid into his warm winter coat. Buttoning it, Larry caught the peculiar scent of snow and its otherworldly crunching sound as it poured from the heavens to earth. Scooping his blankets off the back seat, he made his bed as tight and as warmly as he could in the elements. He also tossed his groceries and backpack onto the front seat while leaving a grocery bag and a few paper towels on the back seat to take a shit if he had to. He didn't think he could stand going in the snow. Finished, he shoved the back door shut.

Sliding under the covers, Larry slammed the door behind him. He knew his shoes were filthy from kicking hard-packed dirt over his vomit but he wore them to bed anyway. Sitting up, he lit one of his candles and turned off the headlights to conserve power. Blinking hard, he took a few seconds to adjust his vision to the dark.

Sorting through his bags and backpack, Larry laid out his available food on the front seat. He still had an entire breast of roast chicken. Wondering with some concern if it was still safe to eat, he thought, it doesn't matter. I've got what I've got and at this point, I'm not going to get more food easily. If I'm going to make it through this, every bite must count. I must eat my oldest food first. I'll eat it for breakfast, if it doesn't freeze tonight. Sighing, he rubbed his weary eyes with his knuckles. He could envision a rock-hard, inedible lump of meat come morning. The answer was to sleep with it. He tucked its container onto his lap, under his blankets.

It occurred to him that he might not survive the night. He could die tonight and be found weeks from now, frozen to death in his car. As for his food, Larry was fairly sure that everything would freeze overnight. Maybe not his water, as the gallon was dense, but it was probable that the lighter things would. Struggling with these notions, Larry decided to continue preparing his foodstuffs. There was nothing else to do except try to stay alive.

Larry emptied his backpack and repackaged his food. He found a baggie and sealed the precious ham. Since the slices of cheese were already layered in wax paper, he used a plastic grocery bag to wrap the stolen deli sandwich and cheese together.

Surveying his groceries, Larry laid out his chicken breast, cheese, ham, loaf of bread, the small bottles of mustard and ketchup, the couple packets of mayonnaise, his deli sandwich, a can of peaches, two beers, and his gallon of water. Remembering the rains of the forest, he knew he could last two to three days on this food if he were very careful. He would be hungry, but he had more now than he had then . . . except it hadn't been so cold then. After bundling his food back into his pack to keep the items dense and protected, he opened his glove box and extracted the small flashlight. He set it by the candle on the dash.

Feeling fragile and ill, Larry turned off the heat and blew out the candle. Settling back on his pillow, he hugged the plastic chicken container to him. He did not crack the window, for fear of spiders and the cold. Pulling the covers over his head, he fell into an uneasy sleep. Several hours later, he awoke, screaming in the dark, with a vivid horror of black spiders crawling all over him. Sitting up abruptly, he grabbed his flashlight, and shining it over his blanket saw there were none. It was just a nightmare. Even so, the dream lingered, keeping him awake for the rest of the night. He could not stop the tears then, and he sobbed quietly through the remaining hours in the tomb of his car as the snow fell steadily, covering the landscape.

# CHAPTER FIFTEEN

The pale frigid morning saw his burgundy napkin drenched in mucus and tears. The snow did not stop nor did the sun appear. Although the flakes were coming down more softly, they continued to fall all day.

Larry sat up in his bed, shuddering, stiff, and starving. His mouth was dry, his nostrils were leaking, and he was still feeling sick. After blowing his nose, he pulled the gallon of water to him, shaking it hard. It wasn't completely frozen and some of the ice inside broke into smaller pieces, leaving plenty for him to drink. He took a long icy swig. He considered turning on the heat but decided to preserve his battery for later that night when the temperature dropped back into a dangerous freeze. At the moment, it was frosty in the car, but it wasn't unbearable.

Spreading a paper towel over his blanket, he pulled the chicken container from under the blankets and set it on his lap. He popped off the hard plastic top, dug his fingers into the meat, tore off a chunk, and ate until he was full. When he was finished, he glanced at the bird. There was still some left. Closing the container, he set it aside. He rinsed his mouth and wiped his hands and then, leaned back again, needing to sleep. He'd gotten very little of it the night before. As his eyelids closed, Larry heard the roaring silence once more. There were no sounds of twittering birds or traffic. There was nothing but the bizarre absence of any noise—an absence that felt unnatural and dissonant. He felt eerily solitary in his stark snow world . . . scared, overwhelmed, and worried. Without help . . . so utterly alone. His breath came out ragged. Shivering, Larry tugged the covers to his chin and within minutes, he fell into a murky, deep slumber.

He dreamed of his father.

Entering the shabby house of his childhood, Larry stood before the man who had raised him. There was no welcome. Ray Curtis Martin blocked his entrance, a cigarette dangling from his lips as the smoke curled upwards. "You been real bad, Larry," Ray said, his voice gravelly from years of smoking. "I don't take to you stealing my fuckin' food from my refriger-ator. I bought that roast chicken and danish with my hard-earned money, not you."

"But I was hungry . . ." explained an eleven year old Larry.

"You eat what I give you and nothing more, you little dickwad."

"You don't give me enough," Larry returned bluntly. "I'm always hungry. I'm just a kid. You're my father, you're supposed to take care of me."

"I don't owe you my paycheck, you little bastard. How many times do I gotta pound it into your thick, brainless skull? Jesus H. Christ, you're stu-pid. I mean, just damn stupid. You fuckin' never learn. And now, I fuckin' gotta punish you. You make me do it. I almost think you want me to hurt you. Well, two can play that game. Hold out your arm again, you fuckin' little shit . . ."

Larry looked at his father in mute refusal. The back of Ray's hand connected with his jaw. He fell against the wall and Ray was on him, press-ing his cigarette into the flesh of his arm. Ray had always hit him; had always hurt him. Not this time though. Larry smiled vacantly, raising his eyes to stare into those of his father. He knew something his old man did not. Ray no longer had the power to hurt him. Smelling the scent of burn-ing flesh, Larry blinked, feeling dominant against the tortuous sensation. He felt nothing. No pain at all. As if time were in slow motion, Larry began to see things he hadn't really noticed before. His father looked sluggish and slow. His mouth was contemptuous and twisted under squinting brown eyes filled with suspicion. Buzzed gray hair made Ray's scalp look mot-tled. His unshaven jowls descended into his thick grimy neck, making him look old. He used to be a plumber with a big company. A few years back, he'd hurt his neck while squirming under a crawl space in a customer's home. He'd gone on disability, a fact he ignored—Ray was good at ignoring facts—while raging that people who sucked on the government tit were all losers, parasites, and welfare queens. Now, Ray was fat, his flaccid belly hanging like a sack of lard over the low-slung waist of his greasy jeans. He watched TV all day. He rarely bathed. Ray was literally a filthy old man. Larry watched his father's mouth grow into a gaping red hole, his fist slicing up to beat him once more. Unmoved, Larry absorbed the blow for the thousandth time. He felt nothing in his dream.

Larry's lashes fluttered, almost coming awake in the seat of his car. He felt his stomach twist again. Thinking about his father did that to him. Ray had made his life wretched. As a boy, he couldn't fight back. When he had gotten older, he had.

Larry had always been the loser, bruised and bloodied, retreating to his room and locking his door. Most of the fights had been an argument over food. Not all of them. Sometimes Larry had screamed at his father to turn down the fucking TV. Larry couldn't think, couldn't study, couldn't write. Ray had retaliated, punching his son's chest, arms, and ribs so violently, Larry couldn't draw a breath. Larry had been in high school then, hiding his brutal abuse under dirty long sleeve shirts. Larry never spoke of his mistreatment to anyone. No one had asked; not even when he'd held his ribs walking in excruciating pain. Larry had avoided teachers, ashamed to be so weak. He'd had no friends because he was too screwed up. The only person Larry had ever wanted to talk to was Peter Bennett. Larry had almost approached the guy. Twice. He badly needed a friend. Bennett had seemed stable, healthy and happy. And in spite of being popular, a sincerely nice person. Larry was too embarrassed to dump his situation on Peter and some of the good things that Peter had done went against all he thought was true. Then, Peter had graduated and gone on to Georgia State University. Two year later, when Larry had been accepted to Georgia State, he hadn't been able to get away from Ray fast enough.

Settling on his side, Larry sighed in misery, pulling his blankets higher. He began to dream again, picking up where he'd left off ...

He pushed Ray aside and moved to the kitchen, where he gazed at the food-encrusted dishes layered in the sink and smothering the counters. Drifting from room to room, Larry took in the refuse of unwashed clothes choking the furniture and collecting on the floor. In the distance, he could hear the blare of the TV and the echo of his father's swearing screams against Muslims, gays, blacks, immigrants, and women. Especially women. Ray hated women. The bitches would wreck your life every time. According to Ray, feminism had destroyed men. Larry was heartily sick of it. He knew differently now. Women were just trying to scrape by and live like anyone else. In the process, they just didn't want to be sexually abused or paid less at work. It was understandable.

In his dream, Larry saw Peter Bennett enter the room and take a seat in the old armchair in the shadows. Peter looked boyish and handsome in his black shirt and blazer. Peter lit a pipe of cherry tobacco and looked expectantly at Larry.

"I didn't know you smoked," Larry said lamely.

Peter shrugged. "I don't—but it's your dream. Apparently, you need me to smoke."

"What am I going to do, Peter? You are the only good person I know. Help me. I'm a mess, I am a mess, and I don't think I'm going to make it." Larry glanced about, embarrassed and repulsed by the filth and hatred surrounding him in his childhood home. He'd been primed to become a carbon copy of Ray.

Furious and nauseated, Larry cupped his face with his hands. He stumbled a few steps towards Peter, his body rocking with unbearable sadness. "Peter, how am I going to fix this? Tell me what to do. Please, please help me ... "

Peter took another puff of his pipe. He studied Larry with kind eyes. Finally, he said, "Take your hands off your face, Larry, and look at me."

Larry slowly lowered his hands and stopped rocking. Raising his eyes from the floor, he looked at Peter. Their eyes connected.

"Good, good," Peter said, a small smile of approval on his face. "Now, gather yourself, stand straight and find some inner peace. You know how to do it. You've been doing it. Take your time. I'll wait." He blew out another airy puff of fragrant smoke.

Larry fought to calm his heart and breath. The roar in his ears slowly began to cease. He began to let go of his of his heavy scales of weight: his anger, fear and hate . . . all of it. Closing his eyes, he smelled the scent of Peter's smoke bring him back to his forest. He felt a slight breeze like that of early evening. He smelled the comforting fumes of his fire. He saw himself lighting candles in preparation of nightfall. He saw himself admiring the glow of airborne fireflies as the night birds twittered and the crickets began to hum. The solar lights of his camp were starting to shine and they were pretty against the ancient oaks in the twilight. Looking around, his camp was solid, comfortable and neat. He began to smile as he took in his freshly washed clothes hanging on the line to dry and his abundant store of food stacked on his sturdy, plastic shelves. Even his structure looked good, tucked tight with its heavy tarp over his stolen table and chair. He gazed at the books on his table, his mug, and the small bottle of whisky, its amber liquid glistening next to the flickering candles. A blanket, draped over the back of his chair, contributed to the aura of coziness. He had built this. As bad as things had been, he had built this. As temporary as it all was, for a brief moment in time, he had felt in control of his life.

He now knew what it felt like. It wasn't necessarily elusive . . .

Peter puffed again and Larry breathed in the soothing scent of his tobacco. "Come back to me now," Peter urged gently.

Reluctantly, Larry opened his eyes.

"You see," Peter said, setting his pipe on the end table and leaning forward, "it's all about what you do. You are not your father. You have choices. Now it's about going forward to discover them."

"I don't know how to do that."

"You do. You have already begun. I see in you great determination, Larry. Don't give up now. Become who you are. Find a way to do that. Don't come back here."

Larry nodded. "I will never come back." He took a step towards Peter, but Peter was fading. "Don't go yet," Larry pleaded. "Peter, please..."

"It's time. You'll be okay, Larry. Just keep going forward. I'll see you on the other side."

As Peter faded from his sight, Larry sighed, shaking his head. He needed to leave this place. He was finished with his father's alcoholism, sadistic abuse, and sickening style of living. Anger and bile rose in him again. Still dreaming, Larry faced his hatred of his father. He was so filled with loathing, the force of it shook him. Before he departed, he wanted to do one last thing.

Walking to the disheveled closet of his old bedroom, he grabbed the baseball bat of his youth. Stomping into his father's living room, Larry raised the bat in front of the new, blaring 52-inch TV flat screen. Of course his father would spend precious money on a big TV, but never him . . . no, never him. Gritting his teeth, Larry swung hard. With the first swing, the screen collapsed upon itself. With the second and third swing about its edges, his father was roaring and heaving his hulking body off the decaying divan. "Nooo!" Ray screamed, wrapping his arms around the buckling set to protect the remains of his beloved talking heads.

Continuing to swing hard, Larry couldn't care less if the bat was smashing his father's skull or the crushed, compacting screen. He continued to swing, revulsion and resentment spewing from him like hellish lava erupting from a volcano.

Eventually Larry dropped the bat, heaving in exertion. The destroyed TV was coated in a smear of bloody pulp and electronic chemical secretions. His jaw set in satisfaction, Larry unfolded himself to stand tall. Leaving the carnage behind him, he let himself out the front door. As it slammed behind him, Larry stepped into a cleansing rain. Lifting his hands, he watched blood run off his fingers onto the sidewalk. At first it felt good, washing from him the surreptitious horror of the past. Then suddenly, the falling water turned freezing upon his pale skin and buzzed scalp that looked just like his father's. Coming barely awake, Larry whimpered at the grayish brain matter stuck between his fingers. No, no, he thought, staring at the small clinging chunks. I have another way, a better way. Still dreaming, he changed course . . .

He made his father alive again. He made himself rich and content. He would drive up to his father's house in a shiny new car. He would walk into the house dressed in a handsome suit, smelling of spiced cologne, his hair longer and groomed. He would look healthy and strong. He would find his father sitting alone in the darkness, a lonely old man. He would empty the grocery bags he was carrying onto the coffee table in front of Ray. He would bring a case of cold beer and a couple of thick, expensive rib-eye steaks. He would bring deli mashed potatoes and a fresh peach pie. He would bring a whole sack of wonderful food and lay them all out in front of Ray.

He would say, "You are going to die without me, Ray. You could've had me, all of this, and more. All that I could bring to you. You could have helped me with school. We could have gone fishing. We could have been great friends. You could have given me a father's advice on how to succeed in life. You could have loved me. But you were stupid. I mean, just damn stupid, Ray. Instead, you hurt me, belittled me, and starved me. And so, you've lost me. This is the last time I'll ever see you again. The last time I'll ever see you alive. Think about what you've done. Then, think about all that you could have had, if only you'd been a good man, a decent man. I hope you miss me, Ray. I hope you miss me every fucking day of your sad life. But I won't miss you," Larry said softly, leaning in closer to his father's eyes. "No, I won't miss you because here is what I am going to do. I am going to live well. I am going to live happy. I am going to get married and have a beautiful family. But you won't be a part of that, Ray. You'll never see your grandchildren. Never. You've lost it all. My money, my family and your future. You're dead to me now, you pathetic son of a bitch."

The house was depressing in its shadows of darkness, cobwebs and deprivation. He watched silent tears leak from Ray's eyes. Turning, he walked out of his childhood home, back into the rain.

The downpour burned him as it turned to snow. Larry stood on the front walk, face up, allowing the sting of the icy flakes make him come awake.

Slowly, he opened his eyes. He was back in his broken Toyota, parked in the spidery shed of the abandoned homestead. His head ached from his dream. He closed his eyes still sad and angry from the weight and clarity of it. He had no idea of the time. But really, it didn't matter. The time was whatever it was and he was going nowhere. He struggled to sit up. Glancing out his rearview mirror, he saw that it was still snowing. The flakes were still coming down fat and wet but they were sparse enough so that he could walk around if he chose. He shifted slightly and groaned. He was cramping again. He was also hungry. Pulling his backpack to him, he made an open-faced sandwich of ham with a touch of mustard. He thought about adding cheese and another slice of bread, but he didn't out of a need to conserve his food. Eating slowly, he forced himself to taste the soft texture of the wheat bread, the spice of the mustard and the smoothness of the thinly sliced ham. Swirling his mouth with water, his taste buds responded. He closed his eyes over the flavor. It only took six bites and he was done. He wanted more. Six bites weren't enough . . . but he'd already eaten twice today. He needed to control himself.

Sighing, Larry packed up his food and slipped the items into his backpack again for safekeeping. Sitting in the silence, he stared through the windshield at the dingy plank wall in front of him. He desperately wanted to go back to sleep but that was a bad idea. He had to stay awake now if he was going to sleep through the night. Maybe if he got out of his car and walked around for some air and exercise, he might feel better. He needed to piss and maybe explore the old shack if he could get in. Gingerly, he opened his car door and climbed out, clutching the crusty cloth napkin tightly in his hand. Since he was awake, perhaps the spiders were too. If there were any.

Larry quickly walked up to the open front of the decrepit structure, keeping an eye on the ceiling for spiders. He turned his attention to the deep, unmarked snow. The entire landscape was obscured under a massive mantle of glistening white for as far as he could see. Scanning the land, he noticed the branches of trees and bushes were buckling from the great weight of snow and the long heavy teeth of icicles. To Larry, the frozen panorama was as stunning as it was deadly. He realized that he had been extremely lucky to have had cover for the night, awful as it had been. Otherwise, he and his car would probably be buried deep beyond hope in this crystalline freeze. Had that happened, he probably wouldn't be here now, spiders and all.

Stepping into the snow, Larry winced at its burning bite. His old canvas sneakers were no match against the freeze. He heard the snow crunch under his feet. The icy flakes were still drifting downward on the empty, hollow place. The flakes felt like tiny fiery embers as they dusted his stiff cheeks. He wasn't used to this. He had no tolerance for this type of weather. Peering up the road, he saw no trace of humanity in the area, no life of any kind, no squirrel or bird. His aloneness hit him again like a sledgehammer.

The shack felt isolated and rural despite being located just beyond a suburban development. Although people lived just down the road, he saw no immediate neighbors. I could die here, he thought again, and no one would know for a while . . . maybe a long while. This place had been undisturbed for years. It could go on undisturbed for more years.

Larry squatted and scrubbed his crusty napkin clean in the crunchy snow. Shaking violently, hands numb, he leapt back to his car and cranked on the heat. Once the air grew warm, he hung the moist cloth on the dash to dry. After sucking in long breaths of heat, he began to feel strong enough to grapple with the freezing cold again. He clicked off his ignition. Knowing what to expect now, he climbed out of his car and stepped carefully into the snowfall, making his way to the front door of the old wooden shack. It was not locked.

Sticking his head in cautiously, he searched the room for spiders. He saw webs but no scary spiky creatures. Opening the door wider, his nose was assaulted by the foul odor of mold and mildew. Not even the cold could hide the putrid scent. The stench didn't surprise him. After all, the shack was ripe with rot. Larry knew then that the place was poison but he entered anyway. It was a very poor place, roughly built. The plank wood walls seemed slightly bowed under weather and age. There were no windows, just a front door. Glancing around the dim room, he saw a small stone fireplace and wondered if it worked. The room was square and bare, except for a piece of dull gray carpeting in the center that didn't reach the walls. Bending, Larry touched the decaying rug with his fingertips. Soggy. Wiping his fingers on the butt of his jeans, he moved to the only other doorway in the room. The door was open and led to a single bedroom. He realized the place had neither a kitchen or bathroom. Just the two rooms.

Standing in the doorway, he watched the snow falling from the ceiling to the floor. Looking up, he stared at the craterous hole in the roof, its blackened edges rotting downward like a raw, gaping wound. A pile of snow had gathered into a mound in the middle of the room. It would melt, Larry thought, and flood the floorboards, adding to the countless floods from rain the sad little home had already endured. No wonder the house smelled so bad. Suddenly, he felt an ache of sorrow for the old place, some emotional connection. This could have been my cabin in the forest, he thought. Maybe, the person who had lived here had been happy. Maybe they'd even had a dream like I once did and actually built that dream; somewhere to live in the simplest of ways. Maybe this cabin was all they had hoped for. Perhaps with a burning fire, evening candles and comfortable furniture, it had been a refuge from the frenetic, outside world.

Entering the room and stepping around the heap of snow, Larry moved to the door on the wall to his right. Lifting the latch and pulling it open, he gazed at what would be the backyard. Looking down, he saw a few steps leading to the ground. They were nearly invisible under the encasement of snow. He was about to close the door when he spied a brown protrusion in the yard, tucked almost out of sight. At first glance, he had imagined it was just a dead bush . . . but maybe not. The mound wasn't high, just about three feet tall. But if it were a bush, the snow wouldn't be so level, he reasoned. Moved to action, Larry lowered himself to sit in the doorway and with the soles of his shoes, he worked to shove the deep snow off the steps. Huffing frosty breaths, he continued to kick and shove until the step boards were fairly clear.

Getting to his feet, he leaned on the door jam, looking down. I must be very careful now, he thought. The boards could be rotten and break under my weight. I don't need a broken leg. Or, they could be slippery; I mustn't fall.

Grasping the railing, he shook the wood. It didn't move. Holding tight, Larry slowly put his weight on the first step. It held. He began to lower his foot to the next step and suddenly, it slid out from under him. Swinging wildly, his arms circled the railing, preventing his fall. Slowly, he untwisted himself and continued on carefully. Reaching the ground, Larry took deliberate hard steps to break the snow. With each step, he paused to regain his balance. He wasn't afraid of falling now. The steps had been slick with ice, but the ground wasn't so bad. Finally, he came to stand in front of the mystery object. Leaning down, he touched the brown part rising out of the snow. Tarp. Snowflakes drifted down on his bare head. He was freezing. Walking around the snow-covered tarp, he saw it was about four feet in length. Wood? Was it a store of wood for the fireplace? He pushed the snow off the top of the mound with his bare hands. It was torture. He was losing all feeling in his fingers again. He didn't have much time before being forced to retreat to his car once more.

"Peter," Larry cried out in desperation. The snow was falling on him. He was freezing. He could not go on. "Peter," he yelled in the wind," help me get the tarp off!" Squeezing his eyes shut, he envisioned the man. He couldn't stand being alone. "Peter," he choked one last time. From every part of his being and mind, he willed Peter into existence from his imagination. He only knew that he *needed* Peter. He had no one else. He pulled on the tarp, aware that he was delusional.

Peter appeared. He laid his hands over Larry's frozen ones. Together, they grasped a section of the tarp and began to pull. Inch by inch, the weighty tarp began to give. The snow was extremely heavy on its edges and it took a monumental effort to pull the old sheeting clear of what lay beneath. As the tarp slipped free, Larry fell backwards into the snow, gasping for breath. Lying there, he closed his eyes. That's it; I am going insane, he thought. I am truly going insane. And, I am going to die here. I cannot get up.

"Get up, Larry," Peter said quietly.

Looking up, Larry saw Peter standing over him, his expression solemn. "Come on. You must get up or freeze to death. Get up. Now."

Larry heard Peter. He almost said, "I can't," but he couldn't disappoint Peter, could he? The only friend he had? No. He couldn't. Peter expected better of him. Struggling to sit up and jerking with the cold, he grasped Peter's outstretched hand and shakily got to his feet.

"I want you to listen closely now, Larry," Peter said. "You're going to go back to your car and get warm. After you stabilize, you must dress as warmly as possible. Find a shirt to wrap around your neck as a scarf and wrap your head to keep your ears from freezing. Bring a towel with you when you return to this wood pile."

"I am returning?"

"Yes. Did you uncover the wood for no reason?"

"Not just me, Peter. We did it. Together."

Peter smiled at that. "Yes. So we did. But now, about the towel. You're not to touch the wood, ever, with your bare hands. The pile is old and it has inhabitants."

"Spiders?"

"Most likely. They may have been there for a long time, making the undisturbed wood their home. You must pick up each piece of wood using only the towel, and throw each piece onto the snow. With each piece, wait a second to allow anything a chance to crawl off. Maybe nothing will, but take no chances."

"I understand." Larry mumbled, the world spinning around him. He was having trouble staying on his feet.

"Good. Go on then. You know what to do."

Larry blinked against his dizziness and the blinding glare of the snow. Peter was gone.

He stumbled back to his car.

# CHAPTER SIXTEEN

Back in the car, Larry was convulsing from the cold. Shaking violently, he lifted the wet napkin to cover and protect his sore fingers. Then, he clicked on his ignition and the heat. The vents blew air as frigid as outside. Within a minute or so, the flow began to warm. Resting his numb hands on his lap, he waited for them to thaw. His fingers were so frozen, he was afraid any sharp movement might break one off. But he was going to be okay now, just as Peter had said. As he warmed, Larry remained mindful of his battery. As soon as the car was heated, he turned off his ignition. Leaning back, he rested.

Now that Peter was with him, he wasn't so afraid. In a little while, he would get up and dress as Peter had instructed him to do. Fifteen minutes later, Larry was warm enough to wrap a sweater securely around his neck and head. He layered on another shirt over his others and slipped back into his coat. From the backseat, he grabbed his black hand towel. It occurred to him to see if there was anything in the old shed that he could use. Leaning over his steering wheel, he clicked on the ignition and turned on his headlights. Walking to the front of his car, he saw stuff in the right corner. There was an old rake. Not the kind to rake leaves, but one with a metal head of long teeth, maybe to loosen soil and furrow a garden. There was also a tall pile of old, yellowed newspapers. On the papers sat an old metal bucket. Moving closer, he used his towel to grab the rake and rushing to the opening of the shed, he tossed it onto the snow. Waiting, he saw a small black spider crawl off the base and onto the white powder. Slowly, the spider crawled, teetering weirdly on it legs until it curled into a ball and died. When he saw no others, Larry picked up the rake and went back to the old newspapers. Using the rake, he lifted the bucket and set it aside. Then, he used the rake to pull a few inches of paper off the top of the stack and onto the floor. Several spiders spilled out, and Larry crushed them with the metal head of the rake. Carefully, using the rake, he spread the newspapers along the length of his car, patiently turning them over and stomping on them until he was certain nothing alive could have survived. Gathering the papers into a fairly neat stack, he prayed that he had missed nothing. He didn't know if he could die of a spider bite, but he didn't want to find out.

Making his way into the house with his towel, rake, and papers, Larry left the front door open and studied the room. Moving to the bedroom, he closed the door firmly to prevent further snow from drifting into the living room. Before doing anything more, he had to find out if the old fireplace was functional. Setting the papers on the low hearth, Larry pulled off a few sheets, balled them up and set them on the cast iron grate. He knew nothing about fireplaces, never having used one before. Unbuttoning his coat, he slid his hand into his back pocket for his lighter. Lighting the edge of one ball, he waited. The balls caught quickly and smoke poured into the room. Coughing, Larry made for the front door. Sticking his head outside, he drew in a few clean breaths of icy air. Behind him, the loose, crumpled balls were already snuffing out, the smoke starting to settle. Leaning against the door jam, Larry stared at the white landscape, trying to recall anything he knew about fireplaces. It wasn't much. Then he remembered he'd once read where a guy had 'pulled opened the fireplace flue' before setting in his logs to burn. He couldn't remember where he'd read it, but the more important question was . . . what was a flue? Stepping back inside, Larry went to the fireplace. If the logs were below, the flue had to be above. Maybe the flue was an opening to the chimney? Maybe it had a lever of some kind? Leaning towards the fireplace, Larry flicked his lighter. Reaching upward to feel his way, Larry suddenly heard Peter's voice.

"The towel, Larry. Always use the towel."

Nodding gratefully, Larry grabbed his hand towel and covered his open palm. With his lighter in the other hand, he lifted the flame as he warily stuck his head inside the fireplace to look upward. There were cobwebs, which meant there were probably spiders in that dark hole. Then he spied a blackened iron lever ending in a circle. Grasping the metal circle with his towel, he pulled on it abruptly while simultaneously jumping backwards. The flue banged open, dropping dirt and soot and several small shriveled animals onto the iron grate. He then spied a large black widow spider flailing in the mix. Her long legs were trying to reach for safety. She then climbed shakily onto the fire-blackened grate. It was hard for Larry to track the venomous monster in the darkness of the fireplace. Moving quickly, he balled some papers and threw them on the grate. Lighting the last ball, he tossed it onto the others.

He was sorry for burning the big spider to death, but he couldn't just let her go. She was too dangerous.

The old dry papers caught and leapt into bright orange flames. Smoke filtered into the room, making Larry cough again. He slowly added more paper. To his horror, bits of flaming paper began to float upward through the flue. The chimney was drawing now, but he was fearful the burning pieces would settle on the roof. It would take nothing to burn this old shack down, he thought, panicked. He instantly imagined the place roaring on fire, the police coming and him being arrested for arson.

Running outside, Larry swathed through the snow, gazing intently at the snow-laden roof. Circling the house, he saw wisps of smoke rising from the stack, but nothing more. Either the paper had burned itself out or the snow on the roof had snuffed any small fire. Breathing in relief, his fear receding, Larry retraced his steps and went back inside. Now, knowing that the chimney worked, he considered what to do next. The hard part was yet to come.

Larry returned to the shed with his rake. Lifting the old bucket with the long-handled tool, he tossed it on the snow. A long brown spider fell off the underside of the pail, onto the white powder. Watching it thrash in the snow, the creature appeared to die fairly quickly. He pushed the spider deeper into the new fallen snow with his rake to make sure. Still using the rake, he pulled the pail upright and peered in. It was empty. Circling the bucket to determine that no critter was still clinging, he saw that it was clean. Filling the bucket with snow, he carried it inside and set it by the fireplace to melt.

Larry went back to the backyard woodpile with his rake and towel. Wielding the rake, he pulled a number of logs off the top of the pile onto the snow. A dozen or so widows, other spiders, centipedes, and wood beetles writhed before him on top of the glistening white expanse. Larry went after the spiders, smashing them with his rake. Pulling each log to him with the rake, he turned every single one over to inspect it closely. When he was satisfied, he looped the towel in the belt of his coat and carried an armload of wood into the house. Stuffing the grate with more newspaper, Larry set several logs on top to create his first evening fire. Returning to the woodpile, he repeated the process of killing spiders and carried in more armloads until he felt he had enough wood stacked for the long night ahead of him. It was starting to get dark.

Returning to the wood pile, Larry used his rake to pull on the tarp and spread it flat over the snow. Scraping the top with the flat side of the rake, he killed any spider he saw along the way. Then, he leaned on his rake to wait a minute to let the snow do its work on any spiders that were underneath the cloth. He looked up at the sky. Icy flakes were coming down, landing on his frozen face. When would it stop? He was nearly beyond bearing the searing agony of the cold. Shaking violently, he flipped the tough old plastic sheet and straightened it. He could see no spiders, but he scraped it anyway. He figured the tarp was an 8' x 10'. He picked up the edges, dragged the sheet away from the wood pile, and shook it harshly. He rolled it up and carried it inside to the fireplace. Now that the wood was exposed, he decided to get one last load. Moving as fast as he could, Larry carried seven more pieces into the house. This would gain him another hour or two of fire if he needed it.

Larry went to his car. He loaded several grocery bags with anything he thought he might need, including his gallon of water. Running his belongings to the house, he returned to fold up his blankets and towels into a tight pile and carried them into the shack. Returning to his car, he packed up some clothes and hefted his backpack onto his shoulders. He made his way back to the house and shut the door. There, he set the load on the hearth. The house was freezing, his breath was coming out white. The room was almost completely dark. He lit the fire.

In the low glow of flickering flames, he stared at the wet carpet. It was the final thing on his list to accomplish. The carpet had to go. He could not sleep on it. Reluctantly, he stripped down to his briefs. Rolling up his clothes, he set them on the fireplace mantle. He was instantly freezing. Worse, he was depleted and hungry. Still, he was getting so close to being finished, there was nothing to do but continue. He summoned Peter in his mind. Peter came and then, faded before his eyes. He gained strength from him, knowing he was still here.

Bending, Larry began the process of rolling up the soaked, rotten floor covering. It stank so badly, he had to stop often and move away from it. Taking a breath again, he continued to roll the growing wet rotten pile forward. The carpet was extremely heavy. It was like rolling up a wet concrete block. His hands felt slimy and he felt mold and bacteria crawling all over him. His nose began to run, causing him to choke. He kept pushing and rolling. When the carpet was completely rolled, he circled his arms around the end and he dragged it, inch by inch, into the frozen bedroom. Dropping it by the mound of snow, he slammed the door behind him, sealing off the room.

Shivering and empty, Larry hobbled to the stone hearth and sat down. As the fire burned, he began to get warm. But until he washed up thoroughly, he would neither dress or handle food. He felt utterly contaminated and slimy. Grabbing the rolled tarp, Larry spread it over the floor in front of the hot fireplace to dry. As he waited for the bucket of snow-water to heat by the fire, he began to talk to Peter. "I've gotten a lot done, Peter," he mumbled, feeling light-headed and lonely.

Peter was in front of him, sitting cross legged on the tarp. "Yes, I see that. You've done a great job."

"I think the pail water will be warm enough soon for me to rinse off. Then, I'll get dressed and eat dinner. Will you stay for dinner?"

"Perhaps," Peter replied. "Larry, the tarp is drying now and soon, you'll be able to lay out your bed on it. You don't want to get the tarp wet. So, if you're going to wash by the warmth of the fire, you'll need to move it back, out of the way, until you're done bathing. Then, you can slide it back into place and it will still be dry. On top, at least. "

Larry nodded in agreement, glad for Peter's suggestion. He was too drained to think clearly. He lifted his head. The room was dancing and flickering in its shadows. He couldn't make the motion stop. He swallowed, feeling ill.

"Try the water bucket now, Larry. It might not be hot, but it could be tepid enough to bathe."

Obediently, Larry stuck his finger into the water. It was slightly warmer than room temperature. He rested his hands on his lap again.

Rising, Peter said, "Let's move the tarp out of the way now, okay? Come on Larry, up you go. You're very close to getting clean, eating and sleeping. Stand up for me now."

Larry stumbled to his feet and grabbing the tarp with Peter, pulled the vinyl back about four feet from the fireplace.

"I'll leave now for you to wash," Peter said. "I'll come back in time for your dinner and help you make your bed." Handing Larry the napkin, Peter continued, "Use this to bathe. When you're done, you can lay it on the hearth to dry again." Turning, he walked out the front door.

Trembling with weariness, Larry pulled the bucket close to him and wet down his body with the cloth. Using a good amount of soap, he scrubbed his face, torso, limbs and feet. Using his styrofoam cup, he filled it and trickled the water like a tiny shower over his face, beard and the other soapy parts of his body. He wet his hair and with a small amount of shampoo, created a modest lather. Dipping the cup again, Larry rinsed his hair twice until it was clean. Finished with his bath, Larry dried off with his towel and got dressed. He was perched on the hearth again when he heard Peter return.

"Let's eat now," Peter said, sitting back down on the tarp. "Why don't you try half of your deli sandwich? It's all ready for you to eat. You don't have to do anything. Add a few peaches from the can, Larry, and it will be a good dinner. "

"Will you have some?" Larry asked.

"No. While you were bathing, I got a bite to eat. So, I'm good." He pushed the backpack towards Larry. "Go on now, eat. "

Larry dug for the sandwich and the can of peaches. Popping the top, he took a sip of the sweet juice. Setting it on the hearth, he partially unwrapped the sandwich and took a bite. It was good.

As Larry ate, Peter spoke again. "Be mindful of how much you consume. Only eat half, Larry. And, just a few slices of peach. After you're done, put the top back on the peaches and put the can on the mantle. Wrap what's left of your sandwich and return it to your backpack. Then, add a few more sticks to the fire."

Larry did as he was told. Once his food was packed and his dwindling fire was revived, Peter pointed to the wood along the wall. "It would be a good idea to create a small stack in front of the hearth by your bed. This will make it easier to feed the fire throughout the night without having to walk for it." Nodding, Larry moved an armload of wood from the wall and set it by his bed in front of the fire.

"Now," said Peter, "since your bath is over, let's move the tarp back into place and make your bed." They did this quickly. As Larry slid under the covers, Peter walked to the door. Larry imagined that Peter was seeing him nearly asleep. The flames of the fire were casting a warm flaming glow around the room. He couldn't keep Peter here. He was too weak to concentrate.

Larry shivered under his blankets, trying to ignore the fetid air of the room. His bed was hard on the floor but he was grateful to finally be lying down. He hadn't stretched out flat in ages. He groaned as he straightened his legs tightly to ease his aching muscles. His whole body was pulsing with pain from his exertions of the day. He was glad his bed was on the tarp and not the bare floor. Underneath the tarp, he knew the floor was saturated with mold. The thought scared him. He hated this dark strange place. But he had made his bed and was lying in it. Staring at the fire, Larry thought of the vast blanket of snow outside. It would be dark and freezing out there. At least he had a roof over his head, a fire, a bed and some food. He was better off than some folks. Shifting, he groaned again in pain.

"Good night, Larry," Peter said, opening the door.

"Good night, Peter," Larry murmured, dreaming. "And, thank you."

# CHAPTER SEVENTEEN

In the morning, Larry woke up cold and coughing. Peter had walked in and out of his dreams the entire night. Mostly, it was to wake him to feed the fire. But the fire was out now. The room was a freezer. He was stiff from sleeping on the hard floor; his blankets had not protected him. The room smelled putrid and he had tried not to breathe too deeply as he slept. He felt cranky and ill, no doubt from the mold spores filling his lungs. If Peter were here, Larry had no doubt he'd be telling him to get out of bed and get the fire going again.

Sitting up, Larry felt that his head was heavy and stuffy. To ease the pressure, he let his chin drop to his chest. He stayed that way for a while. Finally, he got up and set a new fire. Climbing back under the covers, he waited to get warm. Since there were no windows in the room, he had no idea of the time of morning. It could still be in the wee hours or it could be noon. Larry turned on his side to watch the flames. They were mesmerizing and he was soon asleep again.

When he woke, the fire was out once more. Rising, he built a new fire and took the can of peaches off the mantle. Pulling his backpack to him, Larry sat on his blankets and made breakfast from a slice of bread with a thin layer of mustard and swiss cheese. He ate a few peaches in between bites. When he was finished, he placed his food into his backpack and returned the can of peaches to the mantle. Slipping on his coat, he went to the door and opened it. Looking outside, he saw that the snowfall had stopped. The day was pleasant but still icy cold. It would take a day or two or three before the snow on the land would melt, Larry thought. Stepping outside, he tromped around stretching his legs. Returning to the cabin, Larry quickly grew bored. Sitting on his blankets, he held his head between his hands while staring into the fire. Then he spied the old newspapers. His spirits lifted with something to read. The first paper he picked up was dated May 20th, 1978. Larry marveled that the newspapers were still intact.

Larry read for several hours by the fire. At mid-afternoon, he left the house for more paper and wood. He spread out the papers and stomped on them. He did more or less the same with the woodpile in the backyard. The remaining spiders were slower now. Being exposed to the cold was killing them off. Even so, he still feared them. Replenished in wood and newspaper, Larry fed the fire and settling on his blankets, he continued to read.

As day turned into night, Larry ate the last of his chicken for dinner along with a slice of bread slick with mayonnaise and a few more peach slices. After eating, Larry swished his mouth with water from his gallon and brushed his teeth. The snow pail, refilled earlier, was sitting by the fire and now contained warm water. From this, Larry undressed and took another full bath, including the shampooing of his hair. Being clean was a remarkable sensation.

The fire was high and the room was warm. As a result, he took his time. He had simply pulled the tarp back, blankets and all, away from the fireplace, leaving him free to wash in front of the fire's heat. But he was worried. He had been coughing all day and his cough was getting worse. He had to leave this place. The mold was killing him.

After feeding the fire and restacking some logs in front of the hearth, Larry dragged the tarp back to the fire and slid into his makeshift bed. He pulled the bowl-shaped top of his chicken container close to him. He'd use it to spit into and the napkin for blowing his nose. He also had what was left of his gallon of water and paper towels.

Throughout the night, Larry coughed up mucus balls and spat them into the converted plastic bowl. He blew his runny nose raw and continued to cough, never able to breathe right as he tried to sleep. His mouth grew abraded from his inability to breathe out of his nose. He dozed a bit, but continued to wake up, gagging, as his tongue became painfully glued to the roof of his mouth. He was burning with fever. He was hallucinating.

"Peter," Larry whispered, "I am so sick."

Peter appeared. He leaned over Larry. "I know. I am here." Sliding the snow bucket to Larry's side, Peter tore off a long length of paper towel. He folded it into a neat thick rectangle and dipped the paper cloth into the water. Squeezing out the excess, he laid it, wet and cool, across Larry's burning brow. From Larry's gallon of drinking water, Peter filled the styrofoam cup half full. With the cup at Larry's lips, Peter trickled the cool, clear liquid down Larry's throat. This he did this slowly, several times, until Larry's mouth was temporarily moistened again. Then, he built the dying embers into crackling fire. The room was cold again but soon, it would be warm. The old, dry fire wood burned so fast. Too fast.

In the throes of fever, Larry cried out again, thrashing under his slipping blankets. Peter gathered the blankets and smoothing them, covered Larry once more. "Sleep now," he said gently. Re-wetting Larry's forehead cloth, Peter laid the cool comfort over Larry's feverish eyes. Larry stopped thrashing as Peter stroked his hair. "Sleep now," he urged. "I will stay with you."

Morning found Larry in worse condition. His fever kept him in bed for most of the day. The room remained frozen. As he slept, his fires kept burning out. He lost count of the many fires he had to build throughout the day. His wood supply was growing low again, but he couldn't summon the energy to go out in the cold and gather more. He couldn't battle the spiders. His food supply was also dwindling. His gallon of water was down to the last two inches. Although his lips felt cracked and parched, Larry forced himself to not drink from the water in his rusty snow pail. He wanted to. Badly. But even in his delirium, he knew it wasn't drinkable. The last thing he needed was intestinal trouble on top of his current respiratory problems. The pail water was a death sentence. This he was sure of.

He hobbled to the door to check the time of day and saw the blue realm of twilight setting in against the snowbound land. The dark of night would soon follow. Coughing hard, Larry returned to the fireplace to build another fire. He slid under the covers of his rigid bed and lay on his side, watching the flames leap as the wood caught. Staring at the fire, he felt weak, sweaty, and ill. Feeding the fire all day had taxed him. But without the fire, its light, warmth, and cheer, the barren room turned into a black box of nightmares.

A coughing attack overtook him.

Sitting abruptly, he tried to catch his breath but the assault consumed him to the point of drowning his nose, throat, lungs and loosening his bladder. Hacking uncontrollably, Larry grabbed his burgundy cloth, blowing as best he could as he shot out of bed and stumbled to the front door to pee outside. He was unable to control himself. Urine soaked his underwear and trickled to the floor as he reached for the latch. Gagging from suffocating mucus, Larry yanked the door open and fell to his knees in the snow, coughing and urinating at the same time. Crawling forward, away from the doorway, he choked up slimy globs into the snow and balancing himself, blew his nose when he could. He was raging with fever; his insides and head were burning like an inferno. Dropping to the ground, Larry lay side-faced in the snow. The snow felt good. His coughing attack was subsiding and he could breathe through his mouth again. The cold air helped. I will lay here just for a moment, he thought. He felt his eyes flutter closed. He found comfort in the ice slowly numbing and cooling his smoldering body. He wasn't cold at all as the darkness began to seep in around him. He vaguely heard the night birds sing as he began to dream.

"Larry."

"What is it, Peter?" Larry asked, his eyes remaining closed. He could still think even if he could no longer feel his body. He didn't want to move anyway. He was comfortable right now and no longer in pain. If he moved, he would start coughing again. He couldn't have that. His last attack had been too violent.

"Larry."

"Go away, Peter."

"How will you write for me if you die?"

"I want to write for you, Peter. With all my heart, it is the only thing I want. The only thing. But I know the chances are slim to none and I don't really believe I ever will. It is just a dream."

"You're giving up, Larry? So easily? You'll just let yourself die in the snow, in your underwear, without ever finding out?"

"I peed myself, Peter."

"You're ill. It happens. Your underwear is easily washed . . . but you don't want people to find you like this, do you?"

"No."

"Then get up. Come inside. Let's get you to the fire."

"Peter," Larry uttered sadly, "you are the only good thing I have ever known. Everything else has been a lie. But not you. I think I have loved you for a long time now, even if I didn't realize it. You are all that is good and kind and decent. I appreciate your concern for me. I do. You have helped me. You have been wonderful. But I cannot go on. I want you to let me go now. Really. It doesn't hurt. I am finally in no pain."

"No, Larry. I will not let you go. I will not let you die. It's not your time to die. Get up now, Larry. Get up. *Now.*"

Larry tried to obey. He was not able to move his arms and legs. Opening his eyes, he saw that it was deeply dark. A classic winter night. How long had he been laying here? The snow seemed to be reflecting the stars. Rolling over, he stared blankly at the crescent moon above. "Peter, I cannot get up."

Peter knelt by Larry. "Rub your hands on your chest, Larry, and move your ankles together too. Let's start there. Let's get your circulation going."

On his back, Larry commanded his naked legs to move and, rubbing his stiff ankles together, he felt his blood begin to flow. He still couldn't feel his arms. When he was finally able to lay his numb hands on his chest, they felt like blocks of ice. Careful of his fingers, he began to rub the heel of his hand around the area of his heart. He looked up at Peter. He could see him clearly against the stars.

Peter was nodding in encouragement, patiently waiting for Larry to get some momentum. "Now, bring your knees to your stomach, straighten them and do it again a couple of times. You must get your legs working."

Larry flexed his legs as Peter suggested. Coming more awake, he saw Peter beginning to fade away. "Don't you dare leave me now, Peter," he cried out, coughing white breaths into the hollow air of the freezing night. "Peter, please. If you go, I won't be able to get up on my own."

"I am here, Larry. And, I will help you. You need to get up and move now. It's important that you do. Get to your feet. Larry. Get to your feet."

Larry saw the serious expression on Peter's face. He rolled to his knees and slowly, he climbed shakily to his feet. He felt Peter's arms come around his shoulders. He felt Peter supporting him as he stumbled to the shack. Shuttering the door, he made his way over the cold, blackened hearth. He felt Peter lower him to sit there as he jerked convulsively from the cold.

"Light the fire, Larry."

"I'm too cold, Peter, too sick."

"Do it anyway. Then, at least you won't be cold. You know how fast the fire warms you. Imagine how good the heat will feel. You only have to move a little to change everything, Larry. Once the fire gets going, you will be glad for it. You must do this, Larry. I expect it of you. Do it."

Coughing and shaking, Larry weakly leaned down to grab a few newspapers at his feet. Balling them, his hands jerking from the cold, he placed them on top of the grate. The fireplace was too full of ashes to shove them underneath. The room was so dark, he almost could not see. Rising, he felt his way to the woodpile along the wall. Pulling off a few sticks, he set them on the paper. He lit the fire. As the fire caught, he sat close, hugging himself. His shirt and underwear were wet. As soon as he was warm enough, he got into dry clothes. Rinsing his underwear in the snow pail, he twisted out the water and laid his briefs on the hearth to dry by the new, roaring fire.

He spied a spider on the wooden mantle making its way to the warmth. He tried to kill it and missed. Bracing his hand on the wooden mantle, he wheezed, cursing himself. He felt a tickling sensation. He stared at the black spider walking unsteadily on the back of his hand in horror. He sank cautiously, holding out his hand, praying she wouldn't bite him. He grasped his cloth napkin from the stone hearth. Choking in fear, he brushed the metal mesh of the fireplace open with his free hand. Lowering the spider on his other hand to the fire, he quickly brushed her into the flames feeling inexplicably sad.

Spent and strained, he slid into his chilly bed by the flickering glow. As he shivered in the ambient light, he heard Peter say, "Tomorrow, you must leave this place."

"I will," Larry wheezed, hacking into his napkin. "I hate this place." In his delirium, he heard Peter leave. He heard the front door click closed behind his living apparition.

His eyes were dry as he stared into the fire.

He was all alone again.

He closed his eyes, breathing in against the cold and his pain.

# CHAPTER EIGHTEEN

*Morning.* Peter had come throughout the night to get Larry up to build a fire. He had tried, but at some point, he was no longer able to hear Peter. He had fallen into a deep sleep from which he could not awaken, could not respond. Peter had retreated, leaving him alone. He did not necessarily want to be left alone, but neither could he tolerate Peter's relentless pressure. He was well aware that Peter was trying to save his life. But he had somehow survived the night and now, he forced Peter to retreat to the shadows of his mind.

Larry tried to wake up. He was still so ill. It seemed as though the snow last night had snuffed out some of the raging fire within him. He still burned, but not so hotly, not so out of control. He had to leave this place. It was killing him. Peter had told him to leave. So, he would. He struggled to sit up. His nose flooded again and he began to cough explosively. He came to his knees so he could better manage the attack. He spit out the water and mucus that had accumulated in his lungs during his sleep. He blew his nose into his wet rag of a napkin. His spittoon was revolting.

Heaving, Larry strove to catch his breath. He felt so frail. He needed to start thinking now. He needed to start making a plan, no matter how small it might be. He willed his brain to engage and his vision began to clear. What did he need to do? How would he begin? Lifting his head, he looked around. He needed some fresh air. The room smelled so foul, he couldn't stand it. Getting to his feet, he staggered to the door and pulled it open. The day was blue and crisp and he could hear the birds. He could hear the far away sound of machinery. Leaning against the frame of the door, he took in the land. It was still covered in snow.

He could hear small sounds. Water dripping. Branches crackling as they were being released from their burden of ice. A plane faintly overhead. Breathing in the cold air, he thought of his next moves. He would build his last fire. He would eat. He would decide what he needed the most and load it into his backpack. Without his car, he was going to lose the rest. He was going to lose his bed. He was going to lose his clothes. He was going to have to manage this loss going forward. Life was about to get more difficult.

Turning, he went back into the room. He built a fire with the last of his wood. He took his last bath and he layered up in extra clothing. He ate the last of his ham with the last of his mustard. He allowed himself two pieces of bread this time in making his sandwich. He was going to be on foot now and he needed the extra calories. He ate his last three peaches from the can. He made his last selection of clothing. He had to choose between his hoodie and his jean jacket. He chose the hoodie and said goodbye to his jacket. He brushed his teeth. He combed his hair. He got the smallest begging sign from his car and loaded it into his backpack. He coughed harshly while doing it all.

He slipped on his coat and slung on his backpack. He went to the door and turned to take in the room one last time. "Thank you for having me. It's not your fault that I am sick. You did the best you could." Opening the door, he walked out into the snow and began the next phase of his journey.

Trudging through the snow was difficult. Larry's shoes soon became wet, and then his socks and feet. He figured the temperature was hovering a few degrees above freezing. The snow was melting to prove it. The sun was bright in his eyes. As soon as he could, he walked on the left side of the road so he could see cars coming and move out of their way. The road was mostly clear but snow was packed along its edges and starting to turn dirty. He had no idea where to go but kept his eyes open for somewhere to spend the night. He knew he was in trouble. His cough was hindering him and he found it hard to breathe as he walked. He had traveled some distance now and was approaching the old residential area. He crossed the street to the sidewalk. He was already feeling sweaty and brittle from his long walk up the road.

Larry was walking past a row of hedges now. He continued along until he came to the end. Seeing a gap between the fencepost and the end of the hedge, he stopped, looking into the backyard of a low brick ranch home. He saw a plain swimming pool and a small house in the yard on the other side of the pool. He studied the small building. Turning around, he passed the hedge row again and went to the front yard of the main house. The driveway had no car. He couldn't tell about the garage as the door was down. He went to the front door and knocked. He waited and then, knocked again more loudly. Still no one came.

Returning to the sidewalk, he walked past the tall hedges once more. Stepping through the small gap of bushes and into the back yard, he went to the front door of the small pool house. He knocked and waited. He tried the door. It was locked. He went around to the back knowing there was another entry. He had seen it from the sidewalk. He had seen the small concrete pad and plastic chair on the pad. It would not be there if there were no way to get to them. He tried the door and found it open.

Stepping inside, he glanced around. The simple room was rectangular. Maybe 12' by 15', including the small bathroom. The room held a closet with folding doors, a twin bed with a plain coverlet, and an old chest of drawers painted lime green. That was all. The room smelled of chlorine and age. It wasn't pleasant, but it was tolerable. Larry studied the bed to see precisely how it had been made. He slipped his hand underneath the pillow to measure how far under the pillow the thin coverlet had been tucked. It was his full hand. He noted how many inches from the floor the coverlet hung. He opened the closet. It was empty except for two items: an electric blanket and an old space heater. Larry slipped off his back pack and set it by the back door. He took off his coat and set it on his backpack. He took the blanket from the closet and tore off the coverlet. He smoothed the blanket on the bed. He plugged the wire into the end of the blanket and lifting the mattress, hid the wire until it came out to the wall. He moved the bed slightly and saw there was an outlet. He plugged in the blanket and ran its control to the pillow to be hidden underneath. He turned the control on to seven and replaced the coverlet on top of the blanket so it would be hidden if someone came into the room.

Turning, Larry went to the bathroom to splash his face. He was feeling cold and clammy. He was still very ill and couldn't stop coughing. He needed to rest to move his recovery forward. He would sleep for an hour and then leave to find food. If he could, he would come back here to spend the night. He sat on the bed and took off his shoes and socks. He climbed into the warming bed and slept.

An hour later, Larry got up and made the bed exactly as it had been. He put on his wet socks and shoes. He smoothed the bed. He left the blanket control on so when he came back here later tonight, the bed would be warm. He would always have to think forward now. He would always have to see what was in front of him. He would always have to pay attention to details. It would have to become a part of him. He grabbed his coat and backpack as he walked out the door. He trudged the three miles to Walmart. It was the closest place to get food.

Carrying his coat and wearing his backpack, Larry entered Walmart. He went to the restaurant inside and sat down at a table. He had to catch his breath and control his coughing before he could order. He waited for his heart to calm and his breathing to ease.

Going to the counter, he ordered a hamburger, fries, and a Coke. As he ate, he thought about what to do. First, he would apply for a job and try to talk to a manager to explain that he did not have a computer. Second, he would go begging. Third, he would return to the pool house after the lights had gone out in the main house. Then he would sleep. That would be his day. He would start there.

He looked down at his tray. He had eaten everything and tasted nothing. Standing, he cleared his table and took it to the trash. A coughing attack hit him and he rushed to the bathroom to cough in private. Washing his hands and face, he rinsed his mouth and spat the water into the sink. Then he went to find a manager. The woman was kind but said there were no positions open right now, and maybe he should try back in a few weeks. Larry thanked her. He bought a bottle of water and left the store.

Larry walked three miles alongside the road to his favorite intersection. The exertion left him weak but it had also opened up his lungs. He sat on the grass cross-legged, opened his backpack and pulled out his sign. He remained seated and propped it against his knee. Traffic was very busy with Christmas coming in just two weeks. People were generally generous and kind. Others yelled at him or laughed. It did not upset him. He simply did not care.

Larry spent the rest of the morning and afternoon working. He coughed often, but he controlled it—except when traffic was whizzing by and no one could hear him. The day progressed. He followed the arc of the sun in the sky. He could tell time by it now. He had never paid attention to it before; he hadn't needed to. It was now approaching four o'clock and it was time to go. He packed up his sign. He walked three miles back towards Walmart and in the direction of where he hoped to sleep that night. He stopped at McDonalds on the way, got dinner and moved on. It was dark now but the street lamps provided enough light for him to see as he walked his last three miles to the pool house. The temperature was still above freezing but there was a wind and it hurt him.

Reaching the entry of the hedge, he sat on the sidewalk, positioning himself in the shadows to see the back of the main house. He would see when the lights went off for the night. Covering himself with his coat, he pulled his backpack onto his lap and rested his arms on it. He would be patient. It was probably only seven o'clock or seven-thirty now. It could be hours yet.

Larry rested his spine against the post of the fence running across the back of the property. He dozed and thought of Peter. He wondered what he was doing tonight. He did not try to summon him. The snow on the ground under the moon looked lovely. He was feeling nearly frozen now and another coughing attack rose in him. He pulled the coat to his mouth and he coughed hard into the fabric. As it subsided, he leaned his head back on the post, exhausted.

Finally, in what felt like an eternity, the light of the main house went dark. Larry stood and slipped into the pool house. He took off his shoes and outer layer of clothing. Laying down, he felt that the bed was warm. He slept.

Over the next seven days, Larry kept to this routine.

On the eighth night, he waited as usual and slipped to the pool house. The door was locked. He closed his eyes in misery. He was sure he had left no tracks. But that did not matter now. His stay here was over and he still faced a long winter on the streets. Although the snow was finally gone, the nights would dip into the thirties or below. He was in danger again. Larry let his hand drop from the doorknob.

Turning, he silently left the backyard. He walked the three miles back to Walmart. As he walked, he reflected that his week of sleeping in the pool house had allowed him to recover. His cough was nearly over. He had slept warmly at night and gotten some real rest. The miles of walking had begun to make him strong. Each day was becoming easier than the last. Twelve miles or more in a day was a real number. In the week alone, he had probably walked a hundred miles. The pain of it was changing him. His old canvas sneakers were giving out.

Entering Walmart, he decided that he would do two things. He would swipe a piece of paper from a pad and buy new shoes. In the shoe department, he found a sturdy pair of sneakers and tried them on. He liked them. He placed his old sneakers in the box and carrying the box under his arm, he went to the office supply aisle. Tearing a sheet from a notebook, he rolled it and slid it into the box. He paid for his new sneakers at the self-checkout and went out the front door. He sat down on the concrete floor of the Walmart entry alcove with his back against the wall. Placing the box on his lap, he opened the top and took out the paper. Then, using the box as a writing table, he pulled the pen from his coat pocket. He leaned his head on the wall and thought about what he was going to write. Opening his eyes, he looked down and wrote:

*Hello. I am a homeless man. But there is no harm in me. None.*

· *I have been sleeping in your pool house for the last seven nights. I am so sorry. I was ill and desperate to get out of the cold to sleep warm at night. But I must tell you this: the electric blanket on the bed is still on. You will want to turn it off. The control is under the pillow.*

*I appreciate your hospitality. Again, I am sorry for intruding on your property. I wish you a good Christmas.*

*PS. Have no fear. I will not be back your way again.*

Larry folded the paper in thirds and wrote 'Home Owner' on the outside. He put the paper in the interior breast pocket of his coat. He would deliver it after they had left for work in the morning. Getting to his feet, he slid on his backpack and carried the box of his old shoes and receipt to the dumpster area. He set the box on the ground by the huge, high containers, knowing that someone with less than he had might need the shoes. Or someone else who didn't, would simply throw the box away.

It was a starry and peaceful night as he trudged back up the road towards the pool house. Halfway there, he stepped into a small forested area. He chose a tree and lay down at its base with his backpack under his head. It was his first night of being homeless without protection. But he was tougher and stronger now. His revelation of kindness was working for him. Everyone he encountered in stores or on the street, he treated with gentleness and respect. He had learned to slow his words. No one feared him. In the morning, he tucked his note in the homeowner's front door.

Larry spent Christmas night in the brightly lit alcove of a bank as it rained. His bowed lips were tight as the feeling of sadness and loneliness sank deep within him. He sat with his head curved to his knees.

He was spending his nights now sleeping under bushes and trees, in alcoves, various bathrooms, or behind buildings. He never spent the night in the same place twice. Being so exposed, he was aware of how easily he could be spotted and confronted by police. They were everywhere. It was safer to stay unpredictable. He moved around with his begging too. He washed in some form every day at a gas station or store. He had not been back to Walmart in two weeks. The amount he would get from people from his begging had fallen off after Christmas. He found some small humor in the idea that begging was seasonal too. He still had some money, but he was starting to deplete his wallet a little more each day. It was not good. As much as he was trying to be careful, his clothes were growing more worn from overuse. His beard was full now too. He was once again in pain. His hips hurt from walking on concrete and his back hurt from sleeping in strange places. He ached from the cold. He took to staying away from people as much as possible. He wanted no questions, no prying eyes.

He always rose with the sun. It directed his life. He could tell by the scent of the air if it would rain. After coffee in the morning, his first business of the day was to locate a place to sleep based on the weather. He wanted no surprises. He could not hide from the cold, but he could tuck in from the rain. This morning he knew it was not going to rain. It was going to plunge into deep freeze. He heard people at the coffee shop talking about fourteen degrees. He knew he could not survive it. Anything above freezing, he could . . . but not this. It was the middle of January.

He knew of an abandoned gas station off the Parkway. Actually, he knew of two, but this one was closer. The door to the old bathroom on the exterior left side of the building was open. He hated it because it smelled so foul, like backed-up sewage. The faucet did not work, neither did the toilet. The small room was disgustingly dirty. But it would be his shelter for this night. He would have to prepare.

Larry finished his coffee and walked the three miles to Walmart. He hated to spend his dwindling dollars on things he would probably lose, but there was no fooling around with weather this dangerous. He bought a portable battery-operated heater, two bottles of water, disinfectant spray, a small soft pillow on clearance and an inexpensive bedroll. Crossing the street to the dollar store, he bought a plastic tablecloth, two candles, a bag of nuts, and a spy novel. All of it had cost him forty-one dollars, a third of what he had in his wallet.

He carried his heavy bags back up the road to the filthy bathroom. He disinfected the toilet and the tile floor. He spread his white tablecloth over the tile and unrolled his bedroll over the plastic. He set out his pillow and heater, his water and food. He knew there were other homeless people in the area and it could all be gone by the time he returned to shelter for the night. But he had to take the chance. No one could survive out in the elements tonight. The wind chill factor would be zero and he took it seriously.

But now that he had spent money, he had to work. He decided to return to his favorite intersection. It was his highest paying. He sat on the dormant grass with his sign on his knee. His head was low against the freezing breeze. Hearing a car honk, he ran to it. The man handed him a five-dollar bill. Larry thanked him graciously and returned to his position. His head sunk again from the cold and his exhaustion. He heard a voice say, "Hello there."

Turning his head, Larry saw a man with a friendly face approaching him. The man was holding his ribs in apparent pain. The man sank down beside Larry, huffing a bit. "Cold, ain't it."

"Yes. It is awful."

The man sat back on his heels. For a moment he looked embarrassed. "Say, do you have any spare change? I can't stand long enough to work the cars."

"You homeless?" asked Larry, staring at the traffic flying by.

"Yah, I am. My name is Buddy Melrose. I'm from Piney Flats, Tennessee. I come by way of Knoxville and Chattanooga to here. Took a train and then, hitchhiked. But I got hurt jumping from the train. I think I did something real bad to myself. Guess those are the breaks. It's just that I'm so hungry . . ."

Turning his eyes from the traffic, Larry gazed into Buddy's. He saw an older man, maybe seventy or so. Buddy had on a baseball cap and his brittle gray hair stuck out from under it. His face was round, his skin was weathered, and he had a short white beard. His eyes were as brown as his own. But the lines on his face were what interested Larry. They were lines of smiling, of kindness, of laughter. Larry did not like mean people. He determined that Buddy was not one of those people. He turned his attention back to traffic, his brain continuing to analyze. Another car window lowered and an arm shot out with a bill in hand. Larry was up in an instant, accepting the money gratefully. He looked down at his hand. Another five. He returned to the brittle brown grass and sat down once more.

Buddy saw what he had thought was a young man from his general frame in the distance. But now, up close, he wasn't so sure. There had been something about the way the man had looked at him. It hadn't been with hostility, contempt, or disgust, all the typical things he was used to from regular folk. It had been more like a powerful bear, deciding at a glance, if he were interested or not. Buddy had no other words to describe the man's eyes, his look. But seeing them, Buddy was drawn to them. There was kindness in them. He felt a strange gentleness from the man. He couldn't leave. He was in terrible pain and he was starving. He didn't dare approach normal people for money. He could in a big city, but not in a rich small town. He knew he would be arrested faster than he could say the word 'police.' Buddy knew that he was dying; he could feel it inside him. He just didn't want to do it in jail. But he was nearing his end, so asking another homeless man for help was his only option. He looked at Larry and felt the quiet calm from the man, his thick dark hair ruffling in the wind and his beard, dark and heavy. Maybe that's where I got the notion of a bear, he thought. Then he heard the bear speak.

"I will buy you breakfast."

Buddy blinked, surprised. The bear's voice was low and gentle. He had thought maybe he'd get a dollar, but breakfast was too good to be true. He watched the bear fit his sign into his backpack and rise to his feet. He saw the bear looking down at him. Buddy wanted to get up but he couldn't. His old knees were locked to the ground with the cold. He was sure a rib or two were broken. He raised his eyes to the bear's in a silent plea for help. He heard the bear speak again.

"Buddy Melrose," Larry said gently.

"Yah."

"I will help you up. But you are not in the proper position for me to pull you to standing. So I will lift you from under your shoulders. This means I will come from behind you. Is this okay?"

Buddy nodded gratefully. The bear came behind him. He felt the bear's arms slide under his armpits. He felt the bear's hands lock around his chest. He felt the bear brace his weight against his own body. And, he felt the bear bring him to standing. He sagged against the bear. The bear did not let go; his arms locked tighter around his chest. He heard the bear say in his ear:

"If I let go, can you stand?"

Buddy wasn't sure. He hadn't felt the touch of another human for years. He was light-headed from hunger and the cold and the raw bleeding inside him. He did not want to go to a hospital. He wanted it to be over. He did not want to go on. But he wanted breakfast first. And, the bear would buy it for him. He stiffened his body and planted his feet more firmly. "Yah, Bear, I can stand."

Larry withdrew his arms slowly. He waited a second to see if Buddy could stay on his feet. When Buddy did, he picked up his backpack and slipped it on. "There is a Waffle House not too far up the road. Let's go there." He waited for the old man to get his bearings. Then Buddy's feet began to move. They walked in silence to the restaurant. They sat in a booth in the back of the restaurant, near the restrooms.

Buddy was huffing, trying to breathe. He watched the bear order two breakfasts. The waitress saw two homeless men. She asked if they could pay. Larry took money from his wallet and quietly laid it on the table. She served them coffee, followed by their meals.

"What happened to you?" Larry asked gently.

Buddy shrugged, shoveling eggs into his mouth.

"Buddy, don't eat so fast. Taste your food. We are warm now. We can take it slow." Larry saw Buddy nod and swallow.

"I've been homeless for a long time now, Bear," Buddy said, wincing as he took a sip of coffee. He saw Bear waiting for him to go on with his story. He took another bite and saw Bear begin to eat as well. "Years ago, I lost my farm to bankruptcy. My wife died soon after from heartbreak and cancer. I couldn't pay the medical bills, so I ran."

"And then?"

"I became a drunk. I didn't care. Over the years, I picked up odd jobs here and there. But nothing lasted. I just sank lower. Recently, I had the thought to get out of the cold and go to Florida. I was on my way now, except my jump from the train ended badly. I'm pretty sure my ribs are broken. Maybe more than one or two."

Larry sighed, leaning back in the booth. "I'll pay to get you to a hospital. You cannot stay this way."

"I'm grateful, Bear. But no. I don't want that. Let's just eat and I'll tell you why."

They ate and talked until it was finally time to go.

Larry paid the bill and they left the restaurant. Buddy wanted to go to the bandstand gazebo at the park on Main Street. Could Bear just stay with him for a while? Could they go there and talk some more?

Larry hesitated. The bandstand was more than a mile away. It would mean more than a two-mile trek back to the bathroom of the abandoned filling station. "Buddy," he said, "I have a place to spend the night. It is not much but I think it will keep us warm. Come with me now."

"No, Bear, I understand if you want to go, but I am going to the bandstand. I like it there."

Larry felt the air. He noted the sun and the placement of the clouds. He and Buddy had stayed long at the restaurant. It was one o'clock, the waitress had said. He could give Buddy a little more time, but he had to be in his shelter by four. It was already unbearably cold. He walked Buddy to the bandstand. The gazebo was round with a roof and had built-in benches along its sides.

They sat and talked for an hour. Their breath was coming out white. Larry felt the wind shift. He knew he had to leave. "Come with me now, Buddy. We must go. *Please*. The wind has changed. Dark will come quickly tonight." He stood and gazed down at Buddy.

"I have a place to go, Bear, so you get to yours. Thanks for breakfast and spending time with an old man. I will be here in the morning."

Larry had no choice but to leave. He slid his pack onto his back. Looking at Buddy, he said, "I will be in the bathroom at the old gas station on Templeton. If you change your mind, come on over."

Buddy nodded. He watched Larry turn and leave the gazebo. He watched him walk away until he could see him no more. Then he closed his eyes and waited.

Larry moved along quickly. He could handle the miles but the cold was slowing him down. The temperature was in freefall. He picked up his pace, adjusting to a steady trot. He had to keep his blood moving. His lips were already freezing. The icy air was burning his lungs. He summoned within him more strength and found it. He increased his speed. He summoned within him a calm. The feeling spread through him. He fell into a peaceful pace of swiftness and he stayed that way until he came to Templeton. Making a left, he slowed to a brisk walk until he reached the bathroom door. It was open.

Stepping into the bathroom, he closed the door behind him and locked it. His vision cleared and he lit his candles. He saw the small room was as he had left it. He turned on the space heater. He shed his backpack and coat. He sat on the bedroll and regained his breath. He opened a bottle of water and let the clear liquid slide down his dry mouth and throat. He pulled his coat to him and spread it over his lap, then picked up his spy novel, and began to read.

In the morning, Larry traveled the two miles back to the bandstand. Walking into the gazebo, he gazed down at Buddy lying on the bench. He touched his fingers to his cheek. Buddy was gone. He had already known that he would be. Turning, he left the man in peace. He could do nothing more for him now.

He lowered his head and left.

# CHAPTER NINETEEN

Life for Larry grew darker after Buddy's death. Rationally, he knew he couldn't have forced Buddy to do anything he didn't want to do. Buddy had done just what he wanted. He knew that Buddy had not suffered much. Freezing to death numbs a person first. This much he knew. But, internally, he suffered from a painful guilt. He should have taken action. He could have done better. But Buddy had explained it.

Buddy had said, "I am much older than you, Bear. A hospital might patch me up, but then I'm just back on the streets older and weaker, dying slowly. I have no hope. I just want to go. I want an end to it. The only thing I didn't want was to die hungry, and your generosity took care of that."

"I could call the police, Buddy. I could force you to go to the hospital and get well. You could well find happiness in Florida. You could end up thanking me if I don't allow you to die."

Buddy had smiled and sipped his coffee. "Yah. Great. We both go to jail. I die anyway. You stay there, locked up. You can't pay your bail so you stay there. What good did you do? And then you'd have a record, Bear. You don't want that."

"Why do you call me Bear?"

Buddy shrugged. "It was my first impression of you. You're dark and large and you seem to move with an unusual strength, methodical-like, through the cold. And I *like* bears."

"I don't approve of this, Buddy. You have put me in a difficult situation."

"There is no situation, Bear. I wanted you to know because I knew you'd understand."

"But I do not understand, Buddy."

"If you really don't — and I don't believe that's true — it's only because you are still young and strong. But I'm worn out. I know what I want. I just wanted you to know that *I* want it."

Buddy's death had been two weeks ago. It was now the first of February. A dark depression had settled within Larry. He had slept in the Templeton station bathroom for four nights. On the fifth night, he had returned to find that everything had been stolen. He spent the night huddled in the corner by the toilet. The place disgusted him. A hopelessness entered him and for a long moment, he could see no way out of it. He had understood Buddy. He knew why Buddy wanted to die. He had felt it before at the old homestead. He was feeling the same way now. He was ill at heart. His spirit was being broken. There is always a breaking point, and he saw how easily it could come. But he was not done yet. He was learning things and he was learning rapidly. He was starting to employ his learning. To harness and cultivate it. He just had to survive the misery of this night. Then, he would move on.

Larry returned to sleeping under bushes and under the cover of other dark places. He had become Buddy's bear. He did move with methodical strength through the cold. He moved without feeling. His emotions had become as cold and as numb as his body. He no longer felt anything at all.

Larry's eyes opened as the sun began its early eastern glow. He rose from the cold ground and removed his coat. He shook his garment out, pulling off any detritus that had attached to the cloth from the ground. He slid back into his coat and briefly patted the trunk of the tree that had sheltered him for the night. He picked up his backpack and slid it on his back. He was low on funds and he needed more. He had not been to his favorite intersection since Buddy had died. He would go there this morning after his coffee. He began to walk to carry out his plan.

The intersection was busy. People were still depressed from the holidays and the bills they now had to pay. Larry didn't expect much from the early morning traffic. He knew they were running on autopilot. He could see the exhaustion in their faces as they faced another day. He listened to every word they had to say. Some of them hated their bosses. Some of them were in trouble at work. Some of them had financial problems. The words of the people in the cars that gave him money came out in fragments. But they accumulated inside him. They were afraid of being him.

Larry sat again on the grass, his eyes closed as he propped his sign on his knee. He was so tired and it was so cold. He heard someone yelling in the distance. He couldn't make out the words and he didn't care. The yelling persisted. He slowly opened his eyes, the bear within him awakening. He realized the yelling was being directed at him. It was coming from a man on the opposite corner of the intersection, across the street from him. He waited, alert now, watching warily as the man began to negotiate traffic and make his way towards him. The man came upon him, his hostility an open weapon.

"This is my intersection!" he screamed, his arms moving wildly.

Larry looked up at the man's crazed eyes. He saw they were not focused, that the man's screaming was out of control and his hostility was based on fear and hunger. He unzipped his backpack. Withdrawing a cinnamon twist wrapped in wax paper, Larry held up his roll, letting go of his own breakfast. He did not want to fight the man. He would if he had to, but he didn't want to.

The man grabbed the cinnamon roll and tore at the wrapper. Larry's own hunger rumbled in his stomach. He did not look at the man as he devoured his only breakfast. He kept his eyes on traffic; on business. Then the man spoke, diverting his attention. From the man's gush of words, he learned that the man's name was Gus. The rest of the words he did not care about, not until he heard something about the place Gus had made to stay. The bear in Larry shifted. All bears need a place to hibernate. He would talk to the man. He would listen. He glanced up at the man and said, "Sit down." Larry pointed to the cold ground beside him.

Gus felt compelled to sit. He sank to the ground by Larry. He sat as Larry was sitting, cross-legged, facing the profile of the man in front of him. As he settled into sitting, he stared at Larry. The man was not looking at him. Larry's eyes were already back on traffic. Gus felt a gush of words come out of his mouth again. They were all over the place, but he had no control over them. He never had, and they had gotten him into trouble repeatedly. Finally, he saw the man turn his gaze to him. He saw cold brown emotionless eyes. He saw they were stronger than his own. He fell silent, rare for him.

"You talk without thinking," Larry said quietly.

Gus blinked. He waited for his anger to rise, but it did not come. He felt the calmness of the man slow him down. He wasn't sure what it was. He only knew that the man had taken the words from his mouth and, somehow, he stayed silent. He felt the whoosh and rumble of traffic as it whizzed by. He heard the birds chittering. He saw the breeze ruffle the man's dark hair and how the man stayed so still against it all. The man's voice had been low and gentle. It had not been condemning. It was something else. His eyes opened wide. He did speak without thinking. His brain could never sort out his thoughts. Then, Gus knew he could not speak without thinking to this man.

Larry assessed Gus. He saw that Gus was skinny and wiry. That his complexion and teeth were bad. He saw that Gus had no control over himself. He knew that Gus did drugs. He might be off them now, hence his hunger, but he did do them. He saw that his movements were frenetic and his eyes did not see what was in front of him. He saw that Gus was young. Maybe his own age. But he also knew Gus had something he wanted and it was something that Gus would lose shortly because he had no control over himself. Gus would be picked up by the police any moment now. It was not supposition. It was a fact. Gus had no idea how to be invisible. His running mouth would cause him to fail. His lack of ability to process things around him would open him to that attack. He learned that Gus was new to the streets. That he had found money in begging. That he thought of this intersection as his own territory. But Larry had been here long before Gus. He did not care what Gus thought. Gus posed no threat to him. The man only needed to be silenced and he willed for him to be silent. He saw that Gus was no longer speaking. He could talk now.

He said, "Show me."

Gus wiped his nose with the back of his hand. He wasn't sure what the man wanted him to show.

Larry closed his eyes and sighed internally. "Show me your shelter, Gus."

"Gimme some money."

"I have already paid you. You have eaten my breakfast." Larry packed his sign and rose to his feet. He looked down at Gus as he slid on his backpack. He waited for Gus to get up.

Gus scrambled to his feet, looking at Larry.

"How far is it?" Larry asked gently.

"Not far."

"I will let you lead. I would like to see what you have done."

"It's not much."

"Nevertheless."

Gus felt compelled to lead Larry. He liked this quiet man. He wanted to please him. It was a strange feeling but he felt it. He tried not to talk as they walked. He knew the man would not like it. He stumbled along to Larry's measured pace. He wished he could move like that.

They had walked a mile to the dumpster area behind an empty industrial building.

As they approached Gus's hideout, Larry saw two walls about eight feet tall separated by a space of fourteen feet. The backs of the walls were attached to the building. This area would have held two dumpsters, but it was empty now. The placement of the walls plainly intended to hide the dumpsters from public view of the parking lot. The tarp covering the top of the walls created a ceiling, hanging long over the sides and sagging in the middle. The walls themselves were about twelve feet long.

Larry slowed his pace, studying the area. He turned to Gus. "May I look inside?"

"Uh, there's nothing in there but my bedroll."

"Even so. I would like to look."

"Okay, man. But I gotta have money. I need it! I gotta have and if you wanna look ..."

"Stop, Gus."

Gus paused, wiping his nose again while looking at Larry. "Will you give me money?"

"I will."

Larry stepped forward and lifted the tarp hanging down halfway over the entrance. He looked inside. On the concrete floor lay a grungy bedroll. Trash littered the area. He saw a syringe and a long narrow rubber tube. There was nothing else to see. He knew that Gus would not be back tonight. He knew that Gus was never coming back. Larry lowered his hand. He faced Gus as he straightened his body and peered down into the shorter man's eyes.

"You could change, Gus," he said quietly. "People do. I did. I am. It is a process, but it can be done."

"I'm not you, man," Gus replied nervously. "I don't know *what* you are, but you're, like, not normal. You can take your process and shove it. I don't even know what it means."

"It means that you change, Gus. It means that you find some self-control and cultivate it to become stronger and more disciplined so that you avoid trouble."

"You're crazy, man. Fuck you. People don't do that. People don't change! I'll never be like you." He was starting to fidget with anxious energy.

Larry sighed. "It's not about being me. It's about being a better you."

"Why do you care, man?"

"Because when you leave here, Gus, you are about to wreck your life. And, I don't want you to do that."

"I don't know what you're talking about and you don't know what you're talking about and you don't know that. You promised you'd give me some money and I want it now! No process shit from you, just money, okay?" Gus stuck out his hand, his mouth set in stubborn desperation.

"Listen to me, Gus," Larry said gently, aware he was losing the man. "Let me try to help you. We could both stay here and I could help you." Gus's eyes were starting to look unfocused. "Are you hearing me, Gus?"

"Sure, man, but that's not going to happen. Forget it. I already told you!"

"All right then. If you refuse to let me help you, I cannot force you. But now, I want you to walk twenty paces away from me and sit down. Will you do that, Gus?"

Gus's eyes grew a little wider. How did the dude know? He'd intended to snatch the guy's wallet from his hands when he took it out to pay him. He was going to grab it and run away. He'd done it before. He watched the man stand even taller and square his shoulders. He saw that he could not fight the guy and win. He didn't want to attack him anyway. He still liked him. He nodded. Walking away, he sat down on the asphalt, a distance from the man.

Larry unbuttoned his coat and reached into his back pocket. His eyes did not leave the sitting man. He flipped open his wallet and without looking, pulled out the first bill. He already knew that it was a twenty. He returned his wallet to the back pocket of his jeans and buttoned his coat. He approached Gus and handed him the bill. "Go on now, Gus. Good luck to you."

As Gus ran away, Larry began to move forward, out of the parking lot. The money did not really start flowing at the intersection until nine-thirty after the rush hour traffic was over. He looked at the sun. It was eight o'clock now. He could take his time getting there and buy coffee on the way. He needed to get something to eat too. He thought about the dumpster area as he walked. He liked that it was remote and so empty of life. He began to think about the things he would need to build. It would be hard to do without transportation. He thought of his forest and felt a longing stir inside him. He had built something there. He paused in his tracks. It was only seven miles away. He could see it, could visit it again. He was used to walking now. He had already walked hundreds of miles. Seven miles meant nothing to him. As he walked, he also knew he would steal again. He didn't want to, but he would. He had learned that it's easy not to steal when you can afford not to. He was already feeling regret over the hurt he would soon cause.

Larry covered the miles to his forest, moving along silently, speaking to no one. As he walked, he thought about what was happening to him. He knew that once he'd opened his mind to learning and becoming a different person, his mind had continued to expand. He knew his thinking had grown more far reaching, broader, deeper and higher. He saw people and events now with a greater physical sensory and intellectual acuity. Sometimes, his focus was so sharp, its intensity caused his head to hurt. He was learning to control this and depend on his ability to understand his surroundings with clarity.

He had learned two critically important things.

The first was that he'd discovered some kind of plane of existence. When he had originally encountered the peculiar aperture in his mind, he hadn't known what to make of it. But he hadn't ignored it. He'd found a quiet moment and made himself comfortable under a tree, hidden from the view of others. From this safe vantage point, he relaxed, and closed his eyes, intent on taking the mental step up to explore the hole in his mind with its light shining through.

Making the step up, he'd found only a rough patch of ground like that of a forest. The place had just one tree. He'd walked the small area. After seeing nothing more, he had patted the trunk of the tree and stepped back down. The experience had left him light-headed. He had remained under the tree where he had been sitting. When he opened his eyes again, it had been early evening, his empty stomach aching in hunger. He figured that he must have fallen asleep. Still, he was intrigued. He had discovered something about himself that held great implications.

From then on, he'd practiced going to this plane every day until the dizziness from stepping up and down finally ceased. It had been difficult. For several days, he had hidden in a small forest, hungry and dizzy, but learning.

He'd quickly learned that each time he went, the area in his mind continued to grow and expand. He saw more trees. The land became more extensive. He could walk further now. He began to understand that walking on this plane was, for him, a literal occurrence. It gave him a perspective of looking down. Seeing things before they happened. He knew he had found a form of power. He didn't know how far this power could go. But he also knew it could be dangerous for him. When he was on this transcendental plane, he lost touch with his body and physical needs. He would forget to eat. He didn't feel pain when he was 'there.' Sometimes, he stayed too long. And when he stepped down, he suffered. Fatigue, hunger, and all the aches of his earth-bound body that were waiting for him.

However, being 'there' also allowed him to learn more rapidly. This was what he was most interested in.

Larry decided to call this place in his mind his 'Plain.' He no longer saw his higher state of mind as an elusive euphemism. It wasn't just a plane of existence. To him, his Plain was a tangible place. He could walk there, grounded on a land that changed as he willed. It might be mental, but it was also material and causal. Physical and logoic. It was stimulating and expanding. He liked being 'there' even though he didn't know exactly what it meant for him.

On his Plain, Larry also saw himself. He could achieve deep insights into himself and he did not lie to himself. He saw his weaknesses for what they were. His personal failings that he envisioned as 'scales of weight' like heavy plates of armor encasing him. His meanness, laziness, and dishonesty. His rigidity, ignorance and anger. His defensiveness, insecurity, anxiety and fear. His hatred, and lack of self-control. These were all the things that were holding him back and holding him down. He would let them go, and they would rise again, squeezing and suffocating him, paralyzing him with indecision. Shedding them was a constant and relentless cycle of effort. He knew he still had much to learn. He wondered how long it would take before he understood how to gain perfect control. He knew it all depended on his force of will. And a force of will was exactly what he was discovering.

The second important thing he'd learned was how to walk better on the earth. He used to walk with his shoulders hunched forward and often, looking at the ground. But no more. His learning a new way to walk was born out of physical necessity. He'd been forced to find a way to move that eased his pain while covering hundreds of miles on foot. He had learned to stand up straight with his shoulders square and back, allowing him to breathe more deeply by standing taller. He had opened his stride and slowed his pace. Once he had found this method of movement, he'd worked to perfect his glide so that his feet rolled easily on the land beneath him. And he'd made this new method a part of him until he no longer thought of it.

Larry turned into his forest and came to the area of his old camp. He saw that it was beautiful. The forest had taught him much. Small things. To listen. To feel the air. To hear the air. To see how nature worked. It was persistent. He saw how natural selection depended on a creature's ability to compete, survive, and reproduce. It was Darwin's Theory on a miniature scale. The theory was more far-reaching, of course, but that was its essence. He had always known it, but now he understood it. He touched his trees again. He put his arms around his favorite and laid his head against its proud trunk. He listened to the rhythm of the forest. He breathed the scent of the woods into him.

It was time to go. He left the forest and despised his next move. The young teenage boy could not see him coming. He would take an important thing from him. It was not life-threatening, but it would harm the quality of his life. Temporarily. The same as the old man he had robbed. He was well aware of the harm he had done to that innocent person.

Larry moved forward steadily to the old residential area. He had spent a week in this area. He had seen the bike parked in the front yard on weekdays. In the early hours of the weekend, as he had passed the house to go to work, he'd seen the boy get on his bike and ride away. He hadn't cared where the boy went. He only knew the bike had been his transportation. Now the boy would not have that transportation. And it would cause him harm.

Larry got on the bike and rode away. He would start building tomorrow. For now, he would park the bike at his new shelter. Then he would walk to work. He had to work. He had to make money. He knew he would spend a miserable night in Gus's bacteria, but he would get through it. He would focus his thoughts elsewhere. He would focus on his plan for his building. He had already covered fourteen miles this morning. He had not yet eaten. He was burning calories at an alarming rate.

But he was also growing stronger.

# CHAPTER TWENTY

It had been a miserable night, but Larry had known it would be. Gus's bedroll had smelled of urine, vomit, cum, and rank body odor. The night air had been freezing. But it was over now. The sun was not yet rising and the early hour was frosty and silver. Larry rode his bike around the exterior of the industrial building to see what materials were available to him. The bike was a full-size lightweight 10-speed. The finish was cherry red, but he would not take it out on the road until it had been painted black. It would be unrecognizable then.

He felt its wheels glide smoothly under him as he approached the loading dock on the back side of the building. He saw a side ramp leading up to the elevation where trucks would back up to unload. He rode up the ramp and leaned his bike against the wall. Walking the platform, he stood in front of wooden pallets, stacked high by size against the back wall. He touched the pallets, noting their number and various measurements. An idea came to him. There was nothing else on the loading dock. Getting on his bike, he flew down the ramp and continued to circle the building. He saw a small open field to his left and he rode to its edge. He nudged his kickstand down and began to traverse the field to inspect its debris. He saw an old tire, some cinder blocks, a good bit of trash and an old oil drum. He touched the drum and knelt to inspect the cut-out section in the front. He could smell the faint scent of fire ash. He stood up in the field and glanced at the sky. It was five-thirty in the morning. The rays of sun were muted, still low, not more than a hint on the horizon. It was still dark but he could see in the dark.

He had to go to Walmart. It was four miles away. He wondered briefly if he could get away with using the bike rather than his feet. He closed his eyes, considering the thought. No. It was sloppy and sloppy could get him hurt. He got on his bike and rode back to his new home. He parked the bike inside and emptied the clothes from his backpack, setting them by the bike. He kept his personal products with him in the front flap. He began his trek to Walmart and picked up his speed to a trot. He summoned a strength within him and increased his speed to a swift steady pace. There were runners on the parkway all the time. No one would notice him.

Thirty-eight minutes later, he entered Walmart and went to the men's room. He pinched a new black t-shirt and a pair of boxers on the way. He took wet paper towels along with dry ones into the stall. He stripped. He rinsed his armpits, groin and torso. He dried himself and rolled on his deodorant. He slid into the new t-shirt and underwear. He got back into his outer layers and folded his old undergarments into his backpack. He shook out his coat and held it under the hand dryer a long while to blow off the smell of Gus. He put on his coat and stepped to the sink. He splashed his face, brushed his teeth, ran wet warm fingers through his long dark hair. He blew his hair dry. He combed his hair back from his face. Before leaving the bathroom, he glanced at himself in the mirror. He did not recognize himself. He was still looking at a stranger. He left the bathroom.

He bought a hammer, nails, black spray paint, masking tape, a bike lock, two bottles of water, and a pre-made sub sandwich. He paused at the checkout and went back for work gloves. He checked out, loaded his backpack with his bags, and briskly walked the miles home.

At home, he set down his backpack and unloaded his bags. Except for his food, he laid the items from the bags on the floor. He stripped off his coat, rolled it up and put it in a bag. He did not want his coat to touch anything. He did not mind the dirt of the earth but he did not like the filth of humans. He rolled his bike out of the dumpster area and took it further away. He taped up his bike and put on his gloves. Slowly, he began to spray the frame of his bike black. He left the chrome and the fenders alone. When he was finished, there was black paint on the index finger of his right glove. He was glad he had worn gloves. His fingers were long and strong and his palms were wide. He accepted money only with clean hands. He left the bike to dry and went into the shelter. He dragged out Gus's ratty thin bedroll. Rolling it up tight on the asphalt, he stuffed it into a bag. He would dispose of it on his way to work. He turned the bedroll bag upside down and loaded it into another shopping bag. He could now carry the handles of the bag without his fingers touching the filthy thing again. He lifted the front of the tarp back over itself. He rolled his bike back under the canvas, careful of the drying paint. He took off his gloves and placed them by his hammer. He put on his coat. His empty backpack held only his sign. He slipped the pack onto his back and lowered the canvas. Then he went to work.

Larry went back the four miles to the intersection near Walmart. He couldn't go back to his favorite intersection off the highway, as he had been there yesterday. He was almost afraid to anyway. The last time, he had met a drug addict who wanted to steal his wallet. The time before that, he had met an old man who wanted to die. He wanted no more encounters. He still had eight weeks of winter ahead of him and he had to secure himself. February was notorious for freezing rains. He spent five hours working the Walmart intersection. It was time to go. The day had been good but the wind was shifting again and he felt a significant drop in temperature. He had made enough money. He looked at the sun. It was four o'clock. He was cold and hungry. He slid his sign into his backpack and was in the process of slinging the pack onto his back when he was approached by a little girl. Her eyes looked up at him and he smiled down at her.

"Do you talk?" she asked.

Larry laughed at that. "Of course I do." He sank down to her level on bended knee in order to see her eye to eye.

"My mother says homeless people don't talk."

"Well, in many ways, she is right. But it is complicated."

"Why is it complicated?"

He studied the girl. She was clean and pretty. Her long dark hair lay in a loose ponytail on her shoulder and her inquisitive brown eyes were round and large. Her clothing matched, but the garments she wore were faded and of poor quality.

Larry glanced to his left and saw a woman walking towards them. She was strolling to them, but not running at them. She had plastic grocery bags hanging on her arm. He smiled at her and raised his hand in friendly acknowledgement. He had no doubt she was the child's mother. She nodded back to him as she walked. He turned his attention back to the girl. "How old are you?"

"Six."

"All right. Do you know what complicated means?"

She shook her head. "Not exactly." She held his gaze with his.

"It means that something can be hard to understand. I think what your mother means is that poor people do not have a voice. And that is true."

She looked down at the ground. "I am poor. Mama says we are."

"Well, Anna, you might be poor in some ways, but not in all ways. You have someone who loves you."

She looked up, startled. "How did you know my name?"

"It is on your necklace. Now, your mother is coming. What is it you wanted to say to me?" Larry asked gently.

She held up her hand with a dollar wrapped between her fingers. "I wanted to give you this. I know you need it."

Larry tilted his head slightly, looking at her. He did not take the money. He shook his head, his lips parting slightly. "No," he said softly,

The woman approached to stand at their side. Larry was still on his knee. The girl moved forward to Larry. She put her arms around his neck and whispered, "It's okay. We share."

Larry placed only one hand on her thin back to acknowledge her touch. The other he left by his side. He closed his eyes. No one had touched him in years. He had forgotten what it felt like. Actually, he didn't know at all.

The mother watched her daughter embrace the homeless man. She smiled slightly, perplexed. Anna did not talk to people. She turned away from them. She was a serious, strange child who liked to be left alone. Now here she was, hugging a total stranger? She didn't understand but she let Anna have her moment. Anna saw things differently and would never be hurried. She felt a gentleness from the man anyway. She watched the breeze ruffle his dark hair and she smelled his spicy clean scent. She noted that his hand was broad on her daughter's back, his fingers loosely spread apart, and that they were long and smooth. She watched the man bow his head over her daughter's shoulder. The move was so tender, it almost moved her to tears. It definitely caught her by surprise. What had these two said to each other?

Finally, Anna released Larry and stood before him as he remained on his knee. Her solemn brown eyes gazed into Larry's. She held out the bill again.

Larry touched the girl's cheek gently, "No, Anna. Thank you. But I cannot." He slid his knee back and rose to stand gracefully. He turned to the mother and met her eyes. He was not quite sure what to say. He, a stranger, had touched her daughter. He waited for her to speak. Then he would know what to do.

The mother saw that Larry was not an ordinary homeless man. She worked with plenty of homeless in the soup kitchen of their church. They were generally good people. She had no fear of the homeless. She knew their stories. Most had met with some tragedy. But she couldn't see tragedy on this man. There was an aura of power about him. But it was ethereal, like Anna. She looked at her daughter and then back to Larry. "I . . . I hope she didn't bother you."

"Your daughter is wonderful. I am very glad to have met her," Larry said gently. "But I cannot take her money. I understand it is a gift and that I am rejecting that gift, but it is better for her."

The mother nodded. He was being protective of Anna rather than rejecting charity. She understood him now.

Larry spoke, "I must go. It is getting late." He turned to the girl and inclined his head, "Anna." He began to move forward.

"Stop!" Anna commanded, raising her voice.

Larry stopped, closing his eyes. He squared his shoulders. He did not face Anna.

Anna looked at Larry's back and frowned. Now, he wouldn't talk to her?

Larry turned and came back to Anna. "I am here." He grew silent.

"I want to go with you."

"You cannot."

"I want you to take me there."

"I cannot."

"Why not?"

"You have to find your own way there, Anna," Larry returned softly.

Anna's mother brought her fingers to her open lips watching the exchange. She had no idea what to do with Anna. Anna often talked about 'there' but she had not able to tell her what or where 'there' was. But apparently this man knew what Anna was talking about. She took in their faces, their silent brown eyes locked on each other's silent brown eyes. Both faces unsmiling. She blew out a sigh of frustration and licked her dry lips. "Listen, sir, I beg you . . . tell me about this. Can you tell me where 'there' is? Please. I must know. I must understand."

Larry did not want to discuss this. It was why he did not get involved with strangers. He was distressed. He broke Anna's gaze and looked unhappily away. He felt bad for the mother. The exchange must have been awful for her. Unless she knew how different Anna was. Certainly, she does, he thought.

He did not want this. He wanted to leave. He felt his blood pressure rising. He was upset. He stood in the wind, trying to think of what to do. He looked at the mother's face. She was intelligent and the questions in her eyes were searching rather than frantic. She deserved an answer. He closed his eyes and bowed his head. He breathed in the cold air and let it out slowly. He brought his shoulders down. He felt his scales of weight fall off of him. He summoned a calm and slowed his own heart. He waited for the beat to settle into a steady rhythm. He raised his eyes to meet hers. "What does she tell you?"

"That she wants to go 'there' . . . but, I am at a loss. What does it mean? She can't tell me what it is and I don't know how to help her."

"I almost don't know how to answer you. It's complicated."

"That means it is hard to understand," Anna said knowingly.

Larry smiled briefly. He looked at Anna. "Yes. You learn quickly."

To Anna's mother, he said, "It is about learning. It is about self-control. 'There' is a plane one reaches when she or he exceeds common understanding. To be clear, some people might call it a plane of existence. I do not. I see 'there' as a place I can walk on. So I call it my Plain, plain being spelled in the context of an open field." He smiled slightly, seeing her confused expression. He continued gently, "On this plain, a person can do what they otherwise could not. It surpasses anxiety and fear. They can see what others do not. But it can also become a form of expression that can be misunderstood."

To Anna, he said, "When you walk above others, you can frighten them. Be careful of that. Don't go so far away that you can no longer talk to them or understand them. This is where the balance lays. You can be 'there' but you must also remain here. Your 'there' is going to be where you take yourself as you grow. Go to your plain, Anna, because it is within you to do so, but don't fall out of balance."

To Anna's mother he said, "I have apparently connected with Anna on my Plain. I did not know it could be done. I have never met anyone else on it."

Anna's mother asked, "Is it literal? This plain?"

"Yes. But this is where it gets complicated. And I am running out of time to get settled for the night. It is my intention to allay your fears about

Anna. In many ways, she is right. It is the others who cannot rise to her. And she does not yet know how to control her faculties in the face of outside influences. But she will learn and she will be fine."

Larry turned to Anna and said, "I began my growth late in life. I cannot imagine coming into this power so young. I know it must be very difficult for you. You don't know what to do with yourself. And, I know it." He bowed his head slightly. "I wish I could help you. But. Anna, I am barely hanging on myself."

"But you could teach me."

"No, Anna, I cannot. I am already far above you and I cannot come down. I don't even know where I am now. But I will tell you this. You must control yourself. When you are angry, remember that you do not have to be. Let those scales of weight drop. When you feel anxiety, remember it impedes your judgment. Let those scales fall off of you. If you are being dishonest, your thoughts are on the believability and you cannot see what is in front of you. So, don't be dishonest. Do not lie. Not to others and, especially, not to yourself. And when you feel these things, you must summon a calm within you. A self-honesty. Only then can you know what to do. When I say scales of weight, I mean it is like shedding scales of metal that drag you down. Let them go and you will be light enough to go 'there.'" He knew he had not begun to explain. But it had been the best that he could do within the span of a few minutes.

To Anna's mother, he said, "Self-control on this scale is very difficult to accomplish. It is not infallible. A person can fall off their plain. It is up to them whether they climb back on. Educate her to the best of your ability. And be patient with her when she falls. Now please, I must go. I hope I have helped."

Anna took her mother's hand. She raised her hand in goodbye to Larry.

Anna's mother looked down at her daughter's hand linking with hers. Anna hadn't held her hand in over a year. It had broken her heart. Her daughter didn't seem to be abide being touched. So, when she had seen

Anna put her arms around the man, she had been surprised and puzzled. She knew it was all Anna's doing. She knew the man was innocent in all this. But he had been kind to her daughter. And to her. Now, she had an inkling of this higher plain, although she still did not truly understand. Still, he had given her something to think about.

Larry crossed the street and entered Walmart. He had to get moving. He had things to carry. He invested in a thick red sleeping bag, and a line of rope. He checked out and crossed the street to the dollar store. He bought a plastic tablecloth, two candles, disinfectant, a bag of nuts, and a corporate world novel. Outside the door of the store, he loaded everything into his backpack, cut a length of rope, and tied the bedroll to the top of his backpack. He hadn't gotten everything he wanted, but he was tired and wanted to go home.

He trudged forward. The wind was cold and sharp and it hurt him. He picked up the pace of his walking. It was all he could manage. He covered his miles and came to his dark empty place. It was nearly night around him. He lit his candles and set them on the ground. He set about disinfecting the floor, spreading out the plastic and unrolling his bedroll on top of the plastic. He pulled the entry tarp to the ground and secured it with the wheels of his bike. He grabbed the bag with his water and sub sandwich and moved the candles by his bed. Sinking on top of his bedroll, he ate, his back against the wall, his long legs straight out and crossed in front of him. He decided that he would not read tonight. He would sleep and get an early start in the morning. He stood and shed his coat. He laid it over his bedroll as an extra blanket. He took off his sneakers and placed them beside his bed. He slid into the softness of his new covers.

He sighed thinking of Anna. He didn't want to be her.

He blew out the candles and closed his eyes.

# CHAPTER TWENTY ONE

Larry woke. The room was dark but he was fully awake. He had intended to sleep for ten hours and knew that he had. He slid out of his covers and sat up. He grabbed his bike and moved it aside. He slid through the end of his entry tarp and stepped into the blue darkness of early morning. The air was bitterly cold but not quite freezing. It was the time of morning when the sun was making its eastern arc but had not yet reached the horizon. It would only be an hour until it did. This time, he smelled nothing on the air that disturbed him.

He went back inside and lit his candles. Sitting on his bed, he began to unbutton his two outer shirts. Shrugging out of them, he folded the shirts and set them on his bedroll. Rising, he slowly stripped off his remaining two t-shirts. One was white, the other was the fresh black shirt from yesterday. Bending, he laid the two shirts on his bed. He unbuttoned and unzipped his jeans. He pushed his pants down and stepped out of them. He picked them up, folded them, and set them on his bed. He stepped out of his underwear and laid them on the bedroll. He looked at the clothes on his bedroll. They were his cleanest and he had to protect them.

He stood naked in the candlelight. He was surprised that he did not feel affected by the cold. But he was rested and it was probable that his body had acclimated. He had not been fully naked for a long time. He touched his body. He ran his hands over his strong arms, the width of his chest and down his flat stomach. He had lost fat and gained considerable muscle.

His hands traveled around his firm waist to his low back and to the tight roundness of his buttocks. He moved his hands forward to lightly squeeze the strength of his dense, lean thighs. He was hard with sexual desire. He wanted to make love with a woman. But he had no face in his mind, no real being. No one he could summon. This is about myself anyway, he whispered to himself. About what had happened to his body. About how it had changed over his months of struggle and his hundreds of miles walking and running. He felt that his skin was warm and soft under his palms. He had very little hair except for the dark down covering his shins and calves. He had hair under his arms and covering his groin. He moved his hand to his chest and grew quiet to listen to himself breathe. He felt the beat of his own heart. He closed his eyes and his lips parted. He did not know this body. He could feel it, he was in it, he was glad for it, but he did not know it. He had changed so much, he hardly knew himself. Not only in his attitude, demeanor and speech, but physically as well. How had he changed so much? He used to be undersized and scrawny but he wasn't that now. No. He was tall and muscular, lean and strong. An infinite improvement over his former self. And he felt it profoundly to his core.

Larry lowered his hand, his self-exploration over. He needed to work. He moved to the small pile of clothing on the concrete floor from emptying his backpack. He selected a pair of underwear he liked the least and stepped into them. The underwear was clean.

He washed his underwear and socks in public bathrooms. He twisted the water out and returned them to his backpack wrapped in paper towels. He often hung them on the branch of a tree overnight. They would be stiff and sometimes frozen in the morning but they were dry. This pair was stiff and uncomfortable.

He pulled on his roughest t-shirt and put his legs through his jeans. He had stolen a new pair from Walmart when he could no longer tolerate his old pair. His new pair was tighter in the waist and longer in the leg. These jeans fit his frame nicely. He hoped he would not wreck them. They were the only pair he had. He sank onto his bed and pulled on his socks and shoes. Rising, he lifted his shirt and rolled his deodorant under his arms. He drank some water and brushed his teeth. He stepped outside to spit the peppermint foam from his mouth. Holding a water bottle in his hand, he poured water into his free hand to rinse his face and beard. Lifting his shirt from his stomach, he blotted his face dry. He gazed into the morning. It was still dark. He drank more water and thought about his plan.

An intensity burned in his gut. He knew he would not be homeless much longer. Come spring, he would shave his beard and get presentable again. He would join a landscape or construction crew. He would learn the trade, save his money, and then maybe form his own business. Maybe he would move from that into politics. He realized that he had been going about his job search all wrong. He had been going for small, dead-end jobs that, in time, would have sucked at his soul from boredom and kept him in poverty. He needed something larger. Until then, he would have to survive until he broke out of his situation. But he would break out. This he was sure of.

He now shifted his focus to plan for the day and his current plans for building.

First, he would start moving pallets from the loading dock to his new shelter. Second, when the sun was fully up, he would take his bike to Walmart and the dollar store. He would find a large basket and tie it to his bike so that he could move heavier items. He would get bleach, a large plastic bowl, a large sponge, and a gallon of water. He knew he had to be careful of the weight on the front load on his bike. He knew he would have to make more trips to get water. He would get coffee and food for the rest of the day. He would not beg today. He would work on his home to get settled.

He moved forward swiftly. His feet took him to the loading dock, where he began to unload pallets and carry them to the asphalt in front of his home. He set the pallets down in neat stacks by size. The pallets were heavy and he sweated carrying them. He strained his arms, his back and his legs under their weight. His gloves protected his hands from splinters. He continued to move the heavy wooden structures until his breath heaved from exertion. He could feel the muscles of his stomach ripple and tighten. Bending over, he rested his hands on his thighs to catch his breath. He wiped a trickle of sweat from his temple and glanced at the sun. It was eight-thirty now. He had been at it for three hours. His mouth was dry and he drained his water bottle.

It was time to get food and supplies. He shed his gloves and laid them by his hammer. He dressed again in one of his least favorite button-down shirts and smoothed it against his chest. He pulled on his coat. He might be warm now, but he would not be as he rode against the chill of the morning. As he rode, he liked the way the bike wheels clicked softly under his weight. He reached the stores quickly, took care of his business and returned home. He allowed himself time to enjoy his coffee, his cup of fruit, and his hot biscuit stuffed with bacon and eggs.

Finished with his breakfast, Larry rose from the asphalt outside his home. He went inside to load all his clothing onto his bedding. He slid the plastic base forward, rolled his clothes and bed together, and carried the roll outside. He began to pull on the weighty tarp ceiling. It was large and cumbersome. He finally got it free of the walls and dragged it further away. He patiently spread it out flat over the asphalt. He paced it off and found it to be twenty feet by thirty feet.

He undressed again. He got down to his underwear in the pale morning sun. With his chest bare, he mixed bleach and water in his new large blue plastic bowl. Plunging the large sponge into his bowl, he washed the painted beige walls of the dumpster area with the mixture. He watched as the walls grew lighter, the bleach killing off mold, mildew, splatters, and age. He also washed the concrete floor a section at a time. As the area dried, he rinsed off any bleach that had splashed on him. He took special care of his feet. He changed out of his ruined underwear and into the fresh pair he had set aside. He dressed again in his jeans, t-shirt, and sneakers.

He had seen the light-up sign of a bank on the Parkway indicate that it was thirty-five degrees, but he was beyond the cold in his focus. He began the process of stripping the pallets of their slats and nails, leaving their frames to use as he pleased. It was hard and terrible work. His gloves were already starting to fray under the roughness of the wood. It did not stop him. He fitted the empty frames to the concrete floor inside the walled area. Using the loosened boards stacked on the asphalt by size, he began to lay in a smooth floor on top of the frames. The framed height would spare him from any leaking water when it rained. He worked patiently, but he was growing tired. He needed to eat. He glanced at the sun overhead. Noon. He laid his hammer on the floor.

He went to his backpack to get the sandwich, nuts, and orange juice he'd bought for lunch. He did not rush his eating but neither did he linger over it. He knew he wasn't going to get his building done in one day. He still needed to go to the hardware store. He would go tomorrow. He had food for dinner and he had plenty of water. His floor was secure enough for the night. He only had five hours before it got dark. His lunch gave him a lift of energy and he began to work again.

Larry planned his home to be fourteen feet long by seventeen feet deep when he was finished. He would have to get more pallets in the morning but now, he had enough to frame the outside of the concrete walls and nail them together in order to secure the tarp roof.

He laid out the twelve 4' x 4' pallets he would need to accomplish this. He placed them in two rows of six so he could walk down the middle. He began to remove their slats on one side only. He set all the free boards aside. He had a good many now. When he was done, he moved on to strip the four five-foot pallets required for his design. Again, he stripped them of their boards on only one side.

He looked at the sun. Two o'clock. He was growing tired again and his hands were burning. The place looked like a construction zone. He dropped his gloves to the ground. He poured water over his hands and it felt good.

He laid on his newly installed floor to take a ten-minute rest. He felt the cold on his skin. He had to be careful not to get stiff. Ten minutes, he thought, and I can recharge. He closed his eyes to the bright sky above him while smelling the wood beneath him. He rested. He counted the seconds of the minutes in his mind. It gave him something to do while he rested. It kept him more awake than not. When the last second was finally counted, he got to his feet. He went to the basket attached to his bike and poured himself a small cup of coffee from his new thermos. He opened a grocery bag and withdrew a doughnut from a small box of four. He sat on his floor and ate and drank. He waited for the sugar and caffeine to give him a boost. He went back to work.

He chose to frame the exterior of the left wall first. He carried over three 4' x 4' pallets and placed their empty sides against the concrete wall. He wanted the boarded sides out so he could he could drive a nail wherever he wanted. Moving back to the remaining three pallets, he stacked them on top of the first three. The pallet wall was now twelve feet long by eight feet high, the same as the concrete wall. They were a good fit. He nailed the pallets together so they could neither move nor fall. He had already attached a three-foot slat to the top pallet backing up to the wall. He had made it so this board stood thirteen inches taller than the eight-foot height of the wall. He intended to make his left wall thirteen inches higher than the concrete wall, raising its height to nine feet, two inches tall. His right wall would remain eight feet in height. The slant would create a rain run-off once the tarp was back in place. He nailed a matching header of thirteen inches tall to the top front pallet.

Now he needed to create one long board to sit on top of the two headers. Returning to the loose boards, he nailed together an assembly that created a long board of seventeen feet in length. After he attached it to his headers, the board would stick out another five feet. Under this board, he would set the five foot long by nine foot high section of wall he planned to create. He hadn't gotten there yet. Then, he would nail the top board into this new section to keep it immobile.

He glanced at the sun. Three-thirty.

He decided that it was time to build a ladder. He had to have a way to move around the height of the walls. He chose two three-foot pallets. He stripped their backs and every other board on their fronts. He turned the pallets on their sides and joined them with a board.

Larry increased his pace. He needed to work harder now. He didn't have much time left and he did not want to work in the dark. He framed in the right wall fairly quickly now that he knew what he was doing.

He returned to the pile of loose boards and created one long board of fifteen feet. This board he would use as flashing against the back wall over the tarp. He was getting tired again but this time, he ignored his discomfort.

He moved to the tarp lying flat on the ground. Slowly, he began the tedious process of folding it like a fan to create a long manageable length of thirty feet. He reduced the tarp to a foot wide. Grabbing the end, he rolled up the tarp and carried it to his floor. Setting it down, he went to get his ladder. He carried his ladder inside, his arms aching from the weight. He pitched his ladder against the inside left wall by the back wall. He picked up his tarp and rolled it out over his left riser seven feet to the ground. He lowered the remaining roll to the floor and moved his ladder to the right wall. He picked up his tarp and let it fall over the right wall. He went down the ladder and got his fifteen-foot board. He pulled out the first flap of the underside of the tarp and fitted the length to lie flush against the back wall in a height of three inches. He set his board up against the back wall on top of the tarp. Getting off his ladder, he went outside to the left wall. He nailed the end of the first tarp fold to the wood near the ground. It was flush with the back wall. He moved to the right wall and slowly pulled the folded tarp forward until it was stretched tight. He nailed down that end too, near the ground, and flush to the back wall.

His fifteen-foot board listed as the tarp roof moved into its incline. He went back inside and shoved his board into place against the back wall. He moved to the left and nailed his flashing board to the nine-foot riser. He moved to the right and nailed the other end to the eight-foot wall frame. He saw that his board held the tarp tight, flush against the back wall in its incline. He moved along tucking the grommet lip of the tarp rigid and resolute against the back wall. Inspecting his work, he was satisfied that no rain would leak into his room from the back wall.

Moving left to right, he pulled the folded tarp forward over the walls. When it was done, he moved around the exterior and made the tarp taut and smooth as he worked to nail down the edges near the asphalt. He left the front entry of the tarp loose. He still had to work tomorrow to finish.

Larry's lips were dry and his body was shaking from fatigue and the cold. He glanced at the sun. It was getting dark. The wind was picking up and the temperature was dropping. He carried the plastic roll of his bed and clothes inside and unrolled it on the floor. He moved his bike inside and lowered the tarp across the entry. Stepping back outside, he pulled off his clothes. He quickly washed his hair and rinsed his body. The early evening air was frosty and bit his skin. He dried his hair and body with a t-shirt. In spite of the cold, he did not want to go to bed sweaty and dirty. He shampooed and rinsed his underwear. He twisted out the water and lifting a board, he laid the waistband of his underwear over the edge. Leaning the board against the right side of his home he left his underwear to dry overnight. He was quaking from the cold now and his hands were numb. He badly needed to eat and rest.

He glanced at his construction area. Part of him felt compelled to sort and stack the remaining loose boards scattered over the asphalt. But he knew in ten hours he would be up and working with them again. He still had a lot to do. He turned and left them as they lay. Moving inside, he pulled on fresh underwear and t-shirt. He shook out his jeans, folded them and set them aside. He went to his bike and removed his new oil lamp from the box in the basket. He unscrewed the top holding the wick and carefully poured scented evergreen oil into its base. He capped the bottle of oil and set it aside. He lit the wick and the flame jumped high. He adjusted the flame height to medium low. He didn't need more light than that.

He set the folded clothes on his bed aside and pulled on his soft hoodie. He sat on his bed, his legs bare, and ate his dinner of a ham sandwich, an apple, some nuts, and water. He thought about his day. He had been at it for twelve hours. Tomorrow would be hard but not as hard as today. Still, it would be hard. He needed to sleep for ten hours. Finished with his dinner, he brushed his teeth and turned off the lamp. The room was nearly pitch black as he slid under his covers. It was only a little after five in the afternoon but it was nearly dark.

Sighing with exhaustion, he closed his eyes.

He dreamed of a better life.

# CHAPTER TWENTY TWO

Larry was back at the loading dock before sunrise. He needed two four-foot pallets and seven five-footers. Nine trips of heavy weight. He got started. He went into a deeper trance of movement. He set his mind on automatic as he shifted the pallets one by one from the loading dock to his home. He no longer felt the weight. It was below freezing and he could see his breath as he moved. There was something in the air that disturbed him. Setting down his last pallet, he went inside and pulled on his coat. He crawled into his bedroll and rested for a while. The cold was dragging him down. His throat hurt. The weight of the large five-foot pallets had strained his back and arms. He was strong, but still, the weight had hurt him.

He waited for his breath and heart to stabilize from his exertions. He knew he would not be getting truly warm any time soon. He had no heat source. He thought of the oil drum in the field. That thing would be hell to move. But at least he could roll it. He was weary of using his body to lift everything. He thought about what he was going to do next.

He would eat now and then go to the hardware store. He would buy a hand saw, a 10' x20' tarp, some aluminum exhaust piping, door hinges, screws, and better gloves. He also needed food for another day, some cooking pots, and firewood.

The list made his lips tighten. It would be expensive. But he also had the means to accomplish it. He had money, his bike for traveling and the basket to carry his loads. He shoved away his complaint. He needed to get up and move forward now. He had rested long enough.

Rising, he left the cover of his bedroll, and went to the grocery bag in the basket on his bike. He ate two doughnuts, some dried fruit, and water. It was not enough against his loss of calories. Calories were always on his mind. It was not just about hunger. It was about the maintenance of his weight and strength. He was mindful to give his body something back for how hard it worked. He tried to balance his labor with serious rest and real food. He tried to keep his calorie loss equal to food eaten. He knew he had not eaten enough for what he had burned this morning. But it would have to do for now. He would not be so hungry later. He rolled his bike through the entry corner of his tarp and lowered the kickstand. The morning was still dark but beginning to pale with early light. It was about 6:30. He would begin with a hot breakfast and coffee from a service station. He would get a load of firewood there too.

Stepping inside, Larry brushed his teeth and layered his clothes. He combed his hair and put on his coat. He got on his bike and rode against the wind of the freezing morning. At the gas station, he bought a hot egg and ham biscuit. He filled his thermos with hot coffee. He loaded three bundles of wood into his basket. He had paid for them. He rode home, ate, and unloaded his firewood.

He went to Walmart for a few pans and food for the day. He rode home and unloaded the contents of his basket onto the floor of his home. He got back on his bike and rode five miles to the hardware store. He bought his pipe fittings, a saw, hinges, a pack of screws, a screwdriver, a pair of sturdier gloves, and the tarp. He rode home and set his bike clear from his construction. The bank sign on the Parkway said it was twenty-eight degrees. It was ten o'clock in the morning. He had ridden twenty miles this morning.

Larry reluctantly shed his coat and set it on his bed. He was cold from the bike rides. The last ten-mile round-trip ride to the hardware store had caused him excruciating pain. He prayed the day would rise above the freezing mark. Working in the sub-freezing temperature was agonizing and draining.

He pulled the entry tarp back over itself. He stoically removed the two button-down layers of his outer shirts and set them on the bed. He left on his two layers of t-shirts. His arms were now exposed to the cold. His skin felt instantly bitten and he was in nearly unbearable pain from the freezing air. He tried to stop shaking as he pulled on his new gloves and began to work.

He stripped the slats off two five-foot pallets. He moved their empty frames to attach to his floor. He was now making the front of his home five feet longer. He took loose boards and finished the floor on the top of these frames.

He set a five-foot pallet on its side and connected it a four-footer. Standing at its head, he reached down and slowly lifted the nine-foot structure until it was standing. He dragged it over to the left wall of his home and joined it to his existing framed wood wall. He nailed them tightly together with the extended top board he'd created earlier. He carried his ladder outside to the middle of his framed wall. He secured the riser with four more boards nailed along its width.

He worked for a while, continuing to create the front wall of his home.

He set down his hammer and ran swiftly to the field. He was burning with the cold. The clouds were shifting overhead and the sun was weak against them. Reaching the oil barrel, he shoved it over and rolled it forward. He moved the barrel back and forth so the old ash would spill from the opening on its side. The ash came out in hardened clumps from past rains. He found a stick and cleared out the remaining dried ash from the bottom of the barrel.

He then began to roll it forward, over the field and asphalt toward his home. He was panting with exertion. The metal barrel was extremely heavy. Reaching his home, he stood the 55-gallon drum upright and slid it into place at the end of his front right wall. He washed the exterior of the barrel with soap and water. He went to his bike basket and collected the aluminum pipe fittings. He fitted the longest portion of his piping into the six-inch smoke hole on top of the barrel. It was a tight fit. He extended the piping so it stuck out sideways, facing away from his home and secure from the rain.

He stripped one side of a three-foot pallet and attached it to the floor beside the barrel. He would leave the top slats open to allow water to run off to the asphalt when he bathed by the fire.

Stepping outside again, he worked to finish the front wall of his home until it was completely framed in.

Now, he had to work on creating a doorway. He paused, considering how this was to be done. He decided to strip two four-foot pallets of their slats, leaving just the frames. When he had two empty frames, he removed one side each of the four-foot squares. Then he attached the two frames together, creating a door opening that was eight feet tall and four feet wide. Using the loose boards, he quickly laid in a door, fitting it to the door frame. He hammered the long boards together by three cross sections. He attached the door to the frame with the hinges. He sawed off the end of a slat and then sawed that piece in half. Using these stubs of wood, he created door handles.

Larry was suffering. He could do anything when it was above freezing, but once the temperature fell below, it became dangerous and painful. He was in great pain. His hands were numb despite his gloves. Yesterday had been at least ten degrees warmer. He couldn't stand against the cold any longer. He needed to gather kindling and get his fire barrel working.

He sprang to his bike and emptied the basket of its contents. He rode his bike to the field, the wind in his hair. He moved fast to find kindling from the field and fill his basket. He returned to his home and parked the bike by the entrance. His home looked entirely different now with the newly created front wall. He still had to finish the tarp roof, set in his door frame, and wrap up the details by using the loose boards to make his structure tight. But first he had to get warm. He was shaking hard from the cold.

He dropped some kindling on the bottom of the barrel and set several logs on top. He covered the logs with more kindling and lit the loose bundle with his lighter. He had to see if his smokestack worked before he nailed down the tarp roof. The fire caught quickly. In minutes the flames were leaping to the lid of the metal barrel. The barrel filled with smoke, then suddenly, the chimney began to draw. Larry breathed a sigh of relief. He knelt on the floor by his fire, his head bowed. He felt the warmth of the flames. He stayed there for a while getting warm. He knew he had to eat. He was low again on calories. He was burning them rapidly. He felt it in his head. He was slightly dizzy. There were small scratches on his arms from grazing the rough wooden pallets. The scratches oozed blood. This was why he hadn't worn his shirts. He knew it wasn't wise, and maybe even dangerous to expose his arms to potential infection. But he had too few garments to lose and he hadn't wanted to get his sleeves bloody or torn.

Rising, he got his thermos and a sandwich. Sitting by the fire again, he ate and drank. He did not linger. He only had four hours of daylight left. He did not smell rain, but he did smell the hard freeze of winter. He needed to finish and shut the door against the threat. He arranged the supplies in his room. He readied his bath and set out his food and gallon jugs of water.

He moved forward to finish his work on the exterior.

He created a base for the door frame to be level with his floor. Sawing the wood took time. He installed the base and joined it to the floor. He lifted his heavy framed door from the asphalt to standing. He dragged it to the base. With the force of his straining body, he lifted the frame and set it on the base. Pulling the door open, he screwed the door frame to the base. Using the loose boards, he cut in and finished the front corner and the floor at the entrance of his home. He cut in and fit boards around the exhaust pipe. He was finished with all of his wooden walls and the entire floor now.

He pulled the ceiling tarp back further. He got his new tarp and unfolded the length. He began at the corner of the front door. Nailing the right end near the asphalt, he opened the tarp and shoved it high over the front slat wall of his home. Going inside, he pulled the leftover width of the tarp tighter. Stepping outside again, he smoothed the tarp down the front wall to the asphalt. He nailed the tarp firmly, all across the bottom of the wall. He came around the corner, fitting the canvas to the left section of his slat wall. He nailed it down across the bottom by the asphalt.

Inside his house, he moved left and right with the ladder to pull the remainder of the ceiling tight. The twenty-foot length of the tarp had wrapped around the exterior front of the house. Now he was only dealing with the two feet left of the ten-foot width. Going outside, he nailed the tarp to the top end of his nine-foot wall. Moving to the right wall, he pulled the incline of the tarp tight and nailed the end to his eight-foot wooden frame.

Now he brought the original tarp forward and over the new front wall. Stepping outside, he tugged and nailed until the tarp was stretched tight and smooth and had a proper incline. He folded the corners neatly and nailed them down. Going inside, he closed the door. It worked well.

Stepping back outside, he quickly created a three-foot incline level to the entry of the door. He rolled his bike up the incline and into his house. The door, smoke stack, and wooden incline all faced away from the parking lot. He had built the left wall higher so no one could see the canvas of his roof. All they would see was a nondescript brown wall that hopefully wouldn't be noticed. And that was if anyone even came or paid attention. He expected no one.

He picked up the remaining boards scattered over the asphalt. He stacked them by size against the back-right wall of the industrial building. He would use them later to create furniture. He was too tired to do it now. His hands hurt and his head ached. He surveyed the area and picked up any nails he could find. It was starting to get dark. He scanned the area again and saw it was clean. Going inside, he brought with him a small piece of wood that he screwed into the door frame as a latch and a lock. Finished, he turned and lit his oil lamp. His fire was going strong. He fed the flames another log. Looking around the room, he felt surprised at the outcome.

The room was spacious and a combination of rough and smooth. The painted concrete walls were light and smooth. The wooden floor was smooth. The front slat walls were rough but they had an interesting look of age and permanence. His ceiling was silver and tight. He was sure his incline would be effective in running off the rain.

Larry liked the room. He understood now why the old homestead shack had no windows. Windows were expensive and it would take a lot of work to frame them in. The owner simply did not have the resources or means. Larry knew he could frame in a window in the front wall of his own homestead, but he would not spend the money. This was not his property. He had invested in what he needed to build but nothing more. Mostly, he had invested his labor and the raw materials of his surroundings. It had taken him two days, but he was now secure from the weather. He had a way to heat himself, wash clothes, warm food, and bathe again. He was filled with an immense relief.

He would not go out again today. He would bathe, heat his can of chunky beef soup, and read. He would finally have a hot dinner. He got his larger pan and filled it with a gallon of water. He set the pan on top of the fire barrel. It fit nicely. He opened his can of soup and poured it into a smaller pan. He set the pan next to his warming water. There was no more room left on the top of the barrel, but he had what he needed. The room was starting to warm from the fire. He would read until his water and soup heated.

Over the next week, he worked the cars in the morning and he worked on his home in the afternoons. He bought a broom and a mop. He washed the floor with soap and water. After the floor dried, he mopped his floor with wood oil polish. The oil darkened and smoothed the floor and the scent made the room smell clean.

He created a four-foot square table and a bench to fit underneath. The table held his newspapers, a couple of legal and corporate novels, and his oil lamp. He would eat there and read.

He created a bed frame of regular height to raise his bedroll off the floor. He even built himself a handsome headboard to go with the bed. He could now sit on his bed to take off or put on his socks and shoes.

He created a small end table by his bed where now another new oil lamp sat. He created a set of two shelves and placed them on the wall by his fire barrel. He washed and polished the wood of all his furniture as well.

He bought a foam mattress for under his bed roll. He bought a pillow, a soft blanket, and an attractive comforter in a pattern of beige, black and forest green.

Walmart had a clearance of 5' x 7' carpets. He found a beige one with a border of green leaves. He had placed it in the middle of the room. It made the room look larger and brighter.

One of his shelves held his gallons of water and his growing store of canned foods. It held a few plates, bowls and glasses from the dollar store. Some of the taller glasses held his cooking utensils and silverware. The shelf also held his pans.

The other shelf held his few new hand and bath towels. It held his folded shirts, t-shirts, underwear, hoodie, and coat.

He had created a moveable rack that he could set by the fire to dry the few garments he washed at night. In the morning, he would move it out of his way again. It didn't matter that his wash dripped. That was what the open-slatted section of the floor was for. It was where he bathed too. The water simply ran off onto the asphalt below.

He had gotten his necessary toilet supplies, including a lightweight, inexpensive toilet seat for the top of the bucket. He had built a table to stand beside his lined bucket. The table created privacy for the toilet and held a box of liners, toilet paper, a large plastic bowl that looked like cut glass for washing his face and hands. It also held a beige hand towel. At the back of the table, he had placed a gold framed mirror.

On the ceiling, in the middle of the room, Larry had installed three lightweight push-button lights. They were simple stick-on's, but the group of three together made the ceiling appear more real. There were times when he wanted more light for reading. The battery-operated lights filled the room with soft light.

It was raining outside now. Larry could hear the rhythm of water pounding his tarp ceiling. The tarp did not move. It was nailed down too tight. Not even the wind affected it. He had been here a little over a week, and in that time, he had made his home comfortable. He had all he needed. It was about 6:00 p.m. on a cold February night. The dark still came early.

He was glad he was indoors. He was thrilled with the comfort and sturdiness of his new place. It was actually handsome. Tonight, in this wicked weather, his overhead lights were on. His oil lamps were lit. The opening of the fire barrel was casting its own glow. He was thankful that he was not outside and in this freezing torrential night. He thought of Buddy Melrose and understood that he would have been out in the deadly cold. It would drive a man to get old quick. Hopelessness and physical discomfort kill the body and spirit. He knew this very well.

He thought of Gus and his gush of words. He knew that Gus was in a bad place. He had to be. There could be no other outcome for him. He had been exceptionally lucky in sorting out the man's words. They had led him here. He had listened, something Gus was not able to do. He thought about Anna and wondered if he had helped her at all to deal with her confusion of why she was so different. He had told her the truth; he was barely hanging on to his own place in life, his sanity and self-worth. He might be walking on his own Plain but still, he was not sure why he was 'there', how he had done it or how yet to manage it. It was a place where he could intuitively hear another's thoughts if he stayed quiet enough to hear them. And, he had connected with hers. He was open to learning more. He knew he would continue to grow.

Larry marveled at his simple but important physical pleasures. His bed was one of them. He was intensely conscious of its effect on his mind and body. He was no longer sleeping on the floor. He was sleeping so comfortably, he was in awe. It was as though the world had changed for him. The pleasure of this critical comfort had changed his whole outlook. When he slipped into bed at night, he now looked forward to it. Being asleep no longer left him vulnerable and a threat to his existence. He was now no longer truly homeless in this wonderful place of comfort, even though the place did not belong to him. And on this freezing February night, he was feeling safe, happy and content.

From this position of strength and inner peace, he thought of Peter. Sitting at his table, Larry wondered what Peter was doing tonight. For the first time, he willed a connection to Peter in real life. If his attempt at making a connection on this night did not work in reality, he would never try again. He was aware of his love for the man; a love developed from his perception of Peter's goodness, his kindness in allowing him to write his articles, and his own profound delusions of Peter caring for him at the old abandoned homestead. He had made Peter his only friend. But it wasn't really true. Peter probably never thought of him at all. But tonight, he willed a meeting of their minds. He wanted Peter to want to see him. He wanted Peter to find him, and reach out to him. *Peter,* he thought intently one last time, *please find me. Please be open to a connection. Please want to know me. Please help me. Please want to be with me. Please find me and figure out how to do all this.* He leaned on the table, holding his forehead in thought. If his effort did not work, he would let the man go. He would let go of his love, though not his admiration. It was time. He would have to make his own way. Nothing of his existence was Peter's fault or burden to bear. Only his own.

Larry wondered how long this new place would last. That was something he could not know. He couldn't know everything. It was not possible. He was just a simple man.

He survived the rest of the winter in his home. Two full months of warm and comfortable living. It all ended with a knock on his door on an early spring day. He had not seen it coming, but he should have.

It was April 4th, 2018.

# CHAPTER TWENTY THREE

*Morning.* Larry had not slept well and because of it, he was not feeling well. He had been bothered by his dreams. There had been a specter of some sort, not a foe, but it had been dark. It had not let him sleep.

He moved to open his door and saw that it was still dark. Shutting the door, he turned on his overhead lights and lit his oil lamps. The scent of the evergreen oil was soothing. He lit his fire and began his coffee. He looked around the room. He had recently oiled his floor and furniture. He loved the clean scent of the polish. Everything looked right. Everything looked tight. Left undisturbed, he thought, this place could last many years. He made his bed, smoothing his blankets and comforter.

He went to his wash stand and rinsed his face. He brushed his teeth and combed his hair. He looked at himself in the gold-framed mirror and touched his beard. It was full and too long. It covered too much of his face. He had not paid enough attention to himself. He had been too busy working and saving. His facial hair had been soft and warm over the winter. It had kept him protected. Now the season had shifted. It was winter no more and he would become clean-shaven this morning. It was time.

March had been cold and rainy. But now, in early April, people were becoming active. Landscape crews were out. Roofers were at work. Construction was happening. It was time to find work. He would go out today and find it.

He moved to dress. He changed his underwear. He pulled on a pale blue button-down shirt from his shelf. He tucked the ends of his shirt into his white fitted underwear. He stepped into his jeans. He zipped and buttoned them and adjusted the band around his waist to be neat and flat. He rolled back his long sleeves. He looked at his hands and wondered what they would do in the future.

He went to his coffee pan on the fire top. It was ready. He pulled a mug from his shelf and filled it. He took his coffee to the table and sat down to read the newspaper he had bought on his way home last night. He read that the Trump administration was threatening China with twenty five percent tariffs — about fifty billion — on their technology and other goods unless they made trade concessions. He shook his head, doubting China would give in. He saw a trade war coming.

He heard a knock on his door. He closed his eyes. He now knew who the dark specter of his dreams had been. He could name it. Dread. He cursed himself for not listening to his own instincts. He cursed himself for listening to others but not to himself. It was too late. Trouble had arrived and there was no escape.

Larry went to the door and opened it wide. He stood silently aside, his shoulders square, allowing the man to enter. He looked at the man. He knew that he was a good man. He could read the man's strong character; the look in his clear eyes, the way that he dressed, the kindness of his face, and the composure of his stance. He was older, maybe fifty. His guard was up, but that was to be expected. He was a stranger in a strange place.

The man looked around in wonder. The room surprised him deeply. It was large and well built. It was clean and neat. It was handsome and comfortable. The scent of the place set him instantly at ease. It was wonderful. It smelled of soap, masculine spice, furniture polish, and the warm fragrance of evergreen. There was also the welcoming aroma of coffee. No crazy vagrant smelled like this; no unwise bum had created this. No. This was a room made of personal discipline with an aim towards excellence. He knew excellence when he saw it. He looked at the furniture and then at the floor. The wood was the same. He realized the man had made his own furnishings and that they were good. Everything matched. Everything was functional. Everything had been cut right. There was nothing in the room that was not needed. He liked it all. He was greatly impressed.

He turned to the man himself. He saw that he was neatly dressed and dressed in a variation of his own clothes, including the rolled sleeves. He saw the man was tall, a little more than his own height. He saw the man's beard and hair were too long but that could be fixed. He liked the man's clear calm eyes. He felt the serenity of him. He was going to offer this man a job. If a man could build this, he could learn anything. He needed good men for his construction crew. Maybe more. He moved his hand forward to introduce himself. The man was lifting his own hand in return when he heard a shout from outside. He heard his name being yelled. It was one of his men. Distracted, he stepped outside.

"Slater, stop yelling," Sherman Roberts commanded, stepping onto the asphalt. He was very much annoyed. He did not like Slater. The man was oily and always trying to push around the crew. "What is it now?"

"The men are restless and don't know what to do. They're idiots. You gotta give 'em some direction." Slater tried to peer around Sherman. He wanted to see what the bum looked like. When Sherman left, maybe he'd rough the guy up a bit when he kicked him out of his shanty. The nerve of some homeless druggie squatting on their property. Well, maybe not their property, but it was their work site.

"I've already told them what to do. Why is there any confusion?" Sherman felt his jaw tighten. He knew that Slater had confused them. He would deal with Slater later, but he had to sort out this mess first. "Let's go."

"I'll stay for a minute and deal with this guy," Slater said, jerking his chin. He punched his hand, thinking his boss would be impressed with his toughness.

"No, you will not, Slater," Sherman said in disgust. "You will come with me now. I said, let's go!"

Slater let it go. He would come back later. He would cut the bum's canvas roof. That would really hurt him. He fell in beside Sherman's determined walk. Slater began to speak. But Sherman turned to him and said, "Just be quiet. I think you have upset the men. I don't want to hear from you right now. Let's keep moving."

Slater shut up. He did not want to lose his job. He had tried to tell the men what to do because they were new. They were just damn stupid Mexicans anyway. He tried to keep up with his boss. Sherman Roberts was an architect and a builder. His firm built everything from hospitals and office complexes to industrial buildings and more. He also modified industrial buildings for a refitting of function. And since his boss paid well, he would shut up for now.

Larry watched the men leave. He'd been lucky that it had been the man rather than the police who had come to his door. Standing in the doorway, he watched the men walk farther away. He did not know who the older man was. But he had liked him. The man seemed to walk on a Plain of his own. They had almost connected. Now he had to go. His time here was over. It was likely the police would be involved in evicting him. He did not want that. He would not wait for it to happen. Turning, he felt a terrible sadness grip his heart. He would miss his home. Desperately.

He loaded his backpack with clothes and food. He untied the basket from his bike. He did not need it any longer. He set it against the wall. He turned off his oil lamps. He threw water on his fire. He did not care about the overhead lights. He thought about bringing his bedroll but it would just get wet. He would lose it anyway. He had to leave now. All it took was one phone call and in two minutes the police could come swarming.

He swung on his backpack, got on his bike, rode down the ramp, across the parking lot, and out of sight. He had become invisible again.

*　*　*　*　*　*

Sherman Roberts drove his truck to the homestead from the loading dock. He would be surprised if the man was still there. He wouldn't have been, were he in his shoes. But he wanted to try. He hadn't even learned the man's name. Damn Slater anyway! He parked and climbed out of his Silverado. He went to the door. He saw that it was open. Everything was the same, except for the essential light of the man. He had left the room. He had been the only thing Sherman was interested in. He decided to fire Slater that afternoon. He rarely got angry. But he was angry now. He felt profoundly robbed, as though he had lost someone very valuable. Yet the man had not spoken a word.

*　*　*　*　*　*

Larry tried not to feel as though his heart was broken. He would survive this just as he had everything else. Still, it was a massive setback. He could not stop the claws of depression from sinking in. They were sharp and he was in pain.

He listened to the clicking of his bike underneath him. He tried to think of what to do. He would go to work. He would figure out where to sleep later. It was too much to think about now. He went to his favorite intersection.

As he worked, he felt the specters of tears, dread, and fear battle him all day. They would rise within him and he would fight them down. But they were wearing on him. He had not eaten all day but he was not hungry. He worked longer than he had intended. With nowhere to go, it didn't seem to matter. The days were getting longer and warmer. He continued to work. He watched the sun. It was three o'clock now. He would work until four. Then he would get a bottle at the liquor store. Then he would go to Waffle House and get something to eat. Then he would figure out where to spend the night.

He moved forward with his plan.

Larry had tried to eat at Waffle House, but his plate was mostly full when he left the restaurant. He rode towards Main Street. He did not go to the main road itself, but turned early, making a right onto the small road that separated the parking lots from the stores and restaurants facing Main

Street. He was behind those stores and restaurants now. His bike wheels clicked to a stop. He looked at the picnic tables outside a closed barbecue restaurant. The huge black roasting-smoker was sitting cold.

He decided that he would sit here for a while. Then he would spend the night in the walking park behind him. There was a bench not quite a quarter mile up on the path, easy for his bike to reach. He would sleep on the bench, tucked away from sight. Tomorrow, he would feel better. He always needed time to recover from his traumas. He did not try to kid himself any longer. He was traumatized. A tear slid down his cheek. He sighed, straddling the bike, his face in his hands. It would be a long night.

Larry heard people talking as they made their way to their car in the parking lot on his right. He moved his bike forward, parked it, and sat at a picnic table. He glanced at the sun. It was beginning to set. It was about seven o'clock now. It would be dark in an hour. The breeze was beginning to pick up. He was grateful that it was not cold. Last night had been a full moon. It would begin its first phase of waning tonight. It would be high and clear in the night sky. He would be able to see. He had one candle with him. There were only two hours left on it but he had packed it anyway. He would light it after dark while he took his few sips of his bourbon. When the fire went out, he would move to the park bench to sleep. It was the only plan he could think of now. He bowed his head in misery and waited for the night to come.

He crossed his arms on the table and slowly lowered his forehead to rest on them. He slept for a while. He woke up feeling sad, the darkness all around him, the moon shining down on him. He heard no people, only the raucous cries of a barred owl and the far away barking of a dog.

He pulled his backpack to him and lit the candle. He opened his bottle of whiskey. He had no glass so he would have to drink from the bottle. He didn't mind if he got drunk, but he couldn't get too drunk. He still had to ride his bike to the bench. The breeze was stronger now, but the night was clear and quiet. He opened the bottle and took his first sip.

He saw his candle flicker and die. Two hours had passed.

He began to rise off the bench but the world dipped and spun around him. Oh god, what have I done, he thought, gripping the table. He sank back down slowly, realizing that he was very drunk. He tried to rise again. He tried to move his leg over the picnic bench. He choked with horror as he realized that he was in free fall to the ground. He hit hard but managed to spare his face from hitting the dirt. He rolled over and stared at the moon. He blinked at the glowing whiteness against the black of night. His vision blurred as he heard laughter. He could not raise his guard against them. He was too drunk.

They dragged him up off of the ground. They pushed him around between them as he staggered on his feet. He tried repeatedly to get his brain to engage, but he could not. They were loud and laughing as they each took turns punching him in the ribs and stomach. He absorbed their blows feeling but not feeling. He vaguely understood that they might kill him. He could conjure no defense to their assault.

He got that there were three of them. He got that they were young, in their mid-teens. But he could not get more than that. They were hurting him. They were bringing him down. They were dragging him forward. He felt tears spike down his cheeks at his own helplessness. They laughed at his tears, and hit him harder. Their blows continued to come. Somewhere within him, he could not believe this was happening to him. He fell to the ground. They kicked him over and stomped on his chest, stomach, and ribs with their feet.

\*   \*   \*   \*   \*   \*

Sherman Roberts parked his truck at the loading dock. It was late at night. About eleven o'clock. He had been at his office and needed to go home. He had driven here instead. He let himself into the building, a flashlight in his hand. The cavernous building smelled of emptiness, sawdust, drywall, and fresh wood. He didn't know what he was doing. He could inspect the work of his crew in the morning. He realized then that he had not come for his inspection but for the homeless man. He wanted to try again.

He left the building and walked to his truck. He opened the door and tossed the flashlight on the passenger seat. He looked up at the sky. It was dark but the moon was high. It was still nearly full in its brightness. He could see in front of him. He decided to walk to the man's tarp-covered home. He thought of his perceptions of the early morning. He had been so impressed by the way it felt, the enticing way that it had smelled. He remembered the man's eyes. He had wanted to know him. He moved forward in the night toward the tarp structure. He came around the industrial building. From the shadows, he felt movement. He watched as Slater cut the man's roof. He was standing on the man's home-built ladder with his knife, puncturing and cutting.

Sherman watched as the ceiling slowly collapsed and fell into the room. He saw no one come out the door. He waited for that, staying in the shadows. Slater had a knife and he had been angry that he had been fired. If the homeless man was there, he would step forward to help protect him. If not, he would leave. His hand went to the phone in his pocket. He thought about calling the police over Slater's vandalism. He lowered his hand. Exactly what would he report? There was nothing. They had to tear down the home anyway. He felt a great regret for both the man and his home. He waited another minute to see if the man was there. Surely, he would come out as his roof fell upon him. Nothing happened. Sherman determined that the man was gone. He was filled with contempt for Slater as he returned to his truck, glad that he had fired him. He started his engine. There was nothing more that he could do here. He put his Silverado in reverse, backed out, and drove home.

*　*　*　*　*　*

Larry knew he had to get out from under their feet, their kicks and stomps. He drunkenly rolled and came to his knees. One teen grabbed the collar of his blue shirt. They were on him again, laughing and talking loudly. He felt the buttons of the thin fabric give way under the jerking of his attacker. He moved his arms back and let his shirt slide off him into the hands of the assaulting teen. He had to get away from them before they tore off his white undershirt. He rose to his feet and staggered forward. He made it to an alley between the buildings.

The three boys followed him, taunting him loudly. They brought him down again. He heard himself say the words, "Please stop." The boys found it funny to hear him beg. One teen held him while the others plowed their punches into his stomach and ribs. He sank to his knees, defenseless. The alley was spinning and his vision would not clear. Then something came down hard on the front of his head. He thought of Peter and suddenly, the man of the morning entered his mind as well. He felt one last moment of clarity that this could be his final breath on Earth. He fell slowly forward and hit the pavement of the street.

One teen rifled through Larry's back pocket and came away with his wallet. He held it up, crowing in the moonlight. Another went for Larry's bike. They were proud of themselves that they had beaten up an old home-less man. They looked down at the man lying unconscious in the street. They joked that he would be finished off by a car. They hoped that the worthless old bastard would die as they continued to laugh and went on their way.

*　*　*　*　*

Sherman Roberts, president and owner of a huge architectural firm in Atlanta, slid under the covers of his bed. His wife was already asleep next to him. He thought of Larry, although he did not know Larry's name. He tried to settle down to sleep. He was feeling acutely upset.

Peter Bennett, the director of a massive progressive political web-based newspaper in New York, looked up from his computer at his desk at home. He thought of Larry. He wondered why he couldn't get in touch with him. He had called the man many times.

Both men felt an internal disturbance. Both men felt unsettled. Neither knew exactly why except that their thoughts were on Larry. Both had felt a connection. The disturbance was strong, even as it was dissipating.

Larry's blood ran from above his forehead and dripped onto the street. He was alone under the wane of the moon. He felt nothing at all.

# CHAPTER TWENTY FOUR

Larry gradually regained consciousness. Slowly and painfully, he cracked open his dry, gritty eyes. He felt like his eyeballs were glued to his eyelids. He was lying on his chest and the pavement beneath him was hard and hot. He felt like his head was split open and his body ached all over. He wondered if anything was broken. He thought of Buddy Melrose and for the hundredth time, wondered if Buddy had died from internal injuries or the cold. He would never know, but he could relate to Buddy's pain now. He felt utterly broken. But, he thought, feeling emotionally broken and actually being broken are two different things. He shifted his arms and legs to find out. To his vast relief, everything worked. Breathing heavily, he tried to stand. His vision danced and he was as dizzy as though he were still drunk.

Staggering to his feet, he sagged against a wall in the alley until his head cleared. His ribs hurt and his forehead was itchy with crusty blood. He ran the tip of his tongue over his parched, cracked lips. He needed water and maybe some medical attention but he had no idea how to get either. He realized that the heat of the pavement had probably prevented him from going into shock from his injuries. The heat had kept his heart and feet warm. Glancing at the sun, he knew that he had been out for the entire night. As bad as his condition was, the other truth was, he had survived and things could be worse.

Holding his head, Larry recognized that he was still in one of the narrow alleys in downtown Balfour, directly off Main Street.

Stumbling out of the alley, Larry turned left down a sidewalk on Main Street. Fortunately for him, the streets were still fairly empty. As he passed boutiques and other shops, he glimpsed himself in the reflection of their storefront windows. He looked like a disheveled maniac and he wasn't surprised when the few people he encountered on the sidewalk shrank from him. Two young teenage girls with shopping bags gave him a wide berth as he ambled by, disgust written on their fresh, wholesome faces. Not much later, a twenty-something man lifted his phone and stepping closer, snapped a photo of Larry. Humiliated beyond measure, Larry straightened his shoulders and looked the man in the eye. "Why did you take my picture?"

"I shoot interesting things," he replied, surprised the gentle clearness of Larry's voice. "Not that you're a thing . . . "

"And what do you see?"

The man studied Larry for a moment. "I see a man who has fallen on hard times."

Larry nodded. "Keep my picture as a reminder that hard times can happen swiftly. Be good to everyone so that you have friends to help you when such a time comes upon you."

The man's eyes widened in surprise. "Jesus, I feel like I've just talked to Moses come down from the mountain to give me a message."

Larry almost smiled. He probably did look like Moses with his shaggy brown hair and wild beard. But he was in terrible pain from an aching body, hunger, and dehydration. He needed to find water immediately. With a slight nod of his head, Larry moved on, shuffling painfully down the sidewalk as the younger man stared after him. A few hundred yards ahead, Larry saw a restaurant with covered outdoor seating. Remembering that he still had plenty of money, he considered buying a cold beer and his hand fumbled to his back pocket in search of his wallet. It was gone. The punks had not only beaten him, they had also robbed him. They had laughed as they had beaten him, and they had probably laughed over stealing his wallet as well. Cursing inwardly, Larry wondered if he could at least use the bathroom to wash up. He could drink water from the sink. The thought of wetting his dry mouth consumed him as he made his way to the restaurant.

Reaching the outdoor patio, Larry saw the table area was surrounded by an ornate, white wrought iron fence. As he found the gate to gain entry, he immediately spied a nice-looking couple sitting at a table. The girl was playing with her cell phone and the man was typing on his laptop. Larry zoomed in on the laptop. Coming closer to them, Larry said, "Forgive me for interrupting you."

They both glanced up at Larry in surprise. Larry took a step closer and said, "I've been beaten and robbed. I've been wandering around for some days trying to figure out my name."

"Oh wow," the girl gasped, "Do we need to call the police for you?"

Larry shook his head. "What I would like, if you're willing, is for you to bring up a website called The Political Standard and let me take a quick look at it."

"I know it," the man replied. "I read it and even have it on my toolbar. I'll open it." He did so and the website quickly appeared on his screen.

"May I look?" Larry asked, trembling. "May I come closer to look as you scroll through the site? I am looking for something specific."

"Yes," replied the man, sliding his chair over to allow Larry room to view the laptop screen. When Larry was in place, the man tried not to breathe in Larry's stink as he began to slowly scroll through the site.

Crouching down to see better, Larry remained silent, holding his breath, as the depth bar on the side of the screen went lower and lower. Finally, near the bottom, nearly ready to fall off the page, were the two articles Larry was looking for. Tears leaked from his eyes as he pointed to his education article. His dirty finger was shaking as he choked out through his tears, "That's me. I wrote that . . . and this one too," pointing to his other article on the consequences of the forced reproduction of women. "That's me . . . I am Larry Martin."

"Oh, God . . . you're a journalist for The Standard?" The man's face was a study in both shock and admiration. "You're like, important, then."

"No," Larry said, straightening his back. "No. But if I can use your cell phone, I would like to call my editor."

"Yes. Of course," the man replied, picking up the phone and offering it to Larry.

Larry did not take the phone. "As I don't know my way around your phone, would you dial the number for me? And once I have a connection, would you mind if I took it to that corner over there to have a private conversation? I swear to you I will go no further with your phone. "

"All right. What's the number?"

Larry gave it to him. Peter's number was the only number he had ever bothered to memorize except for his Social Security number. But that wasn't surprising. Peter was also the only person who actually meant something to him. The man dialed the number and when it rang on the other end, he handed the phone to Larry. Taking it, Larry moved to the far corner of the patio by the iron fence, his back to the couple, praying that Peter would answer.

Peter did. "Hello?"

"Peter, it's Larry."

"My God, Larry! Where have you been? I've tried to call you a dozen times with the news that the Board approved your articles and they were published two weeks ago."

"I've been on the streets for a while, Peter. Homeless. It's been rough," Larry said quietly. "I no longer have a phone. I'm using a stranger's phone now. He was kind enough to let me see The Standard on his laptop too. I saw the articles and I was so happy, I called you. Thank you so much."

"I have to ask, Larry . . . are you homeless because of drugs?"

"No. After I left Ellison Bart, I couldn't find another job. Things went downhill fast. Not long after I wrote those articles for you, I was evicted. I've been on the streets ever since."

"I see." Peter went quiet for a second. Then, he said, "I'll bet you've had a real education to the other side of life."

"Yes. I have. You cannot know, Peter. It has been awful . . . but I have learned so much."

"Where are you now?"

"Still in Georgia. In a town called Balfour, not too far from Canton."

Peter pulled the laptop on his desk closer. "I'm looking . . . hold on . . . okay, there is an extended-stay motel on the outskirts of Balfour. I can book you a suite. This is what I am thinking . . . would you be willing to write about your experience? Tell your story honestly?"

"Yes. I can do that. I have much to say." Larry's eyes were leaking again in relief.

"You'll have to find the right angle, and I can't tell you what that is . . . but you'll have to find it. Perhaps we could do a series of articles if you've got enough content to sustain that much."

"I . . . can't know that yet. It depends on my approach and how it goes. I am afraid of any promises except that I will work hard and write it real."

"All right. Good enough. I am booking your room as we speak. I take it you don't have a car . . ."

"No. I don't." The old Larry would have wise-cracked, "My Ferrari's in the shop." But the new Larry had no cockiness. He was close to fainting anyway.

"What is the address where you're at now?"

"Let me find out, Peter. Hold on while I ask someone." Turning around, Larry walked back to the owner of the cell phone. "Do you know the address here?"

The man rose from the table, saying, "Let's go inside and find out." Together, they entered the restaurant. The hostess at the front counter recoiled when she saw the bloodied, filthy man that was Larry. The man by Larry's side barked at her, "Quick, what's the address of this restaurant?" Larry held out the phone so Peter could hear her answer.

"4826 East Main Street," she replied, jerking at the harshness of the man's tone.

Raising the phone to his ear, Larry said, "Did you get that, Peter?"

"Yes. 4826 . . . okay, I am sending you a car. Can I use this number to confirm your ride?" Larry looked at the man, and he was nodding. He had heard Peter's question.

"What's going on here?" the hostess demanded.

Larry held up his hand to her as Peter was still talking, "Let me know when you're in your room, okay? I'll arrange for you to get some necessities as well."

"'Okay. Thank you, Peter. I am very grateful. I will talk to you soon." The call finished, Larry handed the cell phone back to its owner. To the hostess, he said, "In short, I'm a journalist. I have been beaten and robbed and my New York editor is arranging a car for me. May I use your restroom to clean up a bit?"

With her mouth formed in an 'O', she nodded, pointing to where the restrooms were located. To the man, Larry said, "I won't be long. Can you keep an eye out for my ride confirmation?"

The man nodded his agreement and asked, "Say, are you hungry? Can I buy you something to eat?"

"A beer and fries would be great, if it's not too much trouble. Thank you. I am famished. I am also happy to pay you back."

"No, no. It's on me. It's simple enough." the man replied. To the hostess, he asked, "Can you get that ordered immediately and have it brought to my table on the patio?"

"Yes. I'll do it right now. "

"Thanks. I appreciate it." As the hostess went to make the order, the man went back to his table while Larry headed to the restroom.

In the restroom, Larry stripped off his ragged t-shirt. He quickly scrubbed off the crusty blood on his forehead. He washed his face, arms, and armpits. Ignoring the cuts and dark bruises on his chest, ribs, and stomach, he rinsed his mouth several times and spat the water into the sink. Then he lowered his head into the sink and let the warm water run over his hair. Grabbing a handful of paper towels, he dried his hair and body the best he could. After pulling his t-shirt back on, he ran his fingers through his hair in an effort to comb back the length. Then with more towels, he dried up the wet floor and sink area out of respect for the restaurant. Glancing at himself in the mirror, he saw that he looked terrible. But, he thought, smiling wryly, it does feel good to be someone again.

Returning to the couple's table on the patio, the man said, "Please, sit. Your food is here and I got your confirmation. Your ride will be here in 21 minutes."

Sinking into the chair, Larry brought the cold beer to his lips. Never had anything tasted so good in his life. After taking a long swig, he dug into his fries and worked to eat normally as opposed to ravaging them. The man was back on his laptop, allowing Larry to enjoy his food in peace. The girl often looked at Larry but just smiled. She too remained quiet. When he was done eating, Larry closed his eyes and marveled at the miracle that had just taken place. He reflected that if his wallet had not been stolen, he would not have had the right story to tell. As a homeless man, he would have just frightened this couple. But being the victim of robbery and worse, beaten, well, that could elicit sympathy and goodwill from nearly anyone. It was all about the wallet. Literally. Funny how the theft had changed his life, that something so bad could make something so good happen. Those thugs would never know what a great favor they had done him. Larry's eyes were still closed when the man said softly, "Mr. Martin, your car is here."

Rising slowly and agonizingly, Larry held out his hand. "I believe your kindness saved my life. What is your name?"

The man stood and shook Larry's washed hand. "My name is Sam Whittaker. This is my girlfriend, Nell Beaumont. We're very glad for you that things have worked out."

"Well, Mr. Whittaker, you are forever my friend. You too, Miss Nell. I am in your debt. If you ever need anything, don't hesitate to ask. You know where to find me."

"Yes, sir. I do."

With a nod to Nell and a smile at Sam, Larry exited the patio and walked with dignity to the car. He was bruised and battered and dirty but no longer broken. He had hope now. It made all the difference.

Larry smiled when he saw the long, sleek silver Lincoln. Peter had always been first class, he thought.

At the sight of Larry and his bloody shirt, the driver slowly slid out of his seat frowning as he slowly opened the back door. "My name is Alan, Mr. Martin. I am to be your driver for as long as you're in town."

Climbing onto the cool leather of the backseat, Larry tried to sit up straight, keenly aware that Alan looked confused and unhappy and was watching him intently as he stood by the door. Larry quickly analyzed that if Alan was to be his driver for as long as he was in town, it also meant that he worked for Peter. He couldn't see any other service doing this. It would simply cost too much. Alan's concern over him was palpable and he needed to say something at this very moment to put Alan at ease. He settled on the truth. Turning his head to gaze at his driver, he spoke in a voice that was low, calm, and clear. "Alan, your car is beautiful. I am sorry that I am so dirty. But I have traveled a very long road to get here. Please forgive me."

Alan studied Larry eyes. This bloody, filthy man had taken him by surprise. The man had seen violence, something he personally avoided and wanted no part of. As he heard the words, his perception of Martin shifted profoundly. Martin's eyes were clear and focused as they looked back, unwavering, into his own. This man was no bum. And, he was somehow attached to Peter Bennett. He needed to respond. He settled on the truth. "I don't pretend to understand, Mr. Martin, but it's my job to drive you and I will. Your appearance has made me wary and I apologize."

Larry closed his eyes and sighed. "I wish you wouldn't. I saw myself in the mirror in the bathroom of the restaurant. I'm well aware of what I look like. It's not good."

Alan saw the man was exhausted. "Let's get started then. I'm here to help you all I can. I'm going to close the door now." He watched Larry nod and settle back into the seat as he firmly shut the door.

# CHAPTER TWENTY FIVE

Before Alan started the car, he turned to look back at Larry. In his hand was a plain crème colored envelope. "This is for you, sir. Mr. Bennett said you should have this to shop with. I am to take you to any store of your choosing for fresh clothes and personal items."

Taking the envelope, Larry's eyes misted but he was determined to remain professional. If Peter had that much faith in him, he would return the favor by being someone worth investing in. Opening the envelope, Larry saw three one hundred-dollar bills. He suspected the money came from Peter's own pocket rather than the budget of The Political Standard. Raising his eyes to meet Alan's, Larry replied quietly, "Let's just go to Walmart. I can get simple necessities there until I get to New York."

"All right." Alan settled in his seat and turning on the engine of the limo, eased out of the parking lot.

As elated as Larry was over his miracle, his adrenaline was now plummeting from being safe. He suddenly felt deep weariness seep into his bones. As they pulled into the Walmart parking lot, Larry asked Alan for help with his shopping. Alan easily agreed, knowing there was no way Martin could handle shopping for himself. He steered Larry to the men's department. "Choose a few things here and I'll get the rest." Larry's gentle nature had touched him and now, he was feeling concerned. He wasn't at all sure how steady Larry was on his feet. He touched Larry's arm, "You going to make it?"

"Yes. I have to. Go on. I will be okay," Larry responded softly. "Let's do this as fast as we can, so we can get out of here."

Alan nodded. "What size shoe?"

"Eleven."

Alan placed his hands on Larry's shoulders and shook him slightly. "Do not go anywhere. I will come back to you and we'll check out together. Agreed?"

"Yes."

As Alan left, Larry tried to focus. Falling into his task, he chose a few button-down shirts, dark colored tees, a pair of dress slacks, a simple blazer, and a new pair of jeans.

Alan was quickly collecting packaged underwear and socks, a set of cotton pajamas, a terry cloth robe, new sneakers and bedroom slippers. Moving his cart swiftly to the personal products aisle, he also tossed in shaving items, a toothbrush and toothpaste, a hair brush, deodorant, shampoo, and a small bottle of cologne. Between them, they were out of the store in forty minutes and on the road again.

"How about a barber now?" Alan asked, glancing at Larry through the rearview mirror. The man's face was hidden beneath a shaggy dark beard. His hair was greasy, long, and lank. He figured Mr. Martin's age to be in the early forties.

"Yes. Just a simple shop, please, if you know of one."

"There's one up the street. I'll drop you off and go to the grocery for you. After you get your haircut, I'll take you to the hotel and it has a kitchen. You'll want food there, right?"

"Yes. I'm not sure what I'm supposed to be doing there though."

"Mr. Bennett said you were to rest for a few days. Your suite is actually very nice. He said to tell you to call him when you are settled and feel strong enough to talk."

"Okay."

"Anything you want in particular from the store?" Alan asked.

"No. Just the basics, and, please, Alan, don't buy much. I don't know my plans yet. Do you need money?"

"No. I'll use the corporate credit card this time."

Larry closed his eyes and leaned back into the marvelous comfort of his seat. The car smelled like new leather. If he'd had a blanket, he would have gone to sleep on the long, buttery soft seat. But he didn't dare to even think about falling asleep, and his gritty eyes remained alert behind his drooping eyelids. Shopping had further drained him, but he still had a few last fumes of awe and amazement to keep him going.

Alan pulled into a strip mall parking lot. "Here you go, Mr. Martin. I texted the barber shop and they are expecting you."

"Thank you, Alan," Larry said, hiding his surprise at Alan's efficiency. Alan stepped out of the car and opened Larry's door. As Larry got out, he said, "You'll be a new man when you leave this place. I come here fairly often and they do amazing things with hot cloths and flat stones."

Larry nodded and tried to smile. Alan was working so hard for him. He deeply appreciated it. He began to turn to go into the shop. But Alan stopped him with his arm and Larry stopped moving.

"Wait, hold on . . . let's get you into a clean shirt first." Alan went to the trunk and dug through the bags. Grabbing a button-down shirt, he handed the garment to Larry. Larry quickly stripped off his bloody t-shirt and slid into the new light blue plaid, buttoning it slowly. Seeing the damage to Larry's chest, back, stomach and ribs, Alan sucked in his breath and winced. The man had been badly beaten. But why? When Larry was finished fumbling with his buttons, Alan lifted Larry's wrists and gently rolled up the cuffs. To Alan's eye, Larry looked like he was close to sleep-walking. "Better now. You okay?"

"Yes."

"All right. Go, enjoy yourself. Seriously. You'll feel much better when you leave here. I promise. I'll see you shortly."

Forty-five minutes later, Larry walked out of the barber shop. Alan had been right. He touched his smooth cheek and smiled. He did feel like a new man. His face was clean-shaven now and his hair was perfectly cut and layered just above his ears. The barber had been kind and said nothing about his awful appearance. There had been moments when the small gash in his scalp had stung from the soap, and his bruised ribs had pulsed with pain from leaning his head back or sitting too long. But it had been worth it.

Alan drove up then. He got out of the car and slowly walked over to Larry. Sliding off his sunglasses, he asked softly in wonder, "Is it you?"

"Yes. It is. And, you were right, Alan. I feel so much better."

Alan smiled, shaking his head. Never would he have believed such a change was possible. It was purely incredible. "You look good," he said. "Now, come on, let's get you to the hotel."

As Larry climbed into the backseat, Alan said, "I didn't buy you much, but I covered breakfast and one real dinner. The rest is soups, rolls, and butter. You also have a deli tray of cold cuts, salad, cheese, and fruit. The hotel supplies the coffee."

"That's perfect. Thank you, Alan. I greatly appreciate all you have done."

Alan shut Larry's door and got into his own seat. He set the GPS and started the car.

"How long do you suppose I'm here?" Larry asked, as Alan smoothly turned onto the road.

"That's up to Mr. Bennett. Honestly, Mr. Martin, I don't know how long you'll be in Atlanta. But for now, our ride will take about sixteen minutes." Alan fell quiet as he observed Martin through his rearview mirror. The man seemed completely overwhelmed and exhausted. He wanted to ask Martin what had happened to him but he was too professional to do so. He said nothing more as he watched the man sigh several times before closing his eyes.

At the Balfour Suites, Alan left Larry sleeping in the backseat while he carried the numerous shopping bags into the room. He put the groceries in the refrigerator and arranged the nonperishables neatly on the kitchen counter. Dumping the bags of clothes and personal products onto the bed, Alan set the bath supplies in the bathroom and hung the bathrobe on the hook behind the door. The new shirts, pants, and blazer went into in the closet, neatly hung, with the new box of sneakers set below on the floor. He tidily stacked the pajamas, slippers, and underwear on the desk for Mr. Martin to get to easily and immediately.

Alan looked around. He had done his best to get Mr. Martin settled. He really liked the guy. He had expected to pick up some self-absorbed prick. Journalists often were. He wasn't sure what Martin was, but a journalist didn't seem to fit him. In his job, he had driven all sorts of people, from arrogant celebrities, stressed wedding couples, cocky jerks, and rude partiers to the typical businessmen who never looked up and never acknowledged him. But he had never driven anyone like this man. When he'd first seen Martin, dirty, bloody, and unkempt, walking to his car from the restaurant, he was so put off he almost didn't let the man into his lovely new Lincoln. But Peter Bennett was one of his best clients. If Bennett said to pick up Mr. Martin, help him shop and get whatever he needs, he would do it. Still, it was close there. Very close. Martin's eyes and demeanor had quickly changed his mind. The man's gaze had been level and intelligent, his words soft spoken and precise. Alan knew then, Martin was not a bum, druggie, or someone he should not allow into his vehicle.

Martin seems to have this genuine, valiant spirit, Alan mused, but he's so wiped out, it actually affects me. He couldn't put his finger on the guy. He's a walking dichotomy, he thought. Strong but fragile. He looked like a derelict but talked like an intellectual. Yet, while he talks easily enough, he says not one word about himself. Who doesn't talk about themselves? But, of course, the one time I actually want to know . . . I get nothing. Alan pondered the thought. When Martin had come out of the barber shop so transformed, he had not believed his eyes. The man had become shockingly handsome and twenty years younger. He'd been astonished that Martin was his own age. A young guy. He also liked Martin's low laugh and the measured way he parceled out words, thoughtful-like. If he lived in town, Alan thought, I'd pursue him as a friend. With one last glance around the suite, Alan knew he had done all he could for now. It was time to wake Mr. Martin.

Returning to his car, Alan opened the back door and gazed at the sleeping man. Larry was sitting upright, his lashes and brows dark against the pale smoothness of his skin. His bowed lips were relaxed and his hands were resting loosely on his lap. "Mr. Martin," Alan said softly, "I need you to wake up now."

"Okay, Peter," Larry murmured, dreaming, "just give me a minute. I'll build up the fire but I can't battle anymore . . . " His voice drifted off. Larry felt Peter shaking his shoulder. He tried to focus on what Peter was saying: "You're not here anymore, Larry. There are no more battles. Pay attention to where you are now. Wake for Alan."

Alan's brows came together, still gazing at Larry. Wherever Mr. Martin was, it wasn't here. Apparently, he and Mr. Bennett had been in some kind of battle together. Were they war buddies? That would explain why Bennett wanted him to take such good care of Martin.

"Mr. Martin, it's Alan." He shook Larry's shoulder lightly again. "Please wake up now. We've arrived at your suite."

"Okay, Alan," Larry said, trying to open his heavy eyelids. He brought his hands up to massage his pounding temples. "I am awake now. Point me to the trunk and I will carry in some bags."

"No, it's all done. Just hand me your backpack and I'll help you to the room."

Larry grabbed his worn pack off the seat and handed it to Alan. Wearily, he swung his legs out of the car and standing, he drew in a breath of fresh air to clear away the sleepy fog still gripping his brain. He was still feeling dizzy from it all; his miracle, his hunger, the stabbing pain in his ribs, and his sheer exhaustion, but he gave Alan a slight smile. "Okay. You lead, I will follow."

Opening the door to the suite, Alan handed Larry the key and explained what he had done in the room. "I'll leave you now, but here is my card. You're to call me when you need to go anywhere, okay?"

Larry took the business card and said, "Thank you, Alan. I will look forward to seeing you again soon."

Alan stood silently, examining Larry. He knew there was nothing more he could do for him at the moment, except tuck him into bed if he had to.

Larry smiled gently, noting Alan's disquiet. "Go on now, Alan. Really. I am fine. I will call you."

Alan turned to leave and stepping out of the room, he pulled the heavy door closed behind him until heard it latch.

Larry headed straight for the shower. He soaped and let the hot water run over his sore, bruised body for a long ten minutes. His fingers explored the cuts and bruises of his torso. It wasn't good, but neither was it serious. There was nothing that wouldn't heal on its own. Getting out of the shower, he dried up and got into his pajamas. He ate some fruit and a buttered roll to ease the empty knot in his stomach. Then he called Peter.

Peter answered the phone on the second ring. "I was just thinking of you. Are you settled in?"

Larry spoke softly and slowly. "I am. I still can't thank you enough. The suite is wonderful. And, Alan has been the very best; efficient, helpful, kind, and forward-thinking. He is truly impressive, Peter. I wanted you to know."

"Good. I like Alan. He's always been excellent as our Atlanta driver. I'll certainly tip him well on your behalf."

"Thank you, Peter. Now . . . what's next?"

"I thought you might like a few days to recover from your ordeal."

"No. Please, if it's okay, Peter, I want to work. I need to work. As soon as possible. That will help me recover more quickly than anything."

"Then I'll arrange a flight for you to New York. I want to see you and talk business."

Larry emitted a small sound of frustration. "Since my wallet has been stolen, I cannot go anywhere without a replacement driver's license."

"Can you get one?"

"Yes. My car died a while back. If it has not been moved, I have a file of personal documents, my birth certificate and so on in the trunk. That should do it."

"Okay. Get Alan to help you. Keep me informed."

"Okay. Again, Peter, thank you for everything. I will get started first thing." Hanging up, he called Alan to arrange an early morning start. Closing the drapes against the afternoon sun, Larry climbed into bed and slept for fourteen hours straight. He dreamed of Peter, but now they were laughing over a beer at a restaurant. This time, Peter wasn't just a figment of his imagination.

Rising early, Larry made a breakfast of scrambled eggs, a toasted muffin, and orange juice. He turned on the TV, but the noise turned his stomach so he switched the set off. After tidying the kitchen, he showered, shaved, and dressed in new clothes: a black pullover, dark jeans, and white sneakers. He slapped on a touch of cologne and was sliding into his blazer when Alan knocked. Striding to the door, Larry let him in.

Stepping into the room, Alan was deeply astounded at the change in Martin. It was impossible to believe that this was the same man he'd picked up yesterday. This morning, Larry was looking young, healthy, energetic, and sharp. Alan was so used to saying 'Good morning, Boss' to his rides — they liked it; it made them feel important — that the words slipped out now. He had not meant to say it, and wished he could take it back. From the flicker in Larry's eyes, he knew he had made a mistake.

"Good morning, Alan. Pour yourself a cup of coffee and come sit down."

Alan didn't want a cup but he did as he was told. Sinking into the armchair, he set the mug on the coffee table and waited for Larry to speak. Larry moved to the sofa across from him and sat down.

"Listen," Larry began gently, "please just call me Larry. Especially after your wonderful care yesterday. So, not Mr. Martin, not Boss . . . just Larry. Okay?"

"Of course. Have I offended . . . "

"No, no. Nothing like that. It's just that I would be more comfortable. Now, for today . . . I need to get a cell phone. We also must go to my car at an abandoned homestead so I can retrieve a personal file hidden in the trunk. It's not far. Then we need to go to the DMV so I can get a new license. After that, we must go to a post office so I can put in a change of address. Then, I want to get a newspaper and a legal novel."

"A newspaper and a novel?"

Larry lips tightened into an amused grin, showing a small dimple on the left side of his mouth. "People do still read them, Alan."

Alan laughed. "I'm sure. Larry, have you and Mr. Bennett been in a war together?"

Larry blinked, tilting his head slightly, mystified.

"It's just that yesterday, when I tried to wake you in the car, you said something like, 'Peter, I'll build a fire but I can't battle anymore.' So, I figured that 'battle' meant you guys had fought together somewhere . . . "

"I have never been in the military, Alan," Larry said slowly, "but . . . there are all kinds of battles."

"I didn't mean to pry. I'm sorry. "

"No worries. We have a full day ahead of us. Is that okay with you?"

"Yes. Anything you want."

Larry stood up. "Good. Then, let's go."

The cell phone had been easy. Alan put it on the credit card. Larry knew he would pay Peter back. Now he had the means to stay in touch and use the internet. Returning to the abandoned homestead was harder. Approaching the putrid place, Larry's throat tightened and he was nauseated. It looked worse than ever. But he could see his car was just as he had left it.

"Stay put," he instructed Alan. "Do not get out of the car. Nothing good happens here. I will get what I need and we'll move on to the DMV." Sliding out of the Lincoln, Larry went to his trunk and opened it. He knew where the file was and thanked the heavens that he'd had the presence of mind to save his precious personal documents. All things considered, it was another miracle. Slamming the trunk lid closed, he whispered goodbye to his old Toyota as he knelt to remove its license plate to erase his tracks. He could be still found, but he wouldn't make it easy. Now, his Toyota was just an abandoned car. Clutching the file and the metal plate in his hand, he climbed back inside the chilled interior of Alan's sleek, silver car.

That evening, he called Peter, holding a temporary paper license in his hand. "I can fly now."

"Excellent. I'll have Marion, my secretary, call you in the morning with flight arrangements."

"Okay. I got a cell phone today, Peter. I will pay you back. Take my number."

"Yes. Got it. Excellent. See you soon."

Hanging up, Larry dialed Alan.

Alan answered promptly. "Good evening, Larry."

"Good evening, Alan. I'm going to get flight instructions to New York in the morning. I don't know the time, but this is just a heads up . . . "

"Sure thing, Mr. Martin. Just let me know when." The phone went dead.

Larry slowly set his phone on the desk, dismayed at Alan's abruptness. He felt as though he had somehow hurt Alan, but he hadn't a clue how. Whatever it was though, he had upset Alan enough to relegate him back to being Mr. Martin once more. He sighed inwardly, baffled. Why did things have to be so fucking complicated?

# CHAPTER TWENTY SIX

Alan knocked on Larry's door at nine the next morning.

Phone in hand, Larry answered the door. He had just texted Peter that he would arrive at LaGuardia at about 5:30 that evening. While he was letting Alan in, Larry's phone chimed with Peter's text reply: *Driver will meet you at baggage and bring you to my office.* Larry texted back: *Thanks. Looking forward to seeing you.*

Turning his attention to Alan, Larry smiled in delight. Alan had his hand on the handle of a large, black, rolling canvas suitcase. "You're a mind-reader, Alan. I was just about to call you to suggest we go buy some luggage."

"I hope you don't mind that I took the liberty then, Mr. Martin."

Larry looked at Alan, studying him. Alan was just slightly taller than he was, with longish blond hair, a lean frame, and clear tan skin. He was dressed in a black button-down shirt, black jeans, and loafers. At the moment, Alan had on his mirrored sunglasses so Larry couldn't see his eyes, but he knew they were green and expressive. Alan's brows and lashes were only slightly darker than his sun-streaked hair and his lips were well-formed under an aquiline nose and high cheekbones. He was a fine-looking man, and Larry could imagine that girls went wild over him. When Alan smiled, his teeth were straight and white, but he wasn't smiling now. He was standing tall, formal, and professional. Gone was the easy demeanor that Larry found both warm and charming. "Thank you for the suitcase, Alan. It's perfect and I really appreciate that you thought of it."

Alan nodded stiffly. "You're welcome, Mr. Martin."

"Now, will you come and sit down?" For a moment, Larry thought Alan was going to turn and walk out the door. The few seconds of Alan's hesitation told Larry his instinct had been right. Alan was upset with him. "Please, Alan."

Alan moved forward and Larry stepped aside to let him pass. As Alan sank into in the arm chair, Larry took his place on the sofa across from him.

Alan saw that Larry's entire wardrobe had already been folded into neat piles on the king-sized bed. Next to the clothes, his personal products had been efficiently bagged in a fresh white trashcan liner. The bed was made, the kitchen counters were clean, and the room was spotless. Martin was plainly a fastidious man. Alan liked that too. In his profession, he had seen many hotel rooms. Some had been so messy, so destroyed, he had often thought that people who lived like that were deranged. He believed how a person lived reflected their character. Finding good people, especially interesting, intelligent people that he'd like to associate with had always been a struggle. In fact, he had never been successful. Not with a man anyway. He frowned slightly.

"Alan?" Larry's voice was low and gentle. "Please tell me what I have done wrong." Larry leaned forward, resting his arms on his thighs and lacing his fingers loosely together. "Allow me to make it right."

Alan raised his eyes to meet Larry's. "It's difficult."

"How so?"

"You've done nothing wrong, Mr. Martin. Not one thing. It's all on me. I mean, I hardly know you . . ."

Larry shifted uneasily. He wasn't sure where this was going. "But?"

"You're going to leave. I've been so informal with you because I like you. Very much, actually. But it was wrong of me to get personally invested."

Larry wasn't sure what to say. He chose his words carefully and spoke slowly. "When you say 'personally invested' what, exactly, do you mean?"

Alan smiled briefly. "I'm not queer, Mr. Martin, although that's fine. I'm just a nice guy who works hard building a business, lives clean, and looks for like-minded friends. Not surprisingly, it's difficult."

Larry nodded. "I think I understand. We're back to 'Mr. Martin' because although you would like to be my friend, you believe that since I am leaving, the friendship you feel towards me cannot or will not be reciprocated, thus it's safer to retreat back into being strictly professional?"

"Yes. That about sums it up."

"I see. That *is* a difficult position. It would be hard to just come out and ask a guy you barely know to be your friend. Except that, knowing what I do of you, you would be wise about it. Your gut would tell you if you're right or not."

"Have I been wise then?"

Larry smiled warmly. "Certainly. Here's the thing, you hurt me when you pulled away last night. It confused me. I slept badly because of it."

"I am *so* sorry."

Larry waved the thought away. "Listen, Alan, I do not have many friends. I would be honored to count you as one of them."

Alan leaned back in his chair. "Thank you, Larry. Now, can I ask you something?"

"Yes."

"Why won't you tell me anything about yourself?"

Larry dropped his chin to his chest. Of all the questions. Lifting his head to gaze at Alan, he said, "It's complicated." When Alan snorted, Larry continued, "No, no. Come on now. I was patient with you."

"Fair enough."

Larry rubbed his fingertips into his eyes, trying to think. Lowering his hands, he looked at Alan and sighed. "There are a number of reasons. First, I have a story to tell and until I tell it to Peter Bennett, I do not feel free to talk about myself. Second, I am not proud of my history. So much has happened to me, I have not even begun to sort it all out. However, that will soon change. Third, as much as I like you—very much, actually—you are still a stranger. It was better to say nothing. Fourth, and most importantly, you are a contractual driver for Mr. Bennett or perhaps for the company, The Political Standard?"

"Both."

"Yes. Well. I could not be certain that whatever I said to you would not be repeated to the people most critical to my existence."

Alan nodded thoughtfully. "Okay. First, I will never repeat anything you say to anyone. That's my policy anyway. I'd go out of business fast if I did. Second, I understand you can't tell me right now who you are, but you can answer a few questions, yes?"

"I will honestly try."

"Are you a spy of some sort?"

"No. Not even remotely. I am just a simple man as you will soon discover. It seems, perhaps, you have built me up into something I'm not."

"You've never hurt anyone, killed or been in trouble with the law?"

"No to all three."

"What battle did you refer to in your sleep?"

Larry debated whether to answer. He decided to trust Alan. "Spiders. I battled spiders. I was stuck in a bad place and very ill. In fact, you've seen it. I got my file there. Anyway, in my delirium, Peter was with me. The place was infested with black widows. Fortunately, it was in the dead of winter and most of the spiders were tucked in for warmth. However, I still have ongoing dreams of that terrible time and Peter helping me. But he was not really there, you see."

"Why were you bloody when I picked you up?"

"I had been beaten up by some teenage guys the night before. They saw a drunk, filthy old man and thought it would be fun to kick him around."

"Are you a drunk?"

"No. I was very low that night. I intended to get drunk. But I was sitting at a picnic table of an outdoor barbecue joint behind Main Street, minding my own business when they spied me."

"Okay. That's all for now, Larry. Thanks."

"As my friend, Alan, it's important you understand that I am no one. No one important anyway."

"Yes, I get that now. But whatever story you have for Peter Bennett isn't unimportant. He's a powerful man. If he thinks it's important, things are going to change for you."

"We will see."

"All right. What do you want to do now?"

Larry stood, as did Alan. Larry glanced at the suitcase. "Let's pack, get something to eat, then head to the airport."

*   *   *   *   *   *

As Larry entered the baggage claim area at LaGuardia Airport in New York, he saw his driver almost immediately. He was an older man, standing in a loose, fanned-out line with several other drivers. Each driver was holding a sign with the name of the person they were to pick up. Larry let his driver know that he had arrived, then turned to get his bag off the carousel. He was glad to leave the busy airport and very much looking forward to seeing Peter soon. The driver was aloof and silent, but Larry didn't mind. Maybe the aloofness was a New York thing. He wasn't interested in talking anyway. He thought of Alan and smiled. They'd had a companionable lunch together and had done a lot of laughing over a beer and nachos. At the Atlanta airport, Alan had pulled up outside the front doors of Delta Airlines and lifted his bag from the trunk. They had hugged goodbye with a promise to stay in touch.

Larry enjoyed the warm feeling of having another friend. And now he was going to see Peter. Oh, Peter, how I hope I don't disappoint you, he thought, staring out the window. The city was loud and chaotic and the traffic was insane, but his driver was good at negotiating the craziness.

Larry's anxiety rose a touch. He could feel the beat of his heart rising. What would he do if he failed at this? Stop, he commanded himself, just stop. I won't fail. What I'm feeling is perfectly normal given that I'm going into something new. I belong here and I can do this. Peter would tell me to find some calm. Larry drew in a quiet breath and slowly let it out. When his heart began to beat normally again, he began to think of what he'd say to Peter. This time, his imagination failed him. It failed because he wasn't in a place where he could dream anything he wanted and not fail. His dreams were all his to control. But this was different. He was walking into a reality—the real world of Peter Bennett—a world of which he had no knowledge. He decided to close his eyes and give it a rest. It would be what it was.

Fifty minutes later, the driver pulled to the sidewalk in front of a skyscraper that held the corporate offices of The Political Standard. Cars were honking and whizzing by. The streets were crowded. The driver moved surprisingly fast to pull his suitcase from the trunk. Larry offered him his last ten-dollar bill as a tip.

"No sir. Thank you. It's been paid."

With a brief nod, Larry walked into the lobby, his suitcase rolling behind him. He had discarded his backpack in Atlanta with no regrets. From the long curve of the concierge desk, he was directed to the left side elevators down the hall which would take him to the 23rd floor.

Stepping off the elevator, Larry entered the rich world of The Political Standard.

He had once been intimidated by Bart's brightly lit modern office, but Bart's office was *nothing* compared to this. The reception room was two stories high, with walls covered in mirrored glass. The mirrors made the room seem cavernous and reflected the sparkle of the huge chandelier suspended from the ceiling. The furnishings were old-world style; wide leather sofas, arm chairs, and tables of dark wood with inlaid glass tops. Persian style carpets were on the marble floor, with the furniture pulled into working groups. To his left, there was a large mahogany L-shaped desk, an executive chair, and four computer screens—two on the long side of the desk itself and two much larger ones mounted on the wall behind the desk. No one was at the desk or in the room. The atmosphere was cool and the place was quiet. As Larry began to text Peter that he had arrived, a woman came through the double doors on the far wall. Walking towards him briskly, she extended her hand.

"Mr. Martin, I am Marion, Mr. Bennett's secretary." Shaking her hand, Larry smiled. She was five feet tall, slender, and wearing a simple blue dress with a white cashmere sweater. Her feet were encased in beige flats and her steel gray hair was twisted up into a flattering style. Larry couldn't guess her age, but he imagined she was well over sixty, although her face was unlined. Except for a touch of lipstick, she wore no makeup. A pair of reading glasses hung around her neck. He wouldn't want to get on her bad side. She struck him as formidable, but right now she seemed at ease and warm in her greeting.

Shaking Larry's hand, Marion saw an extremely handsome young man with clear brown eyes, long dark lashes any girl would be envious of, and no self-important airs whatsoever. His clothes were a touch country, but that could be fixed. If he was overwhelmed, he didn't show it. She liked that. He was standing straight, his shoulders square, the posture of a confident man. She liked that too. It seemed impossible to her that this lovely man had been homeless. Seeing him belied credibility. When he had smiled at her, her heart had actually missed a beat. His smile was beautiful, but there was something else . . . there was a gentleness about him that made her want to hug him. She never wanted to hug anyone. Her first impression was that Larry Martin was someone very special. Now if he could only write as well as he looked, they would have a winner on their hands and Mr. Bennett's gamble would be successful. Bringing Larry here had been a hard sell to the board.

Marion smiled at Larry as she dropped his hand. Larry let go easily. She noticed that while he had tried to be firm in his handshake, he had been careful not to crush her small fingers. "Shall we go? Peter is waiting for you."

"Please. I cannot wait to see him."

Leading him through the large doors, they turned down a long, wide hall of executive offices. The corridor was lit with small chandeliers above and there were lamps on the various console tables that occasionally lined the walls. The effect was soothing and he was glad of the absence of harsh fluorescent light. As they proceeded along, Larry tried not to look into the open doors of the offices. He did notice though, that some people were still working. To Marion, he said, "It is very quiet here."

Marion laughed lightly. "You'll see differently tomorrow. Most of our executives are at a conference today. Our staff writers are in The Pit, next floor up. It's never quiet there. Here's Peter's office. I'll leave you to go in."

"Thank you, Marion. It has been a pleasure to meet you."

"I'll see you tomorrow. Probably." She patted Larry's arm, knocked on Peter's closed door for him, and turning, went back down the hall to her own office.

Larry's heartbeat began to rise again. He could feel the pounding in his chest and the blood rushing to his ears. Turning the knob, he stepped into Peter's office.

Peter looked up from his computer screen, a smile on his lips. His smile faded and his expression became puzzled as he stared at the stranger who had just entered his office.

"Yes, Peter. It's me. Larry."

"Oh, good God. Yes. Of course." Swiveling his chair, Peter jumped from behind his desk, extending his hand. "You made it. I am so glad to see you, Larry," he exclaimed, shaking Larry's firm, affectionate grip.

Larry smiled tenderly. "And I you, Peter. You cannot know." He fought the urge to embrace Peter and hold on to him for a while in sheer relief. He wanted to feel the strength of his body, turned flesh and bone, no longer apparition. But he knew Peter wouldn't understand. Not yet.

"Please, come sit." Peter patted a burgundy leather chair in front of his desk and moved to sit down in his own chair. "Tell me how you are.

You look remarkable, by the way. I absolutely did not recognize you when you came in."

Feeling the wobble of his ankles, Larry sank into the chair. He was a little dizzy that he was here and that Peter was real, looking just as he had in his delirium and dreams. "I am fine, Peter. Your generosity came at a time when I thought I could not go on. I'm aware a person can thank someone until they're sick of hearing it, but for one last time . . . thank you so much. I am beyond grateful. And, I will not disappoint you."

"Are you up to telling me your story? Not all of it, just some of what you experienced?"

"Yes, certainly."

"Take your time."

"Looking back, it's like I experienced some sort of journey, physically and mentally. I didn't think of my wretched situation like that at the time, but being safe at the moment affords me that luxury. The life of a homeless person is one that continues to get worse, Peter. For me, it was going from loss to loss."

Peter nodded sympathetically but remained silent. Anything he said could only sound patronizing.

Larry continued, "You were with me when things got the worst. I had gotten stuck in an abandoned homestead on December 8th as Atlanta became encased in a bad snowstorm. My car had just blown, but I managed to get it parked in the old garage—it was actually more of a shed—attached to the shack on the property. The loss of my car on top of the loss of my camp I had just been forced out of, sent me into near insanity. So did the rotten place I had somehow landed in." Larry paused. He shuddered slightly, trying to breathe.

"Go on," Peter urged.

"It was snowing hard that night and it was bitterly cold. I spent the first night in my car, in that dark shed, wondering if I would make it alive through the night. The next day I moved into the shack because I discovered it had a working fireplace. But the place was crawling with perilous mold and there were spiders on the property, mostly black widows."

"I hate spiders," Peter said quietly.

"I do too. I lived in terror of them, especially at night. But the mold was perhaps more poisonous. It was foul beyond belief and made me ungodly ill. The task of working to make the place survivable with very little resources seemed impossible. It was amazing to me that when, in desperation, I would call out your name for help and you would appear so clearly, I could actually see you. Really, it was very weird. I acknowledge this. But you assisted me in every way. You helped me to free a tarp covered in snow that was so heavy, I could not move it by myself to get to the old firewood underneath. You made me get up from the snow, twice, so I wouldn't freeze to death. You were there warning me of spiders and to cover my hand when I touched something, so I would not get bitten. You cared for me when I was delirious and burning with fever. You helped me in other ways too. It was a dangerous place and a dangerous situation, but because you were there with me, I did not feel so alone. You gave me strength, Peter. You gave me the strength and the hope to go on when I did not feel I could. I know it was total delirium, but yet, you were so real. I have genuine memories of you that we don't share since, obviously, you were not there . . . except that, to me, you were. Just as real as we're sitting here."

"Why me?"

"Because you were the only decent thing in my life. I had been a terrible person and I had no friends. When you gave me a chance with the articles, it was a slim, but possibly real connection between us. It was a thread back to life, even as I had no expectations. There was no one else, but you. In my sad world, you were everything. The possibilities and hope you offered me kept me going."

Leaning forward on his desk, Peter rested his chin on his hand, contemplating the man sitting in front of him. Larry had never been his friend. He had never understood Larry's way of thinking—a mentality based on cruelty and the dehumanization of other people. He hadn't understood

Larry's hatred of minorities, gays and women. He hadn't understood how the man was all for taking away the rights of others and making them illegal. He had read Larry's articles. Over and over again. They had required very little editing. They weren't spectacular but they were publishable. He had to argue with the board to get it done. Two things stood out in his mind. The first was that Larry could learn. This was a big deal; it was critical. It meant that Larry had the ability to expand his skills as a writer. It also meant that Larry was willing to explore the boundaries of his beliefs. He often found the conservative mindset to be so rigid, conservatives refused to move from their position, even when confronted with the facts. But Larry had moved. The second thing was the evident passion that Larry had put into the arguments in his articles. That had moved him. He had believed Larry. And, he believed him now.

Never had he seen a man change so fundamentally in every way, from mentality to appearance. The change had not only made Larry physically compelling, it seemed to have birthed a good character, a good man. And, from what he could tell so far, a humble and forthcoming man. He could appreciate how hard the change must have been. Finally, Peter rested his arms on his desk.

"If that was the case—and I do believe you—I am very glad I was there for you."

Larry smiled briefly, relieved. For a few seconds during Peter's silence, he had imagined that he had offended Peter with his nonsense.

"What I find remarkable, Larry, is that you're so changed. It's simply incredible. That's the story I want you to tell. I want every detail of the road you've traveled, every emotion and every thought. Can you do that?"

"Yes."

"Good. We'll make it into a long series. Don't worry about length. Just tell your story. I suspect you'll enthrall our readers, and such a stimulating human interest story will give a sorely needed break to our hard grind at politics."

Larry nodded, starting to relax. He knew what Peter wanted. He also understood that he would be picked apart by rabid readers. Some would be sympathetic while others would spew unmitigated hate at him for being a traitor to the conservative cause. To them, there was nothing worse than a conservative turned liberal. There could even be death threats.

"I also stole a lot of small stuff from stores, Peter. But I don't want to incriminate myself. How should I handle this?"

Peter sat back. "What stores?"

"Mostly Walmart and a dollar store. But there were also two other thefts I regret. I stole a bike from a boy that was laying in his front yard and some household goods from an old man."

"You robbed an old man's house?"

"I did. I saw him leave and the door was open. I was desperate at the time so I took some blankets, cookware, and food."

Peter tried to imagine being desperate enough to do that. He couldn't. His whole life had been privileged and protected. He had never suffered deprivation of any kind, at any time. Rising from his chair, he stepped to the windows of his office overlooking the city and stared through the glass, analyzing and thinking.

Larry watched Peter. Peter's frame was tall and trim. He was dressed in a crisp white dress shirt, rolled at the forearms, and tucked into tailored black slacks. His chestnut hair was groomed over dark brows and blue eyes. Peter was a very handsome and intimidating man. His long silences unnerved him. He prayed that Peter was not disgusted with him.

Turning from the window, Peter looked at Larry. His fingers came to his lips. He finally said, "Look, you can't incriminate yourself. You'll use fictional names of stores—turn Walmart into 'Big-Sale' or 'House-Smart' or whatever. You get the idea. I'm surprised you didn't get arrested for shoplifting."

"It was close," Larry said. "But not just for shoplifting. It was when I was living in a forest for eight weeks and cooking with a firepit."

Larry told Peter of his camp, the eventual arrival of the police and his narrow miss of being there when they had arrived. "I loved the forest, Peter. I had made it into something workable and comfortable. It was a huge blow when my home was taken from me. Interestingly enough though, if the police hadn't come, I doubt I would have survived the snowstorm in the woods. Being forced out and ending up at that abandoned homestead turned out to be a good thing. It wasn't at the time though. But by making it to the shed when the snowstorm hit, I survived because the roof of the shed kept my car from being buried. I don't believe much in things happening for a reason, but if there was ever an example of it, that was one of them."

"Why didn't you just go home?" Peter asked, rocking back in his chair.

"No home to go to. My mother left when I was a child. My father was an awful man. He was truly vicious and hated everyone, especially women, gays, and immigrants. He was abusive to me as a child. He often beat me, burned me with cigarettes, and generally starved me. I loathed him so deeply, I even killed him in one of my fevered nightmares."

Peter shook his head. "That's really rough, Larry. I see now where you got your beliefs."

"In that dream, I went back to my childhood home. You were there too, Peter. It was the first time you appeared to me. "

"What did I do?"

"You told me to find calm, stay strong and that you would see me on the other side."

"Jesus. That's some intensely prescient stuff."

"Yes. And, here we are," Larry said, his expression solemn as he gazed at Peter. "The rest of my experience, as I said, was all about loss. I lost my apartment, followed by my laptop and cell phone. I built my camp in the forest and lost it. Then I lost my car. I lost my health and some of my sanity at the old homestead. I slept in secret in a woman's old pool house for a week in the winter, but lost that too when the door was locked one day. I have slept under trees and bushes in the rain and in the cold. I have slept in alcoves of businesses, public restrooms or wherever I could find shelter. I watched a man I had met, another homeless guy, die from being frozen to death on a wicked night in January. After Buddy's death, I built another shelter for myself in the dumpster area behind an empty industrial building. I got it comfortable enough and lived there for two months before I was discovered and ran, so I lost that too. Then, I got beaten up and my wallet was stolen. I lost the little money I had and my ID. I had nothing left at that point. That was when I connected with you on the phone. During all of this, I experienced the relentless struggle of trying to stay clean, warm, and fed. Especially clean. I was almost always hungry. Even when I had food, it was always eaten with an awareness of conservation. The thing of it is, my homeless experience was probably easier than most. Except that I too was dying little by little. I cannot describe the intense humiliation, the loss of self-worth, the fear, or the hopelessness involved. I cannot describe the awful feeling of invisibility. I learned that the loss of one's self is the ultimate loss. But I'll tell you this Peter, it was the kindness of strangers that made all the difference."

"How did you eat?"

"I begged on street corners. Strangers gave me gave money. Without their help, I probably would have starved. Or stolen to the point where I was jailed."

Peter rubbed his eyes with his fingertips. "Well, you certainly have a story to tell. You know it's going to be difficult—not just in the telling, but the reaction of readers as well. They can be brutal."

"Yes. I know too well. I am sorry to say that I have made some of those brutal comments myself in the past. So, I know what can happen. I can deal with it."

"Do you have a title for your series? If you don't, that's fine. We'll get there."

"I do."

Peter raised his eyebrows in surprise. "Okay. Let's have it."

"The Other Shoes of Larry Martin."

Peter leaned back in his chair and sighed in happiness.

# CHAPTER TWENTY SEVEN

Peter was thrilled. Larry had turned out just as he hoped. Better, even. Far better. He hadn't expected the altered appearance. The last time he'd seen Larry in college, he hadn't looked good. He'd been slightly seedy and dressed in clothes that seemed unwashed. He had been somewhat skinny and small in appearance. It was Larry's face, though, that at the moment, intrigued him the most. He had the same face back then, he thought, but I just couldn't see it for all the poisonous things that came out of his mouth. But the man sitting in front of him now was perfect. Not only was he presentable, with his gentle and precise style of talking, he was promotable. He had already just proven himself adept to the conceptual angle of the series he was to write. 'The Other Shoes of Larry Martin.' What a great title. Out of the corner of his eye, he saw Larry stifle a yawn. "I'm sorry, Larry. I bet you've had a day."

"I am okay, Peter."

"Even so, let me show you to your office. It's where you'll be living and working for a while until I can find you a place to stay. Have you had dinner?"

"Not yet."

"All right. Let's get you settled. Then, we'll go down the street. There's a little bar that serves great roast beef sandwiches." When Larry nodded, Peter rose from his desk and began to walk to the door. Larry followed, his suitcase which had been left by Peter's door rolling behind him. They walked down the quiet corridor until it ended. Opening the door, Peter ushered Larry inside.

"You can sleep on the sofa. You have a closet here and a bathroom with a shower there." Peter pointed to the two doors. Walking to the desk, he lifted a business card off the blotter and said, "This is a number for our laundry and dry-cleaning service. They will manage all your laundry. Underwear. Clothes. Everything. Call them in the morning and set up an account. Don't worry about money. The Political Standard will take care of your bill." Peter walked over to the closet and opening the door, pointed to a few shopping bags sitting on the upper rack. "Marion bought you some bedding. Sheets, pillow, blankets. She wanted you to be comfortable, as do I." Peter went back to the desk and held up another business card. "This is the number to Jack's Catering. They deliver breakfast, lunch, and dinner, if you want. They're in the building, so they're fast. Their menu is good and varied and they will keep you fed until you find your own preferences. Again, TPS will pay your bill until your first paycheck. Tomorrow Marion will set you up with forms for HR and the government. Do you have any questions?"

"No. I know where I'm going to sleep, wash, eat, and work, at least to start. That covers it. I admit to being surprised that I'm not in The Pit with the other staff writers, Peter."

"Look, Larry, you have a difficult job to do here. It's not only a lot of writing, it's how you write it that will make the series successful or not. I'm not looking for dry reporting. I want more from you. The telling of your transitions are key here. You can show emotion."

"Like telling if I cried?"

"Did you cry?"

"Yes. A lot."

"Then, tell it. Make the readers feel what you went through. Have them experience your pain. Tell them who you were and how you got there. Make them feel what it's like to be homeless. Get them to understand why you changed in your beliefs. Your mindset is not just human interest, it's also completely political. It'll stir a lot of people up. You know that. The issue of homelessness is just as relevant as ever. It's getting worse in this country by the day and it's also a hot and sensitive political issue. There's a lot of hatred and anger there too, for many reasons. No, this isn't going to be easy, Larry. It just won't." Peter shook his head, looking at Larry.

Larry nodded, his expression sober. He was going to be publicly stripped and torn apart. Peter was hoping that he would be a hornet's nest thrown into a crowd. Could he do it? Could he get through it? Given where I am in life, do I have a choice? If I ran right now, he thought, I'm back on the streets. He couldn't imagine Peter's disappointment if he ran. He might understand, but he would never talk to him again. He didn't want that. But, if I do this right, get past this series, maybe I'll have a career here. I do want that.

But first, he had to expose his failures and humiliations to the world. He had to find the talent to do it well. He wasn't a strong writer. TPS was huge, rich, and overwhelming and he was already feeling the pressure of the corporate expectations of excellence. The combination of it all felt like a setup for failure, from his personal exposure and potential retaliatory attacks to his not being good enough and being fired. He could lose all the way around. Peter was right. It was going to be very, very difficult.

"All I can tell you, Peter, is that I will do my best," Larry replied calmly. He wasn't feeling calm. His heartbeat had risen again from anxiety. But he would control it. He had to.

Peter smiled briefly. He prayed that he knew what he was doing. He was throwing Larry to the wolves. All of them. The man could get crushed. But he had enough faith in himself to guide Larry and do what he could to ensure that did not happen. "Good. That's all I can ask for. As for The Pit, no. I want you in a place where you can live and work undisturbed and stay focused. No one will know you're here, temporarily, apart from HR, myself, Marion, reception, catering, and laundry. Of course, you can go out anytime for fresh air. We writers have to be able to walk around, stomp our feet, and clear our minds in order to dream and find the right words to say what we mean. So feel free to do that. Take breaks. Walk. Stay healthy. But if I threw you in The Pit, everyone would know our business and I don't want that. Not yet. Okay?"

"Okay."

Peter laid his hand lightly on Larry's shoulder. "Good man. Now, let's get something to eat."

Over a dinner of sandwiches and beer, Peter tried to be engaging. He knew Larry could talk easily if he wanted to. He'd just seen it. But Larry was mostly quiet, somber and succinct. He had a way of measuring out his words in slow and thoughtful comments. He had a way of saying only what was necessary and nothing more. Peter found it intriguing. Whatever Larry said, he found himself wanting more. They discussed various events happening in the world. They discussed the President's potential criminality of Russian collusion and the latest indictments from Mueller, the Special Counsel investigating the Russian involvement in the 2016 presidential election. They discussed the rise of white supremacy and the rage of the alt-right. Larry was up to date on his knowledge and Peter was satisfied that Larry knew what he was up against. But the man was starting to look weary and Peter knew it was time to go. He paid the bill and walked Larry back to his office.

"Try to get comfortable and sleep well. I'll be in touch tomorrow." Shaking Larry's hand, Peter looked into Larry's eyes. They showed no fear, but Peter wasn't fooled. He was well aware that Larry had to be feeling besieged from the strangeness and weight of all that was happening to him. Sighing, he pulled Larry close and hugged him. "I'm here for you. Whatever you need, just ask. I think we'll make a great team."

Larry felt Peter's warmth and strength, the reality of it nearly unbelievable to him. He tightened his embrace briefly before stepping back. "I will be fine, Peter. And yes, we are going to make a great team. Go on now. You have had a long day too."

Peter hesitated, still wanting to be with Larry. He thought they might continue to talk while Larry got settled. But Larry had just told him to go, so he would leave.

"Good night, Larry."

"Good night, Peter."

Turning the knob, Larry entered his new world.

His office was spacious, with a wall of windows, a sitting area, a round table with seating for four, and a large executive desk. A wide screen computer sat on the desk with papers next to its keyboard. Lifting the papers, he saw a list of passwords to different accounts and files, including the file in which he was to write. Setting the papers down, he continued to look around. He saw a laptop by the printer. Good. Opening the top drawer of the desk, he saw an envelope with his name on it. Opening it, he saw five one-hundred-dollar bills and a handwritten note from Peter that read, *'Larry, you'll need spending money for the city. Let me know when you need more. Peter.'*

Larry put the envelope back into the drawer and went to make his bed on the sofa, get unpacked and shower. Before getting into bed, he turned on his desk lamp and turned off the overhead lights. The glow of the lamp reminded him of his fires. The room was chilly and silent. It was also pristine and luxurious. Intimidatingly so. He set the alarm on his cell phone for five o'clock in the morning and set it on the coffee table in front of the sofa. Climbing into bed, he stretched out and sighed. The sofa was long, wide, firm and comfortable. He would sleep fine. He felt a little dizzy and his thoughts were spinning. Tomorrow would be a busy day. He didn't know how he could do it all. But here he was. And, finally with Peter. However, Peter was his boss, not his friend. He needed to remember that. Closing his eyes, he slept, exhausted.

The alarm clock woke him in what seemed like only minutes. Larry rose, packed away his bed into the closet, and headed to the shower. After shaving, he dressed in a white dress shirt and his only pair of cheap slacks from Walmart. He realized then that he didn't have a belt. He would get one later. He had to get more clothes too.

He went to his desk, called the caterer, set up his account and ordered coffee, orange juice, and an egg and bacon sandwich. Then he called the laundry. After establishing his new account, he learned they would deliver their white laundry bags to his office around noon. His laundry should be placed in their bags and left outside his door. Delivery and pick up would occur at six in the morning. Service would start tomorrow.

Turning to the papers on his desk, he began to memorize the list. After studying for a while, he got on the computer to read the news and familiarize himself with the various in-house accounts, messaging systems, and files on the list. He saw that an email account had been set up for him. Using his password from the list, Larry opened it and typed an email to Peter:

'Good morning, Peter. I am up and active. Breakfast is ordered. Laundry starts tomorrow. I slept well. Couch is comfortable. I will start writing today. Let me know, aside from Marion and HR, if I need to do anything more. Thanks, Larry.' Send.

A knock on the door made him look up. Rising, Larry strode to the door and flipped on his overhead lights before opening it. "Good morning," he said pleasantly, seeing the delivery girl.

"Good morning, Sir. Jack's." She handed him his food box.

"Do I tip you? I'm new here."

"No sir. The company takes care of it. I'm Emma. I'm sure I'll see you again."

"Larry Martin. Thanks, Emma. Listen, is it possible to set up a weekly breakfast menu to be delivered each morning at six?"

"Yes. Just call Jack's, tell them what you want and it'll be done. They'll put you on a service plan. You can do it for lunch and dinner too, if you like."

"Okay. Thank you. You have been helpful. Have a good day."

He took the box back to his desk and moved the papers aside. Opening it, he set out his breakfast and folded the box into the trash.

Popping the lid off his coffee, Larry took a sip and checked his email. He had two. One from Peter, the other from Marion. Peter wrote:

*'Good morning, Larry. Glad you slept well. Just do the HR thing and write today. Remember to walk. I'm in meetings for the day. Your editor is Tina Hawley. She will contact you soon. Good writing. Peter.'*

From Marion:

*'Good morning, Mr. Martin. I will come to your office at 9:00 am and take you to HR. Your new assistant will be Kate Foster. She is assigned to the office next to yours and will start this afternoon. As your assistant, she is to run your errands, manage your schedule, etc. Best luck in your writing. Marion.'*

It was only 7:40 in the morning and Larry was already feeling tired. He'd barely begun the day. These people moved fast. He prayed he could rise to their pace soon. It seemed to him that New York, indeed, never slept. Right now, he could do one of two things. He could nap for a half hour or take a twenty-minute walk to wake himself up. He opted to walk. Leaving his office, he traversed the executive corridor and the reception area. A young woman was at the desk now and he nodded in greeting as he passed her by and headed to the elevator. Getting to the ground level was fairly quick; only a few stops along the way. Leaving the building, Larry stepped into a beautiful April morning. It was chilly, in the low-forties and the street was already starting to bustle. He wasn't cold. He was used to lower temperatures. He set his cell phone timer for ten minutes and turned right on 33rd Street. He wasn't interested in sightseeing. He just wanted to smell the fresh air, stretch his legs, and think about his opening paragraph. It was Tuesday. He had to start writing today. Lost in thought about his work, his timer went off all too soon. Turning around, he headed back to his office. He had a kernel of an idea.

Marion came to his office at nine and Larry spent forty minutes in HR filling out forms. He received a corporate gift card loaded with $1,000. It was his temporary expense account. He was to keep his receipts and turn in his expense report on the 25th of each month. Sliding the card into his pocket, he thought, I must buy a wallet. That business finished, he returned to his office and closed the door. Sitting at his desk, he opened his writing file and stared at the empty page. He thought about whether he should write the series in first or third person. He wondered if he could use a combination of both. That would be different, like he was narrating his own story and then slip into third person for it to read like a book. He wondered if he could make it work. He had never done anything like this before. Leaning forward, he typed the title: THE OTHER SHOES OF LARRY MARTIN. Deep in thought, his fingers remained suspended above the keyboard, ready to type. The phone on his desk rang. Damn. Answering it, he said, "Hello."

"Mr. Martin, this is Sara Steinman at reception."

"Hello, Sara. I am so sorry I did not stop to introduce myself, but I had limited time," Larry said, his tone low and warm.

"Of course, Mr. Martin. We'll meet properly at your convenience. I wanted to let you know that Kate Foster is here."

"She is early."

"Could be a good thing. Early birds and all that," Sara laughed.

"Yes, you are right." Larry laughed with her. "So how does this work? Do I come down?"

"No. I'll have my assistant lead her to your office now, if that's okay."

"Yes. That's fine. Thank you, Sara."

Sara hung up. Mr. Martin seemed very nice. She already knew he was very good-looking. She called her assistant. "You have a 'lead to.'"

"Be right there."

Sara motioned Kate from her chair. "Miss Foster, my assistant will take you to Mr. Martin. "

"Thank you."

Linda came through the doors and walked Kate companionably to Larry's office. Knocking, she opened the door, allowing Kate to step in.

Larry looked up from his computer. Rising, he said, "Miss Foster, welcome. Please, come sit down." He was pleased. Kate was small and lithe.

Her shoulder length hair looked like copper, and freckles dusted her nose. Like Marion, she wore no makeup, except for a touch of lipstick. But the girl didn't need any. She was very pretty with her green eyes, smooth complexion, and pert nose. He smiled at her.

"I'm so pleased to meet you, Mr. Martin. I know I'm early, but I took a chance. Why waste the morning, if I could be of help."

"It worked out," Larry replied. "I'm very glad you're here, actually. I need your help and I have a terrible thing to ask you to do. But only if you're okay with it."

"What is this terrible thing?"

"I need you to shop for me. Clothes, a few ties, a black belt, a thin wallet, black socks, and size eleven black shoes." He watched her pull out her phone and make a list.

"What kind of clothes?" She hit the record button on her phone and held it up for Larry to see she was recording him.

"Four white dress shirts. Two black slacks. A black jacket that will match both."

"Tailored or not?"

"I don't know."

Kate clicked off her phone. Lifting her purse from the floor, she withdrew a small, rolled, cloth tape measure. "May I touch you, Mr. Martin?"

"Yes." Larry stood up and walked around the desk. Kate tapped the voice record button again and slipped the phone into her breast pocket. As she measured Larry, she said the measurements out loud. When she was done, she turned off her phone and they sat down again.

"Miss Foster ..."

"Kate."

"Okay, Kate. I am Larry. I am new here and I am a poor man. You'll be operating on a very small budget. Anything you can buy me on clearance, go for it. I will basically be giving you my last dollar to shop with."

"I understand."

"Are you done with HR?"

"Yes. Marion helped me yesterday."

"Okay, good. Add to your list a small bottle of aspirin. I must write today. I don't have anything else for you to do. You can take all day to do this chore."

"I'm happy to do it, Larry. The reason I'm here is to help you in any way possible. What else can you think of?"

"My expense report is due on the 25th of every month. Can I give you my receipts and have you manage the report?'"

"Yes."

"Your office is next door to mine. Feel free to explore and move in. Also, tomorrow, I will give you a breakfast menu. Will you call Jack's Catering and arrange a service plan for me? Here's their card."

Kate took it and entered the number into her phone. She put the card back on Larry's desk and looked at him, waiting for more.

"I think that's it for now."

Kate stood, held out her hand, palm up, wiggling her fingers. Larry pulled the envelope from the desk drawer. He had already removed Peter's note. Handing the envelope to her, she quickly counted the contents.

"Can you do it?" Larry asked.

"I'll figure something out."

"It's not enough ..."

"No. I'll have to work a miracle. But, I'm good at that."

Larry smiled at her. She flashed him a smile in return. Turning, she sailed out the door.

Larry sat down and began to work. The hours slipped by quickly. A knock on the door lifted his head as Peter stuck his head in. "Busy?"

"Come in, Peter."

Larry rose from his chair and tried not to groan. His ribs still hurt and his low back was cramping from sitting too long. A quick glance at his screen told him it was 6:30 p.m. How was that possible?

Peter sat down in front of Larry. "Have you eaten?"

"No."

"Want to get something?"

"Yes."

"It's thirty-two degrees outside. Get your coat."

Larry went to the closet and grabbed his Walmart blazer.

Peter eyed the thin garment. "No coat?"

"No. But I am fine, Peter." Pulling on his jacket, he asked, "Where are we going?"

"Shay's Tavern is close by. They have good steaks."

Leaving the building, the two men made their way down to the street. Shay's was just a block away. The street was crowded with people walking against a wind that was blustery and freezing cold. Peter didn't try to make conversation as he and Larry walked. He recognized writer's fog when he saw it and Larry hadn't come out of it yet. Opening the door to the restaurant, Peter let Larry enter first. Shay's was busy, but Marion had called ahead for a table and they were seated immediately. The waiter came to the table and Peter ordered beer, steak, and fries for the both of them.

They didn't talk politics as they ate. Peter kept it to small talk and soon, he had Larry laughing. It was good to see the man animated. He hadn't seen that side of Larry yet and took pleasure in it. In the morning, he would lend him a coat.

# CHAPTER TWENTY EIGHT

Larry's alarm went off at 5:00 a.m. He got up, stripped his bedding, showered, shaved and dressed in the same clothes as yesterday. He had nothing for laundry except two pairs of underwear. He checked his email, read some news, and opened his writing file. Emma delivered his breakfast at 6:00 a.m. He typed out a new breakfast plan for Kate to arrange. Monday would be scrambled eggs and bacon; Tuesday, a BLT with coleslaw; Wednesday, an omelet and so on. He printed the menu and walked it to Kate's desk. At 7:00 a.m., Kate showed up, her arms heavy with shopping bags and plastic encased clothes, followed by a stylish young man loaded down with even more.

"Oh, Kate, what have you done?"

"It's early, Larry. You haven't settled in to write yet, so pay attention to me."

"Okay."

"You're going to have to cooperate and try all this on. What doesn't fit, I'll return immediately. I've pulled favors, so there isn't any choice about it. We have to do it now."

For the next two hours, Larry tried on clothes. Under Kate's approval, he came away with a wardrobe of well-fitting, interchangeable garments. He had two jackets, six shirts, three pairs of slacks, two pairs of shoes, six ties, two belts, a slim designer wallet, two bottles of expensive cologne, and more. The rest would go to alteration.

Kate handed him the wallet and hung the clothes in the closet by style and color. Finally, she set a bottle of aspirin on his desk. "Give me your phone, Larry." She quickly entered her cell number into his favorite contacts. Turning, she directed Jessie to remove the bags of rejected clothes from Larry's office and to wait outside.

"How did you do that?"

Sitting in front of Larry, she replied, "I have friends in the garment district. Other places too. And I shopped." She placed a hundred-dollar bill on the desk and pushed it towards him. "So, I did not spend your last dollar."

"Thank you. You are so extraordinary, Kate, I'm at a loss for words. But at least I have the good sense to know that I owe you," Larry said, slipping the bill into his new designer wallet.

"What now?" Kate asked.

"I don't have anything else for you, Kate. I must write. It is all that I am supposed to be doing right now. Please be patient with me. My breakfast plan is on your desk."

"I'll set it up and return the clothes."

"Good. Take your time and be safe."

Entering her office, she called Jack's and arranged Larry's breakfast plan and, thinking about it, she ordered a service plan for his lunch as well. She did not believe for a second that Larry would leave for lunch while he was writing. Marion had told her that he was going to be under a lot of pressure. Leaving her office, she joined her friend, Jessie, in the hall and picked up some of the shopping bags sitting on the floor. He gathered the rest into his arms and they proceeded down the hall to the elevator. Kate hailed a taxi and they bundled the clothes into the backseat with them. "I know this was a lot to ask of you, Jessie, but thank you so much. After we drop these samples off to Ashia, let me buy you breakfast."

Jessie laughed in surprise. "You can do that? Just leave your office and go out to eat now? You have a great job, Kate. Anyway, I just loved that man. He's as pretty as they come. I almost had a heart attack touching him.

Too bad he's straight. The clothes are really going to make him though. Listen, Kate, that place is seriously corporate. You going to be okay there?"

"Yes. I know it's different for me. But, TPS is in its own way a place of creativity. And I think Larry just might be a work of art. We'll make him look like that anyway. I really appreciate your help, Jessie." Kate looked out the window at the noisy, busy city. If her new boss failed, she would not have a job. She was acutely aware that she was just on temporary assignment with TPS. Larry Martin was her only assignment. But it was a chance to get her foot in the door and she had taken it. Kate thought of Larry. He seemed direct, honest, kind and gentle. But this was New York. Being kind and gentle could get you eaten up. She'd seen no trace of a slick ego, rapier tongue or ambition oozing from him, all the attributes of the more successful. Still. He had something. And it was powerful.

When she had told him that he had to try on the clothes, she had expected the protests of a typical man. Instead, he had immediately leaned down in his chair and silently removed his shoes and socks. He had unbuttoned his shirt and removed it without looking at either her or Jessie. He had slid out of his slacks, folded them, and set them on his desk. He had come around the desk in his t-shirt and underwear and said, "Let's begin."

It had surprised her. This was exactly what she needed him to do. To respond without modesty. He had not been wearing boxers. He had been in fitted white underwear. His t-shirt was tucked into them for a smooth line. She could see his fine body. So could Jessie. He must have felt exposed.

She had dressed many people in her career. She had worked with countless models and photo shoots. She knew all kinds of people. No one could make or alter clothes like Jessie. His tailor and alteration shop was one of the finest. They both knew their business. And Jessie had agreed to help her. She would owe him.

When Larry had come out from behind his desk, they had led him forward. He had stood silently for them, his eyes closed. Before they had even begun to dress him, they saw what he had to offer. And they had touched him. His legs were lean and long. His chest was wide and flat and smooth, yet curved in the right places. Their hands had traveled across his chest down his flat stomach to his waist and to his hips. They had lifted his arms. His arms had been long and lean too. She saw his muscles ripple when they had raised them, opening his hands and straightening his long fingers. They saw the V of his body and knew how to dress him. He did not have the lines of a man who worked out at a gym. He had a body of something else. An overall strength, like a runner. His lines were straight and distinct. They knew what to do for him. And he had not moved during their discussion of him.

Yes, Larry had let Jessie and her touch him. And they did. All over. They had pulled on his collars, smoothed shirts over his chest and managed his buttons. They had slid their hands down the side of his torso in the fitting of shirts. They had put their hands in his pants at his waist. They had traveled down his legs to the hem of his slacks. They had touched him at the groin area and inside his legs as they adjusted inseams. They had run their hands down his arms and pulled on his sleeves and cuffs. They had held his hands to make his arms aloft as they scrutinized any constraints of fabric from his wrist to armpit and to his waist. They had indeed touched him all over. Everywhere but his face. And he had remained silent as they touched him. He had remained silent when she and Jessie talked about what to do for each particular garment. He had offered no opinions.

But he had laughed when Jessie joked, they were going to turn him into a movie star. She had seen his laugh. It was low and engaging. And his laugh had made Jessie fall in love with him. Trying on all the clothes had been a grueling process. He had endured it without complaint. He had been invested and cooperative. He had let her dress him with a calmness of a man who knew himself. And, oh Christ, did he look good! She had killed herself to get that collection. She had begged and wheedled and handed out more markers than she knew she could afford. But it had been worth it. Larry had been smart. He had listened and allowed her to choose his wardrobe. Larry had done so without argument or greed. In the short time they had been together, Kate realized that she liked the man. Very much.

He wasn't a braggart or conceited. He had let Jessie manage his buttoning to expedite the selection process. He had let Jessie run his hands over his body as he pinned the clothes that they would take away for alteration. Many straight men would have never allowed such a flagrantly gay man to touch them so intimately. She knew Jessie's touch had been completely professional, but still. Larry had simply gone with the flow. He had listened instead of talked. When she said 'no', he had taken off the garment and silently handed it to Jessie for the discard pile. She saw that his calm, gentle nature didn't come from weakness, but rather some sort of deep, prepossessing self-control. She liked that. His nature had captivated her. As a result, she would do everything she could to help him succeed, no longer just for herself, but for him too. He had earned her respect.

Kate made her returns and after Jessie had been thanked with a brunch she could not afford, she returned to her office. She spent the rest of the day studying TPS articles, issues and positions. Larry was true to his word; he had nothing for her. Picking up her purse to leave for the day, she went next door to check on him and say good-bye. She stared at his closed door, frowning. Taped to the door was a sheet of paper. The note typed in 12-point font read:

*'I am working. Please do not disturb me. I appreciate it. Larry.'*

Kate was back at the office at seven the next morning. Her day was the same as yesterday. Thursday was no different. By Friday night, Larry still had not emerged. Standing in front of his door, she counted six boxes of unopened Jack's stacked neatly against the wall by the doorframe. Wondering what to do, she returned to her office and called Marion.

Marion listened to Kate's concern and came to a decision. "Let's respect his wishes and let him work. Let's give him the weekend. It's entirely possible that he's so focused on what he's doing, he isn't hungry. Writers can do that. On Monday, we'll reassess the situation."

"Thanks, Marion. I'll keep you informed." Kate went home and poured herself a glass of wine. Her roommates were not home yet and she was glad. Sipping her wine, she decided that she would go to the office tomorrow. Sunday too, if she had to. She was disturbed and worried. She didn't want to upset anything; she wasn't going to break down his door . . . but she had to at least know if he was eating.

The weekend brought no change. There were now ten boxes of Jack's stacked outside Larry's door. Monday couldn't come soon enough for Kate. She, herself, had barely eaten all weekend. She arrived at the office at 6:30 a.m. and called Marion, although it was early.

Marion was in her office early for the same reasons—concern and worry. Kate had texted her over the weekend, at the end of the day, on both Saturday and Sunday. Her text was short and all she had said was: *'Larry is the same. Not out, not eating.'* In turn, Marion had informed Peter. Now they both walked into Kate's office.

Peter felt he knew what was happening with Larry when Marion had informed him of the situation. He had experienced it himself. He was currently writing a novel, a work of fiction, and he would often try to leave the office early on Friday just to get home and write. There were many times when he fell so profoundly into his book, outside reality would cease to exist. Finding this 'roll' or 'flow' was something all serious writers searched for and worked hard to find. It was the holy grail of writing. It was where anything and everything could be done and the words flowed so effortlessly, one couldn't write fast enough. He never wanted to eat when it was happening. He'd find himself not eating until late Sunday, when he would have to force himself to surface and snap out of it. He would do his laundry and make his dinner in a painful fog as he worked to transition back to reality. But, when a writing roll did occur, he was also aware that it was happening. When it did, he might not eat, but he did drink a lot of water. Larry must have fallen into a hell of a roll. He prayed it was true and that he hadn't allowed some horrible, neglectful thing to occur. But the truth was he envied Larry. He had never had the luxury of writing on a roll for days in a row.

Peter quietly opened Larry's door without knocking. Sticking his head in, he took in the scene. Opening the door further, he slipped silently into the room and sank into the seat in front of Larry's desk.

The lamp was on, shining on the desk. The drapes were closed and the overhead lights were off. Larry looked fine, sleeping deeply, upright in his executive chair. He had the makings of a real beard, but six days of not shaving would do that. He had on a fresh long-sleeved black cotton tee and his hair was clean. So. He had been showering but not shaving. A large glass of water was on his desk, along with a manuscript. Reaching for the stack, Peter did not try to read it. He simply turned to the last page. One hundred and sixty-two pages. Rising, Peter came around to stand near Larry's side. Discarded and edited pages were puddled at Larry's feet. Sitting again, Peter studied the man. Then, he noticed the pile of used tissues on the desk and realized that Larry had been crying. Peter was suddenly dismayed and saddened.

What had he done?

He had brought a vulnerable homeless man to New York to write about himself. He had ordered him to tell of his pain and fear. His job was to relive the horrors of his past and he was doing just that. One could argue that Larry had a choice to refuse, but did he really? Guilt rose within Peter, turning his gut sour. Rising soundlessly, he left Larry's office, closing the door gently behind him. Going to Kate's office, Peter explained his observations, thoughts and feelings.

"I don't know what to do," he finished.

"I do," said Kate. "He's come this far. Break it up now and it's all for nothing. Let him finish. He's clean. He's hydrating. You say he looks okay, Mr. Bennett."

"He does. But suddenly, I feel like I am torturing him."

"Obviously, I haven't known Larry long," Kate said. "But, based on what I've seen so far, I'll tell you this —never have I seen a man more determined to do what he must."

Marion agreed. "Let him come out on his own, Peter."

"We'll give him until Wednesday," Peter said. "Then I go in."

The little meeting broke up and they went their separate ways. Marion and Kate were calmer now, knowing that Larry was in control of himself. Peter remained restless though; his conscience was bothering him. He had been looking for something interesting to advance himself in the eyes of the corporation. Larry had stumbled into his world and he had immediately spotted the angle. For him, it had been all about business. Not once had he legitimately considered Larry's feelings. There wasn't any way that he could have anticipated how much he would like and respect Larry Martin. But now it was too late. He was stuck. He had fought with the board to have his way. They had finally consented, but with grave reservations. Somehow, he had to make this right. For everyone concerned. He was intensely worried that he couldn't.

Wednesday morning came. There had been no word from Larry. Fifteen boxes of Jack's were now stacked outside Larry's door. Housekeeping had left them there, not knowing what to do. Jack's had left them there to prove that Larry's orders had been fulfilled. Emma had reported the situation to Jack. Jack had called Peter, concerned that Mr. Martin was unhappy.

Peter buzzed Marion, "Call Jack's and have them make a hearty chicken soup for a delivery at seven o'clock tonight to Mr. Martin's office. I also want hot rolls and butter for Larry. For myself, order a BLT with fries. Add a couple of beers, Marion. Assure Jack again that this is not his fault. His food has been excellent, but Mr. Martin has been intensely busy. Have them come and clear away all the food stacked at Larry's door."

"Yes, very good, Peter," Marion said approvingly. "So, you're going in tonight?"

"I think I'd better."

"I'll call Tina Hawley and let her know Larry's pages are coming," Marion said. "I doubt she's aware of the length of Larry's work."

"Yes, do that. Tell her she may have to get a team together to manage it. If Larry was at a hundred and sixty-two pages on Monday, I can't guess the number he's at now. When he's ready to submit, I want them to move fast."

"How are we going to do this, Peter? The board was expecting a series, but this is approaching a book."

Peter fell silent. Then, he sighed. "I don't know. We have to see if Larry's work is even publishable. Let's start there."

"All right. Go to your meetings today. This will somehow all work out."

Peter hung up the phone and considered his situation. He had thought he knew what he was doing. He had been arrogant in that belief. Now he saw it could all go sideways. Badly. Everything depended on Larry. But then, it always had. Standing, he left his office and began his day. Feeling slightly nauseated, he endured a boring breakfast meeting and the more intense meetings of the afternoon that followed. He struggled to concentrate on the topics and issues that were being discussed. He returned to his office in the late afternoon and finished the article he'd been working up.

At six-thirty, he went to Larry's office and stood in front of his closed door. Sucking in his breath, Peter knocked and waited a few seconds before entering. Stepping in, he saw Larry sitting at his desk, working. Larry glanced up from his computer screen but said nothing.

Peter sank into the chair in front of Larry's desk. He opened with the only thing he could think of. "You are extremely important to me, Larry."

Larry swiveled his chair to look at his boss. "I'm aware of that," he said softly, his voice low.

Peter caught the spicy scent of Larry's cologne. He was shaved and attractively dressed. His white button-down shirt looked crisp and expensive. To Peter's eyes, Larry was more than in control of himself. He was continuing to grow. The angles of his face were a bit sharper, reflecting a slight weight loss. His clear brown eyes were calm as usual.

"I'm not talking just about work," Peter said intently. "You are also my friend and I care about you. Locking yourself away and not eating for so long has frightened me. Kate and Marion have been terribly concerned as well."

Larry gazed at Peter. Drawing in air, he breathed out slowly as his eyes closed. His mind was weary from relentless use, but internally, he felt cleansed as though he had rinsed a thousand toxins from his system. He opened his eyes and saw Peter waiting for him to say something.

Larry's lips curved slightly upward. Peter was sitting in front of him just like he had at the old homestead. And, he had just heard Peter call him his friend. It was all he'd ever wanted. The only way to not disappoint Peter was to write like a madman. At first, it had been difficult but then, something had shifted. He had fallen into his own life and faced his own demons. As he wrote, he began to slay them one by one. The days had slipped by swiftly, but he couldn't stop.

He hadn't felt any hunger for food; his hunger was for something higher. A story, his story. The examination of the emotional and physical abyss of deprivation the homeless suffer. That they were real people, just as he was a real person, and not invisible. The argument against laws and policies which deliberately instigated and perpetuated such misery. He had threaded all this together in a narration of his life turned into story. He had no idea if it was good. He had no idea if it worked. But he was trying.

"Peter," Larry said contritely, "I am so sorry that I frightened you. But you gave me a job to do and a quiet place to do it in. I fell into my work and could not come out of it. I did not want to come out of it." He touched the manuscript on his desk. "I will be going back into it when you leave."

"I'm not leaving, Larry," Peter said firmly. "I can't. Not yet. Please allow me to stay with you for a while longer. I understand what you're experiencing. And, I understand that you must go back. But, as your friend, please let's eat dinner tonight, here, together."

Larry nodded. He wasn't sure that he could face food yet, but maybe it was time. He had to balance things better. Worrying Peter wasn't what he had intended to do but, nevertheless, he had done just that.

Peter sighed, relieved. "Jacks is delivering at seven o'clock. I got you something easy on the stomach, just chicken soup and rolls."

"Thank you. That's perfect." Larry pushed away from his desk and stood up. He touched the button on his desk and the drapes began to slide open. He was cramping and needed to stretch his legs a bit. Walking past Peter, he went to the window. He saw that it was raining and growing dark. He was glad he wasn't in it and thought of all the people on the streets below who were. He touched the glass with his fingertips.

Watching Larry, Peter felt a sudden sting of tears in his eyes. Larry's simple movement of touching the rain through the glass undid him. No matter what happened with Larry's writing, he would do everything in his power to protect this marvelous, brave man. He had done everything right. And, he knew with a clarity that shook him, that he was the only thing standing between Larry being dry inside or put out into the rain again. The thought was unbearable. It wouldn't happen. He wouldn't allow it. He would fight the board, tooth and nail, if he had to, once this assignment was done and the series, if it happened, was over. Larry deserved better. If worse came to worse, Larry could be put in The Pit as a staff writer and still be employed.

Larry lowered his hand to his side. Turning his gaze from the window to Peter, he asked gently, "What are your questions, Peter."

"How far along are you?"

"I need another week."

A knock on the door startled them slightly. Larry strode to the door and accepted the Jack's boxes. Setting them on the desk, he settled into his chair. Peter opened the boxes and slid Larry his dinner. They ate in silence for a while. Finally, Peter asked, "How many pages?"

"I'm approaching 400."

Peter paused, his sandwich at his mouth. Sweet God. How was that humanly possible? Swiftly doing the math, Peter calculated that writing eight days at sixteen hours per day would have Larry producing at least thirty-two pages daily. It approached the impossible. No. It was impossible. Setting his sandwich down, he asked, "Are they good?"

"I don't know."

Peter sat back in his seat. Tina Hawley was going to have a heart attack. He still might too. No one was going to believe this.

# CHAPTER TWENTY NINE

Tina Hawley had that heart attack. Marion had given her a heads-up Martin's pages were coming, that they would be lengthy and she should have an editing team standing by. That was a week ago. Today, the bell rang. Martin's file had arrived.

Tim Jonson, her assistant, was standing over her shoulder as Tina opened the file. She looked at the page count and gasped. Her hand went to her mouth as she scrolled through the document. "I was expecting length, sure, what, fifty, okay, a hundred pages? After all, this is a series. But five hundred pages . . . oh dear God! This is a book!"

Tim leaned in closer to look and murmured, "Didn't this guy start like two weeks ago, Tina?"

"Print it out for me, Tim. I want to sit with it. Get Meyers and Becker to help you. Divide the book between the three of you into different sections. Go." Her team would check for content, structure, grammar, and punctuation. Tina knew full well that Martin had started two weeks ago. She had been notified that he was in town and was writing. She had sent Larry an email introducing herself, welcoming him and asking him to send her his pages when he was ready. She had told him he didn't have to finish before feeding them to her. They could work as they go along. He had written back, '*Nice to meet you, Tina. Thank you.*' Then, no pages had come. And, now this. Her breath caught. He must have written much of it before coming to New York. He had to. No one could do this in two weeks. It wasn't possible.

Studying her screen, Tina realized that Martin was using an interesting technique. His narrative read as though he were talking to you personally. It read simply and easily and drew you in to be his friend. Then he slipped into third person, a story telling mode, so that you could see things through his eyes. His thoughts, his fears, his humiliation and his tears. Scrolling to spot check, she determined quickly that it worked. His transitions seemed flawless, so far. His story was compelling and flowed with no exaggeration of words. It stayed that way no matter where she landed and read a bit. His style was clear, concise, and unpretentious. She was still reading when Tim placed the stack of double-spaced pages three inches high on her desk. She looked at the manuscript and shook her head. "Have Bess take over my current project, Tim. I'm going to concentrate on just this. Are you, Meyers, and Becker set on your divisions?"

"Yeah. They're already working. I'll start in a minute too. I just wanted to get you this first." He touched the stack in wonder, staring at the title page. *The Other Shoes of Larry Martin*. Who was this guy?

Tina looked up and said sharply, "Don't just stand there, Tim. Get to it!"

Tim went to his cubicle, sat, and opened the file on his computer. Yes, he would get started, but first he wanted to read Martin's opening. This project had been so hush-hush, it was unreal. He had been told not to mention it to anyone and he hadn't. Now he would see what all the secrecy had been about. He began to read:

*"My name is Larry Martin. I am a homeless man. I've changed the name of the town in which my story takes place for my own safety. I've also changed the names of the stores that I stole from for the same reason. I do have amends to make, but that will come later.*

*Now I am in New York, coming from the streets of a thriving city in Georgia I'll call Windsor. I thought Atlanta was big, but New York seems huge and strange to me. Peter Bennett of The Political Standard brought me here to write my story. Everyone at TPS has been extremely kind and gener-ous. I even have my own office where I can write to you and think in peace. This is all so astonishing to me because I am a guy with no friends, no money, and no home. The truth is, I am a little overwhelmed and frightened. As I settle in to talk with you, I expect that will go away.*

*I'm here because I have something to tell you. And to show you. I have agreed to expose my beating heart to you because you need to hear what I have to say. Not just for me, but for all the people who live without homes. I want to show you what the loss of all you own feels like. I want you to see how easily it happens. This is what happened to me . . . "*

Tim sat back in his chair, his hand in his hair. He couldn't believe it. A homeless guy. A nobody. And Martin had written the entire fucking book at TPS. He stared at the wall, envy stirring inside him. Sighing, he glanced at the clock. He'd better get to work or Tina would be up his ass. His division was chapters eleven to nineteen. The book had thirty chapters. He shook his head again in disbelief.

*       *       *       *       *       *

A week ago, Larry had closed his door again, note intact, but Marion, Kate, and Peter were no longer concerned. Larry hadn't come out for the entire week, but they all saw that he was eating. No Jack's boxes were stacking at his door. Peter had shared his thoughts and observations about his din-ner with Larry with Marion and Kate. The three were once again seated in Kate's office.

Peter said, "When I entered his office, I saw immediately that I was interrupting him. He told me he had fallen into his work and couldn't come out of it. There was a second there I thought he was going to throw me out. He said something like, 'And, I will be going back into it when you leave.' It was the way he said it—like he was already stepping back into his book and was telling me to go. But I told him I wasn't leaving, that I cared for him and would he please have dinner with me. Things improved from there. He's so calm, it's unnerving," Peter said. "Larry is a genuine enigma.

He's sweet and gentle—well, that's what he shows you—but underneath there's an iron will you don't even see coming." He frowned slightly. "It's hard to describe."

"But he is well?" Kate asked. "Does he look well?"

"Yes. Not eating did not hurt him. In fact, he looks so good, it's extraordinary. He's strong and groomed. He also had on the most handsome clothes. Did you manage that, Kate?"

"Yes. Through friends in the district and the money Larry gave me. He knew he had to have clothes. He had none really, not even a belt, so he basically invested every dollar he had. That's what he told me. It was five hundred dollars, not enough to buy a decent jacket, much less an entire wardrobe. He told me to shop clearance." She smiled at the thought of dressing Larry. "He let me choose his clothes. He was cooperative and grateful. With all those beautiful clothes around him, there wasn't an ounce of greed in him. None. I gave him back a hundred dollars. He couldn't be running around without any money in his pocket."

"Was that hundred your money or his?" Peter asked. He knew the lengths young assistants often went to get their job done. Right or wrong, it was part of the culture.

Kate shrugged. "Mine. But I wanted to help him succeed and I like him."

"I'm going to give you a raise, Kate," Peter said. He turned to Marion. "Will you see to it?" Marion nodded.

"Thank you, Mr. Bennett. I appreciate it. And, it's good to know that Mr. Martin is doing so well. It's a relief, honestly."

"It is." Peter stood, as he had a lot of work to do. Looking at Marion and Kate, he said, "He's going to do it again, you know. He says he needs another week. But now we know what to expect and that he is very much in control of himself."

✳   ✳   ✳   ✳   ✳

Peter rocked in his chair at his desk, consumed with anxiety. Marion had just buzzed him that Larry had just submitted his book. How long would it take for Tina to report her verdict?

He also had to face the board. If Tina said Larry's work was good, he'd have to provide a solution to managing its length. He didn't know how they would react. They didn't know this five hundred page book even existed. They would *not* like that they didn't. They might consider it unworkable. They could refuse to have anything to do with it and Larry's suffering would have been for nothing. But he would fight, and he would win. However, if they were right and the series sank from its own weight, he wouldn't be able to protect Larry at all.

On the other hand, if Tina said, 'No go,' he would be crushed, and possibly Larry with him. Then he'd have a fight on his hands to protect Larry. But he would have failed in the eyes of the board, so his position of protecting Larry would be greatly weakened. Even so, he would fight, and he would win, but it would be a bloody battle from which he wouldn't recover for a long time. His influence and direction would now be suspect.

Either way, he would have to find a way to negotiate it all and not get himself and Larry creamed in the process. Peter cupped his face in his hands and rocked. His head ached.

Larry came through Peter's open office door. He saw Peter was in a state and quietly sighed. He wasn't stupid. He'd already figured out most of the variables that Peter was facing. He knew what he had done but still, he hadn't been able to control himself. Peter had asked for a series, but instead he had produced a work that Peter might not be able to sell to his superiors. This was all his fault. Peter's obvious anxiety pierced him. He had put the man, his friend, in jeopardy. How badly, he wouldn't try to guess. "Peter," Larry said gently. "Take your hands off your face and look at me."

Peter slowly lowered his hands from his face. "I didn't know you were there, Larry. I'm— "

"Do not apologize, Peter. It's me that is sorry. I've given you a rough time and I'm aware of it. You asked me for something and I didn't give it to you. I tried, but I had to tell my story my way. And now you don't know what to do."

Peter wiped at his eyes. "No. I don't. Any ideas?"

"Yes. If Tina approves my book, I have a suggestion for you to sell to your board. It's not complicated."

"I'm listening."

"You'll release three chapters a day. I've designed the chapters so that they equate to approximately fifty pages per day. Each chapter is essentially sixteen pages, basically a twenty-minute read, even for slower readers. I avoided big words deliberately. In ten days, your entire series is completely released. For avid readers, three chapters per day will feed them enough to keep coming back. For those who aren't strong readers, my use of third person story-telling will make the length easier for them to digest."

"So, you're saying a ten-day series."

"Yes. That is what I'm saying. It may be a longer and larger than typical, but so what. The days will go by fast. At any rate, TPS is intellectually, academically, scientifically, and politically grounded in its reporting. Readership is acclimated to a higher mindset. A ten-day series will simply serve up more, but in a different way, which is what you wanted."

Peter nodded. It was a solid pitch and he could sell it. "Thank you, Larry. It's a fine argument and I'll use it."

"Now, we just have to see if my submission is accepted. Meanwhile, Peter, what do I do?"

"How about take a break and rest. You've worked incredibly hard. What you've accomplished is . . . beyond belief. Get out of the building, go see the city, get some fresh air."

"I will do that, but I need something more. I would like an assignment."

Peter massaged his temples. "Larry, please sit. I have a headache and looking up at you isn't helping."

Larry sank into the chair in front of Peter's desk. He was silent. He wanted an assignment for three reasons. First, if his book was rejected, he'd have written another piece that would be published. That would give him three published articles at TPS, enough to ask for a job as a staff writer. Second, he needed to show his worth to TPS to help Peter. If TPS gained something from Peter's gamble on him, at the very least, TPS would have some return on their investment, solidifying Peter's belief in him and TPS's belief in Peter. Third, he would go mad if he didn't have something to work on while he waited to see how his future would look. If Peter didn't assign him something now, this very minute, all this would not come about. The thought of going back to the streets was too much for him. He felt grim as he waited for Peter to respond.

Peter lowered his hands to his lap. "You wrote an education article on charter v. public schools. Follow that with another education-based article. DeVos, the U.S. Secretary of Education, has a new proposal to strip Obama-era guidelines and recodify how sexual harassment in the nation's schools are defined. Research it, attack it, and inform people of the consequences. Do it quickly, if you can. I hear The New York Times will be covering it, so let's get there first if possible."

Larry rose to leave Peter's office.

"Do you have time for a quick dinner tonight?"

"No. I will be working."

Peter smiled briefly. He didn't know why he had even asked.

*　*　*　*　*

Two days later, Tina called Peter. "I wanted you to be the first to know. Mr. Martin's book is excellent. My team and I have covered every inch of it and then, we did it again. We can find no fault. Structurally, it's sound. It reads fast and easy and the damn thing makes you cry."

"Overall, what did you come away with?"

"I will never look at a homeless person the same way again. Mr. Martin's story gave them a voice. He made them real and showed you how they each have their own stories."

She continued:

"He's attacked deliberate policy choices that force people to lose all they have — bankers for predatory lending, lawmakers for denying universal health care and forcing medical bankruptcy, big business for keeping all the profits while forcing employees to barely scrape by. And he did it in such a gentle way, he simply explained rather than lectured. He denounced conservative positions that preserve everything for the ultra-wealthy and leave nothing for anyone else or the country. He showed why their way doesn't work and I believed his argument. I'm not finished, Peter."

"Go on, Tina."

"He exposed—and I do mean laid bare—his own life, his rotten attitude towards others, his hatred, his abuse, his beliefs, his pain, and his gradual change in thinking.

But mostly, I fell for him. He became my friend. He talked with me, held my hand, and walked me through all this. It felt so personal. It was personal. When he cried, so did I. And the sections of his delusions of you, Peter, in the shack, and the killing of his father were so sad, but riveting. Anyway, I love this book. I feel sure that readers will eat it up. Some may even learn something. But."

"Out with it, Tina. But what . . . "

"I fear for him, okay? I mean it. Everyone will know everything about him, and he'll get ripped to shreds. Conservatives, alt-right people, MRAs, pundits, and more will all murder him. Worse, there are crazies out there who will come after him. One way or another, he is going to get very, very badly hurt. This is dangerous, Peter."

"So it's a go."

"Fuck you, Peter," Tina said, unhappily. "But yes, it's a go. What do you want me to do?"

"Inform the board that the series has been approved by you. I will handle the rest."

"They are going to be royally pissed, Peter, when they learn what this series really is."

"I know. But Larry gave me a solution and I can calm them down."

"Good luck. With all of it." Tina hung up.

Peter lifted his phone, called Marion, told her the news and what Tina had said.

Marion was quiet as she listened. Finally, she asked, "Have you told Larry yet?"

"No. Have him come to my office at his convenience." Peter hung up and swiveled his chair to look out the window. He would have gone to Larry's office, but he was always interrupting the man. Larry. He never stopped. Just as he never ceased to astonish him. Larry, who writes a five-hundred-page book in two weeks, never mind one that is publishable. It confounded him. He would never get over it. Not for the rest of his life. Nor would he get over Larry's iron will, self-control, and unstoppable determination. He had never seen such a thing. People worked hard, yes, and many defied the norm, rising above all others due to their dedicated efforts, their long hours and their brilliance, but Larry simply walked on a different level. How on earth did he get there? How did one person become such two distinct people that, if you stood them side by side, they would bear no physical resemblance to one another? But that was Larry. The enigma of him. He had finally found himself. And now, life was about to change drastically for him again.

Peter felt fear rise within him.

Larry came to Peter's open door and observed the man. He could see Peter's chair was turned toward the window. That meant he was lost in thought. He walked to Peter's desk. "I am here, Peter," he said gently.

Peter swiveled his chair and stood up. He walked over to Larry, coming close to stand in front of him. He felt somber as he looked into Larry's eyes, Tina's warning a tolling bell in his ears. "You did it, Larry," he said tenderly. "It's a go. Except I still have to deal with the board."

Larry walked into Peter's arms and rested there for a moment. He was so tired. He had done everything for Peter. He couldn't let him down, could he? It wasn't possible. But he could rest for a moment. He felt the warmth of Peter's body, and he closed his eyes, holding his friend. A tear trickled down his cheek. A sob followed, but he controlled it. Feeling Peter's arms tighten around him, he knew he had done the impossible.

He had made it to the other side.

\* \* \* \* \* \*

Marion buzzed Peter. "It's time. The board is waiting for you."

"Thank you, Marion." Peter rose from his desk and took a breath. It was a long walk down the hall, through the massive reception area, then down another long hall to the board room at its end. They were already arguing when he got there. Neilson Fowler, CEO, sat at the head of the table. His eyes betrayed nothing as he watched Peter enter the room and take his seat. Peter remained quiet as he listened to what was being said. Fowler was silent too, not participating in the argument.

Finally, Marcia Taft, the COO, rapped her pencil on the table, impatiently. "This isn't getting us anywhere. Enough. I want to hear from Peter."

"Why? He says one thing and does another," Gary Kirshal said angrily. "Bennett's gone against all recommendations not to bring that homeless guy here. But he just *had* to have it his way! Now, we've spent a fortune housing and feeding this homeless guy, Larry Martin, who doesn't know what he's doing and produces something we can't use. This is a surprise? I think we've all heard from Bennett enough!"

Bill Kirkland said, "I'm sorry to say it, but I have to agree."

Maxwell Blum looked thoughtful. "Look, the fact is, Mr. Martin has done something outstanding, especially if it's true he wrote his book in two weeks which, frankly, I don't believe. But why does it have to be a total loss? We can excerpt it and run the series that way."

"No." Peter said firmly. "We run it all or not at all."

"Why is that, Peter?" Marcia asked. "Obviously, we are experiencing great doubts that the size of Mr. Martin's work will work in our forum."

"It will work."

Stephan Littleton leaned forward. "Peter, saying so does not make it so. We expected a series. Instead, we got a five hundred page tome. The difference is huge. If you're so convinced it will work, explain to us how it possibly could."

Peter stood and walked to the opposite head of the table, so that he faced Neilson Fowler. He would talk to Fowler most directly but include the others.

"None of you have met Larry Martin," Peter said, looking around the table. "None of you have read his book. Is this true?"

Fowler gave a curt nod. Marcia, Littleton, and Blum nodded. Kirshal and Kirkland made no acknowledgement.

Peter continued, "I have met many people in my life. But, never have I met someone like Larry Martin. If he said he could command all the capitals of the world, I would believe him."

"Oh, for pity's sake," Kirshal uttered, throwing his pen down.

"Gary, you have not met the man, yet you judge him as someone of no worth and no intellect, simply because he is homeless. Then you dismiss my educated observation of him as well. Why?"

"Because you deceived us, Bennett."

"Certainly not. I couldn't know what this extraordinary man would produce in allowing him to express himself the best way he knew how. I will tell you for a fact that he did write his book in two weeks. I watched him do it and it was incredibly painful to behold. There is a stunning intelligence in Larry Martin and he has given us a great gift. He has also provided us with a plan for using his work. Tina Hawley says the book is amazing. Do we dismiss her judgment and educated opinion as well? She knows. Unlike you, she has read and experienced Martin's book."

"What is this plan, Peter?" Marcia asked.

"Three chapters per day for a series length of ten days. Mr. Martin specifically designed it this way to appeal to the intellectual nature of our readership." Peter locked eyes with Neilson Fowler. "Mr. Martin has delivered exactly what we hoped for and he has exceeded every reasonable expectation of TPS. There is not one of us in this room who could do what Larry Martin has done. This is but one part of his many points. We see people without homes and dismiss them as having nothing to offer or they wouldn't be in their position. But Martin has much to show you about this and more."

Bill Kirkland said, "Yet, in spite of his lofty intellect, he's still homeless, Bennett."

"No, Bill. That's another part of the point. He's not. He is here. And he is ours."

Neilson Fowler smiled.

# CHAPTER THIRTY

Bill Kirkland sat back, defeated, shaking his head. He wasn't angry, but he just didn't see how Martin's book would fly. It was too big and too long. No one would read it.

Gary Kirshal squinted at Peter in disdain. "So, when are we going to meet your boy wonder? Tell you what, why don't you bring him in now?"

"No," said Peter. "He is currently working up an article about the DeVos Proposal on a deadline for me. He's focused, so now is not the time. And I won't have him intimidated by all of you."

"We're not the wolves, Peter," Marcia said.

"He's working, Marcia," Peter said, his voice softened. "And he's been through hell. Let's leave him alone and let him do what he does best." Peter looked at the rest of the board. "There will be a right time. Just not now. Please understand this: I want all of you to stay away from Larry until I say differently. Do not go near him. I don't know of any other way to say it."

Neilson Fowler stood, and looking at Peter, he said, "I look forward to the series and meeting Mr. Martin when you're ready." To the others, he said, "We're done here."

*   *   *   *   *

Larry wandered the streets of Manhattan. He'd seen the Empire State Building, Central Park, and he smiled as he strolled down Fifth Avenue. Me, on Fifth Avenue, he thought. How incredible.

He still couldn't believe all that had happened to him. Much of it felt like someone else's dream. His memory of writing the book was still covered in mental gauze. But he remembered his words had poured into his computer like a waterfall into a river. That was because he had known what he wanted to say. It had come from the depths of him. It had been just a matter of his fingers keeping up and moving as fast as his thoughts. The hardest part had been keeping it simple. He had cried a lot during the process. Reliving his fear and pain had, in many ways, been cathartic. He had rarely felt tired, even with only a couple of hours of sleep each day. He knew now what it felt like to be driven beyond one's capacity and still keep going. His exhaustion had come only after he had finished and knew he still had to keep going.

Waiting for Tina's opinion had been hell on earth. He had not been able to eat or sleep. Seeing Peter hold his face in what looked like despair had torn him apart. He was glad he had had the foresight to make a key for Peter to unlock the board. But then, that was something only he could do. Peter had let him run amok and create in his own way. Peter had not tried to manage or reign him in. But this approach had also left Peter in the dark, left out of the process, and open to attack. He couldn't let his friend walk into the proverbial lion's den with a large book that was neither wanted nor expected, without a plan to manage it. Peter would have been defenseless. He couldn't have that.

He would have loved to have been allowed to observe the Board meeting. But whatever Peter had said, he had been successful, and now the series was in its third day of running.

The first day had been slow, only a couple hundred comments, and the readership meter had barely moved. The second day had been better; readership had increased noticeably but some of the comments revolted him. They admired his belief in keeping a woman in her place and ate it up when he struck Marney. Larry understood them because he had known them, had been one of them. He knew why they were furious when she punched his face and left him on the floor holding his bleeding nose. Many commenter's cheered for Marney, others said she was a bitch for rejecting him and the worst of them said he should have beaten and raped her in return. The viciousness turned his stomach and, for a while, he had stopped reading the comments.

Yesterday, there had been a flurry of excitement at TPS. Nine chapters were now published, and readership had taken a serious leap up. He had hoped it would, but it still surprised him. Kate had come into his office and told him the comments were now in the thousands. Her expression had not been pleased though. He knew what it meant without asking her. They were shredding him. He had smiled at her and told her that it would be okay. She had left his office then, to leave him to his writing and research. His DeVos article had been published a day before The New York Times had come out with their own analysis of the proposal. Now he was working on writing up an idea that income inequality might be correlated to violence in the political environment of America. He felt that he was onto something critical. He wanted to write something in-depth. As he was thinking about it, he had laid his head on his arms on his desk. He had slept, maybe. He had woken to Peter standing in front of his desk, his face unsmiling, offering him a cup of coffee. Peter had said he wouldn't give him any more assignments until he took a day off, walked, and got some rest.

Larry began to laugh as he thought of Peter's stubborn expression. But this time he had not argued. It had been a good idea. He did need to get out of the office to clear his head and reset himself. So here he was walking on Fifth Avenue, enjoying this beautiful day in early May. He reflected on how much things had changed. He now had a career with TPS, his book was being published, for better or worse—maybe worse—and he was feeling in control of his life. Peter had mentioned that it was time to start looking for a place for him to live and would call a real estate agent he knew.

Larry had also been pleasantly surprised to learn that his office was his to keep. He had fully expected to be thrown into The Pit, as his office was meant for an executive, and he was nothing of the sort. But he knew it was Peter's doing and he was glad that Peter had wanted to keep him close. That was what he wanted too.

Peter was plainly a powerful man at TPS, but Larry had seen him made vulnerable because of him and he would never forget it. It was the driving force of why he would never let the man down. Not then and not now. He had earned Peter's faith in him and he would keep it.

Larry hailed a cab and had the driver drop him off on 32nd street. He still wanted to walk and think, but now he was closer to his office and could walk home. He loved New York. He loved the restaurants, shops, and museums. He loved the crowded streets, the noise, and the insane traffic. He still had much to learn, but that would come. He wasn't quite ready to go back to his office, so he entered a small art gallery.

He had never believed in love at first sight, didn't think it was possible until he saw her approach, asking if she could help him. Her shoulder length hair was long and dark and glossy. Her eyes were the color of molten gold in contrast to the plain brown of his own. She was petite and she made him feel tall and strong against her smallness. She had looked into his eyes with curiosity and when her rosy lips had parted in a smile, the earth had fallen away from his feet. He wanted to circle his arms around her as he was falling. But he controlled himself and found his footing again.

He introduced himself and told her he was a journalist at TPS. He told her that he was hoping to move into a new place soon and had no idea of how to furnish it. When he had said his name, he had watched her expression closely. He could tell from the flicker of her long, dark lashes and the flash of cloud that came over her eyes that she knew who he was, but she betrayed neither recognition nor condemnation. Her eyes had cleared so swiftly, her recognition of him would have been imperceptible had he not been looking for it. But he did know. She lifted her hand and he lifted his own to embrace her long, slim fingers. He couldn't manage a professional handshake. Holding her warm, steady hand was something more to him. He willed a connection. And he felt it when it happened. Instead of letting go, she had pulled him forward, still holding his hand, under the guise of showing him the gallery. He knew he was being too silent, but he could barely think, could barely form words. She covered for him with easy conversation. Their togetherness flowed, and time went into its own corner, leaving them alone.

He couldn't bear to leave her when his tour was over, and he asked her to lunch with him. She came with him, still holding his hand. Over the meal, he found his voice. He had to. He couldn't let her do all the work. He began to laugh at her witty remarks and leaned into her words. He learned that the little gallery belonged to her and that it was holding its own. He learned that she painted and loved good wine. He learned that she was twenty-three years old. He learned that she was an avid reader of books and politics and that she read TPS daily. She wanted him to know, without saying so, that she knew who he was. They didn't discuss him. Not yet. He was glad for it because he only wanted to know about her. Then she told him what he wanted to hear: she would be glad to manage the furnishing and decoration of his new place when he got it, if he wanted. He felt such relief, he allowed his eyes close as he breathed in to control his pounding heart. He didn't want her to furnish the place just for him. He wanted it for her. It would be her home as well and he wanted her to be comfortable. He looked at her lovely face and smiled. She smiled back, sending his heart racing again. Her name was Susan Wyman.

Leaving her, lunch finished, Larry began to drift back to the office. He called Alan, just to check in. They talked more often now. He had told Alan about writing the book, and what had been happening to him. Alan was reading the series. He knew who Larry Martin was now. Alan had laughed that he could not believe that Larry had once possessed such an awful personality. But he had not laughed at Larry being homeless. It was important to Larry that he cement their relationship. He could only do it by being forthcoming and reaching out to Alan. Alan was warm and embracing in his response. Alan told Larry that he had added another limo to his small but growing business. Larry told Alan that he was thrilled for him but hoped that when he came to Atlanta, which he thought he might soon, that it would be Alan who drove him. Not in a professional way, but just to be with him. Alan had assured Larry that it would be him and no other driver. For now. They agreed to talk again soon.

Larry made it to his building, up the elevator and into reception. He stopped by the desk of Sara Steinman and introduced himself properly. Sara had heard that Larry had written his book in two weeks. Everyone was talking about it. Larry didn't know it, but it had catapulted him into the realm of being a god to the other writers. None of them understood it. None of them knew how he did it. But they all believed that he had done it. Peter Bennett himself had confirmed it. They were in awe of him. Sara was too. But she had the presence of mind to congratulate Larry on his success. He thanked her with a gentle smile and continued to his office. He went to his desk and typed a note. It read:

*"I need to sleep for a while. If possible, please don't disturb me. Thank you, Larry."*

He taped it to the door, made his bed, and got undressed. He washed his face and brushed his teeth. He closed the drapes, turned on his lamp, and turned off his overhead light. Sliding under the covers of his bed, he finally closed his eyes. He was long past the boundaries of fatigue. He intended to sleep for ten hours or more. He needed to recover from it all. He had been still running on fumes of awe and amazement. But the fumes were spent. He was on empty. He had nothing left. He could finally sleep now. It was time.

\* \* \* \* \* \*

Day four. Readership was up nearly thirty percent. It was astounding. The pundits and conservative radio personalities were starting to squawk about Larry and his series. Websites on the right and the left were picking it up as well. Kirshal and Kirkland looked at the numbers and knew they had been wrong. Neilson Fowler sat back in his chair and smiled. He had yet to meet Larry Martin. Peter was still controlling the board and keeping Larry unavailable. They had no choice but to wait. None of them would cross Peter. Not even himself.

Peter was a powerfully effective director and TPS had grown steadily under his guidance. Neilson knew when to get out of the way and let someone do their job. He tried his best to stay out of Peter's way. But the idea of bringing a homeless man to TPS to write and tell his story had strained even his credulity. Still. Peter had seen something in the potential of Mr. Martin, enough to have fought for it. Sometimes people see things others do not. He hadn't seen it himself, personally, but nevertheless, he decided to get out of Peter's way once more. He cast the deciding vote. He trusted Peter, and this could be interesting. It all depended on this homeless man and his ability to do his job, whatever it was. Only Peter knew.

But now he knew. He marveled at Peter's instincts. He marveled at Larry Martin's skillful ability to weave his personal story into a conversational scrutiny of how conservative governmental policies and corporate choices were deliberately creating more people without homes.

Martin had written:

*'I am a simple man, but still, an educated man. I look around me, as you can too, and see what is happening.*

*Let me ask you, do you ever wonder why are there so many people without homes today? There are many reasons, many of them directly connected to conservative policies.*

*Do you remember the housing bubble and the market crash of 2008? Of course you do. But I bet you didn't know that half the nation was affected by it. Think about that. Half. It's not a fluke that half of us lost our homes and our savings. Wall Street and a Republican administration did this to your friends and your family. To you. They did it deliberately. Then they came back and bought up all the foreclosed properties they had caused, only to rent them back to you at ever increasing rents. From a financial perspective, it was brilliant. They got richer. But it was also diabolical.*

*I know I've made some bad choices in my life—I'm on the streets because I was fired from my job and then, lost my home. But this kind of loss is not the only thing at work here.*

*You can work hard, work three jobs even, but what do you do when a bulldozer of law comes—one that you do not see—and scrapes you up, forcing you into a deep, black hole from which you can never recover? Who do you blame? Blacks? Muslims? Immigrants? I will tell you right now, you are being distracted from the truth . . .* '

Martin's book is a fascinating read, Neilson thought, but moreover, it's working for TPS. That was all he cared about. Even so, he was deeply impressed.

\* \* \* \* \* \*

Day five. Three more chapters released.

Right wing pundits, radio and websites started their attack. Martin was a hack, he was in it for the money, he had nothing new to say, he was a fraud. They laughed at his homelessness and twisted it into this guy was such a loser, no one could give him any credence. He was just another loud-mouth slacker, wanting his fifteen minutes of fame by using a gimmick of leaving solid conservative family values for liberal nonsense. He was a nutcase and so incompetent, he had been fired from his job by Ellison Bart and his important website, The Bart Data Report, a mover and a shaker in today's political forums. They all agreed that Martin deserved what had happened to him. They sneered at Larry's tears and asked on national TV, 'What man cries like that?' Martin was just another weak, liberal, whining snowflake. They indignantly declared that Martin should be investigated and prosecuted for theft.

But anyone paying attention noticed that the talking heads of TV, radio, and Web did not attack what Larry was saying, just the man, himself. The Right was hanging Larry Martin up and slicing him alive with their verbal steely knives.

Alt-right commenters, men's rights activists, incels, white nationalists, and other men's groups denounced Larry as a traitor. They whipped themselves into a frenzy, screaming wrathfully that Martin should be hanged, or someone should put him out of his sick, twisted misery and shoot him. They were furious with Larry for his abandonment of all they believed. He used to be one of them. They were incredulous that Martin had written:

'Women are the essence of our society and how we live. Without them, we have no strength, just barbarism. When Conservative laws seek to extinguish them, take away their reproductive control, force them into poverty by paying them less while shredding the safety nets that keep their children fed, what are we doing to ourselves?'

The TPS readership meter was rising, approaching near forty percent. People were listening to Martin. He had countless fans. Women loved him. Others appreciated his calm style of challenging them to think. The Left began their own tidal swell of fighting back on mainstream national TV talk shows and the internet. The odd thing was that no one knew what Larry Martin looked like. His byline at Bart's had no photo. There were no pictures of him on the internet. For the moment, they had fun with pulling Larry's old, vicious comments from the web and comparing them with his new progressive outlook. It drove the Right insane. They did not want Martin's transitional philosophies discussed, they did not want a mirror on his words, old or new. They only wanted Martin discredited as a liar, a thief, and a criminal.

Tina called Peter. "I told you."

"I know it."

"So, how is he? I've emailed him a couple of times just to stay in touch and ask how he's holding up. All I get in response is: I'm fine, Tina. Thank you for asking."

Peter let out a rueful chuckle. "Yes, that's Larry. He's always fine. Don't feel bad, Tina. That's all I get too."

"This has got to be seriously hard on him, Peter. Every aspect of his life is being examined and ripped apart. He's getting flayed alive on national television. Does he say anything?"

"No. Nothing. I think he knows what's going on, but Kate says he refuses to watch it. He absolutely loathes television."

Tina sighed. "Well, we know why. Listen, Peter, I have a favor to ask."

"I'm listening."

"Would it be possible for an informal introduction, say like under the auspices of a tour, to let me meet him? I've heard you've been keeping him under wraps."

Peter was silent. What would it hurt? Larry did need to see more of the workings of TPS. He hadn't even seen The Pit yet. But he didn't know how the staff writers would react to Larry's presence. They were boisterous, rowdy, outspoken, and sharp-tongued. A good group, overall. But Larry was so intensely different from them. Maybe he should start with Tina and her group. See how it went. The board might not be pleased that others had met Larry before them, but they could hardly argue with an office tour. Why not give Tina what she asked for? "All right. I'll let you know when we can come."

"Thanks, Peter." Tina hung up.

Peter rose from his desk and went to Larry's office. The door was open. Kate was in his office and had just said something that made Larry laugh. She saw Peter, smiled broadly, and turned to leave. A delivery man came behind Peter, trying to enter Larry's office, his trolley loaded with cases of paper. Peter stepped aside and let him by, waiting patiently for the man to unload and leave. Kate ushered the delivery man out and motioned for Peter to enter before closing the door behind her.

Peter sank into the chair in front of Larry's desk. "You've been a stranger. I've not seen you for two days."

"I've been working on a new in-depth." He told Peter what he was considering.

Peter nodded, liking it. "Are you up for taking a break this afternoon? I thought you might like to see more of TPS." Peter studied Larry's face. If he was feeling any stress from what was happening, it didn't show. He looked boyish and handsome. His eyes were clear and focused. His movements were composed and steady. His expression was typically serene. Everything was right, but Peter's sharp eyes picked up something more.

"Yes," Larry responded in his gentle way. "I can break. I am very interested in seeing more."

Peter sat back in his chair. Larry voice was low and calm, his meter, measured as always. He looked into his friend's eyes, trying to detect what was behind the subtle shift he was feeling. "Good. How about two o'clock?"

"That's fine." Larry smiled at Peter.

Peter began to rise but, changing his mind, he sat again. "All right. What's going on?"

"I've met someone, Peter. And I intend to marry her."

Peter was stunned. As Larry's news sank in, he began to laugh. Would Larry never cease to surprise him? "How, Larry? How long have you known her?"

"Two days."

"And you're going to marry her?" Peter asked incredulously.

"Yes. She just doesn't know it yet."

Peter gave a bark of laughter as Larry smiled impishly. Standing, he came around Larry's desk and gave his friend a brief hug while clapping him on the back. "I am very happy for you. But I won't say congratulations yet as it's a bit premature."

"I know. I'll take my time to be unquestionably sure. Although I feel sure now."

Peter's laughter faded, looking at Larry. "Oh Jesus, Larry, does she know what's happening with you?"

"We haven't talked about it yet. But yes, she does. She reads TPS."

"I hate to say this . . . but do you think it might be wise to stay away from her while all this is . . . "

"I have thought of it. I'll not take her out in public. I don't want her exposed to any potential craziness. But I will talk to her privately."

"That should work. Just be careful. All right then, I'll see you at two. Meet me at my office." Peter turned and went back to his own office.

At two o'clock, Peter escorted Larry to the editing offices, the next floor up. Stepping off the elevator, they nodded a greeting to the receptionist, and went through a door and down a short hall to its end of double glass doors that read: EDITING. Opening one of the glass doors, they stepped into a large area with a glass walled conference room, offices lining a wall, and a square section of cubicles.

Peter steered Larry to Tina's office. Larry saw it was brightly lit and had a seating area. Tina was at her large mahogany desk. Peter tapped on the open door to announce their presence.

Tina rose in greeting. She was in her late forties with short blond hair. She was athletic and attractive. Seeing Larry, her eyes widened, and her lips opened slightly, unable to hide her surprise. Stepping around her desk, she extended her hand, palm down, aware that she was staring. She had been expecting an older man, maybe with long graying hair, wearing an old Salvation Army jacket. She knew she had been stereotypical in her imaginings, but nothing prepared her for the beautiful boy who was standing in front of her. He smelled so good, she wanted to bury her nose in the area between his neck and shoulder. He wore neither jacket nor tie, but his clothes so stunningly fit his frame, she knew they had cost a fortune. He was standing tall and strong and his eyes were warm and merry, and she could not believe that he was the homeless man from his book. She was astonished and so very, very pleased. She would love working with this man.

Larry received her fingers into his palm and let them rest there.

Feeling the smooth heat of Larry's skin, to Tina, he had just stepped out of the book and into her reality. Tina blinked, emotional, and uttered, "I am so glad to meet you, Larry Martin."

Larry smiled at her sweetly. "I told you I was fine, Tina. But now you can see for yourself. I'm all in one piece." He laid his hand on his chest. His voice was low and teasing.

Tina laughed heartily and moved forward to circle her arms tightly around Larry. She hung onto him, unable to let go.

Larry's eyes misted, returning her hug gently but knowingly. He was profoundly aware of what she was feeling. He knew. It was much like when Peter had finally become alive and real to him, stepping out of his own dreams. There was no word for this experience in any language. And, he knew it would it take her a little time to adjust her fantasy of him to this world. It was not something most people would understand.

Tina let Larry go, wiping at the corners of her eyes. She had been the first one to experience Larry Martin. She had taken the manuscript home and cried over it, for many reasons. She had read the entire book in one night. The entire night. He had touched her deeply. He was her friend. She knew him well. Every word of him.

Down the hall, Stu Pearson scurried in to sit next to Tim Jonson, Tina's assistant. He whispered, "I heard that Larry Martin is here."

"I gotta see this guy for myself," Tim said, rising from his chair.

"Don't do it!" Stu warned. "Don't be stupid, Tim!"

"Don't worry. I'm just going to look."

Stepping out of his cubicle, Tim strode to Tina's office. Sticking his head though her open door, he announced, "Hey, Tina, I'm just going to step out for a bite to eat." He had tried to sound important, but he was focused on the young guy standing so close to his boss that he was nearly chest to chest with her. He seemed to be standing over her, almost protectively, and Tina appeared to be struggling with tears, wiping her eyes. Tim realized the kid had to be Martin. An all-consuming jealousy cut him open. This guy, Martin, was barely more than a boy, maybe nineteen, twenty at most, in comparison to his own young age of thirty-eight. Tim would never know what possessed him to enter Tina's office uninvited, but he couldn't control himself. Approaching Larry, Tim abruptly blocked

Tina with his arm as he shoved out his hand for the boy to shake. "I'm Tim Jonson. It's nice to meet you, Larry."

Larry saw Tina's expression fracture. Tim had broken their moment; her moment. He felt an anger rise within him at her loss. He turned his head and leveled his gaze at Tim.

"Did I interrupt something?" Tim asked, suddenly uncomfortable and suddenly, unaccountably fearful.

"Yes, Tim, you did," Larry said softly. "Perhaps we will meet at a more appropriate time."

As Larry gazed at him, unsmiling and silent, Tim lowered his hand and, for a moment, he stared into Larry's eyes. His mouth moved, beginning an apology, but no words came out. He gave Larry a short nod and backed out the door. Going back to his cubicle, he sat.

"Well," demanded Stu. "What do you think? What did he look like?"

"He's just a kid. Oh God, Stu, I think I did something stupid."

"What the heck, Tim? What did you do?"

"I think I barged in on them in a private moment. Bennett was in Tina's office too. Larry Martin looked at me . . . "

"He looked at you. Okay, so?"

"Nothing. I embarrassed myself. I couldn't talk. I opened my mouth to apologize but nothing came out. I think I really pissed him off. I am going to get fired."

Stu frowned. "No. It can't be that bad. Martin is just another writer."

Tim shook his head, recalling the scorching look in Martin's eyes. "No, Stu. Martin is not just another writer. I don't know what he is, but he isn't that." Tim rocked forward, anxiety slicing at him.

Stu saw he wasn't going to get any more out of his friend. Tim looked too worried, chewing on his fingernail. He sighed and went back to his own cubicle.

Back in Tina's office, Peter said, "I'll take Larry around, introduce him a bit, and then we must go."

Tina nodded, somehow at a loss. "I'll talk with you soon, Larry. I'm so glad to have finally met you."

"And I, you, Tina," Larry replied. He slowly pulled Tina back into his arms. Holding her to him, he closed his eyes and murmured, "I know what you are feeling. There are not many who could know, but I do. I know the moment of first encounter brought real from imagination. I understand, Tina."

Tina nodded against Larry's chest. She listened to the beating of Larry's heart and felt his power. She felt Larry's kindness and understanding. She closed her eyes and felt the stirrings of a deep emotional connection. She said, "I think you and I are going to be very close, Larry."

"It is what I want, Tina." He smiled down at her and watched her smile back at him. He released her.

Peter stepped forward and nodded knowingly to Tina. He turned to Larry. "It's time. We must move on now." He led Larry forward, out of Tina's office, and they visited the other offices and a few cubicles before leaving the division. They did not visit Tim.

Leaving Editing, Peter took Larry across the reception lobby to the large glass double doors forming the entrance to The Pit. It was a busy place with a massive layout of desks and computers. Some people were working, others were in groups talking, cracking jokes and laughing loudly. No one would describe the place as somber. As Larry and Peter entered, a few heads swiveled in their direction. Some, seeing Bennett, immediately quieted down. As the noise level began to drop, others fell quiet too, wondering what was going on. When the room was eventually silent, Peter announced, "Ladies and gentlemen, let me introduce Larry Martin to you."

For a moment, the eyes around the room stared at the man by Peter's side. Larry had a small smile on his face and he nodded briefly in acknowledgement of them. He didn't know what else to do. Gazing at them and feeling peaceful, he took in some of their various faces.

Someone began to clap. Larry blinked in surprise at the sudden sharp sound. Others began clapping too. Then the room stood, with everyone clapping.

Larry stepped forward to his fellow writers and accepted the hand of the nearest person.

Seeing that Larry was open to them, they surged around him with laughter and camaraderie. They patted him, hugged him, kissed his cheek, and shook his hand. Finally, after a while, Peter laughingly pulled Larry from the fray. It wasn't easy. The writers didn't want to let Larry go. They all wanted to touch him and talk with him.

Larry saw that Peter was ready to leave. He knew that Peter likely had his own deadlines and had not expected things to take so long. But Peter had been patient and now his time here was over. Being accepted by fellow writers was one of the most wonderful things he had ever experienced in his life. He would never forget this moment. "Thank you all," he said. "Now I must go." The writers stepped back for Larry, clearing his path. Following Peter to the door, Larry turned. He took in their smiling faces and nodded once more.

He left The Pit with Peter at his side.

# CHAPTER THIRTY ONE

Day six. TPS readership had risen to over sixty percent. Advertising revenue had jumped by seventy percent. Subscriptions by the thousands were flooding in. The money was flowing like a dam released; its rushing water making an already huge river rise even higher. The support for Larry Martin was tremendous. A million people were reading his book and it was having an impact. The Left loved his voice and his story and they were paying for it. The Right upped their attacks on Larry. In doing so, they created more interest in Larry's book that otherwise might have gone unnoticed. As a result, more people on the right began to read too, causing the readership numbers of TPS to swell even higher. Sara Steinman reported to Neilson Fowler and Peter that she was starting to get crank calls and threats against Martin. So far there was nothing serious, but she thought they should know.

Day seven. A note came in the mail with no return address. It was typed on regular printing stock and read: *'Larry Martin is a traitor. Larry Martin is going to die.'* Sara Steinman brought the note to Peter. Peter looked at it and grimaced. "Thank you, Sara."

"There are people coming into reception, Mr. Bennett. Right now, there is a pro-life group wanting to speak with Mr. Martin about his views on abortion."

"No. Tell them Mr. Martin isn't available."

"I understand. But there are also other people here who want Mr. Martin to tell their stories. There are a couple of protestors who say they want to set Mr. Martin straight and a reverend who wants to save Mr. Martin's soul. There are also reporters here demanding to meet Mr. Martin."

"I see." Peter rose from his desk. This was only going to get worse. "Can you clear the room, Sara?"

"Yes. I think so."

"Okay, do it, then call security at the front desk and tell them to lock us down. No one is to come up without permission. If you need help clearing reception, don't hesitate to call security. And, Sara . . . "

"Yes, sir."

"Can you find the envelope this note came in, or has it been discarded?"

"I'll try to find it. It may be in my trash basket."

"Try to find it and save it for Rod Dickson, head of internal security. Expect to hear from him. He may need it. He will instruct you on this and other incoming threats regarding Mr. Martin."

"Yes, sir."

"Keep me informed, Sara."

Sara nodded and left his office. Peter sank into his seat, holding the note. Leaning forward, he buzzed Marion. "Marion, Larry has gotten his first genuine death threat. Please contact Rod Dickson and have him get on top of this and any future threats against Larry. He will know who to inform, the NYPD or the FBI."

"I'll get to it immediately, Peter," responded Marion. "Is it very bad?"

"Yes. It is short and to the point. It says Larry is a traitor and will die." He listened to Marion's few short breaths of fright. Then she said, "Peter, Elliott Charles of MSNBC has invited Larry on his show for his last ten-minute segment at five-twenty tomorrow. Taping is at two o'clock. What do I tell him?"

"Have Larry come to my office at his convenience, Marion. I'll let you know."

Marion buzzed Larry on the intercom system. "Larry, Peter is hoping you can come to his office as soon as possible, but at your convenience."

"Okay, Marion. I won't be long," Larry replied, looking at his computer screen. He just had to secure his thought, then he could break. Typing quickly, he finished his paragraph. Rising, he went down the hall to Peter's office. Standing at the open door, he observed his friend sitting in his chair, lost in thought, looking unhappy. Peter was leaning on his chin, holding a piece of paper.

"Peter," Larry said softly. "I am here."

Peter saw Larry and a small smile brushed his lips. "Shut the door, Larry, come sit and talk with me."

Larry closed the door and sat in front of Peter. Peter leaned forward and handed him the death-threat note. Larry glanced at the paper. He saw now. Peter was suffering again on his behalf. He folded the paper back into its thirds, and laid it on Peter's desk. Raising his eyes to Peter's, he said slowly but firmly, "It means nothing, Peter. It is from someone who lives in their mother's basement with nothing better to do. I know them. Please don't suffer over it."

"We have a bit of a dilemma, Larry. But, it's all up to you."

"It always has been, Peter. Nothing has changed," Larry countered gently. "What is your quandary?"

"I honestly love you, Larry. And, if anything happened to you, I don't think I would get over it. I would not recover."

"I know. I'm glad you love me, Peter. And, I love you too. Very much. But we knew this would happen from the start. Again, nothing has changed."

"Yes. Something has changed." Peter fell silent.

Larry watched Peter closely. He could see his friend was deeply troubled. He felt an ache rise in his heart. Peter's pain did that to him. But he could do nothing to solve this until Peter was ready to speak again. He would wait.

Finally, Peter said, "I've looked all over the internet for a photo of you. There are none."

"No. I had no interest in posting any."

"It means that no one knows what you look like except for those in this office."

Larry was silent, wondering where this was going.

"Elliott Charles of MSNBC has invited you on his show."

Larry saw now. He understood Peter's predicament. "What do you want me to do, Peter?"

"I don't know. Your appearance would be great for TPS, but for you, maybe not." Peter shook his head. "Right now, you're shielded. I had hoped to keep it that way until things died down. But if you go on, that shield is lowered. Everyone will know what you look like. You're fair game after that."

Larry bowed his head, thinking. This was a tough one. If he went on and something bad happened as a result, Peter would drown in a sludge of unrecoverable guilt. He didn't want that. But if he didn't go on, he wasn't doing his job. He didn't want that either. He wasn't truly worried. The guys he had known were always ranting, but most were full of hot air. Still, it only took one to go off the deep end.

He knew there were guys out there who wanted chaos and to burn down all the social systems of government. He knew their core values were rooted in bigotry, racism and hatred of women. They wanted minorities to have nothing and women to be forced back into the home. They wanted it to be a white man's world and to hold onto the power they felt slipping away. Some were killers. They had guns. They shot up schools, churches, night clubs and other places in an effort to start culture wars, be remembered, and do their part in hurting people. Sometimes it didn't matter who died, so long as they killed.

Larry sat still, analyzing the matter. He considered his old online community. He had read some of their comments. They hated him. Felt betrayed by him. They wanted him hung or shot. They had encouraged others to murder him. He had read comments like: *Someone needs to take*

*Larry Martin down. Make the guy suffer and die slowly before handing him his heart and kicking him off the planet.'* He had felt so odd being the object of their violent musings. He had read his name over and over again. They wanted to rip him apart. He now knew what it felt like to be the victim of their rancor. In the end though, did he really believe one of them would come after him? No. He did not. His voice was just one out of many.

Now, this situation was out of Peter's hands. Peter could no longer protect him. Not unless he forbade him to go, which he wouldn't do and couldn't do as the Director of TPS and protecting its financial interests. He had to make a judgment, this very moment. What was it to be . . . potential harm to his life or the further enhancement of TPS?

Larry blinked, his thoughts racing. He could either live in fear or keep moving forward.

He knew he had given the impression that he had risen above it all. But he hadn't. He had been emotionally damaged internally, but had controlled what he showed externally. He had been content to let things ride like that for the last week.

He wanted to remain protected, and he didn't want Peter to worry or to expose Susan to any harassment. However, he had Kate pulling numbers daily from their SEO Group, TPS's own TOAD (Tracking Optimization Analysis Department), and revenue generation reports from Accounting. He was well aware of his impact on TPS, financially and otherwise. He had kept up with the national media TV spew, web conversation sections, and social media hot takes. He was aware that reporters were starting to stalk him. He already knew that he couldn't hide forever. It was just a matter of time. Very little time. They were already closing in on him. He could either get on the air and control things or let things control him. He opted for the former.

*       *       *       *       *       *

Day eight. Larry arrived at Rockefeller Center at one o'clock. He was immediately brought to makeup, where he asked for as little as possible. Then he
was directed to a chair by a desk on the set of *Our Media World*.

Elliott Charles was at the desk and rose to shake Larry's hand. "How
are you, Mr. Martin?" He hadn't known what to expect, but he was genuinely surprised at the presence of this collected, good-looking young man.

"I am fine, Mr. Charles. Thank you for having me."

"Are you ready to begin?"

"Yes."

Elliott gave a thumbs up to the camera crew.

The camera man said: "Okay, rolling 3-2-1. You're on, Mr. Charles."

Elliott turned to the camera and said, "Today we have with us Mr.
Larry Martin of The Political Standard. He has written a book titled The
Other Shoes of Larry Martin, currently being published in a series on The
Political Standard. There's been a lot of coverage on this book for a number
of days now. The book tells the tale of Larry's life, his homelessness, his
political opinions, his transition to liberalism and his philosophical rejection of rigid conservatism, both economically and socially. Would you say
that is a fair assessment, Larry?"

"Yes."

"You killed your father in the book. Let's talk about that."

"To be clear, Elliott, I killed my father in my dream, not in life. Ray
Martin is alive today and perhaps even watching this show. He is, however,
dead to me."

"Can we get into that?" Elliott said, leaning closer to Larry.

"My father is a radical conservative. He is a cruel man and was abusive to me as a child. He didn't have to be, but he chose to be. He hates
everyone: women, gays, blacks, Muslims, and immigrants. He is a fanatical
white supremacist. Growing up, his perspective formed my own conservative beliefs. At some point though, a person needs to think for himself."

"At what point did you start the transition to liberalism?"

"It was actually rather abrupt. Throughout my life, my treatment of people was repulsive and deplorable. I carried my conservative views through college and to The Bart Data Report. I covered the homeless and wrote about them as despicable people. After I was fired, I tried to find a job, but could not. Things went downhill quickly. I was illegally evicted and put on the streets. However, before I was, I had reached out to Peter Bennett, a progressive director at TPS, who believed everything I did not. I asked him for work. He was kind and allowed me to write two articles for him. During my research, I learned things I hadn't known before. I didn't know them because I was so set in my conservative thinking, I had never ventured outside that bubble."

"What did you learn?" Elliott asked, intrigued.

"That conservatism does not work. It's based on savage cruelty and a darkness that embraces authoritarianism. Their idea of morality is to create coalitions against those they consider adversarial outsider groups. Their intention is to dominate and exploit these vulnerable people. You see this, for example, in their treatment of women. Conservatives are obsessed with restraining their sexuality. Why?"

Elliott waved his hand and laughed. "You're on a roll, Larry. You tell me."

Larry did not laugh. Camera Two rolled in for a close up of Larry's face. The camera caught Larry's clear brown eyes and the bow of his lips. Martin was good. He was speaking slow and easy. He was young and handsome. The audience would eat him up.

"It's about control, Elliott. Take away reproductive rights and women are destroyed financially. Their voices are rendered powerless. White men retain the power over them. But nothing good can come of this."

"Why is that, Larry?" Elliott shifted in his chair, looking thoughtful. Camera One was on him.

"Because men will be financially destroyed as well. The cost of raising one child from birth to eighteen is now over a quarter of a million dollars in this country. What does a man do when he is forced to have unwanted children and cannot feed them? At what point is he broken? At what point does his family land on the streets if they have no one to take them in? What does a boy do when his girlfriend gets pregnant and he isn't financially able to be a father? You can continue the scenarios. The point is, men will pay dearly for their loss of reproductive rights as well. Consider that, if millions upon millions of children are forced into life every year that no one wants or can afford, men will also suffer a terrible plague of poverty. Homelessness will increase because wages are stagnant, while their costs to house and feed their families will become unbearable. There is always a breaking point. This breaking point, multiplied by the millions, will affect not only the civil aspects of our entire country, but also our entire economic structure."

Elliott leaned forward. "Listen Larry, conservatives, especially the religious, feel that abortion is murder. What do you say to that?"

Larry looked at Elliott. Camera three swung around to capture them both together.

"Two things. The first is that conservatives and religious people are free to believe what they want. But when their beliefs are forced on others who don't share that belief, their forces become oppressive. It goes back to authoritarianism. Forcing beliefs onto others has been repeatedly carried out in human history, with tragic and often catastrophic results. There is also the question of why a conservative belief is more valid than the belief of a progressive. It's not more valid. Conservatism is based on force, while liberalism seeks a universalism that allows an individual to do what is right for their own circumstances.

Second, there is the matter of our children. While Republicans are busy undermining reproductive rights, they are also busy cutting children's healthcare, Medicaid, the Supplemental Nutrition Assistance Program, Temporary Assistance for Needy Families, and Aid to Families with Needy Children. In short, they want to force Americans to have children they cannot feed, but neither do they want to feed them. It's a moral code that is based on punishment and misery. It cannot work. It cannot be sustained."

"What about birth control, Larry? Doesn't that help to keep the numbers down?" Elliott asked pointedly.

"Certainly. However, if Brett Kavanaugh makes it to the Supreme Court, there could be a problem. He apparently does not believe that Roe v. Wade is settled law. He has referred to birth control as 'abortion-inducing drugs.' This is not the first time Republicans have promoted this drivel. But for a Supreme Court judge to embrace such an anti-scientific lie, and if the Supreme Court becomes a dominant conservative power, birth control access may be in jeopardy as well as Roe. It remains to be seen."

"We're running out of time here. Let's go back to your transition of political beliefs. We just have two minutes."

"When I needed a job, my conservative friends rejected me. A kind, progressive man, one that had no reason to help me, helped me. When I was homeless, it was the kindness of strangers who kept me fed and helped me survive. I'll tell you this, Elliott, one helping hand is better than a million nonexistent bootstraps. It was this realization that pushed me over the edge. Hate does not work. Kindness does."

"Larry Martin, thank you for coming," Elliott said, looking at Larry.

"Thank you for having me."

Looking at the camera, Todd closed, "Again, Mr. Martin's book, The Other Shoes of Larry Martin, is still available and can be read on The Political Standard. Thank you all and have a good night."

The cameraman said, "3-2-1 and cut."

Larry unclipped the mic on his jacket lapel, set it on the desk and stood up. Elliott Charles also stood and came around his desk to stand in front of Larry.

"I appreciate the soft questions, Mr. Charles," Larry said, gazing calmly into his host's eyes. "I have never done an interview before."

"Son, I've watched you get creamed on national media. I thought it only fair that you have your say. And I thought you handled yourself very articulately—surprisingly so. However, I'm not sure I've done you any favors."

"Please explain."

Elliott sighed. He liked this intelligent young man. He hadn't missed a beat. He had been intent, composed, and well-spoken. And he had been self-assessing in a raw, humble way. He decided to be frank. "You called conservatism 'savage cruelty.' And that is what you'll see from them tomorrow in response."

"Thank you, sir. Have a good night." Larry shook Elliott's hand. He left the set, went down the hall to a bathroom, scrubbed his face, and vomited violently into the sink.

\* \* \* \* \* \*

Ray Martin was bored. He had started flipping channels to find something more interesting to watch. He felt listless and hungry. Lumbering to the kitchen, he opened the refrigerator door. Then he heard the talking head say, "Today we have with us Mr. Larry Martin of The Political Standard. He has written a book titled, The Other Shoes of Larry Martin, currently being published in a series on The Political Standard." That was his son's name. Larry Martin. It couldn't be. Food forgotten, Ray raced back to his TV. When the camera zoomed in on Larry's face, at first, he could hardly make his boy out. Larry looked completely different now. He blinked at his TV in disbelief. His son was not only unrecognizable, he looked healthy and rich. How was it possible that Larry had made it to the big leagues? He was stupider than shit. Even so, it seemed that he had.

Greed rose in Ray like a tidal wave. There was some gibberish from the pundit about some book. Ray wasn't able to follow and he didn't care. He was too focused on Larry looking rich. He moved to the sofa to watch his son on TV. Now that Larry has money, he can start forking a bunch of it over to me, he thought, and damn well do it for the rest of my life. Ray instantly saw Larry as his lottery and he began to cackle at the thought.

Then, Ray heard the show host say:

"You killed your father in the book. Let's talk about that."

"To be clear, Elliott, I killed my father in my dream, not in life. Ray Martin is alive today and perhaps even watching this show. He is, however, dead to me." Ray sat back abruptly, what the fuck? He heard his son say:

"My father is a radical conservative. He is a cruel man and was abusive to me as a child. He didn't have to be, but he chose to be."

Ray couldn't believe his ears. The little fucker. Larry had killed him on TV, with everyone watching. Humiliation and anger coursed through his veins. Grabbing his remote, he clicked off the set and threw it brutally against the wall. He heard his son's voice again, taunting him in his piggish brain. "He is, however, dead to me. He was abusive. He didn't have to be but he chose to be."

'Chose to be' stuck in his craw. Larry had deserved everything he had gotten. His boy had always mouthed off to him and stolen from him. Didn't the bible preach spare the rod, spoil the child? Well, he hadn't spared Larry anything. When Larry had been young, he'd forced him pull his down pants so he could whack his little ass, hard. Ray's mouth twisted, remembering. He may have gotten out of control with that a few times, unable to stop himself until the blood had dripped down Larry's legs. Every cry from his son had made him angrier, causing him to whip Larry even harder with his thin metal rod. Only wimps, faggots and women cried. No son of his was going to cry.

Ray remembered when Larry had been about nine years old, he'd caught the boy stealing a can of soup. He'd grabbed Larry's wrist and held his lighter flame under his son's palm. He remembered the smell of his son's burning flesh. Larry had kicked and screamed and cried. Larry had wrenched away and run from him. He had followed Larry into his room and punched him so hard for crying, he'd knocked him out. He had picked the boy up from the floor and tossed him onto the bed. Larry had remained unconscious for much of that afternoon. But the next day, Larry had been right back to stealing his damn food again. Larry had always been a rotten kid, crying too easily. He had done what was right in disciplining his son and trying to turn him into a man.

Sitting on his sofa, Ray looked around his dank, dark living room. He suddenly knew Larry was never coming home again. He had lost his boy and everything that would have come from him. He had lost everything. And he had learned it on TV. He lifted his hands to his face. All alone, Ray began to cry.

\* \* \* \* \* \*

Day nine. Larry rose at five in the morning, packed his bed away, showered, shaved, dressed, checked his emails, read some news, and got his breakfast from Jack's. After Emma delivered his food, he went to his computer and typed a note that read: *'Please don't disturb me.'* Taping the note to his door, he closed it shut.

He was feeling dizzy and ill and feverish. He could taste his vomit from yesterday still stuck in his throat. He had to lie down again. Going to his sofa, he shoved a soft decorator pillow under his head and hugged the other one to his chest. He heard the whispers of voices around him. "Your job is so easy, I bet I could do it with my eyes closed," one voice taunted. Another voice cut into him, "Celebrities are idiots. You got nothing to add. And you're not really even a celebrity, Larry. Just go away, man." Another voice rasped, "You're a nothing writer, Larry. Fake news. Do you know what we do with people like you? We shoot them." The voices began to talk louder and louder until they sounded like they were shrieking all around him. His brow creased as he fell asleep. He reduced the noise to, "Easy. Lazy. Fear. Kill you."

Larry thrashed about, unable to get comfortable. He jerked when he felt the bullet slam into his chest. He cried out, reaching out for Peter. They went down together as Peter was screaming. He felt the life draining from him. Tears leaked out of his eyes, onto his pillow. He came awake, eyes wide, feeling Peter's anguish and horror. Sitting up, he held his head. It was too much for him. Peter's anxiety had brought him down, had finally penetrated him. He understood Peter's fear now and it was terrifying.

It had been a bad nightmare and Larry could barely make it to his sink to splash his face. Glancing at himself in the mirror, he saw that he was shaking and pale. He was surprised that he looked so young. His hair was dark and soft around his face. His eyes were large and brown against the tight angles of his skin. Bracing his hands on the sink, he waited for his nausea to subside. His dream had been so real, he was still feeling the torment of it. The memory sucked at him, making him feel weary. He thought he might be sick again. But it was just a dream. It had been just a dream.

Moving to his door, Larry removed the note and sat down at his desk. He stared at his computer screen, steeling himself to jump in and learn the latest. Kate came in and handed him the hard copies of the TPS's latest readership and revenue numbers. She eyed him, watching his long lashes drop as he glanced at the data. The numbers were crazy, exceeding a hundred and five percent increase in activity. Larry set the papers down and smiled at Kate. "Good morning," he murmured weakly, still feeling nauseous.

She heard the gentle intonation of his voice and wondered what she was picking up on. She didn't have time to find out. Marion was speaking on the ICS, asking Larry to come to Peter's office at his convenience.

"I am coming now, Marion." Rising, Larry nodded to Kate and left his office. At Peter's open door, he waited. Peter was on the phone. He saw Peter wave him in and he sat, trying not to hold his stomach.

Peter hung up and looked at Larry. "Well, you have them going now, Larry."

"I know it."

Peter rubbed his eyes. *Savage cruelty.* The phone operators were reporting pandemonium. Sara Steinman had stopped answering her phone. TPS was on lockdown. Protestors were outside the building. Larry was being crucified on national television. His mouth was dry. He couldn't discern if it was from awe or fear. Two words. Two words had unleashed the wrath of hell. "I'm honestly afraid to let you out of the building, Larry," he said quietly.

Larry remained silent.

Peter leaned back in his chair, closing his eyes for a moment, listening to the pounding of his heart thud in his ears. He didn't know whether to choke Larry or congratulate him.

"Why did you want to see me, Peter?" Larry asked softly.

"Because we're back to a dilemma."

"Who is it?"

"Stephanie Ayers, CNN."

Larry nodded. She was a conservative talk show host who covered hot political issues. Her show was weekly and her forum was a roundtable discussion. "Is it taped?"

"Yes. Taping is at one o'clock this afternoon. You are a sudden and surprise guest. She is re-taping a quick panel for you. Her show will air tonight at nine o'clock."

"What do you want me to do, Peter?"

Peter rolled forward, leaning on his desk, his fingers around his mouth and chin. Finally, he said, "We need to get you out of the building in secrecy. I will not try to restrain you, Larry. Neither in word or action. But you have become a dangerous man, both to them and yourself."

"I'm aware of it."

Peter studied Larry's expression. It was peaceful. Larry's apparent serenity astounded him. He couldn't manage to control his own blood pressure and he wasn't the one facing this afternoon's firing squad. He wasn't the one facing torches and pikes. He debated whether to tell Larry of the death threats that had been phoned in throughout the night. What good would it do? He hadn't even congratulated Larry on his outstanding interview with Elliott Charles. His stomach churned. Part of him was afraid of the primordial scream that was developing inside him. But this man, his friend, seemed to be walking above it all. How, how, how was it possible?

"Peter," Larry said gently. "Please. I am begging you to stop. I can see you are working yourself up again. All of this is going to pass soon. The series ends tomorrow and my fifteen minutes of fame will dissipate."

Peter's eyes flickered. Larry could read him that well. He should expect it. He didn't hide his feelings from Larry, after all. Rising, he came around the desk, his hand out in respect. "You did a great interview with Charles, Larry. But I am not surprised. I don't think you can surprise me anymore. I hate to think of what you'd be doing, if you did."

Larry shook Peter's hand and laughed slightly at his levity.

"I'll have Marion make arrangements to get you safely out of here."

"Okay."

# CHAPTER THIRTY TWO

Charlie Streeter of Fox News came into the studio of CNN and sat down to watch the Ayers roundtable taping, live. He had caught wind that Larry Martin was going to be on as a surprise guest. Fox News had led the attack against Martin. But it wasn't just Fox. All the other conservative forums had thrown their spears, axes, and knives at him as well. Democrats were generally a spineless bunch, in his opinion, but Martin had gained a voice. A loud one. But Martin wasn't a Democrat either. The man wasn't even registered to vote. He was just some poor boy from the south, a nobody, with nothing.

Streeter had even checked out the archives of Ellison Bart's site to see what Martin had written. It wasn't bad, considering the vapidity of the topics. Nothing in-depth, but then, Bart's site was more oriented to being a sound bite, bomb-thrower, stirring up the rabble. Bart's followers were Nazis, KKK members, white nationalists, the far alt-right, conspiracy theorists, flat-earthers, and women-hating men with erection problems. Martin's writing had stood out just a little better than most, but that wasn't saying much. So, how did this simple boy from Atlanta write such a book? He'd heard that Martin had done it in just two weeks. Streeter felt a grudging admiration for the feat. He'd seen Martin on Elliott Charles and now knew what the man looked like. He might not like Charles, but he was older and well-respected in the media industry and could do what he wanted.

Elliott had allowed Martin to do his little dance with no resistance. Martin might have gained a few more points with his drama over men being affected by reproduction rights. It was the one thing the media never touched, never discussed. But Martin had stuck his thumb on it and twisted. Fortunately, he'd only had ten minutes. But his comment claiming that conservatism was 'savage cruelty' had been beyond the pale. Conservatives were rightly howling and throwing all they had against Martin. Now, Martin was venturing into a conservative political forum with Stephanie and her panel and he dearly wanted to see the man humiliated in person.

From the shadows, Streeter's eyes went to the set. The four were now seated and Ayers was introducing her panel: Cal Christopher of the Department of Politics at NYU, Ross Heisman of The National Policy Institute and Larry Martin of The Political Standard. The cameras were rolling.

Stephanie began, "You've recently stated, Mr. Martin, that, and I quote, 'conservatism is savage cruelty.' It's a broad and utterly vicious statement. Why did you make it?"

Larry responded, "It would take a book to answer that in-depth and maybe I should write it—"

"Oh, God no!" exclaimed Ross Heisman, laughing, interrupting Larry, trying to be funny and throw Martin off his game.

The panel laughed too but Larry's calm demeanor did not waver.

"The short answer is," Larry continued, "conservatism is based on intolerance of others, reproductive control, racial injustice, the erosion of worker's rights, voter suppression and predatory banking. It has brought about the destruction of the middle class and the deregulation of big business to pollute the air, destroy the environment, and poison the water for profit. That's just the beginning of this discussion. There is much more. The fact is, conservatism burns down everything it touches for regular people. This is what makes it savage."

Stephanie gasped slightly and turned to Cal Christopher, "What do you say to that?"

Christopher leaned in, "That's ridiculous. Current policies are freeing up more factory jobs under Trump. People are better off with his tax reductions too."

Ross Heisman added, "And, since banking restrictions are also being deregulated, Americans will be able to borrow money more easily as well."

Larry spoke with a slow and measured pace, "People who qualify can already borrow now. Restrictions were put back into place because lenders had created the housing bubble and Great Recession of 2007 to 2009. These catastrophes caused half the country to lose their savings and homes. The laws loosened under the Bush administration made it easy for banks to make subprime loans without income verification, and for Wall Street to bundle and sell these bad mortgages. Obama had to bail out the banks and other industries as well. And now it's being set up to happen again under the Trump administration. It will bring harm to the country once more. Are you suggesting this a good thing?"

"Don't put words into my mouth, Martin!" Heisman retorted.

"I asked you a question, Mr. Heisman," Larry returned mildly. "And, Mr. Christopher, while factory jobs may be up slightly, it doesn't move the income index. Overall, people are doing worse. Rents are escalating, wages are stagnant, and homelessness has become a crisis. It shows that conservative policies of trickle-down economics do not work. Trump's tax cuts gave pennies to regular Americans, and everything else to big business and the wealthy. Income inequality has never been worse. Forty-two people now own the same amount of wealth as the bottom 3.7 billion people in the world. But with conservative economic policies, this is a feature, not a bug. It's done on purpose."

"If it's so bad, Mr. Martin, why is unemployment so low?" Stephanie asked intently.

"Unemployment numbers reflect a certain truth, Ms. Ayers," Larry said gently, "but not the whole truth. For example, let's say you give the entire population one piece of bread per day. The numbers would reflect that a hundred percent of the population is being fed— and that would be true—but the whole truth would be that the population is, in reality, starving. And that is what's happening here."

Ross Heisman yelped, exasperated, "Oh, bosh! I disagree with you, Martin. That's not what's happening here! The economy has never been stronger, and conservative economics are keeping it that way. You are hardly qualified to give your opinion on economic matters, Martin, as you are not an economist. I am, but you're just a barely-surfaced homeless man!"

The camera closed in on Larry's face. Larry remained unruffled; his lips did not tighten. "And yet, Mr. Heisman, I have been asked here to do just that. People can learn about the consequential matters that affect them. It takes effort, but it can be done. People should learn. This is why education is so crucial to our country. But education is just one more thing that conservative policies seek to crush by underfunding public schools. They want to deliberately cause them to fail in a push towards private, often religious, charter schools that discriminate against applicants without recrimination. We haven't felt the effects yet, but as federal education policies continue to shift under DeVos, we will."

Christopher raised his voice at Larry, "You're focused on attacking the economic governance of conservative Republicans without merit—"

Heisman interrupted Cal, "Low taxes are what people want—"

"NO! He's calling conservative policies of governing savage and it's absurd! I won't let him get away with it—"

"It goes back to taxes, Martin," Heisman insisted again, "the prosperity it brings, and Republican's support for it. It helps the country!"

"Let's look at that, Mr. Heisman," Larry said calmly. "Take Oklahoma, a deeply red state, for example. What's happening there is a reflection of what conservative Republicans intend for the entire nation." The camera panned back as Larry continued, "Governor Fallin has been putting into practice the elimination of regulations, deep cuts in social spending, and made it nearly impossible to raise taxes—all GOP platforms. Instead of the prosperity you claim will happen, Oklahoma can hardly keep its schools open. The state is bringing in so little revenue, one in five schools are open just four days a week. Their teachers are paid less than all others in the country. Their hospitals and nursing homes are closing down because of severe cuts to Medicaid providers. The state can't even afford to put gas in the cars of its highway patrol cars, and last year officers were put on a mileage limit. Oklahoma's prisons, according to their director of corrections, are so overpopulated, they are approaching a crisis. Beyond this, the people are so poor, their household income ranks 43rd in the country. What, Mr. Heisman, do you think Governor Fallin is going to do?"

Heisman huffed, "You're obfuscating the issue, Martin, not giving the whole picture!"

"I asked you a question, Mr. Heisman. What is she going to do?"

"She's balancing her budget!" Cal defended angrily, jumping in. "She's doing what she's supposed to do!"

"No, she's backtracking." Larry countered firmly, "She's in debate with her Republican state legislature to raise taxes because the conservative policies she put into motion are not sustainable. And if the lesson of Oklahoma isn't enough for you, let's go to Kansas. In 2010, Sam Brownback was elected governor. Do you recall his public promises of a 'Grand Experiment', Mr. Christopher?"

"People say things in campaigns they can't always carry out in practice, Martin. It happens all the time with the Democrats too!"

"We're discussing conservative Republican policies, so let's stay focused on that," Larry said, regaining control. "Governor Brownback promised that Republican economics would turn the state into a paradise of prosperity. He slashed taxes, most specifically for the wealthy. He did so by eliminating state taxes on pass-through income. This is much like the provision in the recent tax cuts that Congressional Republicans passed on a national scale, even if theirs was a massive deduction rather than a total elimination of the tax. But, back in Kansas, what do you think was the result of Governor Brownback's promise of prosperity, Mr. Christopher?"

"It doesn't matter!" Heisman nearly yelled. "All that matters is the nation is doing fine with affordable taxes and low unemployment!"

"The nation is not doing 'fine', Mr. Heisman. The people of this country are drowning in thirteen trillion dollars of overall debt. Eighty percent of US workers are living paycheck to paycheck with one small crisis ready to bring them down. And, I asked you a question, Mr. Christopher. What was the result?"

Christopher glowered at Larry and said, "Stephanie, you may want to step in here."

Stephanie leaned in, her face composed in a professional manner, "I think I have to agree with Mr. Heisman, Mr. Martin. It's a matter of national application and not just one state."

Larry worked to remain calm. "It seems that none of you are willing to examine the conservative 'experiment' of practical application in Kansas. The result was catastrophic. State income plunged, causing cruel cutbacks in social services. Things got so bad, the state's bond rating was downgraded. The promised growth did not occur. During the Obama years, the state's growth nearly fell off the chart compared to the rest of the nation. The job growth in Kansas fell to less than half of what it was for the rest of America."

Larry turned to Heisman and Christopher. "And when you examine when this happened, you'll find that it did so exactly between when the tax cuts were enacted and when they were reduced in 2017. The drop in Kansas job growth was staggering in the harm to its people. Jobs were diminished to the point of being less than all of its neighbors except one. Tell me, Ms. Ayers, which state was that?"

Stephanie's lips tightened. "Oklahoma."

"This is bull!" yelled Heisman, "You can't—"

"No, Mr. Heisman," Larry cut in, his low voice harder, "it's not bull, it's people's lives. Trickle-down economic policies are savage because they cause unmitigated misery. And when those policies are enacted in conjunction with radical cuts in social services, laws unleashing predatory banking, a massive rise in student debt, and the lack of American savings— it all becomes a recipe for national collapse."

"No one appreciates your drama, Martin, and Democrats have been responsible for this too!"

"I am happy to discuss the Democrat's culpability at another time, if you wish, Mr. Heisman. But for now, I redirect your attention back to the reality of The Great Recession. It happened. And it wasn't caused by my drama. If we are not careful, it will happen again."

Heisman's voice rose in agitation, "It won't happen again, Martin! You don't know that and it's irresponsible for you to say so!"

"The facts don't lie, Mr. Heisman." Larry countered. "But next time, foreign investment—from China, Germany or others—will snap up newly created bundled mortgage derivatives at an even greater rate, and then we will really have a problem."

Cal Christopher yelled over Larry: "I don't know where you get your information from, but you're an idiot—!"

Larry said calmly, "Mr. Christopher, once the U.S. housing market embraced radically shoddy underwriting standards, many mortgages were created and sold fraudulently. It does not take an economist to know this."

Heisman yelled, "This is a complicated issue, Martin and it does take an economist to understand the implications of what happened. You don't—"

"Anyone who reads, Mr. Heisman, now knows that this fraud was created by mortgage brokers, mortgage bankers, aggregators, and various securities underwriters who were all unfortunately assisted by the ratings companies. For a period of three years, everyone had fun making a ton of cash off the fees these bad mortgages generated. And when the market finally crashed, both foreign and domestic investors bought massive amounts of foreclosed homes in bundles at auction. They did this in order to rent them back to the American people at increasing and unaffordable rates. Housing in this country remains a crisis. People have become poor because of Wall Street, lax conservative banking policies, and malicious intent."

Christopher snarled angrily, "People aren't poor, Martin. Jobs are strong and what you're saying is crap!"

Larry drew in a patient breath. "Mr. Christopher, half this country lives paycheck to paycheck. Half this country does not have a thousand dollars in savings. Half this country cannot afford a medical bill of even four hundred dollars."

"Again, Martin," Christopher snorted, "I don't know where you get your information! That's just ludicrous!"

"The Fed, sir. More specifically, the Federal Reserve Board's 2017 report on the economic well-being of U.S. households, researching the financial stability of Americans. That was then. Things are definitely worse now as rents and the cost of living are much higher. Add to this misery of the nearly one and a half trillion dollar debt owed by students who will never get married or own a home as a result. And yet, Republicans just chose to give billionaires a tax rebate of the same amount — 1.5 trillion dollars — that could have been used to help mitigate student debt and thus stimulate the economy. The effect on the economy from both these debacles will, in the future, be awful. But then, you already know this. You read the same reports I do."

Christopher and Heisman shook their heads in frustration.

Ignoring them, Larry turned to his host and continued, "This is about the failures and breakdown of our systems that allowed a malignant narcissist to come to power. And the conservative Republican culpability in supporting him, regardless of his very questionable mental state. It's not my drama that embraces a system that has been careening towards this outcome for decades. We need to examine political corruption, institutional failures, and abuses of power. Conservative abuses of power. Republican deregulation and economic policies are not about the welfare of regular people or boosting economic growth. It's been all about enriching the billionaires, the banks, and Wall Street. Think of the Supreme Court ruling on Citizens United, which made corporations people and turned big money into speech in an effort to kill the voice of the people. Now our congressional representatives are owned by those special interests of big business. It's just another way of rewarding the donor class that keeps Republicans in power at the expense of the American people."

Heisman laughed angrily, shaking his head. "You are so wrong, Martin."

"My evidence is the poor economic condition of this country, Mr. Heisman. You have huffed and puffed and attacked me personally, but you've not given one shred of evidence to prove I'm wrong." The camera rolled up for another close-up of Larry.

Turning to Stephanie, Larry softened his voice, "People like public roads, museums, schools, libraries, and the social services that help them survive, all things the government provides. They like to eat, have a home, and be able to pay their bills. We must somehow all live together. To do so, it must be equitable on some level. You can't slash Medicaid and Medicare and all the social programs that help people in this country and actually believe people will be better off. You can't have fiscal policies that allow billionaires and corporations to buy Congress to do their bidding, especially in terms of deregulation that harms the planet and exploits vulnerable people. You can't have tax policies that place the burden on middle America when the corporations and ultra-wealthy are not paying their fair share. It can't all go to the wealthy few, leaving little to nothing for the rest of us. It is not sustainable. Where is the investment in education, national health care, infrastructure, and green technology to make our nation stronger and smarter? How do people deal with the lies they are being told by this President? How do they function in a world where facts are no longer being considered, science is being silenced, and reason is thrown out the door? Who comes up with the bizarre notion of 'alternative facts'? People are crying, Stephanie. The world, to them, is burning. When laws and policies make people desperate, they will become lawless and do desperate things. They will sleep on the streets. They will self-medicate with opioids. They will fill the jails. People do terrible and sad things when they have no hope. It doesn't have to be like this, Stephanie. The cause of hopelessness is fundamental. It lies in the policy choices that fuel it. And these policies must be overhauled."

Stephanie sighed. "We're done for tonight. Thank you, Mr. Heisman of the National Policy Institute, Mr. Christopher of NYU's Department of Politics and Mr. Larry Martin of The Political Standard, for coming. Until next week." (commercial break.)

Heisman and Christopher left without speaking to Larry. Stephanie came up to Larry, brushed his arm for a moment while looking into his eyes, then turned and walked away, leaving Larry to stand on the set alone. One of the cameramen approached Larry, "I think it was something you said, Mr. Martin," he said, not entirely joking as he extended his hand. As Larry shook it, he said, "Good job, sir. I appreciate you advocating for the people."

"What is your name?" Larry asked.

"Benjamin Case, Mr. Martin."

Thank you, Benjamin. I sincerely appreciate you saying so. Is it possible for you to lead me out of here?"

"Yes, sir. Come with me."

\*   \*   \*   \*   \*   \*

Charlie Streeter called his office. "Arrange an interview with Larry Martin of The Political Standard for my show as soon as possible. And if TPS says no, press them hard on it. Just get it arranged." He slipped his cell phone back into his pocket and shook his head. Stephanie had let Martin step all over her. Heisman and Christopher were just as impotent and useless. He had an idea that would bring Martin down.

\*   \*   \*   \*   \*   \*

Larry was tired and his head hurt. He had never been so frightened in his life. He hoped the taping wouldn't be edited too badly. He would see tonight. He wished that he could see Peter, but he was in meetings for the rest of the day. Now he just wanted to get back to the office and call Susan.

The driver of his car, a plain Volvo that would draw no attention, turned off of Columbia Circle and back to TPS. He didn't try to talk as he could see Mr. Martin's eyes were closed. He took Larry to a different parking deck than that of TPS and let him off.

Larry thanked him and went through the back-entrance elevator and up to his office. He closed the door and sat at his desk. Calling Susan, he hoped that she would pick up. She could be busy at the gallery but he knew she was waiting for him to call. They talked every night. He had promised to call after the CNN taping. She had agreed to be apart from him until this was over. But he wanted so badly to hold her. He listened to her phone ring. Then he heard:

"Larry, I'm here. I didn't mean to take so long but a client was just leaving."

"That's okay, Susan. I'm just glad to hear your voice."

"Larry, things seem bad for you on TV . . . "

"Shhhh, Susan," he said softly, "Let's not talk of that. Tell me, instead, how your day is going." He listened to her chatter, her laughter, and he felt his heart grow lighter.

\*　\*　\*　\*　\*　\*

At 8:45 that evening, Larry left his office and wandered down the hall to reception. He knew the room would be empty and he wanted to sit in Sara's executive chair to watch his interview on one of the big screens mounted on the wall behind her desk. Coming through the doors, he looked up, dismayed. The room was full of people and the mounted TVs were on, their volumes set low. This is not what he wanted. People were approaching him. He felt sick.

"Mr. Martin, I am Neilson Fowler. I hope your interview went well?"

"I did my best, sir. We will see what happens."

Turning, Fowler introduced Larry to the other board members. Each shook Larry's hand. Larry summoned a peace within himself but was too tired to say much or smile. The board saw a serious, calm, quiet young man. They were impressed.

Peter stepped off the elevator into reception from his last meeting of his day, dinner with some advertisers. He quickly scanned the unusual scene. Seeing the board surrounding Larry made his jaw tighten. Larry looked exhausted. Damn them. The rest of the people were writers, secretaries, assistant's, TOADs, and executives left over from a long day's work and not yet gone home.

Walking up to Larry, Peter shook Fowler's hand and their eyes locked. Fowler noted Peter's flicker of anger. Peter nodded abruptly to the other board members and took Larry by the arm to lead him out of the group.

"Peter," Larry uttered softly, "I do not want to be here."

"Stay strong, Larry," Peter whispered. "Don't run. Let me get you to the back of the room, out of sight."

Larry nodded, allowing Peter to guide him. This was worse than he had ever imagined. The pressure was too much for him. His head was splitting and his heart was pounding. Why was the board here? What if he had made an ass of himself on CNN? What if they edited it to make him look stupid? His eyes welled, walking forward. He was very upset.

Peter saw the gloss of tears in Larry's eyes. Propelling Larry forward, they reached a sofa in the back of the room. It was full. "Please allow us to sit here," he said to the girls. "I'm sorry, but find another seat." The secretaries promptly scattered. Peter sat Larry down.

"I'm going to be sick. No, Peter, I am sick," Larry mumbled.

Peter motioned a girl forward, "Quick, please, drawing no attention to yourself, get me some water. Hurry now." The girl turned and moved smoothly through the crowd. She returned equally as smoothly with a bottled water. Peter took it from her and cracked it open. Handing it to Larry, he murmured, "Drink."

The volume rose on the TVs. The roundtable was beginning. CNN music was playing. Stephanie's set appeared and she was introducing her panel:

"Cal Christopher of the Department of Politics at NYU, Ross Heisman of The National Policy Institute and Larry Martin of The Political Standard. Stephanie began, "You've recently stated, Mr. Martin, that, and I quote, 'conservatism is 'savage cruelty'. It's a broad and utterly vicious statement. Why did you make it?"

Larry fell back on the sofa. He closed his eyes. He knew every line of what he had said. He would know if the roundtable had been edited. There was complete silence in the room as everyone listened. The tape continued to run as it had in real time. As it went on, Larry began to breathe again as it finished with no edits. He believed it was possible that Stephanie Ayers was responsible. He would send her roses. But, at the moment, the room was spinning. He was having trouble seeing.

Rising, everyone cheered and clapped loudly as they searched for Larry. Peter and Larry stood and began to make their way back to their offices. As they moved along, people smiled at Larry, shaking his hand, touching his sleeve, clapping his shoulder and the writers shook him with affection.

Neilson Fowler held out his hand and leveled his gaze into Larry's eyes. "I'm glad you're ours, Mr. Martin."

"Thank you, sir," Larry said, shaking Fowler's hand. The room reeled.

Peter gave Fowler a nod and said, "Let's let the man rest now, shall we?"

Fowler smiled slightly. He saw that Peter remained intensely protective of Martin. "Good night then, Larry Martin, and you too, Peter."

He stepped aside and allowed them to go through the door.

# CHAPTER THIRTY THREE

Day ten. Peter was sitting at his desk. It was nine in the morning. He was working on an op-ed but could not concentrate. He leaned back in his chair and swiveled to look out the window. It was dark and raining. His mood was foul.

TPS remained on lockdown and probably would stay that way for another three weeks, if not longer. Larry was getting more death threats than ever. The operators had been instructed to make a note of each and every one. Not one was to be overlooked. There were nine letters now. He wouldn't show them to Larry. But it was the first one that still chilled his blood. Made him afraid. Larry Martin is going to die. It wasn't a suggestion; it wasn't a rant. It was a statement. It made him upset. It made him fearful. He'd had enough of it. He would be glad when all this was over.

He sighed, rubbing his face, thinking of Larry. Last night, seeing the board surrounding him had made him furious. He hadn't been able to keep his anger from his eyes. Neilson had called him at six this morning to apologize. Neilson had said that he and the others hadn't known that Larry would come out to reception to watch. But, since he had, it had seemed like a good opportunity to meet him. They had instantly recognized Larry from his Elliott Charles interview.

He had lost his temper with Fowler:

"I asked you to wait, Neilson. Do you think I had no reason to tell you all to stay away? Do you pay me to have *NO* reasons? All of you could have stayed in the background and not revealed to Larry that you were there. All of you chose to ignore my explicit request, my explicit directive. And, I am deeply disturbed over being ignored. You have me greatly upset! I want you and the others to leave Larry alone until I say otherwise. Do *not* come near him! None of you! DO NOT COME NEAR HIM! *EVER!* Do we have a final understanding on this?"

Fowler had agreed. He had apologized again and emphasized that their reaction to suddenly seeing Martin had been spontaneous rather than an intent to be disrespectful.

It had not mollified him. There were very few things he could control to keep pressure off of Larry. The death threats were one. The board and their air of all-important intimidation was another. Billionaires, they all had that air wrapped around them. It didn't matter where they went, that atmosphere still clung to them.

It wasn't enough that Larry was doing Herculean things. They all knew the simple place from which Larry had come. They all knew that Larry had no experience in this ungodly rich, fast-paced world of New York. They all knew that Larry, regardless of having no background, had pounded out a book for them and had faced MSNBC and CNN for them, all in the space of countable days. They all knew his life was being threatened. They all knew that Larry had enriched them greatly. But still, it was not enough. They had to have more. It angered him that they did. It angered him that they hadn't listened to him. It angered him that they didn't care about Larry, the man himself.

And then, Fowler had lowered his boom:

Fowler wanted Larry to appear on the Charlie Streeter show. He had gotten a call from a higher-up at Fox News asking for this favor.

As he had listened to Neilson, he gleaned that Streeter had known he would be rejected. As a preemptive maneuver, Streeter had called in a marker. That individual had approached Fowler directly, rather than go through the proper channels of invitation. Now Neilson was leaning on him to lean on Larry. He had argued with Neilson that it had to be Larry's decision. That he did not believe Larry could handle it right now. He had argued that it was unreasonable to demand it of Larry, when Larry had already done so much. That, in his opinion, Streeter was a vicious man who loved to decimate his victims on live television. But Fowler had insisted anyway. And now his anger had rolled into fury. Oh, yes, his mood was foul.

Last night with Larry had been nearly unbearable. After CNN and his encounter with the Board, Larry hadn't said a word as they walked back to his office. That he didn't speak wasn't the issue, it was the way he didn't speak. Larry had held on only long enough to get back to his office, away from the eyes of others.

He had led Larry through his office door into the middle of the room. He had come around to stand in front of him. He remembered Larry's face being terrifyingly pale, that his eyes had looked frightened as they blinked in slow motion. As if trying to register what was happening to his body. As if trying to fight to stay conscious. He had seen that Larry was sliding into some form of shock. He remembered thinking it was from pressure overload.

He had watched Larry's system shut down in front of his eyes. Then Larry had looked at him and he had actually watched the light go out of Larry's eyes. It had terrified him.

He remembered how he had murmured in horror, 'no no no no' as Larry had begun to fall. He remembered wrapping his arms around him to stop his fall. He remembered feeling tears on his face, holding his friend against his chest, begging him to come back, to wake. He remembered not knowing what to do. He remembered that Larry had told him he was sick. And that he had done nothing but tell him to stay strong and to give him water.

Standing there, with Larry in his arms, holding him so tightly to prevent his slipping to the floor, the man's cheek against his shoulder, he had cursed himself inwardly while saying, 'I'm so sorry, I'm so sorry, I'm so sorry . . .'

It had seemed like an eternity. But Larry had come back to him. Larry had whispered, "Peter, help me to lie down." His words had been so nearly imperceptible, he almost hadn't heard them. He had slowly and carefully steadied Larry to his own two feet. He had led him to his chair and given him water and aspirin. He had moved fast to make Larry a proper bed so he could have a proper sleep. He had knelt before Larry and taken off his shoes. He had led Larry to the sofa and helped him get out of his clothes down to his t-shirt and boxers. He had felt his friend trembling as he laid him down and covered him. He had left Larry's lamp on, the way he liked it. He had closed the drapes and turned off the overhead lights.

But he had not left Larry.

He had spent the night in Larry's chair at his desk, feeling the presence of Larry's workspace, the way the lamp shone on his pages, and breathing in, as his own eyes closed, the clean hint of Larry's cologne.

At four-thirty in the morning, he had woken. He had gone back to his own office to get the dry-cleaning hanging on the back of his door and a full fresh set of underwear from laundry stacked in the long dresser on the wall. He had come back to Larry's office to shower, shave, and get dressed. He had knelt by Larry, and felt the steady rhythm of his breath. He had laid his hand on Larry's forehead to check for fever. He had handwritten a do not disturb note and taped it to Larry's door and he had left him sleeping.

As he watched the rain through his window, Peter recalled Larry saying on TV, 'There is always a breaking point'. He knew that Larry had reached his. Larry might live on a plain all his own, but he had fallen off of it last night. And now he was faced with telling him to appear on Charlie Streeter. He wondered what Larry's reaction would be.

"Peter," Marion said, coming into his office.

Peter turned his chair to face her. He saw that her expression looked anxious as she sank into the chair in front of him. "I just got a call from Neilson Fowler to arrange for Larry to go on Streeter. Can this be right?"

"No. Arrange nothing. Tell them you will have to check with Mr. Martin and you will get back to them with his answer."

"What is going on, Peter? This is all so out of control. "

"I know. And it's worse than you think." Peter told Marion what had happened to Larry last night. He told her because he needed her help to protect Larry.

Marion sat back in her chair, her mouth slightly open in worry. "Should we get him to a hospital, Peter?"

"I don't know. Neilson doesn't know about this and I don't want him to know. Let's see how Larry is when he wakes up. We'll know what to do then."

Marion's lips tightened. "No. We need to wake him now and find out. Peter, he collapsed! It's enough now!"

Peter looked at Marion. Her expression was immutable. "All right."

They rose and went to Larry's office. The office door was still closed, Peter's note still there. The box from Jack's was on the floor by his door. Peter quietly opened the door without knocking. He saw Larry at his desk, reaching for the phone, fully showered, shaved, and dressed. Larry looked up, and lowering his arm to his lap, said, "Come in, Peter."

Peter and Marion entered the room. Marion shut the door behind her. They both sat in front of Larry.

"Hello, Marion," Larry said gently. He looked at their concerned faces and sought to soothe them. "I am fine now. Peter, I apologize for last night. Marion, I can see that he told you."

"Are you really fine?" Marion asked urgently, leaning forward, searching Larry eyes.

"Yes and no," Larry replied softly. "I don't know what happened to me. The room just gave out. I couldn't control it. I'm glad you were there, Peter. Thank you for catching me. Thank you for helping me to lie down, although I wish you had not seen any of it. But I woke up feeling okay. So, in that respect, I am fine. I had just sat down to call you, Peter, to tell you this, when you both came in."

Peter leaned forward intently. "You have done everything right, Larry. What happened to you was our fault, not yours. And you can never think differently. It's important for you to understand that."

Larry gazed at Peter and Marion. They both still appeared serious and upset. Even in seeing that he was fine, their demeanor had not shifted. There should have been some relief in his assurance. But nothing had changed. So, there was something more. A realization rose within him. They had something to tell him. Whatever it was, he knew he wasn't going to like it. He let his eyes drop from theirs and bowed his head. His hands came to his face, blotting out the world. He just needed a moment of peace before he found out. He tried to summon a sense of calm and felt some scales of weight fall away. It wasn't enough. But he could shed no more than he had. He felt entirely vulnerable. Entirely exposed. It caused him pain. He didn't keep them waiting long. Lowering his hands, he set them on the desk, fingers entwined. Raising his eyes to Peter's, he said quietly, "Tell me."

"You're to appear on Charlie Streeter. I don't think I can control this."

"I am to appear—"

"I am sorry. But yes."

"When?"

Peter glanced at Marion and back to Larry. "It hasn't been determined yet."

"You know this is no good, Peter. I do not like him. I do not want to do live television. I am not prepared for this."

"You weren't prepared for the others either, Larry, but you did them and you did them amazingly well. Going live is really no different."

"Streeter is different. I do not know if I can anticipate him. I at least knew the method of Elliott Charles and I felt I could handle Stephanie Ayers roundtable. Even so, I have had a physical reaction to all of it that I could not control. I have never felt like this. Seeing the board pushed me over the edge. It was too much pressure. I felt it from them, Peter. And I lost myself."

"It won't happen again, Larry. You won't see them again until you say you can. I swear it."

Larry fell silent.

Marion nodded in sympathy.

Larry spoke again gently, "Please don't do this, Peter. Unlike Elliott and Stephanie, Streeter attacks. I won't know how he will come at me."

"I will have Spencer Daniels prep you. You will not be alone in this. Not this time."

Larry touched the button on his desk for the drapes to open. He walked to the window and stared out into the gray, dark rain. The day looked as grim as he was feeling. He placed his palm on the glass. "Please don't do this, Peter," he whispered to the glass.

Both Marion and Peter heard Larry's quiet supplication.

Marion shook her head at what they were doing to Larry. The plea touched her cold, hard heart. She could see that Larry was in full control of himself, but it just wasn't right that he be forced to face another interview without time to regain some balance. When she had first met Larry, she had found him delightfully gentle. But then she had seen him fight. And he was relentless. She had no doubt Larry could go on Streeter and win. No doubt whatsoever. No. This was all about the timing. It was critical that Larry be properly prepped. He needed to eat and rest. The short-circuiting of his brain and his passing out last night had robbed him of some of his self-control, at least in his view. It was also likely that he was still feeling very ill. That would cause him to feel weak, something he could not handle. From all that Larry had shown her, his self-control was the very essence of his being. Now he required time to recharge his power. She would manage the timing of Streeter. Streeter could just damn well take it or leave it. She touched Peter's hand.

Peter swung his head to her.

Marion said, "This is a timing issue, Peter. We will do as we're directed, but we will control that direction. We will buy time for prep and recovery."

Peter nodded. He and Marion stood up, about to leave. They went to Larry.

Larry turned and faced them. "I heard your plan, Marion. Thank you."

Peter said, "I want you to rest, Larry. You had a shock last night and your body needs to recover. It would be good if you got undressed and back into bed. I won't tell you what to do, but it would be good."

"And eat your breakfast, if you can," Marion added firmly.

"I will take your advice. Now go on. I know you have things to do." He turned back to the rain as they left.

*　*　*　*　*　*

Marion's voice came through the ICS. "It's Spencer Daniels, Peter."

"Put him through, Marion."

Marion connected Peter.

"Spencer. Tell me."

"We've put him through everything we could think of for the last week. Every last nasty thing. Every little trick. Every insult and attack. From different angles, even. But it was really odd, Peter. The first day, he was barely present. I mean, he was present, but he seemed far away mentally. So, we took it easy on him. Put in just a few hours, maybe five. Then we ramped it up to all day after that for the rest of the week. He seemed to be watching us, rather than participating. He would say something like, 'what else' and we would have to move to the next tactic. He kept us moving. He kept this up until the end of the third day when we had run out of material to beat him up with. I wasn't sure what he was doing."

"Larry is intensely observation oriented. He zeros in on miniscule details other people tend to miss. It puts him, typically, one step ahead of you. If he was watching you, he was learning. His learning curve is monumental, I've discovered."

"Yes, well, at the start of day four, it was like he woke up. And he said, 'Let's do it again.' So, we did. And we even changed it up. He deflected everything. He's so calm, Peter, it's almost, well, unnatural. He has a way of talking that's so measured and concise, you hardly know what to do with it. He won't give you any extra words. He doesn't say 'um' or stall for time. He lets you say something and then he steps on you and you have to remember to respond because he's already walking away with the ball. But yet, the guy is so gentle. It really throws you. "

"Is he ready or not?"

"I'm concerned about his gentle nature with Streeter. Fundamentally, Larry knew he was safe with us. He won't be safe from whatever Streeter does or pulls. Whatever it is, you know he's setting Larry up."

"Is he ready or not?"

Spencer hesitated and then sighed. "Yes. He can handle himself. I'm cautiously optimistic that he's ready."

"Thanks, Spencer."

"Anytime, Peter."

Rising, Peter walked to Larry's office. He tapped lightly on the open door. He saw that Larry was at his desk, working. There were five stacks of pages on Larry's desk and he was reading from one of the stacks.

Larry glanced up. "Come, Peter."

"Your in-depth?" Peter asked as he sat.

"Yes. It is intersectional. But it is too large. I have included all the data I could find on the topic and worked them up into five sections. Now I need to cut the least important points. How are you, Peter?"

"I'm good. I missed you for the last week. It was very empty without you here."

"I missed you too. Very much. Spencer and his team are good guys. I learned a lot from them. Just so you know, I did stop by your office a number of times in the hopes of seeing you in the evening, but you were not there. When are you closing out the series, Peter? I want to go outside."

"One more week to let people finish up. We have already started a public countdown so people know to finish up or lose it."

"What about lockdown. When will it end?"

"Two weeks after we shut down your book."

"I cannot stay in for three weeks, Peter. I want to see Susan and I need some fresh air."

Peter pulled a slip of paper from his pocket and handed it to Larry. "My real estate agent friend has found you something. It's been tough finding anything that is even remotely affordable. But she knows a friend who knows a friend and this place has surfaced. Go look at it today. Use the same security procedures as before. Marion has arranged it for two o'clock today. Is that good for you?"

"Yes. That's wonderful. Thank you, Peter." He looked at the paper. It had the address and the codes to allow him entry.

"If you like it, take it. We'll work something out."

"Okay. I sent Stephanie Ayers something, Peter. I did because I think she was responsible for the lack of edits in the roundtable. It could have gone badly, but it didn't."

"What did you send her?"

"A crystal vase with a dove on it and one white rose."

Peter smiled. "A symbol of peace."

"Yes. It seemed important. I think she will understand. Any other business, Peter?"

"Yes. A publisher has called. They want to publish your book, Larry."

"I've already been published, here, at TPS."

"This is different. You'll be a legitimately published author, Larry. This would be good for you. TPS does not own your book."

"Have you talked about this with the board?"

'I will handle them."

"Okay. They can send their contract over. Can we have legal go over it?"

"Yes. We can. Larry, are you ready for Charlie Streeter?"

"Yes. I am. Set it up."

Peter smiled broadly. He began to laugh. Larry joined him. Neither Larry or Peter were afraid any longer. Not entirely, anyway.

Peter didn't kid himself that they were free and clear of any problems now. He was still worried. He didn't know how to erase the feeling or when it would end. He only knew it wasn't over. He was still having nightmares over something happening to Larry.

It was taking its toll on him.

# CHAPTER THIRTY FOUR

Watching Peter leave his office, Larry called Susan. He explained that he was going to look at a place to live. Could she break away from the gallery and meet him there? She said she could. She said she couldn't wait to see him. He gave her the address and the entry codes in case she got there before he did. Two o'clock couldn't come soon enough for him.

Hanging up, Larry turned his attention back to his article and fell into his work. Jack's brought him lunch. He ate, and worked some more. At one-twenty, he went to his bathroom, washed his face, shaved again, brushed his teeth, and looked at himself in the mirror. He recognized himself now. He liked what he saw. He thought of Susan. His body was burning with a desire to make love to her. He desperately wanted to this afternoon. They could slip away to a lovely hotel room. But that was not what he wanted. He wanted to make love to her on the first night in their home. He wanted to hold her all night long with no interruptions. He closed his eyes and slowly sighed over the thought of it, imagining what her loving would feel like to him. The thought made him weak. His knees almost buckled from his longing.

He moved forward.

He went down twenty floors and met the driver of the Volvo in the parking deck. He got into the car and gave the man the address. He wished his driver good afternoon and asked the man to forgive him if he was too silent. "I have much on my mind," he explained. The driver nodded. Mr.

Martin was a nice man. Most people treated him like garbage. They began in silence. Coming out of the parking garage, Larry saw there were protesters. Still. But fewer. He wondered about their lives, and why they felt he had hurt them so badly that they would spend their precious days doing this. The car continued on. Fifteen minutes later, they came to an older apartment building nestled between two larger buildings. It was interesting. It had a large, tall wall that was attached to the two buildings on either side. In the middle of the wall was a large archway of entry. The wall was covered in ivy.

Getting out of the car, he went through the archway. There was a small front lawn with a crepe myrtle tree, a walkway, and stairs leading up to double doors. The entry code box was on his left. He punched in the numbers. The door buzzed and he let himself in. He was glad there was no doorman. He didn't want a doorman. He wanted his solitude; to be away from prying eyes. There was a simple foyer with a black and white checkered tile floor, a wall of mailboxes and an elevator. Beyond it was a hall. His apartment was down that hall. He was on the first floor. He moved forward.

He used the code to unlock the lockbox hanging on the doorknob. Retrieving the key from within, he opened the front door. Walking inside, he left the door cracked for Susan. He could see she had not yet come. He could not feel her presence, could not smell the delicate scent of her perfume.

He was standing in the front hall. There was a door to his left. Opening it, he saw a good-sized storage closet. Moving on, he came into the living room. It was not large, but it had a fireplace. He liked that. He could envision a sofa in front of it and further back, a dining table and a chest against the wall to hold linens and other things. On his right was a modern galley kitchen. It opened to the living room with just a long counter dividing the space. Walking to the kitchen, he turned on the light. The kitchen was cheerful and bright and he knew Susan would like it. He moved forward to the hall beyond the living room. On his right were two bedrooms, one larger than the other. The bedrooms shared a bathroom. At the end of the hall, on his left, there was a delightful nook. He could write there. It had a smooth brick floor and a window overlooking a small, walled terrace. He opened the French door that led to the terrace and stepped into the outdoor space. He wondered what Susan could do with it—how she would turn it into something wonderful.

He had seen the entire apartment. It was not large but it worked for him. He would take it. He went back to the living room to wait for Susan. The door came open and she stepped inside. He turned to her, his arms opening for her. She walked into them and he buried his face into her shoulder, into her hair. Her fragrance made him dizzy and he fell off the earth again. She raised her face to his. He kissed her slowly, deeply and gently, savoring the moment. Desire rose in his groin, his stomach, his brain, and his heart. It was overwhelming. He needed to gain control of himself. Releasing her, he brushed her cheek, smiled and said, "I am so glad to see you, Susan."

They walked the place together. She loved it. He asked her again if she wanted to furnish and decorate it. He knew she was busy. She said she did. He gave her a credit card that Peter had arranged for him. It had a fifty thousand dollar limit. He knew she would not spend it all. She could do whatever she wanted. It was important to him that she make the place hers. The writing nook was his. He would need a desk, a comfortable office chair, a lamp on his desk, and a shelf to hold papers. He wanted nothing more in the room. She understood.

He pulled her to him again. "I can't wait to be with you here," he said. "I can't wait to make love to you here. The waiting is almost unbearable, Susan."

"I know. I'm suffering from it too, Larry. I dream about it every night. You get off the phone with me and I ache. I go through my days in a fog. I wonder what you are doing. How you are doing it. What you are touching. I only know it's not me." She could feel his hardness and warmth against her. She looked into his beautiful eyes. Lowering her arm, she moved her hand slowly downward. She laid her hand on him, over his slacks, and listened to the sound of his low groan. She loved the way he closed his eyes. She loved his long, dark lashes. She loved his voice; his deep soft voice and the way that he spoke. She loved the way his mind worked. She loved the soft bow of his lips. Those lips were parted now and she thought she was going to die with wanting. She laid her head on his chest. She heard the powerful rhythm of his beating heart. Larry's heart. Her heart.

She knew from the moment she had first seen him. She couldn't let him go. She ate lunch with him. He had told her he was free and had a relationship with no other. She had told him she was free and had a relationship with no other. Neither had ever been married. That was all it had taken to let the dam of their feelings loose like warm water all over them. And then the trouble from his book had come between them. But it had not shut them down. She had seen the comments. She had seen what they were saying on television. She knew he was suffering from death threats. And he had pushed her back into the shadows. He wanted her to hide. He wanted her to be safe. He wanted her cooperation. He could not be with her until it was safe to be with her. And there could be no argument. She smiled, remembering. How does one argue with Larry?

Now she was finally holding him again. She remembered he had touched his lips to hers after that lunch. She had felt the earth tremble and break away under her feet. His scent, the softness of his lips and the brief moment she had felt his arm come around her had left her unable to breathe as he had walked away. It was all she had to sustain her when he had been ripped from her. All these weeks of waiting. And now, she could not let him go. But he was gently pushing her away, stepping back from her now.

"If you do that again, I will not be able to think," Larry said gently. He was in pain as he gazed at her. "Now, I must go back to the office. You are to wait a few minutes before you come out. Please, Susan."

"How long will this go on, Larry?"

He touched her cheek again. "It will still be a while. Peter is setting up my unfortunate interview with Charlie Streeter. I do not have a date yet. Let's get past that and see what happens." He looked around the room again. "Thank you for managing this. I hope you have fun while doing it."

Susan stepped back into his arms. "Please don't leave me, Larry. Not yet. Please not yet."

Larry circled his arms around her small body. "If I stay," he whispered into her ear, "I will not stop. I will not have you on the floor, Susan. It does not matter that you don't care. I care. Please let me leave. *Please* do not stop me."

Susan slowly released him. "This is just painful."

"I know. But the pain will end."

Susan bowed her head, looking at the floor. Larry sighed looking at her. If she moved to him again, he would stay. He didn't want that. If he spoke her name, she would move to him again. He remained silent. She raised her eyes to look into his own. She was calm. She nodded. He closed his eyes in relief. Turning, he left the apartment and climbed back into the Volvo.

\* \* \* \* \* \*

In the morning, he rose at five, put away his bed, showered, shaved and dressed. He checked his emails and read the news. There was less about him now. His book would drop off the site in six days. He could not wait. As he ate his breakfast from Jack's, he thought of Susan. Leaving her yesterday had been nearly impossible. He had been too close to not managing the situation. He was glad that he had. He had not brought protection with him. He wasn't ready to be a father.

Looking around his office, he was glad that it was his. He was very fond of it. Aside from having to pack up his bed daily, he had lived very comfortably here. The bed pack-up was something he was used to anyway. It reminded him of his homeless days in his old Toyota. But how things had changed. How far he had come. And now he would have a real home too. He could hardly believe it.

From the start of his series, he'd had Kate going upstairs daily to Switchboard to check on the level of the threats being made against him. She had made copies for him of the nine letters and had left the original copies with the operators for their records. So far there had been no more of them. Even the number of phone calls were dropping off now. It would have been all over, or close to it, had it not been for Streeter.

The death threats. He thought of Peter. How Peter must have suffered reading them. Yet, Peter had not shown them to him. He knew why and understood. It would have served no purpose. It would have changed nothing. Just added to the stress. Peter had tried to protect him. Which he did do, except that he already knew about the threats. He also knew the letters were being followed up on by internal security and the authorities. While they had found no fingerprints or DNA on the first one—the sender had used an adhesive closing envelope rather than one that required saliva— the others had been deemed not 'genuinely threatening.' This gave him cautious comfort.

Publishing. It was a big house. They had emailed a contract to Peter late yesterday afternoon. He and Peter had gone to Legal. Legal sent a secretary to Neilson Fowler so he could sign a release relinquishing all rights to the book. Peter had already talked to him about it. Neilson wasn't happy, but Peter told him that he had already made a fortune on the series, that the book belonged to Larry and to give it up. Neilson said he would give it up if Larry were willing to talk to him and the board. He had been in Peter's office during this conversation. He had nodded his agreement. He was amazed how everyone wanted to talk with him. The lawyers had amended the contract for Larry to keep the rights to his work. The publisher could sell the book, promote it, and make money from it, but that was all. The book did not belong to them. The contract stipulated that TPS could not archive the work and that when it was taken down, it was finished. Permanently. He would get a $75,000 advance. That was fine with him. So many people had already read the book, the publishers were taking a chance. He didn't care that he could have gotten more. He would get more anyway if there were royalties. Between his advance, his expense account, and his very generous salary at TPS, he had plenty of money. He felt like a rich man, even if he wasn't yet. He had signed the contract. Peter had hugged him with joy. They would have a celebration dinner soon, when it was safe to be seen in a restaurant. Peter was still worried. His own worry was diminishing.

The board. He did not want to see them. They represented life and death over him. They were dangerous to him. But he was starting to feel more secure now. Soon, he would be able to withstand their pressure, their intimidation. He couldn't before. He was too small and they were too big. He could have easily made a mistake in their eyes without knowing it. It had been safer to keep them away. But now, he had agreed. Amazing that Neilson Fowler had used his own book against him. He admired the move. It had been clever.

Streeter. The man had caused him trouble just by pursuing him. He had researched the man and studied his tactics. He now knew how Streeter was going to come at him, even if Streeter didn't know that he knew. Streeter's move was stupid, in his opinion. A wasted opportunity to demolish him. He would see. But he was no longer afraid of the man or his damn show.

Finishing his breakfast, he threw away the trash. He wiped down his desk and began to lay out his pages. He had several other articles going but they had been easy and short. He had released them to Tina. He was close to finishing his in-depth. He hoped to do that today.

Marion was on the ICS. "Larry, are you busy?"

"Not yet, Marion." Then, for her sake, he added, "I just ate my breakfast." He heard her laugh.

"Good. We have good news for you. Can you come to Peter's office?"

"Yes. I am coming now." Leaving his office, he went to Peter's. He paused at the door to observe the scene. Marion and Peter were there. He walked in and positioned a chair. He wanted to be able to see both of their faces at the same time. He waited for one of them to speak.

Peter began. "By delaying your appearance on Streeter, we knew his program would fill up. It has. It was his intention to devote his entire half hour to you. Marion has negotiated it down to a last ten-minute segment, two weeks from today at 9:20 p.m. This fulfills Fowler's directive to us and gives Fowler a marker in return."

Ten minutes. It was nothing. He could manage that short amount of time with his eyes closed. Larry began to laugh. He reached out to Marion's hand and squeezed it thankfully. "You are a wonder, Marion. Thank you so much."

She was laughing too. "You're so welcome, Larry. I'm glad it has worked out. You are fully recovered and strong now. You are prepped. You'll be just fine."

"Yes. I feel good. I am as I should be." He laid his hand on his chest. "And, I know how he will come at me."

Marion blinked in surprise. Peter laughed. Of course Larry would know. They both leaned forward.

And Larry told them.

*   *   *   *   *   *

It was only a week since he had seen Susan at the apartment. She called him at his office in mid-afternoon. Kate put her though. Susan did not call him in the middle of his day unless he said otherwise. "Is everything all right, Susan?"

"Larry," she said slowly, "I have finished the apartment. Not all the details, but at least it's workable. Can you come home tonight?"

He was past being surprised at how women worked their magic. He knew they just did. He would learn the details later. "Yes. I will come. Oh God, Susan . . . "

She knew. She remained silent, allowing the realization to sink in. He would love her tonight. She listened to his breath catch. She gave him time to think.

"I will be home at six o'clock or thereabouts."

"I'll have a simple dinner made. Do not eat, Larry, okay?"

"All right."

Susan Wyman hung up. She laid her head on her arms on the counter of Larry's kitchen. The last of the delivery men had left. When she had offered to manage his place at their first lunch, she had begun immediately searching for treasures. Thrift stores, antique shops, and gallery clearances. She knew he had no money. He had told her so. She had found his dove gray sofa on clearance at Bloomingdales. It could hold the two of them. She had painted her own pictures for his walls. One was an abstract, a sunset on a forest empty of leaves. She had painted the abandoned homestead as she had envisioned from his description in his book. She had painted a man soothing the brow of another ill man. This had been the most difficult. It was of Peter, a man she did not know, but whom Larry loved with great intensity. This painting she had had filled with the old glow of orange fire light and the pewter of shadows. It had taken the longest as it had far greater detail than the other two, but she had finished by working late into the night, waiting for the days to go by. The rest had been easy. A new pillow top bed, expensive soft bedding, an old writing desk, a lovely brushed carpet in a pattern of grays and clays from an antique store, a brass dining set with a top of thick clear glass and an old mahogany buffet. She had stocked the kitchen with new pots and pans and lovely white dishes. The rest of any decor she would fill in later.

She just wanted Larry to come home and she had a determination that was close to matching his own.

# CHAPTER THIRTY FIVE

The Charlie Streeter Show was in commercial break. Larry was led onto the set as the other guests were led off.

Streeter's set was intentionally uncomfortable. One guest chair was on either side of Streeter's desk. The chairs were placed a little too far back, causing a guest to almost have to rise to see the other. Streeter himself blocked their view. He wanted his guests to stand up and yell at each other. The chair placement also forced a guest to face the audience when sitting. Streeter wanted his audience to see the faces of his guest's dead on. He wanted his audience to see their expressions of anger, surprise, or mortification. Streeter liked it this way. It made for more exciting TV.

Larry entered the set from the left side and went straight to the chair in front of him. He grabbed its back firmly and slid it away from Streeter's desk. He positioned the chair so he could see both Streeter's face and the other guest when he came on. His move happened swiftly and smoothly. The chair ended up being a little farther away from Streeter's desk as well. He sat down, at ease, his back straight, his hands loose on his thighs.

Streeter's head swiveled to Larry, his eyes opening wide. He uttered in shock, "What the hell, Martin!"

Ellison Bart came from the right side of the set then. He went straight to Streeter and placed his hand on Streeter's shoulder. Streeter looked up, distracted from Larry. Bart leaned over and whispered something into Streeter's ear. Whatever he said had taken ten seconds. Larry was counting.

Bart slapped Streeter on the shoulder as if they were old friends. He sat down, looked at the audience, and tried to make himself comfortable. His eyes shifted to Larry. His smile grew confused as he gave Larry a nod. "Martin?"

Larry stayed silent. He counted five seconds.

Streeter swung his head to Larry and said levelly, "You need to move your chair back right now, Martin."

"I am happy where I am. Thank you, Mr. Streeter." Another ten seconds.

Streeter locked eyes with Larry and grimaced.

Larry, unsmiling, held his gaze. Five seconds.

They were going live now. There was nothing Streeter could do.

The light for 'ON AIR' blinked on. The cameras were swiveling quickly to adjust their view. The cameramen could not believe what had just happened. They had never seen it before.

The audience was tittering.

Streeter went into professional mode. "We have Larry Martin of The Political Standard"— he nodded to Larry—"and Mr. Ellison Bart of The Bart Data Report"—he nodded to Ellison. "I understand you men know each other very well," he said to neither in particular. He would just toss the ball out and see who took it first.

Ellison sat back in a slouch of nonchalance as though being on TV was nothing to him.

Larry knew differently. Bart lived in a small world. For the two years he had worked for him, the man had never traveled. He had never been on television. He had never faced anything like the massive, intimidating atmosphere of Fox News in New York that he was experiencing now. He could read Bart's eyes. The man was nervous. He was afraid. His posture in the chair showed he was overcompensating. He would let Bart speak first. Then he would know what to do.

Streeter swung his head between the two. Were neither going to speak? He settled on Ellison. "Mr. Bart, how do you know Larry Martin?"

"Well, I, uh." Ellison began to cough slightly into his fist, trying to loosen his throat. Damn, he needed water. Larry was staring at him. He was staggered that he didn't recognize the man. It was a complete stranger sitting there. He had thought this was going to be easy. But this man . . . this man was someone he didn't know.

Streeter swung his head to Larry. "How about you, Martin?"

Still staring at Ellison, he said softly, "Let him speak."

Streeter swung back to Bart.

Bart swallowed nervously. "Yeah, well, uh, Larry used to work for me at my website, The Bart Data Report. My Report is a, a very important part of, you know, the conservative movement. My site covers . . . you know, all the issues. We stay on top of things. Martin, uh, well, he just was not qualified. He was not a good reporter."

"You don't have any reporters, Ellison," Larry said calmly. "You have hacks who spin lies, innuendo, conspiracies, and hatred. You merely throw slime."

Bart was caught by surprise. "Well then, according to you, that made you a hack too, Martin!"

"Indeed. I was a hack. That was my job. I threw your slime. I regret it and I apologize to the world for doing it." Camera One came in closer.

Streeter touched an eyebrow, staring at the top of his desk. Bart had assured him that he could decimate Larry. It was not happening.

"And you weren't good enough to even be a hack!" Bart fired back, sitting straighter. "That's why I fired you!" Camera Two closed in on Ellison's face.

"You fired me because you were cheap, Ellison."

"*What?*"

"You refused to cover even the most basic of business expenses, like parking," Larry replied, his voice low and measured. "You wanted me to pay your expenses out of the low wage you paid me. Finally, when I could not afford it, as downtown Atlanta parking is very expensive and I was very poor—something you were well aware of, Ellison—I could not get you your photos. That is why you fired me. Had you paid your business bills, you would have had them. But it was up to you. And now, I can't thank you enough."

Ellison gasped in alarm. *Who was this guy?* He didn't know what to say. He had expected nothing like this. He stared at Larry, bug-eyed. He had expected Larry to be surprised, cowed, and embarrassed that he had gotten fired. He had intended to say some nasty things and pound Larry on his incompetence. He intended to have the audience laugh with him over Larry's discomfort. But Larry wasn't looking cowed or embarrassed. Not even remotely. Instead of being a blubbering mess, the man appeared soundly calm and supreme in his self-governance. This guy was not the Larry he knew. This guy had just crushed him. Easily and neatly. Larry was cool and prepared. He didn't know how to recover. He glanced at the audience, open-mouthed, his mind drawing a blank.

The audience, mostly simple working-class people, rose to their feet. They hooted with laughter, clapping loudly. An ex-boss getting reamed on national television was great. Many of them had old bosses they would have loved to tell off, but would never get the chance or have the guts to do it. They were keen on Martin. Bart's shocked expression sent them into joyful viciousness.

Streeter, in tune with his rowdy crowd, let them laugh for a minute. He knew the interview was over. There was nothing he could do to save it. Martin wasn't going to be pushed around. The man was in complete control of himself. Ellison was an idiot. Finally, he turned to Bart and said, "You didn't tell me that. It was an important detail."

Bart swung to Charlie angrily. "It doesn't matter! I fired him! He had to go! Martin was a lousy reporter, I tell you! He couldn't meet his assignments! He was incompetent! There was nothing more to tell!"

"Apparently, there was," Streeter said, looking disgusted. "While I might not care for Mr. Martin's politics, being a lousy reporter is most definitely not one of his faults."

Ellison jerked back, gaping at Streeter. "Charlie . . . what the . . . what are you saying?" It dawned on him that Streeter looked annoyed. Streeter would save his show and throw him under the bus? Well, he wouldn't fucking tolerate it. This was sabotage. Fuck him. Shaking his head, Ellison abruptly got to his feet. He was livid. He didn't dare look at Martin again. The man had just humiliated him on national TV and he had no comeback. He jabbed an agitated finger at Charlie. "I did my part here, Streeter. I don't appreciate you turning tables on me like this. I don't have to take this." He strode off the set.

The audience howled in laughter after him.

Charlie raised his arm to the crowd, instigating them more as he watched Ellison leave. With his eye on the timer, he let them loose. He needed to fill time. After a minute, he smiled and quieted his audience down with his hand. He was in control of them. Then, turning to Larry, he said, "Well, I guess that's over. I appreciate you coming on, Mr. Martin."

The camera rolled in for a close up of Larry's face. It caught the flicker of his eyes. For one brief second, they turned hard. But he spoke softly, the consummate professional, and said to Streeter, "Thank you for inviting me, Charlie. It was an invitation I will never forget."

Streeter blinked, then laughed. He knew what Larry meant. Turning to the camera, he said cheerfully, "Okay. Good night, everyone! Mr. Larry Martin of The Political Standard. God bless!"

The audience clapped loudly and happily for Larry.

The 'OFF AIR' light came on.

As the audience began to get up and tumble out of the studio, Streeter moved to stand in front of Larry. "I do have some admiration for you, Larry." He held out his hand.

Larry did not smile. He shook Streeter's hand. "Thank you, Charlie. I appreciate that," he said gently. "But please do not invite me again. I do not care for live television."

Streeter smiled. "You handled yourself just fine. You got me with that chair thing though."

"I had to."

Streeter threw his head back in laughter. He wagged his finger at Larry, "You're good, very good." He patted Larry's arm. "Come on. I'll walk you out."

\*   \*   \*   \*   \*   \*

The Volvo took Larry home to his apartment. He entered and saw that Susan was not home. She had an art show at the gallery tonight, a champagne affair for a local artist she liked. Going to the kitchen, he poured himself a brandy. He was tired. He would catch his interview on the internet tomorrow. But, then again, as stupid as it had been, why bother.

He went down the hall to his writing nook. His phone buzzed in his pocket. He pulled it out and looked at the number. It was vaguely familiar. Marney? He still had his old phone number. It was possible. Sinking into his leather chair, he set his glass on his desk and answered the call. "Hello."

There was a sigh. "Hello Larry."

"Marney. How are you?"

"Good." She paused. "I've seen your interviews, Larry. You've changed so much."

"I know. It had to happen. I apologize to you, Marney, for being such an awful person. I know better now, and I am truly sorry."

"I . . . well, I'm calling to find out if I'm too late. I wanted to call you a while ago, but I was scared."

"Scared? Why, Marney?"

"You're . . . well, you're important now. "

Larry was quiet. "I see. I know it makes a difference. In fact, I know it well." His voice was kind. "I have experienced that myself."

"Am I too late, Larry?"

"Yes, Marney, you are. I love someone now."

She gave a little laugh. "Story of my life."

"No," said Larry gently, "it's not. You will find the right person for you. I hope you do. You deserve that."

"Oh, Larry . . . "

"Goodbye, Marney. And, best of luck to you," he said softly.

"Goodbye, Larry." Marney hung up.

Larry took a sip of his drink. He thought of how he had treated her and was ashamed. He could not imagine being like he used to be. But now, he wasn't, and she was in the past. He deleted her number. He set his phone on the desk and touched his keyboard, bringing his computer screen alive. His phone vibrated again, lighting up. Swiping the screen, he recognized the number. Raising the phone to his ear, he said, "Hello Ellison."

Ellison Bart was all business. "Listen Larry, I've been thinking it over and I want to give you your job back. With a raise." Then he added, "And, an expense account."

Larry understood why he was offering. What better way to have an opponent controlled, under his thumb, and be able to save face? He would give the man no hope. "No, Ellison. You are far too late. You can't begin to afford me now. "

"Aw, shit, Larry. You can't survive in New York. They'll eat you alive and spit you out."

Larry thought of Peter and Susan. He smiled and said gently, "I understand why *you* would say that. But I am doing just fine. And soon, I am to marry a beautiful woman."

Bart hesitated. He couldn't fight that. Nothing would drag a man away from his woman, especially a beautiful one. He felt a stab of jealousy. He didn't have a girlfriend, but when he finally did, she'd be beautiful too. Ugly women disgusted him. Back to business. "Look Larry, come back to me and I'll throw in a five thousand dollar bonus." Let Martin refuse *that*.

"No."

Bart paused. This wasn't going well. "Fuck, Martin, I hope you know what you're doing. But if you change your mind . . ."

"I won't, Ellison."

Ellison Bart saw Larry slipping through his fingers. Getting him back was his only hope of not being completely politically and publicly embarrassed. "Well, Larry, if you change your mind, you know where to find me."

Larry said softly, his voice low and serene, "I do, Ellison. But we will never talk again."

"Jesus, Larry . . ."

"Good night, Ellison." Larry clicked off his phone and laid it by his keyboard. He heard the front door unlatch. He stood up and went to the living room.

Susan was coming in, dressed in her evening gown and carrying a sparkling little purse. She walked into Larry's arms. "How was your show?" she asked in his ear.

"Short," Larry murmured, holding her. He closed his eyes. He didn't want to think of Streeter and Ellison Bart now. He had better things to do.

Susan left him to get a small brandy of her own. Coming back to him, she led him to the terrace. They sat and talked for a while. She told him that she had sold six works. Two of her own and four of the artist she was promoting. It had been a good and successful night.

Larry congratulated her warmly. He felt great pride in her accomplishments. She told him that she wanted to shower now. She left him alone in the outdoor room. He sat, sipping his drink. He loved what she had done with the outdoor space. It now had a stone floor and furniture covered in pillows of tan and black stripes. She had kept things simple. The room held large stone pots of colorful flowers. In the corners were tall fichus trees. She had laced them with little white lights. He was sitting at a table with four chairs. He was comfortable and feeling peaceful. He listened to the sounds of the night birds and felt the evening air on his face. He listened for the sound of her shower to go off. Setting his drink on the table, he went his writing nook. He unbuttoned his shirt and removed all his clothes, setting them neatly on his office chair. He entered the bathroom through the hallway and stepped into the hot water of the shower to wash off Streeter and his day. He soaped his body and washed his hair. He rinsed well, enjoying the soothing heat of the water. After stepping out of the shower, he shaved, brushed his teeth and blew his hair dry. He added a touch of cologne. And pulling a thick white towel about his waist, he entered his bedroom.

Susan was sitting at her vanity, brushing her hair. The room was dim except for the candles she was burning. Looking up, she smiled at Larry. Standing, she moved to him and put a finger in the waist of his towel. She tugged on the cloth and the towel fell to the carpet. She kept him standing as she moved her fingers over his skin, exploring his body. He stood silently, letting her do to him what she wanted. She ran her hands over his shoulders, then down his chest. She ran her hands under his arms and down his ribs. She smiled into his eyes as her hand went lower to hold his hardness and cup his warm testicles in her palm. She began to lightly massage while moving her hand back and forth around him.

It was too much for him. He was trembling under her touch as he slipped the thin straps of her slip off her shoulders. The slip drifted to the floor and she stepped out of it. He led her to the bed and pulled back the covers. He wrapped his arms around her small body and gently laid her down. He lay alongside her, touching her skin. He kissed her deeply as his hand traveled down her belly and beyond. He searched for her suppleness and found it. His fingers explored, bringing her to being warm and wet. He slowly inserted his finger, circling in her softness. His thumb massaged her button of sensitivity. He watched her low moans and gently increased his pressure. He watched her until she was nearly sobbing. He wanted her to be ready to receive him. She cried out against his sweet torture. Rising, he positioned himself to enter her. They had made love before and he knew what he was doing. He pushed forward slowly, sliding in and out, but only to up a point. He stayed there for a while, wanting the sensation to last. When he saw she could no longer bear what he was doing to her, he grew still and began to brush his lips over her body. He kissed her breasts, her neck, her smooth cheek and coming to her lips, he kissed her again. He felt her quiver under him. Rising a little, he was mindful not to put his weight on her. He slid his hands into hers and raised them high, palm to palm, on the pillows. He moved his hips again, sliding forward, in and out. Each time he went a little deeper. Finally, he plunged ahead, filling her completely. He had her trapped on him and he felt her legs slide down alongside of his own. He met her eyes and watched her expression of surprise and wonder. He moved higher into her.

Susan looked at him. She saw him smile as the warm white light of intensity burst through her body. She lost all control and it overwhelmed her. The sensation shattered her into a thousand pieces and she let it happen. She went limp against the pillows.

Larry let go of her hands and eased his pressure. He lay beside her and let her rest. He slid his head onto her chest, listening to her heart running wild and the small gasps of her breath. He waited patiently for her heartbeat and breathing to calm. "I love you, Susan," he murmured. "I will love you forever."

"I think I have died, Larry. I think you have killed me. I can't feel anything."

Larry chuckled, gathering her to him. "I hope you always feel this way." Susan laughed weakly in his arms. He continued to let her rest. After a short while, he asked, "Can I go on?"

"Yes. I love you too, Larry. With all my heart. I am only yours."

"That's all I want," he breathed. He released her and let her lay back. "Let me come in." Rising, he rose above her, bracing on his hands. She opened her legs to him, still feeling sensitive. He positioned himself and entered her. Slowly, he began to slide back and forth. He wanted this indescribable sensation to last. She felt so good to him; he didn't have the words to describe what he was feeling. He was grateful she was on birth control now and he didn't have to stop for a condom. He felt the pressure build. He tried to go slowly but he knew he was not going to last long. He slid in and out of the length of her. With one final plunge he felt his world come apart like stars exploding in a massive supernova. He lowered his head, gasping. He fell sideways, careful not to crush her. With his cheek against her breast, he thought, I will look forward to this for the rest of my life.

\*    \*    \*    \*    \*    \*

The next morning, Larry stopped by Peter's office on the way to his own. Peter waved him in. He sat. He spoke slowly, "Why are we still on lockdown, Peter? People are weary of being frisked. I am hearing some complaints. Please. Let it go. Nothing will happen. It is over."

Peter gazed at Larry. He heard the gentleness of Larry's low voice. He noticed that Larry was continuing to grow. There was a new air about him. And it was calmer and more powerful than it had been before. But he couldn't let it go. Larry was still being driven in the Volvo. Security measures were still in place. Larry should not yet walk the streets. He remembered the letter: *Larry Martin is going to die.* Neither the NYPD nor the FBI had any leads on this letter except that it had been mailed in Manhattan. He remained intensely disturbed by this. It meant the potential killer was close by. He saw how Larry could be harmed, how it could easily happen. He would lower their guard. He would let go of all protections. He saw how the two of them could be walking, maybe laughing, until their attacker came upon them on the street. Larry is shot in the chest or maybe stabbed from behind. He had ongoing nightmares over it. He couldn't bear the possibility of it happening. It wasn't just Larry. This crazy person could come into the building, hurting others as he searched for Larry. He had a duty to protect everyone. It was his burden to bear. There were still death threats trickling in. Things were still active. No. He couldn't let it go.

Larry looked at Peter. He saw that Peter was struggling. He wasn't stupid. He knew from Kate about the death threats still straggling in. They were much less, but they were still there. Yet, Peter still did not speak of them. He was absorbing them all by himself. He read Peter's eyes and expression. He grew quiet to feel Peter's thoughts. He got them, and sighed. "Forgive me, Peter. I know you must do as you have to."

"Yes, Larry. I do. There will be a time when I can let go. Meanwhile, the protections will remain in place, not just for you but for everyone. I know you understand," Peter said quietly. "That is what I want."

"What do we do then?"

"I am sending you to DC for a short while to get a feel for it. I want you to see how it works."

"I have never been to the Capitol. I would like to see Washington. What is a short while, Peter?"

"A month."

A month. Larry blinked, looking away. He swallowed.

"I need some rest, Larry. I want you safe but I can't relax with you here. And there are things you need too. I know you understand me."

Larry nodded. He did. It was about his protection. It was about his continuing to learn and grow. It was about a reprieve from the board. "Okay." He couldn't stand that Peter was still suffering on his behalf.

"I'll set it up for you then. I'll have John Lester show you around. He knows the White House. He can introduce you to people."

"Okay."

"You saw Streeter coming all right."

"It had to be Bart. There was no one else he could have used against me for his circus. But Bart is a limited person. There was nothing he could do against me. And I knew moving the chair would throw off Streeter. I was prepared for all of it. And Marion's negotiation for ten minutes made the whole thing easy. I want to go to Atlanta first, Peter, before DC."

"Ah," Peter said knowingly. "The old man and the boy?"

"Yes."

"When do you want to go?"

"I have a few things to finish up. The middle of next week would be good."

"I'll tell Marion."

Larry rose to his feet. He went to Peter. Peter stood and Larry pulled him close. "I will do as you want. Get some rest. I appreciate your concern. I do. But I will miss you terribly, Peter."

Peter sighed, hugging Larry tightly. He knew he was doing the right thing in sending Larry away. It was just that it would be very empty without him. Still, a month would pass. He needed time to decide what to do. While

Larry was gone, he would ease the office back into normal life and see what happened. He let go of Larry's shoulders and smiled at his friend. Larry was always easy, always cooperative. They would get past this.

Larry left Peter. He went to his own office and thought of Susan. He knew she would understand. They would survive this short time apart. They had a lifetime together to look forward to.

* * * * * *

*Atlanta.* Alan, blonde and tan, was standing in Delta baggage claim waiting for Larry. He looked handsome and sharp in his peach button-down, rolled sleeves, and black slacks. As Larry approached, he took off his mirrored sunglasses, smiled broadly, and opened his arms.

Larry walked into Alan's arms, hugging him hard.

Alan released Larry and said, "My, my, you've been having fun."

Larry laughed. "It's been that. Or, something." He spied his suitcase coming around the belt. "Let me get that, Alan."

Leaving baggage claim, they walked into the bright, hot Georgia day and made their way to the parking garage that held Alan's car. Using his fob, Alan popped the locks on his personal Mercedes. He put Larry's suitcase in his trunk as Larry waited. They got in the car together and buckled up.

Alan rested his arm on the steering wheel. He turned to Larry. "I can take you to your hotel or you can stay at my place. Which do you prefer?"

Larry was surprised by the offer. He didn't hesitate. "Your place."

Alan nodded. "Good." Pulling his sunglasses from his shirt, he slid them on. "I got some steaks just in case." He started his engine. "Let's go to Windsor, Larry."

# CHAPTER THIRTY SIX

Windsor. The city of his book. The city where he had exposed his heart and his suffering to the public. Balfour. The reality of Windsor. They were going to Balfour. Alan knew what Larry wanted to do. To accomplish his reparations to the old man and the boy.

Larry did not care too much about Walmart. He had been wrong in his small thefts and there was no rationalizing them to be right. He did feel some remorse. But their owners were mega-billionaires who had more money than they could spend in a thousand lifetimes. They kept so much money for themselves and paid their employees so little, their employees often had to apply for food stamps. The taxpayers of America, in essence, paid for the feeding of their workers; the people who stocked their shelves, cleaned their floors, checked out their customers, and kept their stores running. He had no way to pay his debt to the corporation anyway without potential exposure to legal trouble. The same for the massive corporation that owned the dollar store. The corporations would survive the small damage he had done them. But he could make reparations to the two individuals that he had directly harmed. Then he thought of his old Toyota. "Alan, thank you again for managing the towing of my car. It was good of you and I know it was not your problem."

"It was easy enough, Larry. The charity was prompt in picking it up and with the title you sent me, the paperwork was a breeze."

"I am glad it is gone and cannot be traced back to me. I worried about it sitting there. I did not want to be associated to Balfour in any way. I seriously doubt any issue would have arisen, but it is safer for me that no one knows about Balfour."

Alan nodded, his eyes on the road. "I agree. If someone *had* put it together by finding your old car and checked local stores for security footage of you, it might have led to some trouble for you. But that concern is over now."

Larry leaned back in the luxury of Alan's car and shut his eyes. He felt himself relax and grow quiet, listening to the power of the car. As time went by, he admired Alan's ability to smoothly negotiate Atlanta's twelve-lane highway. He realized then that he had not spoken in a while. Maybe too long. He was too used to riding in silence, tucked into his own thoughts. He had to come out of it and speak to Alan.

Alan glanced at Larry. His friend's eyes were still closed. They had been riding for nearly an hour and would reach Balfour in less than half that. He knew that Larry was not asleep. Larry's eyes had opened a few times as though to check their location, then they had closed again. He didn't mind. He knew from before that Larry often didn't talk while they drove and that Larry would talk when he felt like it. Meanwhile, their silence was companionable, allowing him to pay attention to the high volume of traffic.

Larry's phone pinged. He opened his eyes. He maneuvered to pull his phone from the front pocket of his pants. Looking at this phone, he swiped sideways and opened the email. His brows came together as he read:

*Dear Mr. Martin,*

*My name is Sherman Roberts. I am the president and owner of a large architectural firm in Atlanta. I find myself writing you, although I'm not quite sure why. I found your email address at The Political Standard.*

*I believe that you and I came close to meeting at your well-built homestead at the industrial park off Bashton Road in Balfour on April 4th of this year. I could be mistaken. Forgive me if I am.*

*I have read your book in The Political Standard. The description of your industrial park homestead matches what I saw on that morning. The names, Windsor and Balfour, are similar in cadence. It is not a stretch to imagine they are one and the same.*

*It had been my intention to offer you a job that morning. I knew from your work and my impression of you that you were no ordinary man. Our introduction was interrupted and prevented by an ill-timed employee I'll just call Slater. I fired him later that afternoon, not just for this, but for many other reasons as well.*

*That morning, by the time I came back to your home, after I had dealt with the mess he had created, you were gone. It upset me that you were but I understood. I would have left too. I came back twice to look for you. The second time was at 11:00 that night. I didn't think you would be there, but I took the chance. This is where it gets both sad and interesting. It actually horrifies me.*

Larry's hand came to his lips as he read. He remembered the man. He remembered what he looked like and that he had liked him. He remembered that they had been interrupted by Slater. He remembered that he had not yet spoken when the man had left his home to tell Slater to stop yelling. He remembered that they had missed their connection. He remembered fleeing his home on his bike to become invisible again. And he remembered that he had thought of this man and Peter, just a flash in his brain seconds before he fell to the pavement, unconscious, after being beaten. Now he knew the man's name.

Alan glanced at Larry. He could tell by Larry's expression that whatever he was reading held him suspended by concern and disbelief. He hoped it was nothing bad but he would not ask. Larry would tell him later. Maybe. He saw Larry look up and blink a few times. Then he watched him lower his head to continue reading.

*The moon was high that night. There was plenty of light. My truck was parked at the loading dock. I decided to walk to your home. Coming around the building, I saw Slater on your ladder cutting the canvas of your roof. His viciousness galled me. I waited to see if you were there. It concerned me that Slater had a knife. I knew he was angry from being fired. I didn't want him to harm you if you were there. I was ready to step forward to protect you if you were. But you were not, and I went home.*

*I tried to sleep but I couldn't. I kept coming back to thoughts of you. My wife knew I was not at ease and tried to calm me with a hot tea. She is a wonderful woman. I have pieced together that my disquiet was taking place as you were being beaten. Your roof had been cut and then that. I wish I had not been a part of it all. The attacks on you made me ill at heart.*

*I know you are in New York now, safe and sound. It seems Peter Bennett got you before I did. That's the interesting part. A few more seconds and you would be here with me now. Funny how life works out.*

*If you ever get to Atlanta and you have the time and interest, I would like to meet you again. I understand if I don't hear from you. Perhaps I would remind you of a painful time.*

*Best Wishes, Sherman Roberts*

Larry looked up. Sherman's phone number was under his name. Turning to Alan, he said: "I will let you read this letter later after we get settled. It is startling."

Alan nodded, his eyes on the road. "Larry, we're coming up on Balfour in eleven minutes. What's our plan?"

"First, I want to go to an old residential section on Beauchamp where I stole the bicycle. I want to get the house number on the street and see if the boy already has a replacement. Second, we will stop by the old man's house in that same area. I have an envelope for him which I would like you to give to him, Alan, if you do not mind. Tell him it comes with regrets from the thief who stole from him. Tell him that he hopes that this will make up for his loss. Tell him the thief is never coming back and deeply apologizes for his violation. Third, if the boy does not have a replacement, we will go to the bike shop on Main Street and have them deliver one to him. Then, we can go home."

"All right," Alan said. He glanced at Larry. "You okay? You look a little shook up."

Larry laughed slightly, shaking his head. "It is funny how life works out. How one bad thing can lead to another good thing. You will see, Alan, when you read this letter how a few seconds changed everything. If not for those few seconds, I might be living in Atlanta working for an architectural firm—doing what, I do not know. But, actually, this would not be true. I would have eventually gotten on a computer to discover my articles on TPS. Even if they had fallen off the front page, I would have been curious enough to check the archives. Peter Bennett and I would have connected anyway. Nothing could stop this. It was already in motion." Larry looked thoughtful for a moment. He looked at Alan. "But here's another thought. With the job offer from Sherman Roberts, I would also have likely spent that night in my home at the industrial park until something better could be arranged. There was a man with a knife who came looking for me, Alan. Roberts would not have been there and I could have quite possibly have been killed. So, for me, the beating was better. Just amazing."

"I'll have to read this letter to catch up with your thoughts, Larry. But it does sound rather astonishing. I hate that you were beaten but I'm glad that you weren't killed."

Larry fell quiet. It was something to digest. Slater would have been fired that afternoon regardless of him. He would have hated to face an angry man with a knife.

"You lead an interesting life, Larry," Alan said quietly. "I also see how easy it is for a homeless person to get attacked."

"All the time, Alan. In one form or another."

"I don't think I could make it if I ever became homeless," Alan murmured, glancing in his rearview mirror.

"You will never be homeless, Alan. First, you have friends that would help you. I, personally, would never allow you to be on the streets if I could prevent it. Second, you would find within you a strength you didn't know you possessed. You would continue to rise to your strength until you escaped your homelessness. Your experience would give you insight and knowledge to exceed common understanding. You would reach it faster because you are already an intelligent man. I was not an intelligent man when I began my journey. I had to become one. Still. Such a journey is not one that I would wish on anyone."

Alan picked up his speed and merging, he watched and maneuvered as the exit for Balfour came up. The Mercedes moved smoothly off the highway.

As they moved forward, Larry recognized the streets of Balfour. He was glad that he was with Alan. Otherwise, the sight might have made him queasy. He had suffered so much here. But it was over.

Alan turned right at Walmart. He followed the two-lane road, then slowed his car and made a slow left onto Beauchamp.

"Stop now, Alan." Larry saw the street number of the house was 421. There was no bike. "Go now, to the next street over and let's take care of the old man." Larry directed Alan to the man's house. He handed Alan an envelope from the inside breast pocket of his jacket.

Alan took the envelope, got out of the car and walked to the house. He knocked on the door and the old man answered. Alan gave him the envelope and told him what Larry had directed him to say.

The old man counted the $1,000 in the envelope. His eyes welled with tears. He was on a small fixed income and had not been able to replace much of what had been taken from him. The theft had made his life harder. He had suffered from a constant fear that the thief would return. "He will never come back?"

"No," said Alan. "He is actually a good man who was desperate at the time. But he has always regretted what he had done to you. Hopefully, this makes things right and relieves your fear."

"It does," said the old man in wonder. "Tell him thank you for me."

Alan nodded. "I will. Good afternoon, sir." He walked back to his car. Sliding in, he buckled himself and started his engine. "You did a good thing, Larry. He had been living in fear of your return. Now, for him, it's over. He said to thank you. We'll go to the bike shop now." He headed his car towards Main Street. On the way there, he asked, "How does one exceed common understanding? How is it done?"

Larry closed his eyes, thinking and analyzing the most direct approach to Alan's question. "You've read my book. You read what I explained to Anna."

"Yes."

"Let's start there. I think it is possible for most anyone with undiminished capacity to do it. It takes great effort. Those who have found their plane of existence know it. They already know how to listen, learn, and grow. They see around them and in front of them. They pay attention to details and apply them to their accumulating knowledge. They do not lie to themselves. They open their boundaries of belief. They take their learning and apply it to their lives. They think ahead. They see what they are facing. And then they face it without panic or fear. They know how to control themselves. They understand that, by this application, they move to a different level. How high they go is up to them. Too high, too narrow in knowledge, they become a savant." Larry glanced at Alan. "Does any of this strike a bell?"

Alan was staring ahead. He was listening intently. But he also saw there was a possibility he did not want to see. The light turned green. "Continue," he said.

"A savant is not necessarily a bad thing. It may be the only talent that person has so they move forward with it until they can no longer communicate with others. That is not what you want. There must be a balance. We are all human, so we must be able to understand one another. What you know should not be a weapon. It should be understanding. When you walk above others, they know it. The best case is they will respect you for it. The worst case is they will fear you. But if they fear you, you are doing something wrong. It is in your favor to disarm their fear. Then they won't see you when you don't want them to. Or they will not see you coming if you must but still prefer that they do not see you." Larry sighed. "This is a heavy conversation."

"You have more."

"Yes. There is more."

Alan pulled into a parking space in front of the bike shop. He felt dread accumulate within him. He bowed his head. They were quiet for a moment. He raised his head. Turning to Larry, he said, "Let's go get the bike."

Larry told the shop owner that he wanted an excellent red, light-weight ten-speed. The shop owner showed him a bike. Larry paid for the bike and gave the man the boy's address. "This is a private gift," he told the shop owner. "Please do not reveal who this bike came from. If no one answers the door, leave the bike under the tree in the front yard."

"I understand, sir. I'll keep your confidence."

"Very good. Thank you. Have a good day."

Larry and Alan got back into Alan's car. "Let's go home, Alan."

Alan was quiet as they drove to his home. Ten minutes later, he turned up the drive of a lovely brick two-story home. Unloading Larry's suitcase, he showed Larry to his guest room. "I am down the hall. Get comfortable and I'll meet you at the pool in the backyard."

"Alan," Larry said, placing his hand on Alan's arm. "There is nothing to be afraid of. You should stop now with your dread."

Alan sighed. "You don't know what I'm thinking."

"No. I do not. But I do know it is wrong. I will see you at the pool."

Larry and Alan met at the pool at about the same time. Both were in pullover dark t-shirts and jeans. Both had on sneakers.

Alan went to the refrigerator and got a couple of beers. He handed one to Larry and they sat at a table by the pool.

"Your home is beautiful, Alan. But then, I knew it would be."

The breeze ruffled Alan's hair as he settled into his chair with his beer. "Thank you. Where do you go from here, Larry?"

"To DC. I will learn the Capital and the city. It's Peter's way of keeping me from the board. He is buying me more time. To continue to grow. I am forced to see them now." He told Alan about Fowler using his own book against him. "So, I have to see them soon. But it will be when I am ready."

"How long will you stay in DC?"

"A month."

Alan nodded. "It will be a good experience for you."

"It will. And now you have added to your fleet? Tell me about that."

Alan told him. He had enough business to add yet another car at the end of the month as well. "Things are changing all the time, Larry. My SEO is good on the internet. I'm on Google's first page now for limo searches. And, I'm doing some local advertising on TV and radio."

Larry smiled broadly and leaning forward to Alan, clinked his bottle to Alan's. "It is so good to hear, Alan. Congratulations. But it does not surprise me. Now. What is troubling you."

Alan let air slide between his teeth. He closed his eyes, feeling the beat of his heart. He would tell the truth. "You are growing too fast, Larry. You are outgrowing me. I have just found you. And already you're so changed from when I drove you before."

"Alan . . ." Larry said, his voice low in alarm.

"No. Let me finish. I am upset because I know you are going to forget me. I saw it at the airport, the way people . . ."

Larry felt his blood pressure rise at his friend's distress. This would not do. He lowered his shoulders and let his metaphorical scales of weight fall off of him: his alarm, and his instant anxiety from that alarm. He summoned a calm and felt it when it flooded through him. He would have to be open to listening to Alan and his fears. Then he would know what to do. But he would have to direct that guidance if he was to help his friend. "Alan," Larry asked gently, "what did you see?"

Alan leaned back in his chair. He took a breath and swung his gaze from Larry to the pool.

"Take your time."

"I saw you coming down the corridor before you saw me. People watched you move, Larry. They stopped in their tracks and they gazed at you. They stepped back to give you a wide berth. You didn't seem to notice. You were just walking. No one moves the way you do. Then some began to touch your sleeve as you went by. Then, from the crowd, an old woman stepped up to you. She was not well put together; she did not look clean. She lowered her head to you. And you bent and put your arms around her. She began to cry. You held her to you for a while, Larry, until she stopped. All the people around you did not move on with their lives. Instead, they just stood around you. Respectfully. They didn't go away until you walked clear of the corridor and you came to me. I don't know what that was. I have never seen such a thing."

Larry placed his beer on the table. He leaned forward, his arms on his thighs and his fingers laced together and looked at Alan. "During my time as a homeless person, Alan, I had to work to learn my new self as I grew. I did not know myself. I was changing rapidly, both mentally and physically. I lost weight and my legs became long and lean from the many miles I walked. I began to stand differently, taller and more square of shoulder to accept my new frame. I began to walk differently to absorb the miles. Hundreds of them. I had to find a way to walk to ease the pain. I learned how to find my movement out of necessity. I found it and it became a part of me. For survival, I needed to find a way to become invisible. Not that people did not see me but that they did not fear me. The answer was in being kind. I learned that kindness transcends all other human emotions. It is the essence of what people can be if they want to be. People are so often cruel to one another; they have become used to it. They expect it. After this realization—another leap in understanding that exceeds the common—I moved from being an awful person to being a genuinely better one. I cultivated gentleness and kindness until it became a part of me. I saw that it worked. I could *never* go back to who I was. Then I found that I could go where I wanted without fear. Because people no longer feared me, they were disarmed. As a homeless person, it was vital to surviving. And this is something I continue to cultivate, even now. It continues to be a growth of understanding. I have not discovered all I need to know. Maybe I never will."

"What about the people, Larry. Why did they touch you like that?"

"I think the answer would be they were simply moved to kindness. Which is one part of my point. People respond to kindness. They can feel it. Only the truly evil have no use for it."

"Did you know the old woman?"

"No. But I saw that she was homeless. One aspect of the plight of the homeless is that they are rarely, if ever, touched in kindness. I could do that for her."

A tear spiked down Alan's cheek. He was deeply upset. His hand moved quickly to brush it away. "When I first saw you, I was not going to let you into my car. I was going to tell Mr. Bennett you were an unacceptable ride. I did fear you and your bloody appearance. But then you spoke and you won me, just like that." Alan snapped his fingers. He felt a fury gather inside him. His voice rose. "My move to you, my taking care of you, my wanting to be your friend happened so fast and it does not happen!" he yelled, pounding the table. "It does not happen! Do you understand, Larry?

In all my life of driving, since I was a teen, it has NEVER happened! I didn't see you coming, not a mile away, and I let you in . . . *again*."

Larry sighed, staring at the ground. He remained silent. He felt a pain grip his heart for his friend. He would be patient. He knew they had the time to work this through. And the privacy in which to do it. Alan was loaded with insecurity and fears and he would have to sort them out one by one. He would wait for Alan to speak and see where it went. He would just have to be ready to move fast to keep him here.

Alan shuddered between sadness and anger. He took a few breaths, then said, "I nearly pulled away. I nearly got free. I came close. I nearly walked out the door after I delivered your suitcase. I would have sent you another driver to take you to the airport. But I could not leave you. I dared to let you in again. And, I knew you would hurt me."

"Why, Alan."

"Because I can read people. I've seen enough of them. But I'd never met anyone like you. You had mystery written all over you. I could not read you! It was enough to set off my alarm bells." His voice rose again in anger. He could not control himself. "I knew you were special. I knew you were different. I don't like people. In many ways, I absolutely hate them. I work long hours. Crazy hours. My girlfriend tries not to complain, but it affects her. Then you come along, my first male friend in my whole fucking entire life. Someone I could believe in and give my heart to. But now, we've barely begun our friendship and I don't know how to keep up with you. I see you slipping through my fingers. The fact is, I am not special like you, Larry. I know you are growing and growing tremendously and that you will grow to become a very important man on this earth, and I know that you *WILL* forget me," Alan shouted. "I KNOW IT!"

Turning from Larry, Alan shuddered again, drawing in a ragged breath. He was furious at himself. He had just made an utter ass of himself, raging like that at Larry. Men did not act like this. They weren't so needy. He wasn't equipped to explain to Larry how much he needed him. But he did, on so many levels. Larry had come into his life and he had felt shaken. Affected. He couldn't explain why, only that the feelings were there. Painfully, powerfully, and deeply there. He didn't care how a man was supposed to feel about sentiment or friendship, he only knew what he wanted. He stared at the pool, then abruptly rose to his feet. He couldn't bear to be here. He was acutely embarrassed. He moved to leave.

Larry was swift on his feet, blocking Alan. He knew every emotion Alan was feeling, every facet of what he was experiencing. He would not let him leave. He swept his arms around Alan firmly and steadily. "You have had your say, Alan," he said harshly into Alan's ear, securing his friend tightly to his body. "Now, you will let me have mine. Fair is fair. Sit down. And do not leave me again. We must work this out."

Larry did not let go of Alan. Not until he felt Alan stop resisting him. Not until he felt Alan surrender. Not until he felt Alan lay his head on his shoulder. Not until he heard Alan murmur, "All right." He released Alan slowly. He pointed to Alan's chair. He watched Alan move to it and sit.

He sat himself then. He laid his hand against his chest, breathing. And to hold his heart. Alan had been very strong. It had been extremely hard to control him. Now he had to find the right thing to say. What was Alan's largest fear? There were several. One was the largest. He would start there. He leaned forward and looked intently at Alan. He settled his body into a calm posture. He swallowed. He wondered if Alan was going to hurt him. He would find out. It had to be done. "Look at me now, Alan. "

Alan raised his head and met Larry's eyes.

"I will not hurt you, Alan," Larry began gently. "Not unless you twist me into that position. That is up to you. You control that. Only you. If you reject me, I will leave right now. Do not lie to me. What is it to be?"

Alan laughed incredulously and resentfully. He shook his head. "You make me come back to you again."

"I do not. It is your choice. But know this: If you throw our friendship away out of your fears and insecurities, you will have broken my heart. I will leave. I will not talk to you again. I will not trust you. I will not trust that you can rise above it all when you must."

"How does Peter Bennett deal with you, Larry?" Alan asked bitterly.

Larry jerked slightly. He had not seen the question coming. "Peter," he uttered softly. "Like you, Alan, Peter is an extremely strong personality. Like you, he had some adjusting to do with me. But he did it rapidly. He simply accepted who I am. He opened his heart to me. It caused him pain. He became afraid of what might happen to me. But, he did not back away from his fear. He shielded me. He took all the blows on my behalf."

"I am not like Peter Bennett."

"I am not asking you to be like Peter Bennett. There is no one like Peter Bennett. Peter was my inspiration in life. All I ever wanted was to be his friend. But he walked so far above me, I had no way of reaching him. Not until, in his kindness, he allowed me a connection. But it was my responsibility to rise to him. I could not tear him down to me. It would never happen. Do you see?" Larry drew in his breath, waiting. He parted his lips, breathing. He glanced at the sky in pain and looked at Alan.

Alan gazed back at Larry. He had never felt such intimidation. He was frightened of Larry. Larry was saying that he would have to rise to him. That he would have to step up above himself. He would have to find a new level if he were to keep Larry as his friend. He saw that now. And he saw that Larry was bending him to face his own insecurities. He didn't have to be insecure as Larry continued to grow, to rise even further. They both knew he would. He could either continue being fearful of getting hurt, or simply accept the friendship Larry was offering. That Larry was just who he was. No more. No less. It would mean that he would have to believe in himself. And do it well enough that Larry could trust him again not to fall. He did believe in himself to some degree. But it was limited and he had never been pushed beyond it. But now, he was being pushed. How did he meet Larry's mind? How did he adjust to Larry's level? He saw the stricken look on Larry's face and saw that he was hurting his friend. And he knew it had to stop. "I am so sorry, Larry. I know I've hurt you." He bowed his head. "I will rise to you and continue to rise as you need it. It's just that this is very new to me."

Larry swallowed in relief. His mouth was dry, waiting for Alan to speak. He instantly shed his hurt. "One day soon you will meet Peter Bennet. You will like him. Very much. On that same day Peter Bennett will meet you, Alan. He will like you. Very much. You are both your own men. Both my friends. Both people I love. And you will rise too, Alan. I am bringing you with me. It is all I can do."

Alan nodded mutely, feeling reassured and relieved. He believed Larry.

"As for the rest of it, now you have some understanding why I could not meet the board. I did not know if I could rise to them. I have my own struggles too. The intimidation is awful. But I will have to find the strength within myself to manage them. There are always new levels of understanding. There are always new levels that you must physically control so that you can step up. It is all about self-control. And it is seriously difficult. It is also important to know when the time is right. Things don't just happen because we want them to. They happen because we make them so. There is no perfection. There is no infallibility. There will be failure. It cannot be helped. But then, you get back on your Plain—the place in your mind that encompasses a higher level of thinking and perception—and keep climbing. It is all about your perspective. It is all about how you treat people. It is all about yourself. Who you are and how you move. Do these things and you will get there."

"I understand."

"I know you do. It is who you are. You just did not recognize it. But I did. And I do. Now. I believe you mentioned steaks. And I am starving."

Alan sighed. He lowered his shoulders, shaking his head in wonder. He began to laugh.

Larry laughed too.

Larry now had everything he wanted. His relationship with Alan had just been cemented. He knew Alan would struggle through changes. He knew they would be hard. He knew Alan would succeed. He knew Alan would find his own walk and then, walk on his own Plain. They would connect there.

Peter still walked far above him. Peter was his friend, mentor, and protector. He would change nothing.

Susan also had her own Plain. She knew who she was and what she was doing. They had already connected. He intuitively knew her every thought. But she intended for him to know. Larry was not only content. He was blissful. It was a marvelous feeling. A first in his life. And he was still climbing.

He would go to DC. The capital. He would see firsthand where the center of power was. There were many capitals of the world. But this capital was in his world. It represented his country. He remembered what he had said on national television:

"*We must somehow all live together. To do so, it must be equitable on some level. It can't all go to the wealthy few, leaving little to nothing for the rest of us. How do people deal with the lies they are being told? How do they function in a world where facts are no longer considered? People are crying, Stephanie. The world to them is burning.*"

Stephanie had not cut him. He knew she and her producers could have. Somebody had argued not to. He had a voice. And it would get louder.

He would learn more in Washington. Maybe there was something he could do to help stop the burning. Maybe there was nothing. But he knew he would try. He would climb higher. He wondered where it would lead. He turned to Alan and said, "Tonight I will call Sherman Roberts."

Larry took out his phone and opened to Sherman's letter. He handed his phone to Alan. Alan read the email. He read it twice.

Alan nodded. He felt his world shift.

# CHAPTER THIRTY SEVEN

Sherman felt the phone ring in his pocket. He looked at his phone. He did not know the number. It could be a scam or sales. But it was a local number. He slid his finger on the phone screen to the answer call. "Yes."

"Mr. Roberts. This is Larry Martin."

Roberts heard the low voice. The tone was warm and friendly. He was astonished. He rocked back in his office chair with a brief laugh of pleasure. He hadn't really expected Martin to call. "I am so pleased to hear from you, Mr. Martin. Where are you now?"

"I am in Balfour, sir. "

"You came back?" Roberts asked in awe.

"I had business to attend to. It is done. I leave Atlanta tomorrow."

"Is there any way you can squeeze me in before you leave?"

"Yes, Mr. Roberts, I can. If it fits your schedule, I will be at your office at ten o'clock in the morning."

"It does. That's perfect. My wife will be glad this has happened. She can stop serving me teas now."

Larry laughed. "Give her my regards. I appreciate her concern. But I am truly fine now."

Roberts shook his head in marvel. "This is just amazing."

"Sir. Tomorrow morning, I will have a dear and close friend with me. It is my intention to introduce him to you. His name is Alan Thomas Roth. He is president and owner of Atlanta Limo Fleet Services. He is a very good man. He will not stay with us while we talk. But I would like to take the opportunity to connect the two of you together."

"By all means. Bring him. It would be my pleasure to meet him. And, it would also be my pleasure if you would call me Sherman."

"Thank you, Sherman. I extend the same to you."

"Larry," Sherman breathed, "I can't wait to meet you. And, Alan, of course. But I do look forward to our meeting."

Larry gave a low laugh. "As do I, Sherman. It should be interesting. Have a good night."

"You too, Larry. See you in the morning." Sherman hung up the phone. He felt like a miracle had just happened. He called his wife.

*   *   *   *   *   *

Larry and Alan were led through the enormous offices of Roberts Architectural and Construction, Incorporated. The furnishings were modern with splashes of vivid color on the walls and in the art displayed on them. It had a sense of urgent workspace, but the place was well designed, comfortable, and welcoming. The firm had grossed a little over two billion last year. It would be more this year. The assistant stopped at Sherman's door. "Here we are. Have a good day." She turned and went down the hall.

Alan let Larry enter first. Sherman was standing in front of his desk, waiting.

Sherman watched as Larry came to stand in front of him. He saw Larry smile gently and look straight back into his own eyes. He heard Larry say his name, his head slightly tilted, the same way he often tilted his own. The mannerism was small, but he was drawn to its peculiar familiarity. He saw Larry offer his hand to him and he took it. He felt the firmness of Larry's handshake. The connection impacted him greatly and he felt captive to it. He was incredulous that the beautiful boy standing before him was the same man who had been homeless, bearded, and older-looking. He felt shaken and astounded. But it wasn't just that. There was something more. Much more. He felt so many things all at once. Larry's gentleness, kindness, power, and warmth. He also felt a sense of Larry's inner strength and peace and sharp intellect. He suddenly knew he would truly feel a loss if he failed to establish a permanent relationship with this boy before he allowed him to leave his office. He knew he wouldn't allow it. He would find a way. But he didn't even know this boy, except that he was essentially looking at himself twenty-five years ago. Larry's physical similarities to himself were uncanny. Lowering his head, he opened his eyes in realization as he stared at the floor. This boy could be his son. He wasn't. But he could be. He knew from Larry's book that Larry had made his birth father dead to him and he felt a rise of hope. He was a man who knew what he wanted. He didn't get to where he was—the multi-billionaire owner of an international architecture firm—by not knowing. He knew without any doubt that he wanted Larry. He did not have a son. He would never have a son. But, Larry, so like him, might be his only chance, even this late in life. He came to a decision.

Sherman raised his eyes to the blonde man standing behind Larry. He was also young and tall and handsome. Very different from Larry, but he had his own presence. His expression was knowing. Sherman sighed, letting go of Larry's hand. He felt as though he held on too long anyway. But Larry's patience had allowed him to feel unhurried as he had searched his own mind. He stepped to Alan, his hand outstretched. "Thank you for coming, Alan. It's so good to meet you." He felt an instant connection to this young man as well, if only because he was important to Larry.

Alan shook Sherman's hand. He had observed Larry's impact on Sherman. The man still appeared slightly stunned. At least he was not alone in feeling the planetary pull of Larry's influence. It gratified him to see that someone older and wiser was noticeably dazed by Larry's company. He found the fact comforting. It caused him to feel a swift kinsmanship with Sherman. He felt himself smiling. He glanced at Larry and felt his calmness while he waited for his connection to Sherman to take place. He looked back at Sherman. He saw a fine-looking man with a full head of dark brown hair starting to gray at his temples. He saw that Sherman was dressed in expensive gray slacks and a matching shirt of patterned gray and crème, tucked in at the waist and rolled at the cuff. He saw that the man physically resembled an older Larry. That he stood tall and calm like Larry. He liked the man instantly. The man's gray eyes were sharp and intelligent; the eyes of someone who missed nothing. Pushing his intimidation aside, he felt himself rise to the man's level. That if Larry were connecting them, he would be someone worth connecting to. As he acknowledged the thought, he knew that he had much to learn. "And I, you, Sherman. You know I won't be staying, but here is my card if you ever need me." He handed the man his business card and watched Sherman place it carefully into his wallet.

Sherman shook Alan's hand again. "Perhaps we could have lunch sometime, Alan? I would like to get to know you better."

"We'll do that, sir. And I'll look forward to it. If you like, I'll call you in a day or two and we can set something up at your convenience."

"I'll look for your call then, Alan. We will definitely set it up. Thank you again." Sherman watched as Alan left his office and he turned to Larry. "Please sit, Larry." He touched a chair in front of his desk and moved to his own chair.

Larry sat. He would let Sherman talk first.

Sherman sat and got comfortable in his chair as he gazed at Larry. He saw that Larry was dressed in a beautifully tailored black business suit with a beige silk tie, monochrome to his beige button-down shirt. Larry looked very elegant; his cuffs just a hint longer than the sleeves of his jacket, crisp and perfect. He suddenly didn't know how to begin. The boy was just too prepossessing. He could not get over it. He just could not get over the way he looked. It was terribly difficult to correlate this man of wealth to the homeless man he had been. The young man before him was a study in serenity. A living work of art. A thing of beauty. And he knew beauty well. He dealt in it.

Larry saw Sherman struggling. He spoke before it became awkward. It was something he rarely did, but there was no threat here. Just a friend in need. "Thank you for your letter, Sherman. It was enlightening and yes, both sad and interesting as well."

Sherman shook his head. "What happened to you, Larry, was a terrible thing. Reading your account of your beating upset me. Especially knowing that you didn't know about Slater cutting your canvas about the same time. But I saw the whole picture. I debated whether to write you. I wasn't sure if it would serve any purpose."

"And yet it did, Sherman. It brought us together. Had you not written, our encounter would not be taking place now."

Sherman smiled wryly. "I was relieved to know you survived and ended up so well. I don't envy men, but I had the thought that I might envy Peter Bennett. I had the thought that you could be here, starting wherever you were inclined, and working your way up the ladder in either sales, marketing, construction, or administration. It would have been your choice."

"I will be forthright with you, Sherman. I would have given anything for such a career here. Anything. I cannot tell you how deeply grateful I am, how indebted I feel for your generosity and potential protection of me on that awful night. But the wheels were already in motion for me to go to Peter Bennett. Nothing could have stopped them. Even if I had started with you, Bennett's pull would have been too great. I would have gone to him. It was better that I did not start with you. Saying goodbye would have been traumatizing and difficult. I would not have wanted that for either of us."

Sherman sighed. He played with the edge of a paper on his desk. "What is to be done then? Do I just let you leave and never see you again? That is not what I want."

Larry nodded. "What would you like, Sherman? I am open to new relationships. You know from my book that I come from nothing. I have no family. But I would like very much for that to change. The same goes for friendships. For the first time in my life, I am only starting to cultivate some. Doing so is vastly important to me."

Sherman looked up and watched Larry for a moment. He sat back in his chair and looked away, thinking. Finally, he looked back at Larry and said, "Look, Larry. I'm going to be direct with you. I find this to be a very unusual circumstance. I'm never so forward in pursuing a relationship. But from the first moment I saw you in Balfour, I knew I wanted something from you. That feeling was strong enough to make me reach out to you in my email. You would either respond because you felt a potential connection too . . . or not. I felt it was worth a try and the chips would fall as they would. Now that you are here, I find my first impression of you is even stronger. But I have no interest in pushing you beyond what you feel you can give."

"Sherman," Larry said gently, "I am here because I do feel our connection. I welcome it and I understand that it is rare. But you must tell me what it is you hope for from me. I cannot lead on this."

Sherman leaned forward. He said calmly, "Larry, I own and run a multi-billion dollar corporation. I make quick decisions all the time, every day. I can do this because I know myself. I know what I want. I do know what I want from you, however, the last thing I want to do is to run you off by moving too fast. But, in your case, I feel I have to because by the time you leave my office, I would like to have a genuine understanding. A meeting of the minds."

"I won't run, Sherman. I feel you are a good man and would not ask anything of me that is unreasonable."

Sherman smiled briefly. "Not unreasonable . . . but still, life changing. The fact is I don't have a son, Larry. I see me in you. I am drawn to you in that way. A son is the only thing I don't have. I don't require a snap decision from you. This is something that takes time to cultivate. But, to get there, I have to be frank about my interest."

Larry sat back in surprise. He had expected Sherman to establish with him a better level of friendship. Perhaps some definition of it that he could acknowledge and accept and take into the future. He definitely wanted that. But Sherman was right; he was moving fast. "Sherman," he said softly, looking at the man, "you don't know me. How can you be so sure you want that?"

Sherman sat straighter. "I think I've been more involved with you, Larry, than you have with me. First, I've read your book so I know your history. I see how you think, how you've managed to get this far, your determination, your mindset towards others, and your political beliefs, which align with my own.

Second, I know you are beginning a career as a successful journalist with a very powerful paper, and that you've accomplished this despite coming from nothing.

Third, I saw what you built in Balfour and I found it impressive. So impressive that, on the spot, I had decided to take you in, even if it was just to give you work. This was my first emotional connection to you.

Fourth, my second emotional connection to you was when you were being beaten and Slater cut your canvas roof. I actually suffered over these events. I wasn't joking about my wife's teas.

Fifth, I know you have no father or family . . . so, we fit. You have a need·and I have a want. This is my third emotional connection with you.

Sixth, I see that you are very intelligent and forthright and I like that. And now that you are here with me—my fourth emotional connection with you—I can either ask if you are interested or let the opportunity pass by. I choose the former. This is where we have a meeting of the minds or you tell me if I'm entirely out of mine. I won't be offended if you reject my offer. I fully understand that it is sudden and unusual, if not too much to ask."

Larry sat still, digesting Sherman's reasoning. It wasn't so different than what had happened with Peter. He had felt Peter become real to him from his imagination. He had wanted a relationship with Peter very badly. For Sherman, he had not only come from his book, but Sherman had already felt things beyond it. Yes, Sherman knew him far better than he knew Sherman. But he also knew himself. And he was confident that Sherman was a fine and very generous man. He could find in Sherman someone he had never known. A real father. But he also wanted to take his time to get to know the man before he committed to such a huge step. He knew he had to answer and he spoke slowly, "Thank you, Sherman. I am deeply moved and honored by your request. And I am not turning it down.

But you understand that I need some time before committing to it. So I have a proposal that would take us forward in your hope."

Sherman smiled. He had not been rejected. That was all that mattered. He knew the rest would come in time and it was enough. "What is your proposal, Larry? Tell me."

"I am on my way now to DC for the next month. My time there will not be my own, as I will be under the guidance of John Lester. But after that, I will return to New York. It is my intention to ask Susan—Susan Wyman —to be my wife." He thought of Susan, recalling how he had wanted her on sight. Much like Sherman wanted him now. He recognized there were different kinds of love. His love for Peter and Alan was entirely different than his love for Susan. The love between a father and son was something he didn't know. But he knew from Susan that love at first sight was possible. He would be a part of her family, just as Sherman was asking him to be a part of his. He understood Sherman better in that moment. "Her father, William, is the owner of Wyman Industries. I know you know of it."

Sherman gave a slight laugh. "I know William Wyman. We have met in Washington on a number of occasions."

"It's a small world. I have not met him yet, Sherman, so I ask that you keep my confidence."

"Certainly."

"To the point, it will likely take a year or so for this wedding to come about. As much as I prefer a small event, I have sense enough to know it will not happen that way. It is beyond my control. I will do as Susan and her mother want. But I would like for you to stand for me as my father, if you are willing. The year, in the meantime, will give us time to know one another better. And I definitely want that. What do you think?"

Sherman nodded. "I'm in favor of anything that moves our relationship forward, Larry. And I want you to be comfortable in that. As for your wedding, yes, I will stand for you. My wife too, so you will have family on your side."

Larry smiled, relieved. "Good. That means so much to me. Actually, I am knocked a bit sideways by all this."

Sherman laughed. "I can imagine. Still, it's a good beginning. Don't you think?"

Larry nodded, smiling. "I do. But now, I must go. Alan is waiting and I am to the airport. But I will call you in early July." He rose to his feet.

Sherman stood as well. He walked around his desk to Larry and searched Larry's eyes. "You are giving me a great gift, Larry."

"It is all I can do, Sherman," Larry said gently.

Sherman looked down at Larry's shoes. They were a soft black, made of Italian leather. "You are wearing another pair of shoes now, Larry. I sense that great responsibility will come with them. Does that frighten you, moving forward?"

"Yes. I am fairly terrified."

Sherman's hand came to his mouth in thought. He could not imagine what Larry must be feeling. The transition of this young man's life had been rapid and startling. It had been monumental. He would have been terrified too. He sighed. He laid his hand on Larry's arm. It was warm and firm beneath his touch. He said, "People have different perspectives, Larry. Everyone is accountable to someone and no one knows it all."

Larry bowed his head in acquiescence. He did know this. He remained silent and listened.

"You are being well met with guidance. I know John Lester and he is a fine man. I have met him through various steel lobbyist meetings in Washington. He gets around. I do not know Peter Bennett. However, his reputation for excellence is well known. You have begun to approach the halls of power. It is a dangerous place to be and I don't know what you will do with your voice. You have a massive platform from which to speak, through The Political Standard. I am not concerned with your negotiation of all this, but I can fathom its weight. Do you understand what I am saying?"

"Yes, Sherman. I do. And, I would appreciate your perspective any-time you are willing to share it."

"Don't hesitate to ask, Larry. I mean it. I know these people and they can be seriously spiteful. Just be careful. Anything I can do to protect and advance you, I will. But I'll have to understand what is happening with you. You will be caught up in things beyond your control. For many reasons. My unsolicited advice to you is to lay low for a while. Be silent. Learn the lay of the land. Pay attention to the details. Keep to yourself and observe. See who is who and what is what. Do not let them see you coming."

"Yes, sir."

Sherman sighed and moved his hand to rest on Larry's shoulder. "I am actually afraid for you, Larry. There is nothing I can do but let you find your own way. Still. I am here. And, I will be with you as well, as long as you keep me informed. I do wonder though, what you will do."

Larry smiled thoughtfully at his new father. A good man who would be there for him. A thoughtful man who would help to protect and guide him as a father should, something he had never known. But he would know now. Sherman was his choice too. He saw the future with clarity. His children would have grandparents—Sherman and his wonderful wife. He had already felt the cementing of their relationship take place. And he already knew that he and Sherman were of the same mind. "I don't know, Sherman," he said softly. "But we will find out."

Sherman laughed, dropping his hand. "Go on now. I know you have things to do. Know that I will meet with Alan soon. He and I will continue on. We will both no doubt miss you. Very much."

Larry stepped back from Sherman. He gazed at the man; his eyes tender. "Thank you for everything, Sherman. We will talk soon."

"I will be waiting, Larry."

Larry nodded. Turning, he left Sherman's office. He walked down the long hall and back into the lobby. He saw Alan sitting in a chair, reading on the laptop he had brought with him. He approached his friend. "We go now, Alan."

Alan closed his laptop and stood. "What do you want to do now, Larry."

Larry laid his hand on Alan's shoulder. "I think . . . "

Alan watched the eyes of his friend cloud over. He waited for them to clear.

Larry saw a long road loom ahead of him. It was dark and empty. He saw nothing at the other end. His heart rose in anxiety. He did not lie to himself. It was going to be very, very difficult to take on. He was going to enter a world of untold corruption, although he was only there to observe and learn. For now. He would watch people who gorged themselves on wealth. They would do anything and everything to stay in power, even to the ends of supporting an unfit president.

This administration had never helped the people. It had become an evil thing. It was taking an extreme right turn towards Fascism. A form of government that stood against democracy. An authoritarian government moving towards the destruction of vulnerable coalitions of people. Women. Minorities. Immigrants. Muslims. The elderly. The poor.

Scientists were saying that there were only twelve years left until the irreversible destruction of the planet. This administration was working to make sure that it happened. They had wiped from the books all facts relating to this catastrophe and the harm it would bring.

They would make the Supreme Court a dominant conservative power to move their agenda forward in their favor. There were almost no remaining checks and balances of government. It was a dangerous and frightening thing. Sherman was right to be scared for him. He was scared for himself. He didn't know what he was doing.

But he had survived to get to this point. A resting point.

He had secured to himself all the people in his life that he could. He had Alan, a chosen best friend. He had Susan, a wonderful future wife to complete his life. He had Sherman, a strong, new father whose relationship with him would continue to grow. Then there was Peter, a man he would continue to rise to.

All this would come about. He would make it so.

He saw that it would take great effort to balance and maintain it all. It was all extraordinary to him.

He saw the four pillars of his life: Rise, choose, complete, adopt.

He could stand on these pillars. He had a future and a family. He would love them, care for them and cultivate their love for him. He would nurture their separate and combined knowledge. He would be covered in their massive web of security. They would keep him grounded so that he remained 'here'. He would find the balance between 'there,' the plane of existence in his mind and 'here,' the reality of life.

His life was about to become very complicated. He felt the weight of it all. Especially his current worry over Peter. Moving forward, he would lessen his pace. He would step slowly and deliberately until he knew what he was doing. He would take one day at a time until he could see beyond it.

But now, he had to eat. He was hungry. His eyes cleared. "Let's go to a restaurant, Alan. Let's get a good meal. Then, we will go to the airport. And I will continue on to the next phase of my journey, whatever that may be."

Alan nodded.

Turning together, they began the walk to Alan's car.

# QUOTES FROM THE MANY ARTICLES OF LARRY MARTIN / INTERVIEWS

1. When laws and policies make people desperate, they will become lawless and do desperate things.

2. It's easy not to steal when you can afford not to.

3. One helping hand is better than a million nonexistent bootstraps.

4. Serious adversity typically leads to more adversity. If you think things can't get worse, I have learned they can and will.

5. If you are a person without friends, examine why. Clean up your act and cultivate some. Everyone will have a low point in life. Without friends, you are alone and lost.

6. People tend to kill what they don't understand. And, when someone has no understanding, it means they are ignorant. This is why ignorance is so deadly.

7. How do you follow the law, when the laws are designed to kill you?

8. If you have to lie to make your point, you don't have a point, just a lie. *Just a lie.*

# AFTERWARD

I apologize to MSNBC, CNN and FOX news. I do not know anything of their schedules of recording. The programs and anchors in this work are completely fictional. I have taken literary license to move my story forward. All ludicrous mistakes are my own.

But this does need to be said to Fox News from Larry Martin:

*"You are deliberately and knowingly supporting the control of Fascism. You are leading this country to a dangerous precipice. I cannot fathom your purpose. You would have your own power anyway. You have an audience. How you use your power is up to you. But, if you continue on this course of destruction, you will ultimately fail. And you will help our country to fail.*
*There can be no other outcome.*
*Not for any of us.*
*It doesn't have to be this way.*
***It is a choice."***

*- Larry Martin*